PRAISE FOR JENNIFER PROBST

"For a sexy, fun-filled, warmhearted read, look no further than Jennifer Probst!"

—Jill Shalvis, *New York Times* bestselling author

"Jennifer Probst is an absolute auto-buy author for me."

—J. Kenner, *New York Times* bestselling author

"Jennifer Probst knows how to bring the swoons and the sexy."

—Amy E. Reichert, author of *The Coincidence of Coconut Cake*

"As always, Jennifer Probst never fails to deliver romance that sizzles and has a way of tugging those emotional heartstrings."

—*Four Chicks Flipping Pages*

"Jennifer Probst's books remind me of delicious chocolate cake. Bursting with flavor, decadently rich . . . very satisfying."

—*Love Affair with an e-Reader*

PRAISE FOR *THE START OF SOMETHING GOOD*

"The must-ha   2018!"

—*Gina's Bookshelf*

"Achingly roman   ng, realistic, and just plain beautiful, *The Start of Something Good* lingers with you long after you turn the last page."

—Katy Evans, *New York Times* bestselling author

Love

on

Beach

Avenue

OTHER BOOKS BY JENNIFER PROBST

The Stay Series

The Start of Something Good
A Brand New Ending
All Roads Lead to You
Something Just Like This

Nonfiction

Write Naked: A Bestseller's Secrets to Writing Romance &
Navigating the Path to Success

The Billionaire Builders Series

Everywhere and Every Way
Any Time, Any Place
Somehow, Some Way
All or Nothing at All

The Searching for . . . Series

Searching for Someday
Searching for Perfect
Searching for Beautiful
Searching for Always
Searching for You
Searching for Mine
Searching for Disaster

The Marriage to a Billionaire Series

The Marriage Bargain
The Marriage Trap

Love

on

Beach

Avenue

JENNIFER PROBST

 Montlake

Text copyright © 2020 by Triple J Publishing Inc.
All rights reserved.

Published by Montlake, Seattle

www.apub.com

Amazon, the Amazon logo, and Montlake are trademarks of Amazon.com, Inc., or its affiliates.

ISBN-13: 9781542015912
ISBN-10: 154201591X

Cover design by Caroline Teagle Johnson

Cover photography by Regina Wamba

Printed in the United States of America

For my person, Jodi Prada.
Cape May will always be our place—
a magical destination of memories, friendship, adventure,
and love. Thanks for being with me on this journey.
I love you.

Writers begin with a grain of sand, and then create a beach.

—*Robert Black*

Chapter One

"If anyone objects to this marriage, let them speak now, or forever hold their peace."

Avery Alyssa Sunshine stood at the back of the church, her practiced gaze sweeping over the large crowd sitting in the pews. The church was small and intimate, with soaring ceilings and elaborate stained-glass windows, giving the guests a taste of old-school religion and tradition. The lilies were creamy white and bursting with bloom. The faint scent of incense hung in the air. And her bride looked perfect—from the flowing trail of her sheer lace veil to the elaborate pearl-encrusted train that filled the chancel. The bride and groom gazed at each other with evident love, their beaming faces a reminder of why she loved her job as a wedding planner.

And then it happened.

"I object." The lone male voice boomed in the air.

The crowd gasped, and the bride jerked around, china-blue eyes filled with horror.

No. No, no, no . . .

Dressed in a sharp black suit, the man stood up, arms extended as if in a last-minute plea, which it was. Avery glimpsed only the back of his head, his golden-blond hair a bit long and brushing the nape of his neck. "Susan, I tried to move on, but you're the only one I've ever loved. I can't let you marry him if there's still a chance for us."

For one endless, horrifying moment, everything went dead quiet. Avery froze, her mind unable to compute this disaster since it was brand new and fell under the heading of *Shit That Hasn't Happened Yet, Thank God*.

Nothing like an on-the-job education.

The bride's face turned from horror to fury. Her teeth ground together, and her perfect rosy complexion flushed dark red. "You bastard!" she hissed through the delicate veil. "You cheated on me."

Another gasp from the crowd. The priest's jaw dropped. It was like the entire church was filming a rom-com and everyone knew their lines except Avery.

Oh, hell no. This was not going to become a *Runaway Bride* situation. Not on her watch.

She whipped out her phone and sent the text her sisters dreaded: **Code Red. Code Red in the church.**

The groom dropped his future wife's hand and shot her a puzzled look. "Baby, who is this guy? Do you still have feelings for him?"

Avery shot into action, knowing there was precious little time to save the wedding. Launching down the aisle in her three-inch heels, she reached the interloper in seconds, and before he could make another earth-shattering plea, she firmly yet politely placed a hand on his arm. "Sir, please come with me," she said quietly, smile pasted in place. "Let's talk about this in private."

The bride let out a distressed cry, and the sudden hushed dialogue between the bride and groom echoed from the high ceilings and bounced straight to the ears of the crowd. Right on cue, Avery's sister Bella popped out of the private room to the side of the altar and headed toward the organist. Within seconds, the beautiful strains of "Ave Maria" floated in the air, followed by the singer's soaring soprano.

Avery prayed the interloper wouldn't fight her—she didn't want to tackle the guy in the aisle—but he seemed to realize actually breaking up a wedding wasn't as much fun as in the movies. With a ducked head, he began to follow her out of the church.

Whispering soothing phrases to the cheater, she guided him into the small room where the brides are usually held before the ceremony, and shut the door behind them. She pointed to the bench. "Have a seat. I'm sorry, I didn't get your name?"

The man rubbed his head with both hands, messing up his too-long hair even more. "Ben Larson. I've known Susan since college. We promised to marry each other, but I was too young. I think we're meant to be together."

Her mind clicked through the guest list, snagged on the name, and brought up her mental notes. Ben Larson—an old college friend who'd broken up with her after college and recently reconnected. He helped out her mother, who'd pressured Susan to invite him. Was supposed to attend with his girlfriend.

Dammit. She hadn't seen a red flag on this one.

The slight scent of beer on his breath indicated he'd had a few before the ceremony. A disjointed puzzle slowly came together: Ben breaks up with his current girlfriend. Feels sentimental, maybe a bit scared over still being alone. Has too much to drink, decides to attend the wedding alone, and in a spectacular, stupid move, impulsively convinces himself he still loves Susan.

"I understand, Ben," Avery said in a warm voice. "Hang on."

Bella would have quietly taken the bride and groom aside by now to mediate a discussion. The crowd needed one last distraction to buy them some time. Quickly, Avery tapped out a text to her other sister, Taylor.

Bring in the champagne. Need five more minutes.

Avery always made sure there were a few trays of poured champagne ready to go for any crisis. It was the ultimate distraction.

3

Her sister texted back. **Allowed in the church?**

Don't care. Go.

Snapping her gaze away from the phone, she studied the cheating interloper in front of her. Time to de-bomb the situation. "Ben, did you and your girlfriend break up recently?"

A ragged sigh. His lips curved downward in a bit of a sulk. "Well, yeah, but that has nothing to do with this."

"I think it does. Don't you think if you had these feelings for Susan, you would have said something sooner? Maybe it's not Susan you truly miss. Maybe it's . . ." She trailed off, looking for help.

"Melissa?"

"Yes, Melissa. You see, Susan always considered you a good friend, especially to her mother. She appreciates that relationship, but never believed you were meant to be together. Now, Melissa, I bet she was a better match. It must've been hard losing her."

He nodded, looking miserable. "Yeah, it was. I got scared. Was afraid she'd end up hurting me, so I broke up with her first. Stupid, huh?"

"Sometimes we do stupid things because we're afraid. But I think if you're brave enough to stand up in church and proclaim your feelings, you're brave enough to go after Melissa. The one you truly love." She paused for a beat. "Don't you?"

He looked up. His eyes sparked with a hint of determination. "Yeah, I do. You're right. I gotta get her back."

"I agree." Already, she was on her phone, getting an Uber to the front of the church. "A black SUV will be out front to take you where you need. To take you to Melissa."

"I have my car."

She shook her head. "No, you've had a few beers, and you want to make sure you practice your speech on the way over. Now, come with me. We'll go out the side door."

4

"Thanks." Worry flickered over his face. "Hey, I didn't mess up Susan's wedding or anything, did I? Can you tell her I made a mistake? That I love Melissa instead?"

"Of course, I'll fix it. Off you go."

She pushed him out the door and dragged in a breath. Smoothing her hair, she composed herself, reentered the church, and assessed the situation.

Guests happily sipping champagne while the soloist kept singing her heart out.

Bride and groom smiling at each other again while Bella looked on.

Priest holding his stance at the altar, Bible open, ready to continue.

Bridesmaids and groomsmen standing still, probably due to Taylor threatening them if they uttered a word or took a step off the line.

Avery met her sisters' gazes. They nodded. Order had been restored.

Bella escorted the couple back front and center the exact moment the last lingering note of music trailed off.

The priest smiled and skipped over the question he'd already asked, smoothly transitioning to the most important part of the ceremony. "And now, repeat after me . . ."

The vows were recited.

And once again, Avery relished a rush of satisfaction knowing she'd managed to provide the happily ever after her job required.

"That was intense."

Avery glanced at her youngest sister, who'd uttered the declaration. They were settled in the private room at Sunshine Bridal. Taylor sprawled on the blush-pink leather couch, deliberately leaving no room for anyone else. She'd already ripped off her standard uniform of black skirt, dark tights, and pearl-colored silk blouse, replaced with jeans and a tank. Bella squished herself into the smallest chair in the official war room, always the first one to make a sacrifice. Avery was too tired to be noble, so she sank down in the last chair, the perfect oversize-recliner outfit with a cup holder for the usual needed cocktail.

Avery carefully peeled off the heels that had been molded to her feet and winced at the pain. She'd forgotten to bring her Tieks to change into. After the explosive ceremony, she'd been vibrating at a high intensity, focused on making sure no other errors slipped past her. The midnight reception had run well past, and they'd just finished up distributing payments and closing down shop.

It was 3:00 a.m.

She was too old for this crap.

"My head won't stop pounding," Bella moaned. "Who plays endless hip-hop at a Catholic wedding?"

Avery snorted, swallowing past the dryness in her throat that no amount of water seemed able to take away. Not after an eighteen-hour workday with no time to sit. "I think that's discriminatory. We asked the DJ to bleep out all the expletives."

"Which was unnecessary since they didn't even play Drake," Taylor pointed out. "I thought you talked the bride into including some songs her grandparents could dance to. They were getting bored."

Avery arched a brow. "Is that why you started a Bingo game at the back table?"

"Yep."

Bella shook her head. Lustrous blonde strands of hair that rivaled Goldilocks's swung across her shoulders. "You're brilliant, T. I don't know why you keep saying you hate your job. You have a natural talent for giving people what they want before they know it."

Avery caught the slight flush of pleasure in her youngest sister's cheeks, but it was quickly squashed. Taylor's usual sarcastic sneer settled on her red lips, which complemented her pink hair. "After today's debacle, you're still wondering why I don't believe in marriage? Honestly, I don't get you two. It's obvious the bride still has feelings for the cheater.

She just chose the good guy because she wanted a settled relationship. What was once safe will eventually become boring, and they'll be divorced within five years. It's textbook."

Avery swore she wouldn't fight, not at this hour, but it was hard not to defend and explain. "No, I told you I spoke with him, and he was just feeling lonely."

"I said *her*. Not him. His douchey move intrigued her enough to start thinking of the cheater, which is the beginning of the end."

Bella groaned. "Stop. I don't have the energy to listen to your conspiracies against love and marriage. I have to get up in three hours for Zoe, and you both stuck me with the afternoon tea party. Can we just cut this meeting short and go to bed?"

At the end of an event they worked together, they'd meet in the war room to go over the details—both good and bad—and give themselves some time to come down from the exhausted high of a wedding. Many times, they toasted with a glass of champagne, spent some time bonding, then retired to bed. But right now, Avery sensed an aura of impatience with her sisters. A weariness that wasn't physical but mental. Were they beginning to regret their choices to take over the business?

When their parents announced they were moving to Florida and leaving Sunshine Bridal in their daughters' capable hands, they'd all agreed on an even split. At first, Taylor had refused, citing her dream to travel and experience a worldly life without social constraints, but big plans required big money. She'd told them she would give it three years and planned to take off after that, giving them enough time to replace her. Bella had always expressed an interest in being part of the family business, and as a single mother of a five-year-old, this gave her the stability she needed.

As for Avery? She had been born to be a wedding coordinator. She'd believed in fairy-tale love and marriage from the time she was young. Watching her parents grow and change as they raised their children, yet still retain the close bond between them, proved it existed. Sure, she was thirty-two and hadn't experienced her own fairy-tale relationship, but dammit, she believed.

Her past relationships had been basically healthy, but she'd never fallen in love. Caring and deep affection? Yes. Passion? Yes. But not the vibrating knowledge in her core that told her she'd met her soul mate. She dreamed of the day she'd finally find her true companion. She didn't want a string of one-night stands or men who didn't believe in commitment. When she fell, it needed to be with a man who was brave enough to love her back and say it out loud—preferably with a ring and on bended knee not too long afterward.

That's why she loved all the trappings and rituals that revolved around a wedding ceremony, even with the craziness popping up amid difficult relatives, jealous bridesmaids, other PITAs (Pain in the Asses), and endless minutiae. It all became worth it each time Avery watched someone walk down the aisle with all that wild hope, joy, and love etched on his or her face. Knowing she was a part of their permanent memories gave her a slice of immortality.

Still, her parents moaned about her pickiness. Her sisters rolled their eyes at her stubborn belief in perfection. Her friends begged her to freeze her eggs, just in case. But she didn't care.

She'd wait for *the one*.

He'd come eventually. And he didn't have to save her or give her some stupid glass slipper. She just wanted a man who saw all aspects of her—including her crazy—and loved her anyway. She wanted a man who'd be in it with her wholeheartedly: the bad, the good, and all the in-between.

Maybe that's why she'd become the natural leader of the group. It felt good to be respected by her sisters, but sometimes, she'd love to just take a long break and let them make the important decisions for a while. She hadn't taken a real vacation in years. As her parents had begun to slow down and make numerous mistakes, she'd taken the helm and worked endlessly to stave off any disasters. By the time her parents felt it was safe to finally leave, Avery had transitioned to director, adviser, and everything in between for Sunshine Bridal.

She pushed aside the thought and mentally shrugged. She loved her job and rarely bitched. It was only the beginning of April, and the burgeoning wedding season had just begun. For the next six months, there'd barely be time to breathe, let alone try and analyze the unspoken change in dynamics she sensed with her sisters.

She offered a smile. "You're right. Let's skip the rundown and call it a night. Bella, did you need help with Zoe tomorrow?"

"No, she's got a birthday party, and Daisy's taking her afterward for a playdate." Daisy was a close friend of the family. She'd been pregnant the same time as Bella, and they'd raised their daughters together.

"Good. Hey, T, want to have dinner and go over the résumés for the new hires? I culled the best but would love to have a second opinion before I begin calling them in for interviews. We need to be prepared if we're losing Gabe as an assistant soon."

Her youngest sister slid off the couch and scowled. "No."

Avery blinked. "Why not?"

"Because I'm not working tomorrow, psycho. I have something called a date. Maybe you've heard of it?"

Used to Taylor's sarcasm, she ignored the sting and tried to be nice. "Oh, with who?"

"Just a guy I met at a bar. No one important."

"Do you want to meet for drinks before your date? It won't take long."

Taylor groaned, shaking her head and heading toward the door. "No. I want to spend the time prepping to look hot and not thinking about work on my one lousy day off. You should try it sometime. Does wonders for your personality."

"Really? I'm not seeing the evidence," Avery said innocently.

Bella giggled, but took up the defense. She was the peacekeeping middle child and loyal to her role. "T's right. Once the high season hits, you won't be able to have much fun or socialize. Go do something crazy, Avery."

Annoyance flashed. She had no time for crazy. Her schedule was crammed, her phone buzzed nonstop, and even her sleep was disturbed by crazed brides and grooms who had midnight panic attacks and figured their wedding coordinator was the perfect person to talk to.

She knew Taylor wasn't committed to the business long term, and Bella had her daughter to care about, but ganging up on her because she wasn't dating or doing reckless things was not cool. Was she the only one who cared that the family business needed to come first? That everything their parents had worked for and cultivated was important? Fun could come later, when their bank accounts were fat and they had solidified themselves as the premier wedding planners for the Jersey shore—not just Cape May. Yes, they'd achieved some success, but there was always a competitor ready to take over. They needed to be consistently sharp and on their game. The only way to accomplish this was by working their asses off, and that meant missing an occasional day off.

She opened her mouth, then firmly shut it. No. She wouldn't go on a tirade when they were tired and cranky. Best to attack it in the brightness of the morning, after a few cups of coffee. "I am," she said brightly. "This meeting is adjourned. I'm getting my ass to bed. Personally, I think that's enough crazy from me."

She marched past her sisters, the first in line to leave and not even checking to see if the front door was locked behind her.

Yeah. Take that crazy.

Chapter Two

"I'm getting married!"

Carter Ross pulled his cell phone away from his ear and stared at the offending object. His usual steady heartbeat began exploding from his chest, and he wondered if all those damn chocolate croissants he loved so much had finally done their job.

He was having a heart attack.

Gripping the edge of his sleek walnut desk, he focused on his breathing, barely hearing his sister's voice ramble on. Sweat beaded his forehead. Should he hang up and dial 911? No, he refused to kick it when he was the only family Ally had left. He'd probably just had too much coffee. He made a mental note to switch to half-decaf, shut his eyes, and slowly got his body back under control. Until the next wave of disaster hit in the form of emotion, which he despised. God knew anything messy and unpredictable had no place in his life, but here it was, crashing in with gaudy neon lights.

Anger. Pride. Helplessness. Grief.

Denial.

He pressed the phone back to his ear. "Ally, slow down," he commanded. "What are you talking about? Who do you think you're marrying?"

A frustrated hiss echoed over the line. "Are you serious? I'm marrying Jason, you idiot!"

His mind flashed on the image of a tall, slender man with dark hair and blue eyes that gazed at his sister with affection. Yes, Carter had met him a few times and actually liked him. The guy was the head of some big marketing firm, and he didn't act like an asshole even though he was rich. But they hadn't been dating long. Why get married so fast? Unless . . .

His heart rate sped up again.

"Ally-Cat, you can tell me the truth. Are you pregnant?"

A laugh burst out, and he almost fell out of the chair in relief. "Oh my God, you are so dramatic. No, I'm not pregnant. We're doing this the traditional way. Maybe you'll do it one day, too, if you ever decide to go out on an actual date. With a human, not canine."

He relaxed in the worn leather chair, which squeaked a bit too loudly. He mentally added fixing it to his to-do list. "Lucy would take offense. And just because I don't talk about my love life doesn't mean I don't have one."

"Is your right foot shaking?" she asked, a smile in her voice.

He looked down and immediately stilled his twitching foot. "You're changing the subject. Jason never called me to ask for permission to marry you."

"I'm over thirty. I think we're past that stage, don't you?" she asked softly.

The image of his sister's face floated in his mind. She'd always been bigger than life, as full of temper and vitality as her shock of red hair. Her brown eyes held dreams of glory but were always so kind. She'd always been the type to pull lost mutts to his doorstep, invite lonely kids to dinner, and forgive everyone before they deserved it. He'd tried to protect her from the known scum, but it was hard getting respect as her brother, even though he'd been more of a father than sibling to her after their parents died when she was only ten years old.

Unfortunately, he wasn't able to keep tabs on her anymore or scare any assholes away since she'd moved to Texas. He made a mental note to call his private detective to get a check on Jason and make sure there weren't any past zombies hidden in his closet. "Bring me up to speed. How long have you two been dating?"

"A year."

"Barely enough time to know if he leaves the cap off the toothpaste."

"He does, and I don't care. Not like you, who threatened me with sticky notes in the bathroom."

He winced. Not one of his better moves, but Carter found that being thorough was quite helpful in the majority of life, as opposed to Ally, who claimed she did her best work within chaos. He shuddered at the thought. "Fine, but there are bigger issues to consider. Does he gamble? Flirt with other women? Leave a bad tip at restaurants? Obsess with those ridiculous phone apps or social-media networks? I don't want you to get caught off guard, because hiring a hit man to kill him isn't as easy as the movies make it seem."

"I know him." Her familiar tone took on a misty longing and dancing joy.

Damn. She was in love. It had finally happened, and he wasn't around to share her happiness or be close to support her. Guilt rippled across his nerve endings.

"He's a good man, Carter. I think I knew the moment we met. I got those crazy butterflies, and when we shook hands, it was like the world faded out for a moment. My whole being shuddered. I just knew."

This time, he was grateful they weren't face-to-face. He couldn't hide the cynicism regarding such fanciful ideas as instant love or finding one's soul mate. Statistically, it didn't even properly calculate as decent odds. People liked to wrap up attraction in pretty packages to sell movies, TV shows, or book ideas, especially for women. But he loved his sister, and if she was happy believing unicorns flew when their gazes met, he wasn't about to contradict her. "I'm glad. But what if—"

"Carter." She cut him off. The sudden silence jangled with raw emotion and a longing he could feel even with the miles between them. "Please be happy for me. It's . . . important."

He swallowed past the lump in his throat. *Ah, hell.* Did he have a choice? His baby sister was going to get married, and damned if he'd be the one to make her unhappy or ruin her moment. "I *am* happy for you. I'm just being a bit of a dick because I'm not there to hear the news in person. I miss you, Ally-Cat."

"Miss you, too," she said. "If you'd do FaceTime, I could show you the ring."

He grinned. "You know I hate being on camera. Text me. Is it the size of Texas?"

"Bigger, and badder, and more sparkles than I ever imagined."

His grin widened. Ally cared little for surface trappings, but she did have a weakness for things that glittered. "Tell me the details. Are you having a long engagement? Party? Is the date set yet? Shall I fly out soon?"

"Actually, we're getting married this August."

He fell silent, frowning. "Wait, I thought it took at least a year to plan a wedding. Are you sure you're not forgetting to tell me something?"

"I'm sure. And yes, usually a big wedding takes time to plan, but we don't want to wait. We're in love, and I always dreamed of an outdoor summer wedding by the beach. I put in a call to Avery, and she agreed to take me on, even though it's only four months to do everything."

The name triggered a faded memory. "Avery?"

"Avery Sunshine, my best friend from college. Don't you remember? She practically lived with us one semester when she had problems with her roommate. Please don't tell me forty is affecting your memory," she teased.

"Brat. Of course I remember." Avery Sunshine. How could he forget his sister's partner in crime? He'd worried so much when Ally began to run a bit wild in college, expressing her inner badass and late-teen angst. When she had brought Avery home one evening to hang out and introduced them, he'd hoped the girl would be the calming influence his sister needed.

He'd been wrong.

Instead, she was the fire that lit the match and made his sister burn. Suddenly, the double *As* (the ridiculous nickname they'd dubbed themselves) were sneaking alcohol, running around with boys, and turning into social partygoers. Sure, he'd expected some trouble in college—it was part of a ritual he'd read about and studied up on before sending his sister off to Georgetown University. But not at the level where grades were sacrificed.

When she'd brought home a C in biology, he did what needed to be done: He installed a curfew. Insisted on meeting every boy she wanted to date. And did his best to keep Avery Sunshine away from his home.

Her image danced in his mind. She reminded him of Tigger. Wild honey curls that sprang in every direction, bouncing over her shoulders as she zipped around with boundless energy. Flashing quick limbs and a mischievous grin. Stunning hazel eyes that seemed too large in her small face. A scattering of freckles over a pert nose that used to wrinkle whenever she was forced to talk to him.

Yeah, it was instant dislike on both of their parts.

In a crazy way, he'd almost felt like she was competing with him for Ally's attention, determined to be her favorite. Ridiculous.

He'd tried explaining how important grades were, how they needed to keep their reputations spotless for future jobs and relationships, but she'd just tip up her head like she smelled something bad and pretend to listen.

Once, he'd overheard her call him *old*. His temper had hit until reality slammed him full force: she was right. He'd been the oldest twenty-six-year-old on the planet. But she still pissed him off.

Carter shook off his thoughts and refocused. "I didn't think you two spoke anymore. You graduated a decade ago."

"We've always kept in touch. I even went to see her in Cape May once for the weekend. Oh, Carter, you'd love it there. The beach is gorgeous, and there's these Victorian inns that line the street. Quaint shops and five-star restaurants. It's magical."

He rarely got to see the beach. Growing up and working in DC, there wasn't time or money for vacations, let alone an ocean getaway in New Jersey. "Sounds beautiful. But what does Avery have to do with your wedding?"

"She's a wedding planner. She runs a business with her two sisters, and I've decided that's where I want to get married. Can you picture an oceanfront ceremony paired with a glamorous reception? Jason loved the idea."

He struggled to keep up with all the sudden plans. "I'm surprised you don't want to get married in Texas."

"I've only been here a year, and it's not yet home. Jason's family is scattered, so there was nothing holding us back from having a destination wedding. Even better, I've decided as soon as the semester ends, I'm heading to Cape May. Since we don't have much time, and there's endless decisions to be made, I rented a house for the summer!"

Ally worked as a professor of economics. When she'd graduated with her PhD, Carter realized all the work and sacrifice to give his sister the type of life she deserved had been worth it. "Ally-Cat, I'm so happy you can take a break, but you shouldn't be stressed planning a wedding. I can pay for any planner you want—the best of the best. It's sweet you want to give the business to Avery, but this is too important."

A tinkling laugh rose to his ears. "Sunshine Bridal *is* the best of the best in Cape May. Avery's the one doing *me* a favor by squeezing me into her schedule."

He couldn't imagine the girl he'd known running a successful wedding agency. She was too scattered, too intent on pursuing fun at the expense of responsibility. He'd assumed her family had spoiled her rotten, allowing her to waste an expensive education at Georgetown to pursue some fun and experience the novelty of living away from home. Unease settled over him. "Is Jason coming with you, too?"

"No, he has to work, but he'll fly out for some long weekends. It'll be exciting to steep myself in wedding details and hang with Avery again. We always have so much fun together."

"Hmm, yes, you do."

"You're worried, aren't you? Afraid I'm going to get into trouble at some dive bar or get caught skinny-dipping in the ocean?"

"Like the time I had to bail you two out after you were arrested for trespassing at the gardens?"

He could practically see her wince. "Okay, admittedly that was not a good idea. Avery and I just wanted to see what the gardens were like in the moonlight. It was harmless."

"It was the Enid A. Haupt Garden. But sure, almost having a criminal record is completely harmless. I wonder why I'm concerned you'll be traipsing around all summer with this woman."

Her words came out in a harsh whisper, and he was sure she was gritting her teeth. "Stop treating me like a child or I won't ask you to be my man of honor. Why do you always have to hold this crap over me? I have a respectable job and I'm getting married."

His heart stilled. "Man of what?"

"Man of honor. I had a nice speech planned before I asked you, but you managed to piss me off once again, so this is the best you're gonna get. Carter, my overbearing, pain-in-the-ass brother, will you be my man of honor for my wedding?"

He blinked. His throat tightened with emotion. His sister had been his entire world for most of his life. To be asked to stand beside her through her wedding meant everything to him. It took him a few moments before he was able to respond. "I don't have to wear a dress, do I?"

She laughed. "Not unless you want to. No, your job will be to help me make decisions and just be my emotional rock. Avery will take care of everything else, but I really want your input. Oh, how I'd love for you to spend some time with me this summer. It's been forever since we hung out. When was the last time you took a vacation?"

Never. Not that it mattered. His job was satisfying, and he'd been able to stop worrying as much these last five years as Ally settled into being an adult and building her own life. "Besides the team-building project at Logan Circle?"

"That wasn't a vacation. Please tell me you know that."

"But the scavenger hunt and escape-room activities really helped us bond."

"Okay, I have an outrageous suggestion: take some time off and spend the summer with me. You never take vacations, and we'd have so much fun!"

He opened his mouth, automatically ready to decline, then shut it. For the first time in a while, he was a bit restless. He loved his job as a hacker, but there was an odd stirring in his gut. Almost as if he were searching for . . . more. He just wasn't sure what it was.

Spending time with his sister might be the solution. She was his only family, and helping her plan the most important day of her life would be like stepping back into the past, when they were together 24-7. Getting the time off shouldn't be a problem. He'd accumulated a ton of vacation days, and he'd finish up this latest project by the end of the month.

"Let me see what I can do. Are you sure I wouldn't be crashing in on your time with Avery?" He knew he was a bit overprotective and overwhelming at times.

"As long as you don't give me a curfew or limit my alcohol intake, I'd love it."

"Okay, Ally-Cat, you convinced me. Let's do it."

Her squeal made him grin. "This is going to be the best summer of our lives."

Carter wondered why her words suddenly seemed like a forewarning of something to come. He shook off the odd thought, said goodbye to his sister, and began to make a list to prepare for his time off.

Avery selected a croissant from the platter. The flaky crust and buttery texture showed a perfect bake, and just a hint of chocolate peeked from the sides. She licked her lips and settled at the head of the conference table—a gorgeous mahogany antique that she'd grabbed at an estate sale and repurposed. The standout centerpiece of the room was paired with softer touches: fresh blush roses, lavender-mint soy candles, soft buttercream carpeting, and delicate lace curtains. The walls were adorned with black-and-white photographs of some of their most esteemed weddings, clad in ornate frames that beckoned new clients.

This was different from the war room, since they brought all prospective clients here for meetings. Avery had learned that showcasing a ruthless business purpose paired with appealing to all five senses was a winning combination in the wedding business.

She flipped open her planner and laptop, then glanced around the room. Her sisters were all seated and ready for the meeting, along with Gabe, her full-time assistant and right-hand man. "Good morning, ladies and gentleman! Let's make this a great day! Bella, do you want to start?"

Her sister's calm energy blanketed the room. Avery didn't know if it was being a mother or the tragic past of losing her husband, but she was continually impressed by Bella's ability to keep focused in any crazy situation. It was like she owned a yogi's heart, though she'd never taken up the practice, preferring to run on the boardwalk every morning before Zoe awoke.

"I have the Cameron wedding this upcoming weekend, and everything is on schedule. We discovered there are two nut allergies, so we changed out the cake. The family descends on the Chalfonte Hotel on Thursday, so I'll need all hands on deck. The MOG offered to treat the wedding party to a spa treatment on Friday, and the FOB requested jet skiing."

Avery winced. "Well, the mother of the groom will earn points, but you couldn't talk the father of the bride into a safe golf outing instead?"

"Nope," Bella said. "He was insistent, but I spoke with Ralph at the marina, and they'll send a guide to make sure no one goes daredevil in the water."

Taylor snorted into her coffee cup. "Let's just hope they fare better than the Sullivans. I still think that ranks as one of our worst weddings."

Avery lifted a brow. "Really? What about the Cruz ceremony during Hurricane Sandy?" The bride's veil had been ripped off by the wind, the reception flooded, and a bridesmaid got hit in the face with part of the trellis. Thank God for their liability clause or they'd be bankrupt.

Gabe put down his latte, no doubt doctored with a double shot of espresso, and cut in. "Sorry, boss, but Taylor is right. The Sullivan FOG ended up stealing a Jet Ski and crashing it, remember? Broke his leg and couldn't walk his daughter down the aisle. I never took him for a wild one, but he got on that thing when nobody was looking, jumped the roped-off area, and headed for the wild blue ocean beyond. Ralph thought he'd drowned by the time he caught up to him."

"True," Avery said. She popped the rest of the croissant in her mouth and tamped down the urge to have one more. She loved morning breakfast meetings with pastries.

"And the bride was a crier," Taylor added.

"I hate the criers," Bella said. "Everything takes so much longer when you have to calm them down."

Gabe shrugged. "I don't mind the weepy ones. Most of them are easy to handle, especially compared to the divas."

"I don't think there's a woman you can't handle," Avery teased. Gabe embraced all things bridal and owned it. He was charming with the ladies, best friends with the guys, and adept at sewing up loose ends that could end up biting them in the ass. The entire town of Cape May was madly in love with him, as evidenced by his being named Bachelor of the Cape for two years in a row in *Exit Zero* magazine.

Avery scratched a note into her calendar. "Okay, we'll keep a tight watch on the FOB. Let us know if you need any backup. T?"

Taylor casually glanced at her purple glitter Passion Planner and tapped her matching purple nail. "I just have the afternoon tea service on Sunday for a bridal party, but next weekend is Elsa's bachelorette party in Wildwood."

Avery stared. "Wildwood?"

Taylor gave a snort of laughter. "Yep. The bride wants an old-fashioned boardwalk experience with fast food, cotton candy, and rides. It'll be easy, but you know Jersey girls can get a bit wild. Anyone care to jump in and help?"

Avery and Bella both shook their heads. "I think you got this one," Avery said, hoping her sister didn't insist. Taylor was the best with bachelorette parties, entertainment, social media, and intimidating the hell out of wayward grooms and bitchy maids of honor. Still, they had instituted a rule of always having a backup in case of emergencies. "Gabe, would you mind being on call in case T needs an extra chaperone?"

"Yep, not a problem."

"Excellent," Avery said. "I've got the Peretti wedding at the Pelican Club. They're forecasting rain, and I've already fielded a bunch of calls regarding their plan for outside photographs. I spoke with Pierce about a plan B, and he set up an alternate studio on-site with those professional beach backgrounds he made that work really well."

"Let's hope it's just a drizzle. I love when the mist settles and gives that dreamy glow," Bella said.

Avery noticed Gabe was looking at Bella with an odd expression as she spoke, but she didn't call him out on it, wanting to get the last part of their meeting over and done with. "Agreed. Our final agenda item is the summer schedules. Let's get a rundown," she said.

As each of them rattled off a full list of weddings and bridal events for every weekend through Labor Day, her heartbeat sped up. They were not going to be happy with her announcement. Was there a way to spin it in a positive light? Dammit, she should have plied everyone with mimosas beforehand. She was losing her touch.

She pasted a smile on her face. "Isn't it wonderful how well we're doing? And I have even more good news!"

Her sisters looked up from their planners.

Gabe narrowed his gaze in suspicion. "What news?"

Avery clapped her hands together, pretending they were going to be thrilled. "I got a call from Ally Ross. She was my best friend back in college. You met her two years ago when she came to stay with me, remember?"

"Yeah," Taylor said slowly. "What about her?"

"She's getting married and asked if I'd take her on as a full-service client."

Everyone relaxed in their chairs. "Oh, that's nice," Bella said. "If they haven't settled on a date yet, you may want to encourage her to look for something after next summer. It'd be tough to fit her into the schedule next year."

Nerves jumped in her belly. She shook them off and reminded herself Taylor and Bella couldn't really hurt her. Gabe would protect her, right? "Actually, it's this summer. August twentieth. Isn't that wonderful? We'll finish the season with a bang."

Silence descended.

Avery closed her laptop and stood up. "Okay, meeting adjourned. See you guys later."

"Stop right there!" Taylor jabbed her finger in the air. "Sit your ass back down."

She reluctantly obeyed. "What's the problem?"

Taylor glared. "Problem? We cannot handle another full-service wedding this summer! We're already over capacity, and so are the vendors. She'll never get a venue, or food, or . . . anything. Have you lost your mind?"

Bella lifted her hands in the air. "Maybe you can explain it's impossible to fit her in, but you'd make it happen next year?"

Avery shot an imploring look at Gabe, her last ally. He was always up for a challenge. He thrived on doing the impossible.

He sipped his latte and quirked a brow. "I don't know what you're looking at me for. I'm good, but even I can't produce a time-turner to save us all. I'm no Harry Potter."

"Hermione was the one who had the time-turner. She let Harry use it," Taylor pointed out.

"Really? We're going to have an argument over who's more powerful, Hermione or Harry?" he asked dryly.

"Hermione," Taylor and Bella said together.

Gabe glowered but refused to rise to the bait, and everyone was once again staring at Avery.

Damn, she was on her own. Avery decided there was only one way out of this: complete and utter positivity. She refused to back down just because it was more work. She'd read Rachel Hollis's *Girl, Stop Apologizing*, so she'd channel Rachel and handle it. "Guys, it's going to be amazing. First off, she'll bring us more income, so we can cut back our schedule for the winter. Imagine being able to say no to a last-minute Christmas ceremony. How good will that feel, right?"

Her team stayed silent and definitely disgruntled. She'd have to rely on their emotions to convince them.

"Okay, I understand it's a lot, but Ally is a really important person to me. I couldn't say no. Besides, this is going to be easy. Her fiancé basically gave her full command of choices, and she's rented a house on Beach Avenue for the summer, so she's available at our convenience. Plenty of people in town owe me favors. I'll just collect—I know I can make it work." She allowed a slight tremble in her lips for Bella's benefit. "Please. I promise this wedding will go off without a hitch. I can do it all by myself, and you don't have to worry about a thing."

Taylor slammed her planner closed in disgust. "Fine. But that fake almost-cry didn't convince me. As long as you know you're in this one alone. I mean it, Avery. I'm too damn busy with my own clients."

Avery beamed. "I understand. Bella?"

Bella sighed. "If you think you can handle an extra full-service client and plan a wedding in three months, go for it."

She glanced over at her assistant. "Gabe? The only things I may ask for help with are the tuxedos and if they need direction with the bachelor party."

He grunted. "Have I ever been able to say no to you?"

"No, which is why I adore you. Thanks, guys. You're the best. She's coming in later this week."

"Let's just hope she doesn't spring any surprises on you," Taylor muttered.

"She won't. This wedding is going to be smooth sailing the whole way. I can just feel it."

Her sisters shared a glance. Then burst into laughter.

"Said no other wedding planner—ever," Bella quipped.

"You're a hoot," Taylor said, shaking her head.

Gabe scooped up his latte and laptop. "You do realize you probably jinxed the event by saying that, right?"

"Oh, ye of little faith," Avery announced. "I can't wait to prove you all wrong."

She meant every word. Sure, wedding planning for close friends or family members could sometimes be challenging, but Ally was easygoing and rarely worried about the small things. It was another reason they'd bonded so closely in college and kept up a solid friendship in the years apart.

No, she had a good feeling about this wedding.

Maybe it could even be fun.

Chapter Three

Avery flung open the door, threw back her head, and yelled, "The Double *A*s are back!"

With a squeal of delight, her friend dove into her arms, and they hugged while jumping up and down. Giggling like a teen, she tugged Ally inside her house and managed to step back, grinning.

"I can't believe I'm here," Ally said, gripping Avery's arms. "We get to spend a whole summer together planning my wedding."

"I know! You look amazing."

"So do you."

Avery took in her friend's vivid red hair, cut in a chic bob, and fashionable dark-washed jeans with a gauzy white top. Her almond-brown eyes tilted slightly upward at the corners, framed by thick, lush lashes. Avery loved her familiar signature scent of Light Blue, a fresh fragrance that matched her personality. But her real beauty came straight from her heart. "Come in and sit down. Is it too early for wine?"

Ally wrinkled her nose. "Darling, it's never too early for wine. Especially rosé?"

"I have some Whispering Angel chilling right now," Avery said, heading to the kitchen. "How was your trip?"

"Uneventful. The moment I turned on Beach Avenue, my whole body began to relax. I'd almost forgotten how beautiful it is here. Very different from our crazy days in DC."

Crazy, indeed. Whenever they jumped on the phone or spent time together, the years melted away, and brought Avery back to that kick-ass, wild young woman she had once been. Even she admitted she'd gone a bit crazy during her time away from home. Her parents had always been strict, so finally having her freedom in DC had been a heady cocktail that had gotten her a bit drunk.

Avery poured two crystal glasses, pulled a cheese plate from the refrigerator, and walked to the aqua-blue sectional with tons of yellow throw pillows. She had a thing for bright color and couldn't imagine living in a home with neutrals. Life was too short for beige. "True. But DC had a type of energy I needed to experience. Fast paced, aggressive, and goal oriented. Striking in its tainted glory but with an American pride I really loved."

Her friend laughed and took the offered glass. "No wonder you got an A in poetry," she teased. "I don't remember any of that. I always dreamed of living by the ocean."

Avery took a seat across the faded beach-white coffee table. "Yeah, but I needed to see what else was out there to know I wanted to come back. I felt trapped here growing up. At least, Georgetown made me realize I truly did want to run the family business. How's Texas?"

"Hot as hell, with real gun-toting cowboys. But full of character and good-hearted people who'd do anything for their neighbors and friends. For the first time, I feel like I belong to a real community. Jason's marketing business is booming. And my students? Amazing. They're going to change the world one day."

Avery's heart squeezed at the joy on her friend's face. "I'm so happy for you, babe," she said softly, raising her glass in a toast. "All your dreams have come true. To you."

"To friendship."

They clinked glasses and settled back on the fat cushions, kicking off their shoes. For the next half hour, they chatted nonstop, catching up and then finally settling on the wedding. "I can't thank you enough for doing this, Avery. I know how busy you are. I just hope I don't cause you undue stress."

Avery shook her head. So typical of her friend to be worried about others. "First up, I think it's important for you to remember you're paying me. Yes, I squeezed you in, but you're a client, and I need you to be a little selfish for once in your life. I took all of the pictures you sent me over the past few weeks and already created lists of vendors and items I think you'll love. I've got files for your dress, cake, favors, centerpieces, flowers—all of it, so don't panic. If you don't like something or disagree, tell me. If you want something specific, tell me. If you hate one of my suggestions, tell me. There're no hurt feelings. My job is to give you the wedding of your dreams—that's what makes me happy. Sound fair?"

Ally smiled. "Yeah. I'll try to be a bitch."

She laughed. "Your resting bitch face looks like a kid going to Disney World."

"Okay, I'll practice." They giggled again and tore into the cheese. "I love your house. Reminds me of a fairy tale."

"Thanks! When this cottage went up for sale, I had to grab it. Living in my parents' house was too weird. I needed my own space to do me."

The purple Victorian cottage had a small fenced-in yard, a tiny porch, and charming tilted shutters. The roof sloped. It was cold in the winter and too hot in the summer. The floors creaked, the radiator hissed, and the upstairs bathroom leaked. She didn't have a tub, and the closet was a postage stamp. The yard seemed to yield only colorful wildflowers that burst from every corner and were technically called weeds. But the cottage vibrated with a goodness and joyous vitality that had obsessed her from the age of ten. When she was young, she'd sworn to her mother one day she'd live in the purple fairy-tale cottage with her prince.

A few years ago, she'd finally bought it. Alone. And it was the proudest damn moment of her life.

"It was a perfect choice. Do your sisters still live close?"

"Yes. Bella and Taylor actually rent a two-family a few blocks down."

"That's so great. Okay, let me know what we do next. I was never one of those girls to fuss about a future wedding day, but now I'm nervous. One of my colleagues brought in a stack of magazines, and I had to breathe into a paper bag afterward."

Avery laughed. "My job is to keep you sane and breakdown-free. Even relaxed and happy, by my standards. But let's not talk shop today. We'll have our first official meeting tomorrow at my office at one p.m. for that. Right now, I just want you to relax, eat cheese, and give me all of the good gossip. I heard Texans were good at that."

Ally sighed with relief. "Sounds awesome. But we're going to need more wine."

Avery laughed, refilled their glasses, and settled into the cushy pillows. The next few hours flew by, and she felt as if a piece of her had snapped back into place being with her best friend again.

Ally stood up. "Now that I've eaten all your cheese and drunk all the wine, I better get going. I know you have appointments."

"I wish we could hang out all afternoon, but at least I know we'll be able to see each other regularly. We're going to have the best summer!"

They hugged and Avery escorted her to the door. It had been a long time since she'd planned a wedding for someone she loved. Sure, they had the occasional local who booked her, but the majority of her clientele was unknown, with dreams of a destination beach wedding planned to perfection being the true goal. She was close to her brides when they worked together, and was proud of her Love Wall, where she posted all her cards, notes, and pictures from grateful brides. But with Ally, she had a personal desire to make it beautiful, even though she had a squeezed schedule and little free time to savor.

Seeing Ally again reminded her it'd be worth it.

With a deep breath, Avery cleaned up and headed to the office.

The next day, she was running late. She'd crammed in back-to-back appointments, and all her weddings were beginning to blur together. The cake tasting ran into the invitation consultation, and after dealing with a bride who hated making decisions without texting every single one of her bridesmaids for their input, Avery's vision couldn't handle another calligraphy option. God, she'd give anything for a pastry right now.

Even though the wedding craze of May had passed, June was almost as bad. Casting a longing glance at the café, she hurried past, skipping a coffee refill in exchange for precious minutes. Her red silk blouse and cream skirt stuck to her damp skin, and her hair rebelled in the humidity. She could practically feel strands poking out of the dozen hair clips she'd tried to use to tame it. Sometimes she hated Bella for inheriting her smooth golden locks. Maybe she should cut it short like Taylor. Except she'd probably look like a demonic Orphan Annie.

Glancing at her watch, she quickened her pace. Ally wouldn't mind if she was a bit late, but she hated beginning a new partnership on weak ground. Respecting a client's time was essential in running a successful business, even if this client was her best friend on a summer beach vacation.

Her heel caught in one of the deadly uneven pavements that defined Cape May sidewalks, and she did a two-step shuffle, averting disaster. She finally reached the bright yellow-and-pink scrolled sign that announced SUNSHINE BRIDAL and headed toward the door.

"There she is!"

The shout took her off guard, and she teetered again on her shoes. Damn pumps. She preferred flats or sandals, but these red-soled designers went perfectly with her outfit. With four-inch heels, they put her at a respectable height, but her clumsiness threatened to ruin her fashion statement.

Two women faced her—one on the verge of tears, the other glaring with anger. She recognized the curvy brunette immediately, but the other woman was a stranger. She shifted her focus to her bride. "Delilah, what's wrong?"

The petite woman pointed a trembling finger to her right. "She says the Majesty Hotel booking never went through. She said I can't get married June eleventh because she already reserved that date and time for *her* reception."

Avery shook her head. "No, I'm sorry, that's not possible. I've already received the confirmation, and the deposit went through. I'm sorry, Ms. . . ."

"Papadalle. And *you're* wrong." She stabbed her finger right back at Delilah. "I called first to reserve that date, and the sales rep put it in the book. But yesterday, the guy I spoke to wasn't there, and I was told there was no record of my wedding."

Sympathy shot through Avery. "That's terrible. Are you sure you didn't give him the wrong date?"

The woman curled back her lips and spit venom. "I'm not stupid! I'm doing this on my own on a tight budget, and I can prove I booked it. I have my credit-card receipt." She reached in her purse and pulled out a crumpled piece of white paper, shaking it in the air. "I know what's going on here. You fancy wedding planners pushed him to *forget* my date because you paid more. But I'm not going away, so the joke's on you. I'll sue you all. I'll stand outside your wedding and protest. I'll get on the news."

Delilah gasped. "You wouldn't!"

"Hell yes, I would!"

"Ladies, please, let's calm down and try to figure this out." Avery faced Ms. Papadalle and tried to radiate authority and reassurance. "Did you go to the Majesty with your receipt to discuss the problem?"

"Of course I did! A guy named Steve told me the planners at Sunshine Bridal were the only ones who could fix the mix-up."

Avery tapped her foot and tried to ignore her pounding head. *Dammit.* She knew Steve was a part-time student working for extra cash. God help them all if he'd taken the booking without informing the owner. Seemed like he couldn't handle confrontation and wanted to keep his job, so he'd sent an upset bride straight to her doorstep. Sure, blame the wedding planner. Wasn't that standard? The kid had no thought to the disasters that could occur. "Wait. Delilah, how did you even hear about this?"

"She called me and said to meet her here at one p.m.," Delilah said.

She swiveled her gaze back to Ms. Papadalle, still confused. "But how did you get Delilah's number? The booking is under my business name, not Delilah's."

"I told Steve I wanted her information and refused to leave until he gave it to me!" the woman yelled.

Oh yeah, Steve was definitely getting fired over this breach of protocol. Her head pounded harder.

Delilah trembled. "I'm sorry, Avery. I was afraid not to show. She scared me."

Delilah was soft-spoken and shy. The poor thing was clearly terrified, and the whole scene was unfolding in front of Avery's respectable business. She had to get them off the street before the town gossips realized a bride war was brewing.

Avery cleared her throat. "Okay, let's go inside. We'll get a cool drink, I'll make some phone calls, and we'll straighten it all out."

Ms. Papadalle ignored her calm entreaty. Bracing her feet, she threw her shoulders back and announced her ultimatum. "There's only one way to solve this. Change your date."

Delilah's voice broke. "But I can't. It would ruin everything."

"Then I'm bringing you all down. This is America. I deserve an equal shot even if I don't hire a fancy-schmancy wedding planner."

Delilah's lower lip shook, and her eyes filled with tears. "But my family already bought airline tickets. They're nonrefundable."

"Too bad. I have proof I booked it first." She shook the receipt wildly in the air like a baby bird trying to fly. "I'm taking the date. Deal with it." Ms. Papadalle towered over Delilah, face masked in righteous fury.

Before Avery could take a step forward to defuse the tension, comfort her bride, and take control of the situation, Delilah launched herself at the woman. Ms. Papadalle stumbled under the surprise attack and fell back on her ass, landing in a tangled mess of limbs on the sidewalk. Delilah stared in shock, blinking as if she'd come out of a fugue state. She opened her mouth, maybe to apologize, but it was too late.

"I'll kill you!" Ms. Papadalle sprang up from the ground and came at Delilah with a roar, but instead of running away, Avery's once-shy, reserved bride let out a matching warrior cry, and they fell into a tangle of fists, hair-pulling, and nail-scratching.

Holy shit.

She'd witnessed wicked arguments before, along with many drunken threats she'd always been able to resolve, but never two women in a real catfight. Knowing she had little time and no help, she went with her instincts and dove in.

"Stop it!" she yelled, wishing she had a hose to spray them with water like she'd seen on television with warring dogs. "You're both making a scene!" She tried inserting herself into the middle, but a flashing nail caught her on the cheek, and then someone hit her in the head and ripped out the clips holding her hair. Gritting her teeth, she used all her strength and managed to push them away from each other with one mighty shove.

Both staggered back, eyes wide as if just realizing what they'd done on a public sidewalk. Avery moved to keep herself in between them, but her heel wobbled in the crack of the sidewalk.

Ah, hell.

Balance lost, she waved her arms in the air like a crazed chicken, then crashed to the ground. A litany of curse words blasted from her mouth, each one dirtier than the last, as she crawled indelicately to her scraped knees and looked up with a glower.

She registered the matching chagrined expressions on the two women staring down at her, then let her gaze travel past them to the couple framed in the open doorway. Ally took in the scene with a dropped jaw and eyes filled with shock. A man flanked her friend's side, tall and lean and slightly familiar. His gaze assessed the situation with a flare of mockery and judgment that immediately pissed Avery off.

He turned to Ally. His voice was deep and velvety smooth, but his words cut deep without apology. "Please don't tell me this is your wedding planner."

And then she remembered who he was. Carter Ross. Her best friend's older brother. Dread punched her stomach.

A groan of disgust rose to her lips as she straightened up and regarded the man she'd disliked from the moment they'd met. Carter was rude, arrogant, and always trying to boss them both around. He'd consistently judged her and found her lacking, believing she wasn't good enough to be friends with Ally. His cool gaze hadn't changed, even behind those new nerdy black glasses, and it still made her vaguely uncomfortable.

Lips slightly pursed, as if he'd tasted something bad, he shook his head and marched over. "Okay, ladies, fight's over. Let's see if we can solve the problem." Guiding them both firmly under the elbow, he began to direct them inside.

Responding to the magic of his commanding voice, Delilah and Ms. Papadalle quietly climbed the stairs and went through the door. With a furious glare, Avery followed.

Ally took her hand, fussing and asking a million questions, but it was Carter's gaze that assessed, judged, and gave his final verdict. And once again, she knew he'd found her lacking.

She tried to regain control of the situation, indicating to the women to follow her into the back private room to talk, but he interrupted in his usual domineering manner.

"I don't know the circumstances of what caused such a public scenario, but I do know one thing." He paused, his gaze weighing heavily on them. "Your husbands-to-be would be mortified by your behavior. Nothing is worth losing your dignity and kindness. I hope you'll both apologize to the other and work it out."

Avery almost closed her eyes in horror. How dare he talk to them like wayward children? She opened her mouth to apologize, but the two future brides ducked their heads in shame and began to babble.

"You're right, I'm so sorry. I can't believe I lost my temper over something like this—"

"This wedding has made me insane. I'm doing things I've never done before—"

"Acting ridiculous—"

"So childish, please forgive me—"

They began madly exchanging apologies, gripping each other's hands, and Carter nodded in approval.

WTF? Why were they apologizing to *him*? She was the one who fell on her ass and tried to help them! And did he always have to be so condescending?

Desperate to get them away from him, Avery interrupted in a loud, chirpy voice. "If you can both head to the room on the right and take a seat, I promise it will all work out. I'll take care of everything."

Still murmuring apologies, the women disappeared into the back private room.

She dragged in a breath and tried to register calm. Then directed her words to her friend. "I'm so sorry, Ally. If you wait in the conference room, I'll be there in a few minutes."

"Of course! Not a problem, take your time."

She began to turn, relieved her friend was so easygoing, until Carter's voice stopped her cold.

"Still getting yourself into catfights?" he asked, brow arched in mockery.

His remark made her want to howl in rage and frustration. The memory of that night hit full force. Drunk in a college bar, a group of catty girls had begun taunting Ally, and she hadn't been able to curb her impulse to defend her best friend. Avery had jumped at them, fists flying. Carter had been the one to pick them up and talk the group of girls out of pressing any charges. God, she still remembered sitting in the back seat while he lectured her on reckless behavior, growing up, and acting responsibly.

Her ears burned as humiliation leaked through her. Again. "I've got this handled," she shot back, glaring up at him even with her four-inch heels.

"Sure." His voice and look registered skepticism. "But hurry it up. You're already late for our appointment, and I can't afford to have a delay in my itinerary."

Oh yeah.

She despised Carter Ross.

Chapter Four

Carter studied the woman across the gleaming conference table. She'd restored her hair back into a neat little bun, reapplied lipstick, and exuded a calm, confident air that contradicted the fierce wildcat persona he'd seen outside minutes ago.

At first glance, Avery hadn't changed at all. Her physical attributes were the same—from her curly honey-blonde hair and too-wide hazel eyes to her small build. Her curves had turned killer, especially emphasized in the tight pencil skirt and fire engine–red top, or maybe it was simply that he'd never noticed before because she'd been so young back then. Yes, she'd grown up well.

Not that it mattered.

A brawl on the porch of her business establishment was career suicide in his mind. He'd immediately decided to talk Ally out of using Avery's services, no matter how many five-star reviews her business boasted.

But now, it was as if he were staring at a different woman. Fat folders surrounded Avery, all color coded and marked with various headers. A detailed calendar of events that needed to be completed was brought up on her laptop, counting down to D-Day, a red heart marking the date of the wedding. The conference room was beautifully decorated, and they'd been served sparkling water with lemon along with petits fours on delicate china while they waited. She'd apologized for the public display, excused herself for fifteen more minutes, and returned in professional mode. She had an air of confidence that hadn't been there when she'd attended Georgetown, as if she'd finally settled into herself. The way she spoke with authority and walked with her shoulders back, posture strong. He assumed the two women had either left or killed each other, but when Avery entered the conference room, she acted like nothing had ever happened.

Still, he didn't trust anyone who couldn't handle her clients. He'd just seen proof that if things went wonky during his sister's wedding, Avery wouldn't be up to the task.

He'd tried to tell Ally this, but she was adamant it wouldn't be an issue for them and was intent on using Avery. She also warned him about giving Avery a hard time. His sister wasn't about to budge, determined to give her friend the business. *Fine.* Carter would have to make sure things were taken care of. Just like he always did.

"The main goal of today is to figure out your personal style and how you want it reflected in your wedding. Are you still obsessed with purple and silver?"

Ally laughed. "Guilty as charged. But is that overdone or tacky?"

Avery cocked her head. "It's a classic combination that's cool and sophisticated. There's one important thing you need to remember. I don't care if you come to me with zebra patterns—if it's what you want, I will make sure it looks beautiful. That's my job. Your job is to tell me everything you love and would like to incorporate for your day. Okay?"

Ally beamed. "Yes. Isn't this exciting, Carter?"

He caught Avery's gaze. Oh, she was good at this. Dislike shone in her eyes, but it was banked just enough that someone not looking for it wouldn't notice. But he did. "Extremely. I can't wait to see what's next," he drawled.

Avery's chin tilted up. She turned in her chair, directing her attention toward Ally, refusing to include him in the discussion. The snub teased a smirk out of him. At least she was amusing.

"Tell me a little about how you see your day unfolding—from ceremony to reception to everything in between?"

His sister gave a sigh. "I really want to say our vows on the beach. I know weather can throw us a curveball, but I'd like to try. I'm imagining the ocean in the background with a beautiful white trellis. Simple, but elegant. Same thing with the reception. I'd love something that makes everyone feel like they're in a garden, with tons of flowers and stone walkways, and a fabulous dinner. The food is really important. I can't stand regular wedding fare with the traditional three options. I want something outside the box."

Avery nodded, her fingers flying over the keyboard. "Got it. Unique cuisine—sit-down or buffet?"

"I guess sit-down, but I don't want the guests to feel stuck for too many hours while they wait for food. Oh, and I want a DJ, not a band, and none of those traditional things that have been overdone. No bouquet-throwing, or garter toss, or ridiculous themed dances with props."

"Not even the Macarena?" he teased. "That's a fan fave."

His sister grinned. "Not unless you lead the charge, big brother."

"Right. No Macarena."

Avery didn't even bother to look at him. "How many guests do you want to invite?"

"About seventy-five. I love intimate round tables so people can talk. I don't want those giant ones where no one can hear you speak over the music."

"Got it. Because of the timing, I'm restricted to certain vendors, but I have a few ideas. There's this amazing gourmet restaurant with a terrace that may be able to fit that many guests. Would you be willing to cut the list to fifty if you liked the place?"

Ally wrinkled her nose. "I don't know."

"Why should she have to make such a sacrifice?" he said. "I'm sure you have enough contacts to give her both—right?"

Ally hit her brother's shoulder. "Shush. I told you no fighting."

He threw up his hands in defeat. "I'm not! I'm just asking an important question about her vendor list."

Avery smiled at his sister, but her voice flicked with ice. "My contacts are substantial, but I like knowing what aspects are flexible since it's rare to find a venue that is an exact match to all of the bride's wishes. Wedding planning is quite complicated. It's totally understandable if you can't keep up. I can finish with Ally if you'd like to wander around town and get a cup of coffee."

Amusement flickered again. Damned if she wasn't trying to get rid of him. He crossed his arms in front of his chest and settled deeper into his chair. "No, thanks. I find this fascinating. I'm learning so much."

Her smile never slipped. "Good. Now, I've always pegged you as daring but elegant. You'll take risks as long as they don't run the verge of tacky. Correct?"

"Exactly."

"What about Jason? Likes, dislikes, anything I need to avoid?"

"No, he's totally open."

"Great. Anything specific you'd like to incorporate for yourself?"

His sister's face clouded, though a smile touched her lips. "Yes. Before our mother passed, she wrote me a letter. I'd like this quote included someway in my wedding theme." She reached in her purse and pulled out a piece of paper, carefully smoothing it out and handing it over.

A lump rose in his throat, and the familiar grief shook through him—the undeniable realization that their parents wouldn't watch Ally walk down the aisle, and the frustration that he had to be both mother and father to her. He was afraid he'd fail on both fronts on the most important day of her life.

Avery read the quote aloud, her voice a mix of smoke and honey, drifting and pouring over his ears. "'I love thee with the breath, smiles, tears, of all my life; and, if God choose, I shall but love thee better after death.'"

The Elizabeth Barrett Browning quote hit him like a sucker punch. He reached over and squeezed his sister's hand, trying to impart strength.

"It's beautiful," Avery said. "I think I can do something special with this if you give me some time to brainstorm."

"Thanks. Mom loved poetry. She always said she was a terrible poet, but I loved the stuff she wrote. It made her happy."

Avery gave her an encouraging nod. "She'll be part of your day because it's filled with love. Whenever I see a couple exchange vows, it's like the air vibrates with the people in their life, all gathering around to bless them. Your mom and dad will see it all. I just know it."

Carter jerked slightly at the emotional words that should have sounded cheesy and fake. It was probably a canned response she used on all her clients who'd lost their parents. But why did it feel like she was sharing a piece of herself, as if her heart meant every sentiment she uttered? Either she was wicked good at her job or the woman had drunk the Kool-Aid on this lovefest thing.

Sure, he was happy his sister had met the man she wanted to build a life with, but he simply didn't believe in all the hearts-and-flowers junk that came with the decision to marry. The more someone allowed pumped-up sentiments like poetry and fiction and pretty trappings to affect their relationship, the more danger threatened.

God knew he'd seen it firsthand.

He vowed to protect his sister, so keeping this entire process logical and real was his priority. He wouldn't allow Avery to fill his sister's head with unreal expectations, either of her wedding day or her actual married life.

He watched Avery finish typing, take a sip of water, and flip some pages in her big book. "Now, how about the wedding party? Have you picked them yet?"

"Yes, Jason will have his brother as his best man and three friends as groomsmen." Ally rattled off the names. "Since you're my wedding planner, I didn't get to ask you to be in my bridal party."

"Oh, you're so sweet," Avery said. Her face flickered with emotion. "That means a lot to me, but this is even better. I can be involved in everything."

"True. I'll be having two friends from Texas as my bridesmaids, Judith and Noelle, and Jason's sister, Maddie. And of course, Carter will be my man of honor."

Avery blinked. Slowly, her gaze fastened on him, and a sudden connection seared between them, fiery hot and full of dislike, animosity, and something else—something he refused to delve into or try to name. "Man of honor?" she questioned.

"Yes, that's okay, right? I read that Ryan Seacrest was the man of honor at his sister's wedding, and Carter is my only family."

Avery ripped her gaze away. "No problem," she said crisply. "I'll collect everyone's emails so we can keep the whole wedding party informed of decisions that affect them, and of course, you can FaceTime your brother anytime you'd like his opinion."

His sister laughed. "Are you kidding? He has video phobia. Thank goodness I convinced him to stay with me the whole summer and help with everything." Her phone rang and she glanced down. "I'm sorry, do you mind if I step out for a bit? It's Jason."

Avery nodded, and Ally walked out, shutting the door behind her.

Thick silence settled over the room. Curiously, Carter watched Avery's face. She'd managed to school it into a calm expression, pretending the announcement didn't affect her, but he knew better.

She was pissed.

Those eyes couldn't lie no matter how hard she tried. Sparks of temper flew at him like jagged pieces of glass, looking to wound. Her features were tight, and her shoulders squared as if ready for battle.

Carter held back a grin. It was kind of fun torturing her a bit. As the bride's most important person, he was suddenly the one she had to please, which was completely different from their relationship back in DC. No, back then she had loved making fun of him, dragging his sister into dangerous situations in the name of adventure, and encouraging Ally to live big and rebel against her big brother's strict and unfair rules.

She cleared her throat, but he didn't speak, knowing quiet was a more powerful weapon than speech. Finally, she forced out words. "It's nice of you to be here for your sister this summer to support her. The good news is you won't have much to do. I'll have guided appointments set up, and I know already what Ally's taste is, so you can just enjoy a beach vacation and leave all this boring wedding planning to us." Her smile was bright and completely fake.

He cocked his head. "Is that so?"

"Of course. I'll be sure to keep you in the loop, but I want to assure you, I have everything covered."

He straightened the knot on his tie. Shot his cuffs. Adjusted his glasses. Then peered over the lenses to address her. "I'm sure you think you do. But after that debacle I saw on the street, I beg to differ. My sister's wedding means everything to her, and I intend to see she gets what she wants. I'm not here for a beach vacation. I'm here to be involved in every single step of planning this wedding. I'll be going to every appointment, every tasting, and every fitting. I'll help with the parties, the favors, the flowers, and everything in between. Do we understand each other?"

He pushed back from the table, crossed one ankle over his knee, and waited for her response.

Damn, he was enjoying this.

Maybe this summer would be more interesting than he'd thought.

Avery refused to flinch. Refused to back off from his mocking blue-gray eyes or his smug grin. Oh, he was a bigger ass than she'd remembered—a complete control freak who'd try to muck up her processes and drive her insane just for the fun of it. No way was he about to intimidate her. She was an expert in taming fierce mama bears, overprotective fathers, and zealous bridesmaids. Handling one older brother should be a cakewalk.

Unfortunately, she was still off her game after being completely humiliated by that awful scene he'd witnessed. Even worse? He'd taken charge when she'd floundered, exhibiting a natural command that was part of his DNA. In all her years of dealing with PITAs and planning snafus, she'd never seen such a turnaround from a stern lecture. She'd made a call to Al, the Majesty owner, and found a smaller room at a large discount that satisfied Ms. Pappadelle's requirements. They'd retreated, chattering away like old friends, leaving her head spinning like those old cartoons with little birdies circling above.

Some cakewalk. Carter had exploited her moment of weakness in order to convince Ally to let him help plan the wedding. Now Avery was stuck with him.

He kept staring, not budging an inch while he waited for her response. The only thing that stopped her from giving him a verbal tongue-lashing was his obvious love for Ally. He'd taken her hand with no pause, his presence a comfort to her friend when she spoke about their mother. It was the only redeeming quality the man had.

Still, she needed to teach him how the game rules worked.

"You like being in charge, don't you?" she asked, tilting her head to study him.

He smirked. "So do you."

"When it involves my business and clients, yes. Personally, I think you're just pissed you're being forced to listen to me. I have the expertise and knowledge you simply don't have. It'd be best for all of us moving forward if you stepped back and let me guide Ally without your interference. I promise to take good care of her."

He gave a deep laugh, and her nerve endings tingled. *Bastard.*

It was eighty degrees out and the man was dressed in a slim tailored suit like he worked on Wall Street. The charcoal fabric fit him snugly, emphasizing his lean, whipcord length. He radiated a calm intensity that had always thrown her off, even when she was young. Those misty blue-and-gray eyes seemed to hold all the answers, even hidden behind glasses. As if the deeper and longer he stared at her, the more secrets he'd catch. As if he were imagining things she had no access to but wished for a hint.

Back then, the only thing she'd focused on was her irritation with his unfair demands on Ally. No boys, no frat parties, no staying out past curfew. No drinking, no smoking, and no fun. He'd treated Ally like a high school student rather than a college woman, so Avery had made sure to drag her friend on adventures and allow her to experience life.

Now her brother wanted to do the same thing with her wedding.

Too bad there was a new sheriff in town.

He pushed his glasses up his nose and regarded her with disdain. "Taking care of her once ended with my sister in jail. Remember that? When I specifically asked you to promise you'd be home by midnight for her biology test the next day?"

"I was nineteen then! What do you think I'm going to do before her wedding? Get her arrested for drunken misbehavior? Propositioning a stripper? Cheating at cards?"

"All of those are possibilities," he said dryly. "After all, I just witnessed a bride war on your front steps."

Those glasses only made him look stodgier and intimidating. Hadn't he heard of contact lenses?

"It's simple. I don't trust you, Avery. I never did. There's only one person who can take the best care of my sister." A grim smile rested on his lips. "Me."

She growled low in her throat, fisted her hands, and almost blasted a tirade at his arrogant declaration, but Ally came back through the door.

"Jason says hello to both of you," she sang merrily, flopping back in the chair next to her brother. "What'd I miss?"

Carter smiled and draped his arm across the back of her chair. "Not much. Avery was just telling me how happy she was to work with both of us on the wedding. She understands how important me being the man of honor is for you and felt I should be involved in every step of the planning. That's okay with you, right?"

"Yes! I love that we're doing this together," Ally said.

Carter threw Avery a triumphant look, and she smothered a groan. Damn, he was good.

Avery had no choice but to smile back, pretending she was on board. Being older, he had more experience than she did in the business world, honing his slick moves to get a client to do what he wanted. But this wasn't her first rodeo. She reminded herself she'd handled far worse clients. He might be a challenge, but she'd win eventually. For now, she'd let him believe he'd bested her.

"This is going to be so much fun," she said, smiling even brighter. "Our three most time-sensitive tasks are booking the venue, getting your dress, and picking out invitations. I contacted Vera's Bridal, and she can fit you in Wednesday at two."

"What if Vera doesn't have what she wants?" Carter asked.

"I doubt Ally will have a problem finding the perfect dress there." She smiled at her friend. "Vera has an amazing assortment of dresses in various styles you can get right off the rack, and she does all the alterations. As you probably know, extensive changes or delivery issues can be detrimental in wedding planning. We wouldn't want you to end up without your perfect dress because we ignored the time crunch. You didn't have your heart set on some glamorous Alexander McQueen from Paris, did you?"

Ally laughed. "God, no. There are a few styles I'd like to try out, but I'm open."

"Great. We can meet tomorrow at the shop. Here's the address." She whipped out a business card and handed it to Ally. "Like I said before, I went through all of the pictures you forwarded and made a list of specific vendors that matched your style and budget. I'll book an array of appointments throughout the next few weeks." She lifted a fat binder and placed it in front of them. "Here's some invitation designs that are in stock and can be sent out quickly. Look them over tonight, if possible, and tell me if you like any tomorrow. The rest will unfold as we move forward."

Emotion filled her friend's eyes. "Thanks so much, Avery. You've already made this whole thing feel special."

"That's what wedding planners are for." She reached across and held Ally's hand. "And best friends, of course."

They stood up and hugged. She caught Carter's judging look—the same one he used to give her when she came to pick up Ally to go out—and she couldn't help it. She stuck out her tongue.

He thought she was still a juvenile hell-raiser? *Fine.* She'd let him believe it, and then dazzle him while he watched her do the job she was born to do. A job she was great at.

When he smothered a laugh, the gleam of humor in those pewter eyes made her pause, but it disappeared so quickly she figured she'd imagined the whole thing.

Carter Ross was hardly human enough to get the joke.

Chapter Five

Avery arrived at Vera's Bridal early. The boutique displayed a stunning pearl-and-lace vintage gown in the window, and already the place was packed, with a small line forming to get in. Thank God Vera always gave her first dibs on last-minute appointments, managing to squeeze her in amid the chaos of endless summer brides clamoring for their dream gowns.

She wove through the line and made her way inside. The racks were jammed with plastic-encased gowns, and the sounds of chattering, excited women filled the air. Three main dressing rooms were set apart with full-size mirrors, a fitting platform, and white fabric-covered chairs clustered around. She checked in at the front desk and waited for Vera.

"Darling!" She was greeted with enthusiasm. Avery rose and gave the older woman a hug, wrapped in her signature scent of cherry blossoms. With her sophisticated silver hair in a tight chignon, the carved classic features of the former prima ballerina still held a jarring presence that hadn't left with age. Vera's birdlike frame was dressed in a tight black dress with a long strand of pearls looped twice around her swanlike neck. Her long fingers fluttered in the air, the flash of a fat diamond ring and matching tennis bracelet a symbol of her success. At seventy-eight years old, Vera had lived a life of glamour—a lead dancer at the Metropolitan who then retired to open up her own bridal shop by the beach. She was an inspiration to Avery, and a reminder that you were never too old to pivot and claim success on your own terms.

"I haven't seen you in a while," Avery said, smiling. "How did you manage to squeeze in a vacation in the middle of rush season?"

Vera's laugh tinkled like scattered glass. "Darling, you never say no to Paris. Besides, I was able to steal a few special gowns that aren't available in the States yet. Now, who are you here with today? Are we doing the full treatment?"

"Yes, she's my best friend. Ally Ross. She's coming with her brother."

"How lovely! I do adore when a man is involved as long as he doesn't act like an ass. I'll get champagne set up in fitting room three. Ring me when she arrives and we'll have a chat."

"Thank you."

A few minutes later, Ally walked in, features flushed with anticipation and the buzz of nerves every prospective bride experienced. Carter towered from behind, dwarfing the space. Avery noticed a few women stop and stare, his dynamic presence like a vibration in the room. As usual, his lips were tight in disapproval, like he'd already found a dozen reasons not to like her choice of bridal salons.

Trying not to roll her eyes, she went over to greet them. "Welcome to Vera's! We're all set for dressing room three, so I can lead you back. Or if you'd like, feel free to poke around and explore a bit before we settle."

"It's a bit small, don't you think?" Carter asked.

"Small but mighty," she chirped back, flashing her brightest smile. "Vera is a legend and can help us find the perfect dress."

"How interesting," he drawled. "What makes her a legend?"

She kept her tone cool and professional. "Besides being a famous prima ballerina who traveled all over the world, she learned how to sew from her grandmother, who worked at Dior. Vera has consulted with the top designers and is on call for the queen."

Ally widened her eyes. "Of England?"

"Correct." She shot Carter a look. "Hopefully that's a solid-enough résumé."

Ally clapped her hands. "It is for me! I can't believe I'm the actual bride—I feel kind of giddy."

"Good, I want you to be excited and enjoy yourself." She whipped out her iPad and tapped to the screen of Ally's preferred styles. "I already gave Vera an initial list of gowns to pull, especially strapless ones with an A-line skirt that you seem to like best. Let's have a quick chat with her first, and then we'll get started. I'll go grab her."

Ally and Carter wandered off to investigate. Vera was engaged deeply in conversation with a client, so Avery made the signal they were ready and began pulling a few dresses from the list that incorporated the features her friend liked. She hummed under her breath, flitting through the racks with an expertise that rivaled Vera's attendants. She loved helping pull wedding dresses and assisted Vera with many of her brides.

Avery hung the dresses in the fitting room, and they gathered together for the initial chat. Vera poured champagne, and took a few minutes getting to know them both, her easy charm allowing Ally to relax while she sipped her bubbly.

"Avery picked out a few dresses to start us with based on the pictures you liked, but I want you to know bridal shopping can sometimes be frustrating. Many brides see something in a picture, but it doesn't look like they imagined on them. Let's use this time as a journey to explore and have fun figuring out what you like. We'll find the right dress, but why rush through the experience feeling impatient and desperate?"

"I know we don't have the normal time schedule, though," Ally said. "Will that cut out a lot of my options?"

"I'll make sure to only show you dresses that don't have to be special ordered. Your size is an asset since it's common to find off the rack and easily alter. Now, is there anything you don't like in a wedding dress?"

Avery wrinkled her nose. "Nothing tight or formfitting. No mermaid. Nothing too flashy or too—"

"Weird," Carter finished. "I've seen some of those wedding shows on TLC. Sometimes more isn't a good thing."

Vera laughed. "Understood. Now, let's whisk your brother off to the waiting area and get started. Avery, why don't you keep Mr. Ross company?"

"Of course." She grabbed the whole bottle of champagne and led him out while she let Vera do her job.

The waiting room held pristine white chairs, a velvet couch with raspberry throw pillows, and plush vanilla carpet. The chandelier dripped elegant crystals and pearls. The full-length mirrors were gilded with silver scrolling. The entire room was elegant and classy.

Carter hooked his ankle over his knee, glass held gracefully between his long fingers. Irritation bristled. Why was he dressed like he had a job interview? Today, it was a navy-blue suit with a pink tie that should have looked ridiculous but instead was a tiny bit hot. His polished wing-tipped shoes exposed no imperfections under the gleaming light.

"Don't you own a pair of shorts?"

He blinked, then slowly swiveled his head around. His gaze flicked over her body in pure dismissal. "Yes."

She waited for more, but he remained silent, just sipping his champagne. "Then why are you wearing a suit on vacation?"

"Because I'm not on vacation yet. I'm still working on a project. Therefore, I'm technically required to dress for my job."

Her mouth dropped open. "That's ridiculous. You're in a different state, and no one from the office is going to see you. Why wouldn't you dress comfortably?"

He looked at her like she'd asked a stupid question. "I *am* comfortable."

"Why am I not surprised?" she muttered under her breath. Did he even know how to kick back and relax? Tamping down her frustration, she resolved to try and get along with him. He was her friend's ManOH, and she knew the next three months would be easier if they formed a truce. "Are you still doing computer stuff?"

"Yes."

"What exactly is your job?"

"I'm a hacker."

"Isn't that illegal?"

"Not if you work for the good guys. I'm termed an ethical hacker. I do jobs for the government to stop bad people from infiltrating our economy and computer systems."

Hmm, that was actually interesting. She'd figured he did quality assurance or something similarly yawn-worthy. "Did you want to make a difference? Is that why you got into that field of work?"

The judging gaze was back. "No, Avery. I needed to make a lot of money and have the ability to be mobile. It fit my needs." End of subject. He returned his attention to his glass, swirling the bubbly liquid around like it held all the answers.

Oh, how she despised the way he addressed her, like she was completely beneath him. She was about to make a cutting remark when Ally appeared in her first dress and stepped up on the platform.

"What do you think?" she asked, facing them and smoothing her palms down the thick satin skirt. It was a stunning dress. A strapless shirred bodice flared gently out to a full skirt with a simple train. The lines were beautifully cut, and it screamed classic elegance.

"It's gorgeous on you," Avery said. "Do you like it?"

"I love it. Carter?"

Those stormy eyes were hooded. "It's nice."

Avery gritted her teeth. If Carter got in his sister's head to make her doubt her decisions, she'd kill him.

Vera launched into some of the aspects of the dress, touching on the designer but allowing Ally to come to her own conclusion.

She turned around a few times. "I really love it, but I'd like to see more."

"Of course," Avery said. "That's the best way to figure out your favorite. Try on as many as possible."

Ally gathered the full skirt and disappeared back into the dressing room with Vera.

Avery whirled on her heel. "'It's nice'?" she growled. "That's the reaction you give your sister when you see her in a wedding dress for the first time?"

He shrugged. "It *was* nice. Would you prefer I whip out my internal thesaurus to dazzle you both with my vocabulary?"

She swallowed a groan. "No, but a little enthusiasm is required as her support system. I know you don't have many emotions, but here's a bit of advice from the wedding planner: fake it."

He cocked his head. "You seem a bit high strung. I thought you were supposed to be the calm in the storm for all involved in the wedding. Isn't that your job?"

"My job is to protect the bride at all times, even if it's from her brother. Here she comes. Do better this time."

Ally came out in the second A-line gown, but this one had a bigger, more elaborate train, and the bodice was encrusted with pearls. Once again, the style complemented her figure. "Okay, here's dress number two. What do you think?"

"Gorgeous," Avery said, walking around to see it from all sides.

"Carter?"

"It's quite picturesque."

Ah, hell. She was going to kill him.

Thankfully, Ally didn't seem to notice the odd word, because she was looking in the mirror, studying her reflection with intense concentration.

"Do you like this one better, sweets?" Avery asked.

"I love this one, too."

"As much as the last?" Vera prodded.

"Yes, I think so. I mean, there's nothing wrong with them. They're really nice."

Avery shared a look with Vera. "We don't want you to feel 'nice.' We want you to feel like the hottest bride on the planet."

Her friend laughed, spinning around one more time. "Maybe we can try another style I like to get a comparison? That may help narrow me down."

"Absolutely," Vera said. "Let's get you back in the dressing room."

The moment they left, Avery stomped over to Carter's chair. "I cannot believe you said that."

He looked bored. "What now? I gave a different response. Listen, I'll know when it's the dress, and so will she. I'm not about to mimic a cheerleader for the next twenty dresses she may parade out in."

"Oh, I see. We wouldn't want you to waste any real emotion by faking some enthusiasm. What if you run out of the surplus you stored up for the winter? You may not even be able to smile for a month."

He arched a brow. "Do you do yoga?"

"No, why?"

"I heard it's good for hidden anger issues and stress. It also helps to keep you looking young."

She smiled. "Guess that means you don't practice, either. Aren't you forty-five by now?"

He gave a tiny jerk, but she caught it and her smile widened. "I just turned forty."

"Really? Huh, I thought you were fifteen years older than us."

"Eight." His answer was clipped and touched with temper. "Only eight."

"Of course. My bad."

She barely had time to savor the victory when Ally reappeared. This time, she'd gone for a full-out ball gown. The billowing skirt, endless beading, and off-the-shoulder bodice made her look like the redheaded princess from *Brave* in all her glory.

"Oh, Ally, you look stunning," Avery breathed. "Is there any gown you don't look good in?"

Ally laughed a bit nervously, tugging at the material. "I know, I feel like I dropped off a wedding cake. It's like a work of art. What do you think, Carter?"

Avery held her breath.

He waited one beat, then two. "I think it's superb." His voice held no excited inflection, a complete contradiction to his words.

Jerk.

Again, Ally didn't seem to care, either used to her brother or too caught up in her own opinion. "I love this dress. Like, really love it. I think Jason would, too."

Vera did her spiel, buying Ally more time to make up her mind, but it was obvious she didn't love it enough to stop trying on more dresses. And so, they continued.

She tried on every A-line, every ball gown, and every strapless dress they were able to find. They tried one of the designer gowns Vera had snatched from Paris. They tried expensive, middle of the road, and downright simple. Ally loved every dress she put on, complimenting the fit and the designer, but never getting any closer to calling it *the one*.

And that's when Avery began to panic.

Vera had already spent more than the allocated time for the appointment and gave her a look that told her she might need to bring in the closure strategy. Avery nodded, crossing her fingers that it'd work.

"Darling, you seemed to like the third gown the most. Why don't you slip back into that, and we'll do a little embellishing so you can get an idea of what it'd be like on your wedding day? Sound good?" Vera asked.

Her friend agreed and headed back to the dressing room.

Avery began to pace the lush white carpet and decided one last glass of bubbly wouldn't hurt. They'd find the dress. She'd worked with the pickiest brides and was always able to find them a match. Ally loved every one. This wouldn't be too hard of a sell.

"She doesn't like any of those dresses, you know."

She whirled around and faced her verbal torturer. "You're draining all the magical, positive energy from this entire experience," she hissed. "Can't you just try and believe?"

That caused him to treat her to half a smile. The man would be so much more approachable if he'd just loosen up a bit and show his teeth.

"Please tell me you don't believe in that crap," he said.

"I do. It's powerful stuff, and I think you're blocking Ally's ability to connect with her perfect dress."

His smile broadened. Slowly, he set down his glass and stretched out his legs. She spotted his plain black dress socks. Had he ever worn such a loud color? Gotten crazy drunk? Broken the rules in the pursuit of fun? Or had he just been born old and boring? Ally had only told her he worked in computers, had been an early recruit in DC, and was her legal guardian—who took the job seriously.

"I hate to tell you this, but you haven't been picking out the right dresses for her," he said.

Her jaw dropped. "We've tried various styles, and they all look amazing. She's just scared to make a commitment. Many brides are like that."

He shook his head. The crisp strands of his hair gleamed a deep blue-black, emphasizing his heavy brows and olive-toned skin. He looked nothing like Ally, with her bright hair and freckles. From the pictures her friend had shown her, Carter resembled their father, and Ally their mother.

"Ally is pretending to know what she wants because she's afraid the real type of dress she'd like to try wouldn't look good on her."

Amusement cut through her. Oh, he thought he was a professional now, huh? Figured he could pick his sister a wedding dress after two hours of watching her and Vera empty the inventory. She crossed her arms in front of her chest and regarded him with pursed lips. "I see. Let me guess. *You* know what type of dress she really wants."

"Correct."

A laugh escaped her. "If you knew, why didn't you share this important information with us?"

He shrugged. "I wanted to see if you'd impress me." He paused. "You didn't."

Shock battled with the thirst for justice. She couldn't let such an insult go by without challenging him. "Care to make a bet?" she drawled.

He leaned in, seemingly intrigued. "What kind?"

"I'll give you two shots. If Vera's sleight of hand doesn't work, you go and pick out two dresses you think Ally will like. If she picks one as *the* dress, you win."

"What do I get?"

She shot him a look. "Really? How about your sister's happiness."

"And you buy me dinner."

Avery stared in astonishment. "You want to take me to dinner?"

"No, I want you to buy *me* dinner. There's a big difference."

Her cheeks burned. Oh, he was a monster. Able to humiliate her with his cutting, casual words and bored demeanor. "What if I win?"

"Besides my sister's happiness? How about I keep my many opinions to myself?"

She perked up. "Really? You'd stop complaining and second-guessing me and following us around with that lemon face?"

He grunted. "I don't have a lemon face."

"Yeah, you do. You remind me of Debbie Downer on *Saturday Night Live. Wah-waaah!*"

Now he looked irritated. "You're being ridiculous. I'll take the bet."

Ally came back out, but this time she had all the extras to make her look like a real bride. Vera had swept up her hair and secured it with a headpiece and veil that trailed behind her in sheer lacy glory. Tiny pearls were clipped to her ears. A shimmery necklace accentuated the low bodice.

Avery sighed. "You're stunning," she said. "What do you think?"

"Oh, I feel beautiful," she said with a smile. "I love the veil, and I think this is definitely my favorite out of all of them. Carter?"

"Dazzling," he said.

"What do you think, sweets? Is this the one?" Avery asked.

Ally hesitated. Stared into the mirror. Opened her mouth. "I don't know."

The statement held a tad of desperation, and suddenly, Avery felt horrible. Had she been pushing her friend in the wrong direction? Pressured her to pick too soon? With the tight time schedule, it was vital to find a dress this week, but she didn't want Ally not to love and adore it. That was primary.

Vera gave her a warm smile. "It's okay not to know. This is your first trip, and sometimes it can be overwhelming. Why don't we reschedule for Friday so you can take some time to think? I have two more dresses I can have overnighted to me for you to try."

Carter unrolled his long frame from the chair. "Ally-Cat, just hang out for a few. I want you to try on a dress for me, okay?"

His sister laughed. "Are you looking for a new career or something?"

"Sure, maybe I'll partner up with Avery." He winked. "Be right back."

He strode out toward the main salon with the racks as if he knew exactly how to shop for a wedding dress. As if he could tell fit, design, and what Ally would like from viewing it behind a thick plastic wrap. Vera chatted with Ally, trying to see if there was another style she'd like to try on Friday, and before long, Carter came trudging back with one dress.

"How about giving this one a go?"

Avery stared at it and almost burst into laughter. Vera looked thoughtful as she picked up the dress and began clucking under her tongue. "How interesting," she murmured.

His sister cleared her throat. "Um, Carter, it's not even white," she said worriedly.

"I know, but you always said white washed your skin out. Will you try it?"

Ally's face softened. "Of course. Be right back." She trudged back into the fitting room with Vera by her side.

Avery shook her head. "You're so arrogant, you didn't even pick out a backup?"

One shoulder lifted in a half shrug. "I saw that one and had a gut feeling. You term it arrogance. I term it confidence."

"It has none of the things she wants. It's lace, it's tight. She's gonna hate it."

"You'd like that, wouldn't you?" he asked.

She squirmed under his probing gaze and tossed her head. Why did she get a weird tingly feeling when he did that? It freaked her out. "No. I want Ally to find her dress no matter who wins," she corrected. "I just don't think that's the one."

"We'll see."

She gave a *humph* and turned away from him. She swore she'd be nice when Ally came out, no matter how bad it looked. She swore she'd even be a graceful winner and not lord it over him. But all her vows died the instant she saw her friend.

My God, she is beautiful.

Her throat tightened at the way the cream lace hugged Ally's body, emphasizing the swell of her breasts and the curve of her hips, then fell into an elegant full train that swept behind her. The lace was exquisite, done in a vanilla cream that made her skin glow and her hair catch fire. Tiny capped sleeves were positioned a tad off the shoulder, and the neckline was square, giving her a shape and silhouette the dresses before had only covered up. She looked regal and elegant and unique. It was a dress not everyone could wear, but it was made for Ally.

Avery's voice broke. "Oh, babe. I have no words."

This time, her friend's smile was full of excitement, and her eyes shone with a joy that hadn't been there before. "I can't believe it. I actually look good in this, and the lace is so . . ." She drifted off in a dreamy haze, her fingers skimming down her hips, a bubbly laugh spilling from her lips. "I feel like a bride. What do you think, Carter?"

Avery swiveled her head, already prepared for his smug victory.

Her heart stopped.

He looked at his sister with a naked adoration and pride that made a wave of longing crash through her. In disbelief, she watched as a slow smile curved those full lips, lighting up his face and making her tummy tumble around and drop. "It's perfect," he said gruffly. "You found your dress."

"I found my dress," she whispered, eyes filling up with tears. "I found my dress!"

Avery laughed, closing the distance to squeeze her hands in shared excitement. "You found your dress!" she cried out, and they laughed and jumped up and down, not caring that they looked silly or might be causing a scene.

Vera chuckled at their antics, finally ushering Ally back to undress.

Silence stretched between Avery and Carter. Now that the high of her friend finding her dress faded, she realized it meant Carter had won the challenge. Even worse? He'd proved an untrained nonprofessional could waltz into a bridal store and find the one perfect gown after the expensive wedding planner had failed.

Avery had failed.

Heat gathered within her and bloomed outward. Her skin felt hot, and the sting of loss was almost painful with humiliation. First the fiasco in front of her business, and now her failure over the dress. Defeat mocked her, but she was too damn stubborn to give up so easily. She'd take this loss with grace, and make sure to dazzle him in the next round. After all, there were a million more details he wasn't ready for.

He'd gotten lucky.

When she finally gathered her composure, she faced him head-on. "Congratulations," she said. "Well done."

"Thank you. I'm glad she's so happy."

"Me, too."

Tension vibrated in the air, but it had a strange twist of awareness. They were standing close. She studied the perfect square of his jaw, cleanly shaven and smooth. She noticed his cologne was subtle but carried a hint of the salty ocean breeze, one of her favorite scents. His intense gaze was trained on hers, and it was getting harder to draw breath into her lungs. The ground vibrated slightly underneath.

What the hell was going on here?

"Avery?" he whispered. His dark, husky tone soothed her ears.

Her heart pounded, and her voice came out rough, jagged. "Yes?"

A smile touched his lips.

She stared helplessly back, afraid of what he was about to say, excited about what he was about to say.

"I heard that Peter Shields Inn is excellent. Let me know when your next open evening is. I'm flexible." Then he turned on his extremely polished heel and disappeared.

She blinked, slowly coming to her senses. Dinner. She was paying for his dinner, and he wanted to go to a five-star restaurant. Not for her company. No—in order to keep humiliating and reminding her he'd won on her turf.

Bastard.

It was time for war.

Chapter Six

Avery walked into the conference room, grabbed a chocolate croissant, and slammed into her chair. She flipped open her planner, muttering under her breath, and tried to get her head clear for the jam-packed day ahead. "Where's Gabe?" she demanded.

"Covering the bridesmaid brunch at Mad Batter," Taylor said. "Remember?"

No, she'd forgotten, which wasn't like her. Trying to change her mood, she indulged in an extra-large bite of the flaky pastry and looked up. "What do we have going on?"

Bella and Taylor shared a look. "Um, what happened to your normal, happy 'Good morning, ladies—let's make it a great day!'? Is everything okay?" Bella asked.

She waved a hand in the air. "Whatever."

Taylor rubbed her hands together and leaned in. "Oh, I have to know what's going on. Did a PITA finally get to you? Did you lose a client? Did the two crazy catfighting brides come back with a new beef? Tell us every detail."

Avery sighed. She'd told her sisters about the double-booked reception debacle, but instead of praising her for solving the problem, they kept chattering about how awesome Carter had responded to the crisis. *Ridiculous.* They had no idea he was truly a liability. "I had Ally's dress appointment yesterday."

"I love dress shopping," Bella said dreamily. "I swear it's magic when a bride finds her fit. Did Vera pick out something wonderful?"

Avery took another bite of her croissant, and fortified with the sweet, creamy filling, she managed to tell the rest of the story. How Ally had liked but not loved any of the dresses she and Vera had picked. How Carter had ended up finding the dress. "Now, why don't we get started? We're all set for the Johns' wedding this weekend, but I need all hands on deck, especially with the threat of rain. How about—"

"Wait a minute. How did Carter find the dress?" Taylor interrupted.

She glared. "Because he's pushy. He made some silly declaration he knew exactly what Ally wanted, hit the racks, and got lucky. It's not worth discussing. At least Ally's happy and found her dress. That's what truly matters."

Her sisters stared at her. Then burst into laughter.

"What's so damn funny?" she demanded.

Taylor shook her pink hair and let out a half snort. "You must've been so pissed! You hate when people intrude. Remember that MOH who kept dragging in dresses she liked for the bride to try on, and you got her deliberately drunk so you could get rid of her?"

Avery tilted her chin and narrowed her gaze. "What's our motto? 'Protect the bride at all costs.' I simply had no choice. And I was not pissed."

"Liar," Taylor sang.

"Leave her alone, T," Bella said, but her blue eyes danced with humor. "Is Carter cute? Maybe he can be your summer assistant."

That awful prickle of heat skated down her spine. It was probably her body's way of reminding her it had been almost a year since she'd hooked up with a man. She'd been too busy and hadn't needed any distractions. Work fulfilled her. Why go looking for trouble?

But maybe she'd passed the limit of when her body rebelled. Maybe after this summer, she'd go on a date.

"God, no, he's not cute," she said. "He's a nerd and a bit subhuman in his ability to hide and control all of his emotions. I wish he'd go back to DC and leave me with Ally. Plus, he's old."

"Oh, too bad," Bella said.

Taylor cocked her head. "Gray-hair old?"

Avery shifted in her seat and concentrated on her croissant. "Just old. Now, if you're done teasing me, can we move on? I need this wedding tight in all aspects. Let's go over your tasks one more time."

Her sisters rolled their eyes but followed orders. They knew it was the only way to end the meeting, while Avery knew it was her exact scheduling, distribution of tasks, and ruthless double-checking that made Sunshine Bridal the best.

She intended to keep it that way.

The next day, Avery drove down Beach Avenue and scored a parking space right across from Bagel Time Cafe. She was meeting Ally and Carter to take them to see two vendors for the reception venue. After working her contacts hard, she'd been able to score the appointments and get the date held temporarily. Every weekend in August had long been snatched up, but there'd been a cancellation at one, and a rare open spot at the other, giving her an opportunity to get Ally the perfect place in town. If they didn't like either of them, she'd have to look farther out of Cape May.

She got out of the car, crossed the street, and popped into the café. The line twisted out the door, but she squeezed her way to the counter and flagged down Christina.

"Hey, Avery, what can I get you?" The girl had a casual ponytail, bright smile, and fresh, dewy skin that screamed YOUNG.

"Tuna salad on a sesame bagel, please. Lettuce and tomato, no sides."

Christina scratched the order on her pad and stuck the pen behind her ear. "Give me five?"

"Thank you. And just add it to my tab. I'm already receiving death stares."

Christina laughed. "Beach-rush time. No worries. Locals need to have some perks, right?"

"God, yes. When you get married, I'll give you a discount."

"No, thanks. I plan to remain hopelessly, happily single." Her ponytail bobbed as she disappeared into the kitchen.

Avery headed outside to wait, scrolling through her phone messages and answering emails with lightning-quick fingers. Finally, she looked up, leaned against the building, and took in the familiar sights and sounds of the small beach town she'd grown up in.

Summer was in full swing, and the beach was already packed—a sea of brightly colored umbrellas set up to witness the magnificent waves crashing over the surf. The air was sharp with sea salt and sunscreen. Small shops lined both sides of the street, selling beach gear, ice cream, pizza, and the all-essential fudge. Sandals slapped against concrete, seagulls screeched and dove for leftovers, and bikes rang their tinkly bells as families pedaled down the roads.

Most of the time, living by the ocean was as magical as everyone believed. Other times, getting stuck with a rush of tourists cramming the streets and overtaking the shops and cafés was just frustrating. The locals had to fight for space and ended up retreating to a few spots that were hidden from visitors.

Cape May was a tourist attraction all the way through Christmas, but then everything pretty much shut down until spring. For those few months, a deep hush blanketed the town, and people stayed indoors. Unfortunately, the bridal business was still busy during the break, when careful planning was critical to getting through the wedding season smoothly.

Avery stared longingly at the beach right across the street. When was the last time she'd grabbed a few hours to lie out in the sun or take a swim? Bella took Zoe regularly. Taylor carved out an entire day a week to play—no matter what the schedule. Avery had no right to feel jealous of their free time when she chose to work.

Wasn't it worth it? Sunshine Bridal had just been announced as one of the top planners for beach weddings on the Knot. They were famous. Overbooked. Brides begged to be taken as clients. She'd gotten everything she ever wanted.

Christina waved her in. She thanked her, grabbed the sandwich, and found an open table next to a group of college-age girls. The girls let out a loud whoop, then burst into hysterical giggles without shame or apology. She smiled, shaking her head, until the image of her running wild and free back in college hit her full force. The heady hit of dancing past midnight, learning new subjects that sparked her creativity, and the endless spill of time spread before her. Even with a full-time class schedule and a part-time job, Avery had felt as if she were discovering herself and blooming in DC. The world was a giant mystery waiting to be deciphered.

When had she lost that excitement? Sure, she adored most aspects of her job, but if she kept up her constant schedule, would she eventually burn out?

She finished her bagel, popped a breath mint, and pushed the endless questions aside. She had appointments throughout the evening, and then the three-day weekend would begin, full of back-to-back activities for the Johns' wedding.

Right now, she had no time for doubts.

Kind of ironic.

She headed down the sidewalk toward Congress Hall, where she was supposed to meet Ally and Carter. The sprawling, elegant, sunny-yellow hotel had been transformed years ago from a horror house and was now one of the top-rated venues for weddings and receptions in Cape May.

As she approached the sign, she squinted in the light, trying to focus. Was that Carter? He was dressed in his usual suit—at least today he was sporting cream linen pants, a white shirt, and a casual jacket— but he was carrying something in a bag. Something that . . . moved.

A dog.

A very tiny dog.

Avery blinked a few times, but the image still registered. He had a large square bag with a strap slung over his shoulder. The material was durable soft leather in a cognac color. A small head peeked out from the top, and Avery saw it was a Yorkie. A bright-pink bow twisted a few locks of hair on top of her head, flopping back and forth as she moved. Her features were tiny, her nose a twitchy black dot surrounded by long strands of gray, black, and brown fur. Her collar was sterling silver and blinked madly in the sunlight, emphasizing a few glitzy charms that dangled.

The Yorkie stared back at her, a touch of arrogance in her face as she seemed to check out her new visitor. When Avery finally managed to tear her gaze away from the dog, she noticed that Carter was looking at her with the same arrogance.

"Ally should be here any moment."

"What is that?" she asked, pointing to his bag.

"A dog. What's the problem? Are you afraid of dogs?" His voice was rich, deep, and full of arrogance and demand.

The touch of sarcasm flicked at her nerves and brought her back to her college days, when he'd always spoken down to her. She changed course and decided to annoy him back. "Is that a man's purse?"

He flinched. The glee of kicking him off-balance was like a sweet wave of adrenaline. "No. It's an oversized briefcase with a detachable strap."

She smirked. "Looks like a man purse to me. And your dog? She's so . . . delicate."

That lush lower lip curled. "Her name is Lucy."

"How sweet. I love how her pink bow is so . . . feminine."

His gaze narrowed with a touch of danger. A sizzle shot through her at the spark in those blue-gray eyes. Why did sparring with him bring such a rush of excitement? "You disappoint me, Avery."

"Huh? What are you talking about?"

"Dog discrimination and profiling. I bet you go the other way when you see a pit bull, too, assuming it's aggressive and dangerous."

Her jaw dropped. "I do not! I love dogs—*all* dogs! I don't discriminate."

He peered over his glasses, lips tight with disapproval. "You are making assumptions that as a male, I should have a big, burly type of dog. But I happen to like Yorkshire terriers. They're refined, highly skilled mouse hunters, and fierce of heart. And Ally bought her the bow, which happens to be pink. Would you like to make fun of me now?"

Her cheeks burned. Damn him. He was always twisting her words! "I'm not making fun of you," she said stiffly. "I was only making an observation."

"Do you have a dog?"

"No. But only because I'm too busy with work. I have no time to take care of one. I'm a huge animal lover." She decided to prove it, reaching over to pet Lucy. "Hey, sweetie, how are you?" she crooned.

Lucy bared her tiny, sharp teeth and growled.

She jerked her hand back.

"Small doesn't necessarily mean delicate. She's extremely picky about who she allows to touch her. After she gets to know you, you may offer your hand, palm up, and allow her to learn your scent."

Irritation flowed through her. He was such a know-it-all. "Hmm, you're a big dog expert, too? Just like with wedding planning?" she practically sneered.

He cocked his head and studied her. Lucy copied his exact image, so it was like staring in duplicate. "No, it's quite difficult to be a dog expert."

She sucked in her breath at the jab, got ready to give him hell, and was interrupted by her best friend.

"My two favorite people in the world!" Ally said, drawing them in for a hug. "And Lucy, of course. How are you, baby?" She reached out and pressed a kiss on the dog's nose, then scratched under her chin.

Lucy accepted the petting like a queen allowing her subjects to serve her. Seemed like Carter had found a dog with the same condescending personality. God knew he'd never be able to find a woman to put up with his crap. Lucy was the perfect companion.

Avery forced a smile. "We have two wonderful reception venues to see today. Are we ready?"

"Let's go," Carter said.

"Um, don't you need to take your dog home?"

His voice chilled. "Lucy doesn't like being left alone for too long. I'm going to bring her with."

"Do you think it's a good idea to bring her into a restaurant?"

Ally laughed. "She's well behaved and stays in her carrier with no fuss. I'm sure she won't bother us."

Avery flicked her gaze to the man purse and back to the man, who seemed to silently dare her to make another comment about his accessory bag. Lucy tossed her pink-bowed head, gave a snort, and sank down for a nap.

Unbelievable.

Avery spun on her heel. "Fine, let's go. My car's over here."

They got into her white SUV and headed out. "This first venue is the Ocean Club. Their SeaSalt restaurant has amazing cuisine, and I think it gives the flavor of elegance combined with the beach fun you may be looking for. They had a last-minute cancellation, so they're holding it for us for twenty-four hours."

"What if they didn't have a cancellation?" Carter asked from the back seat. "Would Ally have no choices at all?"

Her shoulders stiffened, but she kept her voice light. "No, I have another vendor we'll see next."

"And if she doesn't like that one?"

Her fingers gripped tight around the steering wheel. "I'd get creative. This late in the season I have limited choices, but we got lucky."

"Huh. Didn't realize luck was a huge part of the wedding-planning business."

"Stop busting her chops, Carter," his sister called out. "You have no idea how much stress we've put poor Avery under to plan this in three months. Don't add to it."

She smiled at her friend, who tossed her a wink. Carter remained blessedly quiet for the rest of the drive. It was nice to see Ally stand up to her older sibling, and Avery enjoyed every moment of the king's temporary knockdown.

When they arrived at the Ocean Club, she introduced them to Peter, who took them through the space with his usual enthusiasm and charm. She'd built a long-term relationship with multiple vendors in Cape May and loved when one of her favorites was able to work with her. Whenever they had a cancellation, they immediately called Avery because she always had a bride ready to jump on the spot. Personally, this was the reception site she believed would fit her friend's vision best.

The massive open room where the reception would be held boasted a gorgeous bar; huge windows open to views of the beach; and gleaming, warm, polished wood floors. Her heels tapped as she began to paint a picture of the space to fit Ally and Jason's needs. "You can definitely go with a smaller space with your number of guests, but this allows endless possibilities for decor and setup without feeling dwarfed. The dance floor could go here, or over there," she pointed out. "We'd put the tables scattered by those windows so the guests have plenty of breathing room while they watch the sunset over the beach. I'd suggest doing silver tablecloths with black-raspberry accents."

"I love that," Ally said. "What about cocktail hour?"

"We can do it outside on the sundeck so you get a nice combination of inside and out. I'd also suggest doing various appetizer stations that are a bit unique, such as martini cakes, a full raw bar, and a special cocktail named for events you and Jason experienced together. The possibilities are endless."

"I can picture the whole thing." Ally gave a sigh. "I'm torn on what to do about the main dinner, though."

"Chef Gordon can customize a menu that works," she said. "If you didn't want a sit-down or buffet, we could do a full tasting instead, where he'd make various bites that are served throughout the evening. That would give you more of a party atmosphere if you want to avoid the formalities of a sit-down."

Ally swung around and grabbed Carter's hand. "It sounds perfect, but do you think it's too weird?" she asked. "Do you think Jason's family would question the lack of a full sit-down dinner?"

Avery held her breath and prayed Carter would be supportive, even if he disagreed. He frowned, as if seriously considering it, and nodded. "No. If the food is good and plentiful, I don't think they'll care how it's served. What if you do a formal gourmet rehearsal dinner? That way, you get both, but it's more intimate with just us, the wedding party, and Jason's immediate family."

Damn him. She'd been about to suggest the same idea, but opening her mouth now would make her look petty and juvenile.

She kept smiling as Ally clapped her hands. "Yes! I love that idea!"

He tipped his head in acknowledgment. Lucy popped her head up from the bag to lick his hand, and he smiled and patted her head with pure affection.

Oh, how she disliked this man.

After a productive appointment, Avery took them to their second option. The restaurant was gorgeous and intimate, with a fine menu and old-world feel. It marked all of Ally's boxes, but Avery sensed the SeaSalt had captivated her friend. In the end, the decision was easy.

"I love the SeaSalt," Ally said as they walked out of their second appointment. "I know Jason would feel the most comfortable there. He doesn't like being boxed in, so having all that extra room available with the views sold it for me."

"It's a great choice," Avery said, giving Ally a tight hug. "I'll call Peter and get it booked. I also ordered the invitations you picked, so our top three critical tasks are officially done. The rest will just be fun."

For Ally, that is.

The endless tasks to keep Ally's wedding on track were overwhelming, but there was no way she was giving her friend a hint of the stress to bring it all together.

"Let's celebrate," Ally said. "Can we grab a cocktail or dinner? My treat."

"*My* treat," Carter corrected, offering a rare smile.

Avery glanced at her watch and sighed. "I'm sorry, sweets, but I'm working all night long. I have a conference call at six and a huge wedding this upcoming weekend. I'll be swamped for the next three days."

"But you have to eat!" Ally said. "Just one drink and a salad? Look, we can head right into Fins. You'll be out in an hour tops and be fortified for the night."

She hesitated, but the pleading look on her friend's face got her. "Okay, one hour. But I'm not sure if Fins allows dogs."

Carter dismissed this with an elegant wave of his hand. "Lucy is a certified therapy dog. It's fine," he said.

"You're kidding. What's your diagnosis?"

He didn't look at her, just forged ahead with those long, measured strides. "Anxiety."

Avery stumbled on her heel, and he reached out to steady her with superhero speed. His fingers burned into her upper arm, and she gasped at the contact on her bare skin.

What the hell was that about? Her arm tingled, and heat shimmered in her core. She'd never had such a reaction to a man's touch. Is that what loathing felt like?

"You don't have anxiety," she said, refusing to analyze her strange response.

"How would you know?"

She snorted. "'Cause you're like a robot."

Ally burst into laughter. "Priceless. You know my brother too well. Lucy's actually the one with anxiety when she's away from him for too long. She's also supersmart, so he pulled some strings, got her certified, and now gets to take her everywhere."

He paused before the entrance and slipped a tiny jacket over Lucy's body that signified her as a therapy dog. *Unbelievable.*

"That's illegal," Avery said. And surprising. She never would have imagined Carter breaking any rules—he was always respectful of authority.

"Yes, it is. And I'm sure you've never broken the law before." He snapped his fingers. "Oh, wait, you've been to jail. Guess you can't judge."

Ally punched him lightly in the arm. "Are you ever going to get over that tiny mishap?"

"No. When you have to bail someone you love out of prison at three a.m., come talk to me. Then we'll be even."

Avery and Ally rolled their eyes and entered Fins.

They were seated immediately on the back patio. The scorching heat was fading as the sun drifted downward, and a light breeze teased and tugged at Avery's hair, pulling some strands free. She ordered a vodka and seltzer, oysters, and a side salad, and allowed her body to relax into the chair.

"I'll be right back. I want to hit the restroom and call Jason to let him know where we booked," Ally said. Her hair gleamed bright red and bounced as she left, and Avery smiled at the open, beautiful joy reflected on her friend's face.

Avery turned toward Carter, and the question popped out of her mouth. "Has she always been this happy?"

He regarded her with his usual serious expression. "She was born happy. My parents always said she had a gift of seeing the bigger picture in the world. Made it easy for her to forgive. Made it easy for her to fail because she always concentrated on the wins. She was like a light in the household."

His words struck her hard, said so matter-of-factly about his sister. "What about you?"

He cocked his head. "What about me?"

"If she was the light, what were you?"

His stormy ultramarine gaze crashed into hers. Her chest tightened, and fire zipped through her. "The realist. What else would I be?"

The waiter interrupted, dropping their drinks and appetizers on the table, then gliding off. The serious mood broke, and her breath finally reached her lungs.

Losing their parents at such a young age must have affected both of them, but Ally was always open about her grief, and grateful to her brother for raising her. After their mother had died of cancer, their father passed shortly afterward of a heart attack. Ally said Carter rarely spoke about their father's death, as if the tragedy of losing both parents within a few short months was too much for him to process. Curiosity stirred. Avery wished she could ask Carter many questions, but they didn't have that type of relationship.

He fed a few pieces of bread to Lucy, who remained quiet, her head cocked and tilted up in a mix of need and adoration. "How'd you end up getting Lucy?" she asked, forking up an oyster and enjoying the mild, sweet taste mixed with a touch of salt on her tongue. It was so fresh, she skipped the cocktail sauce and enjoyed it with only a drizzle of lemon. "Breeder, pet store, or shelter?"

He swirled his ruby-red pinot noir, then took a sip. "I was away at a work conference and walking to my hotel. I saw a man with Lucy on a leash. She barked, and he kicked her hard. Knocked her against a tree. I called out, but he didn't hear me. Lucy got up, and you know what she did? Looked straight at that asshole and let out another loud bark. It pretty much screamed *Fuck you*. And then he kicked her again."

"Oh my God, why are there such cruel people in the world?" She stared at Lucy with a new respect. "What did you do?"

"I went over and began telling him how my daughter had been begging for a Yorkie forever, but we couldn't find one at the shelter. I kissed his ass and offered him three hundred bucks for the dog right then."

"I'm surprised you didn't beat the crap out of him."

He shook his head. "Then he wouldn't have given me the dog. Even if I accused him of animal abuse, it's pretty hard to get it to stick. Lucy would've been right back with him. My goal was to get her away from him, permanently."

"So he accepted your offer?"

A smile touched his lips. "Not until he negotiated to five hundred dollars. As soon as he took my money, I picked her up and snuck her into the hotel. I ordered us room service, named her Lucy, and she slept in the bed with me that night. We've been inseparable ever since."

Emotion roared over her in choppy waves. The way he looked after Ally and Lucy told her there was more depth than what he showed. Why was she intrigued to learn more about that part of him?

"Why Lucy?"

"From *Peanuts*. I like the way she's always pulling the football away from Charlie Brown. She's feisty and never apologizes. It was perfect for her."

Avery grinned. "Yeah, I guess it is. She's a little bit mean, though."

"Not if she finds you worthy."

Lucy took that exact moment to gaze across the table at her, curl her lips back, and show her teeth in warning. When Carter looked back down at her, she nosed his hand with sweetness and affection.

A combination of respect and irritation mingled at the dog's obvious dislike for her. It seemed she was quite possessive of her man.

What a bitch.

He took a bite of his crab cake. "Well, now that we booked the reception venue, you can relax. I can handle the rest with Ally if you just want to give us your preferred contacts."

"What do you mean I 'can relax'? There's still a long list of things to accomplish in a short amount of time."

"I'm sure, but as you stated before, the rest are minor details. We can do the flowers, cake, rehearsal dinner, and favors on our own. That will open up more time for you to devote to your other brides."

The patronizing, smug smile was back, and her heart sank. He had no respect for her job or what was involved. Probably thought she was a glorified secretary, running around to confirm a bride's choices.

She dabbed her mouth with her napkin and tried for patience. "I know it may seem you have the bulk behind you, but there are millions of details that crop up that I handle."

"Like what?"

She steeled her shoulders. "Like coordinating over a dozen vendors' schedules so everything arrives the way we ordered and on time. Like being the main contact in case anything upsets your sister or she has any questions, rather than floundering about and trying to figure out who to call. It's not just choosing cake and flowers, Carter. It's photos, videos, ceremony, transportation, rehearsal dinner, makeup, hair, musicians, caterer, and hotels for the family to stay at. This isn't about visiting a few vendors."

"Understood. If your assistant can give me a list, I'll handle it. I'll be finished with my project this week, and I can devote the rest of the summer to dealing with these details. Honestly, it's not a problem."

Slowly, the horror of his true intention unfolded. Her fork dropped and clattered to her plate. Lucy jumped and peered over the edge of her carrier to see what was going on. "You don't want me to plan Ally's wedding," she said, the shock still barreling through her. "You still don't think I can handle it."

The coldness was back. Like a turtle crawling back into his shell, he surrounded himself with an icy distance and disapproval. "I'm only trying to take care of my sister."

"So am I. As her damn wedding planner. You may think you know everything, but you have no idea what's involved with a wedding. Do twenty-four hours in my shoes and you'd be in full retreat, crying like a little baby."

His gaze narrowed. "I doubt it."

"I don't. Just because you got lucky with a dress and one lousy suggestion for the rehearsal dinner doesn't mean diddly-squat."

"Diddly-squat, huh? You're quite the linguist."

Her voice shook. "You're quite the control freak."

His jaw locked. "Once again, your penchant for drama is not a good look. If you're losing it now, how will you deal with the multiple crises you keep telling me happen at a wedding?"

She tried desperately to remind herself he was a client—the ManOH—and she couldn't lose her temper for Ally's sake. She dropped her voice to a harsh whisper. "I'm giving you a free pass today for your sister's sake, but be warned, robot man. You want a war? You're on the wrong battlefield, because I have the home advantage. And I've never lost a skirmish."

He sat back, staring at her with renewed interest. "Robot man, huh?" he finally said. "Interesting. Threats using war metaphors aren't very original, though, but I appreciate the visual effect. I'm more of a bottom-line person, so I'll get to the point. You're not getting rid of me, Avery. I'm going to be in this every step of the way until my sister walks down the aisle. You can either accept it gracefully or keep having these little tantrums, which is only wasting a good amount of energy you can put into planning the perfect wedding. I'd advise the former."

She shook with the effort of not launching across the table and throttling him. He was unlike any ManOH she'd ever dealt with—worse than awful MOBs and PITA brides. He was all of them encompassed in one giant nightmare she couldn't get rid of.

And he'd be here the entire summer. In her face.

All the goodwill from their initial conversation drained away, and she was left with one goal in mind: destroy him without ruining Ally's wedding.

On cue, her friend came back, but her face didn't reflect the happiness of a bride who'd just booked her reception venue. She slid into the chair, pocketed her phone, and faced them with a worried look. "I just got terrible news. Jason's mother broke her leg."

"Oh no, is she all right?" Avery asked, reaching out to squeeze her hand.

"Yes, she's home now in a cast, but she needs round-the-clock care for the next few weeks until she's able to get around on crutches. Jason can't get the time off because of the wedding and honeymoon, and his brother just had a new baby. Maddie started a new job in California, so she can't help, either. It's a mess."

"Can you hire a nurse to stay with her?" Carter suggested.

"We were discussing it, but honestly? She hates dealing with strangers in her house due to anxiety. Jason and I were talking, and we think the best solution is for me to go back home and stay with her until the wedding."

Avery and Carter were silent for a while. Her mind raced through the rest of the summer, quickly sorting out what still needed to be decided on. "I think that's a good idea," she said firmly. "You'll only worry if you stay, and I handle most of my clients' weddings virtually, anyway. Like I said, we've decided on the most important things. I'll put together a spreadsheet, and we'll do the rest via email, text, FaceTime, whatever works for you. I got this."

Ally smiled in gratitude and let out a breath. "Thank you. I loved the idea of spending the summer here, but she needs me now. And Jason's mom is like . . ." She trailed off, emotion choking her throat.

"A second mom," Carter finished, nodding his head. "I get it. She's lucky to have you as a future daughter-in-law. I agree with Avery. We can handle the rest of the wedding planning together."

A slow roaring began in her head. Gripping the edge of the table, she tried to mask the desperation tinged in her voice. "Um, there's really no reason for Carter to stay, either," she said, directing her words at Ally. "It'd be a waste of his time when I can speak directly with you about the rest of the details."

Ally turned to her brother. "She's right, you know. If I'm leaving, there's no need for you to spend the summer away from work."

Carter smiled, lifting up his hands. "I already reassigned the rest of my projects until the end of the summer. Besides, you were right, Ally-Cat. I haven't had a vacation for years and could use some beach time. I'll stay here and help Avery. That way, it'll be like you're still here. I'll make sure to involve myself in every detail."

OH. HELL. NO.

Avery spoke up. Loudly. "I really don't think that's—"

"What a great idea!" Ally practically squealed. "Oh, I'm so relieved. This way, Avery will get some extra help, and we can still all do this together, just like I envisioned. I can't thank you both enough."

The protests died on her lips. She watched in horror as Carter turned and met her gaze.

Triumph carved out the lines of his face. Smug satisfaction gleamed from pewter eyes. And Avery swore to make him pay.

Game on.

Chapter Seven

She was avoiding him.

Carter looked out over his balcony at the crashing waves and analyzed his next move. Since that fateful dinner a week ago, when Ally had announced she needed to leave, it was obvious her wedding planner was not thrilled with his offer to help. Not that he'd termed it as an offer. More like a demand.

She definitely disliked taking orders, even though her entire career revolved around pleasing high-maintenance clients. Unless it was just him she disliked. Quite possible, since the moment they'd seen each other, she seemed determined to piss him off. From her judgy looks and cool disregard, he'd known immediately she wasn't happy to see him, let alone learn he was Ally's man of honor. Her attitude set off his usually nonexistent temper, touching deep, dark parts inside that flared to life. Things that contained raw, untamed stuff and something even worse.

Want.

A groan escaped his lips and he fisted his hands. One casual touch outside Fins had set his body off like a firecracker. Just a simple brush of skin on skin, the subtle scent of lavender mint drifting to his nostrils, and he was suddenly, horrifyingly hard.

He was fucked-up.

Only he'd become sexually attracted to a woman who drove him batty and personally disliked him. Of course, it could be a fluke. He'd read that anger could warp into arousal, so maybe the challenge of winning each skirmish had gotten his body mis-wired. It was a logical conclusion and the only one he'd accept. Because there was no way he'd get involved with Avery Sunshine.

Ever.

He glanced with frustration at his phone. The string of texts he'd sent was met with savvy nonanswers created to make him go away.

C: Narrowed down three possible restaurants for rehearsal. Here are the links. Can you make appointments at each and let me know when?

A: Sure. I'll get back to you. ☺

C: Ally liked these centerpieces (see attachment). When is the floral appointment?

A: Let me check on that. ☺

C: I called this photographer, whose work received high reviews. Would like to meet with him next week. When are you free?

A: I'll peek at my schedule and let you know. ☺

C: A full week has passed, and I still haven't heard from you on these important issues. I've left you a voice mail on your business phone to contact me ASAP. Please forward me a spreadsheet and updated schedule of all appointments immediately.

A: Already spoke with your sister. Will let you know if I need you. ☺

No spreadsheet. No tasks, vendor list, or appointment dates. She was shutting him out, and the smiley faces proved it. Her hand had been well played. If he went complaining to his sister, Avery would play dumb and pretend to get upset. It'd also make him look like a ridiculous whiner. She'd been smart to disappear.

It was time to take back control.

He didn't question why it was important for him to be involved in every step. He trusted Ally to make the right decisions and knew Jason would support her. Weddings had never been on his radar, other than the ceremonial horror of committing yourself to forever. He'd never cared about the actual details, but knowing their mother wasn't around to offer opinions and guidance to Ally hurt him. He didn't want his sister to feel as if she were lacking, so he'd be mother, father, and best friend in one shot.

He refused to fail her.

Decision made, he settled Lucy with one of her favorite bones, promising to be back early, and headed out. He'd camp out in Avery's office until someone had to deal with him, then lodge his complaint about not having his phone calls or text messages returned.

The sun beamed hot on his bare arms, and he enjoyed being out of his restrictive suit, officially on vacation now. Today, he'd donned white board shorts, a blue T-shirt, and leather sandals. Trading in his glasses for a pair of prescription Ray-Bans, he took in the sights and sounds of the busy streets.

No wonder his sister had raved about Cape May. It emanated quirky charm and combined gorgeously restored Victorian homes with old-school beach flavor. It'd managed to avoid the tacky boardwalk filled with rides and overpriced food, offering visitors a clean beach, unique shops, and delicious cafés. Other than a small arcade, the town mostly catered to families rather than teens. Horses and carriages clopped by, taking people on mini tours, and red surreys holding six people pedaling madly mixed in with the cars and foot traffic.

He walked out of the hubbub of town and toward the quieter streets, shielded in shade by massive oak trees that lined the curbs. He passed multiple bed-and-breakfasts painted in Crayola-type color. People relaxed on oversize porches, sipping tea and eating cookies in wicker rockers. Many waved as he strolled by, and he was surprised to find himself smiling and waving back. When he finally reached Sunshine Bridal, his mind was clear and focused.

He walked through the front door and headed directly into the office. A young woman with short pink hair was tapping madly on a laptop, muttering softly under her breath.

"Excuse me? I'm looking for Avery."

She jerked around. Golden-brown eyes stared back at him with a tinge of angst, as if she wasn't thrilled at being interrupted. "She's on an appointment. Not sure when she'll return. Can I take a message?"

"Maybe you can help me."

He tried not to grin at her annoyed exhaled breath, which was followed up by a huge fake smile. "Sure. What can I do for you?"

"I'm Carter Ross. Ally's brother."

Recognition lit up, and the stressed lines of her face smoothed out. "Oh, thank goodness! I cannot deal with one more grouchy client today. I'm Taylor, Avery's sister. It's nice to meet you. We all adore Ally and are so happy for her."

"Thanks, me, too. Um, I'm having some issues with Avery getting back in touch with me. She doesn't return my messages, and I'm supposed to be accompanying her on several appointments."

Taylor frowned. "That's weird and not like Avery at all. She's so damn organized, she color-codes her pens. Let me bring up her calendar." She punched a few keys and stared at the screen. "She should be back within the hour. Are you going with her to the bakery at three?"

He snapped his fingers. "Yes, I am. Could you do me a favor? Does she have any other appointments set up for my sister? I'd love a printout so I don't miss anything."

"Of course. I'll whip this out. Looks like you'll be in back-to-back appointments all next week, but then things will calm down a bit. I'm glad you got the SeaSalt for the reception. Pulling off a wedding in under three months is a challenge."

"I'm beginning to see that."

Taylor handed him the list. "Do you mind waiting here for her unaccompanied? I have to go meet a client."

He opened his mouth to agree, but was interrupted by a woman rushing in with a child snugly nestled in her arms. Though her hair was long and golden blonde, and her eyes a bright blue, he spotted the similarities in their faces immediately. Definitely the last sister of the crew. Her daughter looked like a tiny miniature, dressed in a Cinderella dress, plastic blue heels, and a tiara perched on her head. He pegged her as about five years old.

"T, you have to watch Zoe for me. I got an SOS from Samantha, who's having a panic attack at her bridal fitting. The MOG mentioned she'd gained some weight, and Samantha's hysterical."

"You let her do the fitting with the MOG?" Taylor asked, shaking her head. "Dude, bad decision."

The blonde glared. "Yeah, I know. Here, take her." She shoved the little girl into her sister's arms. Zoe tilted her rosy face up, her lips smeared with something that resembled pink frosting. "Hi, Aunt TT! Mama said a bad word."

"Hi, munchkin. Let's wash Mama's mouth out with soap later." This caused an array of giggles to erupt. "Bella, I can't watch her! I'm already running late for an appointment, and Avery isn't here yet."

"Oh my God, this is so bad." Bella leaned over and began to drag in deep breaths. "You think I can take her with me?"

"Into a meltdown with a hysterical bride and clueless MOG?"

"I'll bring her Kindle! Maybe promise her one of those gourmet lollipops if she's good! I have to get there ASAP, or the whole appointment will blow up and—"

"I can watch her."

All three females jerked around to stare at Carter.

He regarded the little girl with a smile and hunkered down so he didn't look so intimidating. "Are you Cinderella, or do you dress like that all the time for school?" he asked.

Another giggle. "It's summer! There's no school in summer. And I'm not really Cinderella since she's a pretend character, but I like to look pretty. Are you getting married?"

"No, my sister is. I'm waiting for your aunt Avery. Do you think you'd be okay to hang with me for a bit until she gets here?"

"Wait—who are you?" Bella demanded, eyes narrowed in suspicion.

"Carter Ross. I'm Ally's brother, the man of honor."

Bella's face cleared. "Oh yes, Avery told us all about Ally's wedding. I'm sorry we haven't met before now. I'm Bella."

"Nice to meet you. Listen, I know you don't know me, but I don't mind watching her until Avery arrives. Here's my ID." He slid out his driver's license and handed his phone over. "You can put my number in your contacts. Does she have her Kindle with her?"

Bella bit her lip. "Yes. Are you sure you don't mind?"

"I wouldn't offer if I did. I promise to keep her right here and not move."

Taylor cocked her head and regarded him with respect. "That's really cool. I think it'd be okay. Bella?"

"Sweetheart, this is Carter. Do you want to stay with him for a little while? You can't leave the office, but you can read or play your games."

Zoe nodded. "Will Carter read *Fancy Nancy* with me?"

"I love *Fancy Nancy*," he said solemnly.

Bella looked back and forth between them, then made her decision. "I owe you big-time," she said, hurriedly grabbing his phone and exchanging numbers. He noticed she studied his ID carefully, then took a picture of it with her phone. *Good.* He was glad she was being thorough. She gave Zoe a hug and kiss goodbye, warning her to behave, and then disappeared in a frenzy with Taylor at her side.

The door banged shut behind them.

Carter stared down at his new charge. Her bright-blue eyes studied him with the open curiosity of the very young. "Do you really like *Fancy Nancy*?" she finally asked suspiciously.

He smothered a laugh. Damn, she was adorable. "I really do. Why don't you open it up and I'll read. Want to sit on the couch?"

"Sure." She scrambled up, fishing her pink Kindle out of her *PAW Patrol* backpack. He stretched out his legs, crossed his ankles, and hit the button to put the cover in full size.

"I like her outfit, but yours is nicer," he said, tapping the screen.

"Thanks! Pink is my favorite color, even though I'm mostly wearing blue today."

"I can tell because you had pink cupcakes today with sprinkles, right?"

Her eyes widened. Her soft voice came out in a hush. "How did you know that?"

His lips twitched. "I have some magic powers, but I don't like to use them often."

"Do you have a wand?"

"Nope, I just use my mind. Should we read?"

"Oh yes." She crossed her legs, rearranged her dress, and leaned her head close to see the pictures. The scent of strawberry shampoo made him smile.

Carter read the book, using his funny voices like he used to do when Ally was little, and got lost in the moment. Kids were good for that. And dogs. It was too bad he wasn't keen on having a child alone—after raising Ally with no support, he knew how difficult being a single parent was. That's why he believed in a two-parent household if at all possible. He had no desire to get married, though, or engage in a serious, committed relationship. Therefore, kids weren't in the picture for him.

A sudden flicker of regret cut deep at the thought, but he pushed the feeling away and concentrated on the story. He rarely allowed any messy emotions to throw him off-balance. There was no point, so it was much easier to push them away until they disappeared.

They'd gotten to book three in the series when the door flung open and Avery rushed in. She threw her purse on the table, kicked off her heels, and began tearing through a huge pile of thick folders stuffed with papers and mismatched fabrics. He looked down at Zoe, who was grinning at the fact her aunt hadn't spotted them on the couch.

"Hi, Aunt Avery!" she shouted.

86

"Holy crap!" The files flew from her hands and scattered on the floor. "Wh-What's going on?"

Zoe gave a deep sigh. "She says bad words, too, but I can't say 'em 'cause I'm too little. Aunt TT says when I'm old, I can say all the bad words."

"At least seven," he said, nodding.

"At least."

"What's going on?" Avery demanded again, this time much louder. She stared at them in shock. "Carter, why are you here? Zoe, where's your mom?"

"Your sisters had to both run out, so I told them I'd watch Zoe until you got back. It's lucky I stopped in, since I would have missed the appointment at the bakery."

The surge of pink in her cheeks confirmed her attempt at treachery. "How did you know about that?"

"Taylor looked up your schedule. She was kind enough to give me a printout so I can be aware of any future appointments. I'll be honest, I expected more organization and follow-up from my sister's wedding planner."

She winced. "It's not a big deal. I intended to overnight a few samples she can taste with Jason and make her final decision."

"Ah, but what samples? What if you give her the wrong three choices because I wasn't there, telling you what she likes and doesn't like?"

"Can I have cake, too?" the little girl chimed in. "I like chocolate and vanilla and pink cupcakes with rainbows."

"I think we should all have cake. It's been a disappointing day."

Avery looked like she was going to scream, but Zoe reached over and patted his hand. "At least we got to read *Fancy Nancy*."

"That was my highlight." Oh, how he adored a precocious child. They made life so much more interesting. Bella and her husband were blessed to have her. "Is your aunt always so riled up?"

Zoe wrinkled her nose. "She runs around a lot."

He laughed.

Avery groaned and walked over to the couch. "Hey, munchkin," she said, "how about I put on *PAW Patrol* in the other room?"

"Yes!" The little girl shot up, and he knew he'd been replaced by the lure of cartoon puppies. Not a bad choice. "Thanks for reading with me, Carter. Can we eat cake later?"

"Yes, it's a date. Wait. Are you old enough to date?"

She gave another charming giggle. "No, silly, but we can be friends."

"Awesome. Catch ya later."

She bounced out of the room, holding Avery's hand. Carter got up from the couch and stretched, then spotted the Keurig coffee station. He could use a shot of caffeine for what lay ahead. He had a gut feeling Avery was going to make her disapproval of his visit loudly known.

Might as well get ready for the show.

He whistled and made himself a fresh mug.

When she stomped back in the room, he was perched halfway on the desk, drinking coffee. With his hip cocked out and legs casually crossed, it took her a moment to regather her forces.

He looked . . . different.

The suit was gone and replaced with shorts that showed off lean muscled legs and olive-toned skin. His T-shirt was a dark blue, stretching tight over an impressive broad chest and making his eyes appear less gray and more cerulean, adding a depth that threw her off. His usual shaven jaw now held a shadow of dark stubble. The glasses were gone, and a pair of trendy black sunglasses was perched on top of his head. He should've looked less intimidating, but awareness skated over her nerve endings, causing a vibration in her core that puzzled her. What was it about him that made her body buzz? Was it just dislike she was mistakenly dubbing as physical attraction?

She couldn't be attracted to Carter Ross. He was everything she didn't like in a man: rude, arrogant, boring, and her best friend's pain-in-the-ass brother. Dear Lord, she had to get her dating life back in order or she was going to fall apart.

She gathered all those disturbing, rambling thoughts, balled them up into a tight knot, and shoved them in a lockbox. Then focused on something that made sense.

Her annoyance.

"You can't barge into my place of business and get involved with my family," she said, hands on her hips as she faced him down. "You should have never been watching Zoe. I can't believe Bella left her with you!"

His gaze flicked over her body with a lazy assessment, as if he were bored by her outburst. "I tried calling and texting first. You chose to ignore me, even though I'm your client just as much as my sister."

"No, you're not. You're just the ManOH." She practically spat out the words. "Ally's happy with our current arrangement; I haven't gotten any complaints from her."

"Yet. Let me make things crystal clear so there are no longer any misunderstandings." He sipped his coffee and took his time. "I spoke with Ally before she left and confirmed I'd be involved with every step of this process. I'm her only family, so you're stuck with me. I will attend every vendor appointment from now on. And if you somehow forget to include me, this time I'll be sure to jump on the phone and tell Ally you're cutting me out on purpose. I've been kind enough to spare you the discomfort of a confrontation in order to protect my sister, but if it continues, I won't be as forgiving."

She gasped. He wouldn't dare. He'd never deliberately stress out his sister. Would he? Or maybe he'd grab the opportunity to once again prove she was lousy at her job and that he'd been right about her all along. Was he that mean and twisted?

Yeah. He was.

Her quick afternoon at the bakery suddenly took a bad turn. She thought of all the appointments she had lined up the next two weeks for Ally's wedding and wanted to weep. This was her fault. She'd been so sure he'd just go away if she ignored him. She should have known Carter had too big of an ego to leave her alone. Somehow they'd gotten into a weird competition over Ally's wedding, and he viewed it as a challenge. *Ridiculous.*

She needed to regather control and create a plan B. Maybe if she ran him ragged, he'd get tired of the endless choices over minute details. It happened to grooms and FOBs all the time. They'd be enthusiastic about the decor in the beginning, until they needed to view dozens of centerpieces, discussing the benefits and disadvantages of lilies versus roses, white versus pink, and tall vases versus small bowls. Give the men one or two of those appointments and they'd beg off the rest, deciding to trust the bride and the planner, and go play some golf.

Yes, Carter would be the same exact way. Eventually, he'd retreat and she could finish planning this wedding on her own.

"Fine," she said. "You win. I won't ditch you anymore."

"Such lofty standards you have," he drawled.

She gritted her teeth. "We need to be at the bakery at three. I'll text my sisters to see when they're coming back for Zoe. For now, feel free to finish your coffee and relax in the conference room."

"I feel so pampered."

His dry wit threatened a laugh from her, but she managed to squash it in time. After a few texts to her sisters, she checked on Zoe and gathered up her stack of folders, slipping it into a sleek black bag with the Sunshine Bridal logo.

After what felt like an eternity, Bella flew through the front door and collapsed on the couch, sweat dampening her forehead. "Oh my God, what a nightmare."

"What happened? Is everything okay?"

"The sitter got sick, so I had to move some of my appointments, but then I got a crazy text from Samantha at Vera's. She had a meltdown and refused to come out of the dressing room because the MOG called her fat in a roundabout way."

Avery covered her mouth with her fingers. "No. You should have called me."

"You were slammed with appointments this morning, so I didn't want to bother you."

Avery shook her head. Her sister hated leaning on anyone for help, determined to handle her own clients. "Next time bother me," she said.

Bella waved a hand in the air. "It all worked out fine. I rushed over there and managed to get Samantha to let me in the dressing room, coaxed her into a different dress, and when she came out, everyone burst into tears and called her the most beautiful bride in the world. Holy shit."

"Mama, Aunt TT said you're gonna get the soap!"

Avery watched her sister's face fall into pure joy as she picked up Zoe and gave her a snuggle. Her vibrating tension calmed. Honestly, Bella rarely got worked up over a client disaster. Avery wondered if she was feeling a bit overwhelmed and made a mental note to try and check in with her more. "You're right, no dessert for me tonight. Did you have fun with Carter?"

"Oh yes, we read *Fancy Nancy* and talked about cake."

"Perfect." Her sister's eyes sparked with mischief. "Did Aunt Avery have fun with Carter?"

Avery sucked in a breath and glared. "Not funny," she muttered. "Why on earth would you leave her with him? I told you he was difficult and a PITA."

"And here I thought you were beginning to like me. Why am I thinking, in this case, a *PITA* isn't the term used for a sandwich?"

Avery closed her eyes in horror. The man was always lurking or stalking or eavesdropping. Anyone else would have stayed in the damn conference room, but here he was again, prowling around and getting in her business.

Bella actually laughed. "'Cause it's not, but if I tell you, I'll need to invest in more soap. Thanks again for helping me out."

"Carter, I like you lots. Why don't you like him, Aunt Avery?" Zoe asked.

Her heart stuttered at the adorable face staring back at her with a worried look. Even at five, Zoe was kind to everyone and hated when any child was left out. Swallowing back her frustration, she gave her niece a smile. "I like Carter just fine."

"Oh, good. He's not getting married, Mama. You think he can be my dad?"

Silence fell.

Besides being kind, Zoe was also brutally truthful about not having a father.

Avery waited for the shocked look on Carter's face and the endless questions, but he surprised her by taking the announcement with ease. "How about we be friends? I'm staying in Cape May the whole summer. If it's okay with your mom, we can spend more time together. Unless you think I'm too old." He pulled a face and Zoe laughed.

The tension in the room dissipated, and her sister managed a grateful smile. "Sounds good to me. What do you think, Zoe?" Bella asked.

"I can take you to the beach and show you how to build castles," the little girl announced.

"Deal."

"Well, I better get this little munchkin home. I'll call you later, Avery. Thanks again, Carter." Bella disappeared with her daughter and left them alone.

The air shifted, and the sudden silence pressed down upon them.

Avery dared a glance from under her lashes. He was staring at her hard, as if trying to figure something out. For some reason, the intense blue of his eyes mixed with the clean scent of his skin made her a tiny bit woozy. He smelled like soap and man and ocean-salt breeze. This close, she noticed that the scruff hugging his chiseled jaw emphasized the full curve of his bottom lip.

"What's *PITA* mean, Avery?" His voice deepened, silky and low with a touch of gravel.

A shiver shook through her. She wrapped her arms in front of her chest and tipped her chin up. He still towered over her. "Pain in the Ass."

She waited for the sarcasm, but he surprised her again by laughing. "Of course it does."

Chapter Eight

"Are we ready for the cake tasting?" he asked.

She blinked like she'd been taken off guard. "Oh. Yes. Let's go." Grabbing her stuff, she led him out and toward her car. "It's a few blocks—do you want to walk or ride?"

"I don't mind the walk as long as you don't." He glanced at her teetering strappy sandals. "How do you even navigate the sidewalks in those? It's like someone who was permanently off-balance paved them."

She smiled. "It's always been that way here. You get used to it."

He plucked her heavy bag from her shoulder and transferred it to his, ignoring her protests. "Was growing up in a beach town as idyllic as it sounds?"

"Pretty much. The locals are close-knit and take care of one another through winter. The tourists can drive us nuts, but they also bring in the business we all need. My family has been here through two generations, so the ocean is part of our blood."

She'd rarely talked about her family's business or beach home years ago. Curiosity stirred. "Why did you go to college in DC?" he asked. "It's a contradiction to how you grew up."

She tilted her head and gave him a knowing glance. "That's exactly why. I wanted a city where I could be in the middle of it all. I craved fast-paced, loud, dirty, surrounded by passionate people proclaiming their opinions. My parents fought me, but I was eighteen, and all I wanted was to be different. I didn't know if I wanted to go back to my childhood home and run the family business."

Jagged misfit pieces clicked into place. She'd been running away. Afraid of getting stuck in a small ocean town, doing the same job for years on end out of responsibility. No wonder she'd embraced DC and all her wildness. He let the silence settle between them, but it was comfortable, as if she'd accepted that he was analyzing her response.

She spoke suddenly. "Ally and I talked about running off and starting our own business."

He snapped his fingers. "I remember. A bookstore with an attached café, right?"

"Yep. We wanted to serve organic foods, handmade chocolates, and sell primarily romance novels and poetry."

He groaned. "I almost had a heart attack. You both had no business plan and no money. You also couldn't cook and had no clue about location. Ally and I got into a big fight over it."

"Oh, she had a few choice words to use about you," she said, laughing. "We swore we'd open the business ourselves, become successful, and prove you wrong. We called it the Broken Cupid."

"You didn't."

"Yep. We imagined poetry readings with broody, talented artists filling the spaces. Reading and discussing great literature and drinking the espressos we made at our café."

"You're killing me here. Dare I ask what finally destroyed this great vision?"

"I'm not sure. We both got jobs to begin saving, and planned to get a business loan. But then Ally began dating that guy Ben, and got caught up in her romance. I came home for a visit, and my mother begged me to give the bridal business a try before I went back to DC. By the time I spoke with Ally about it, she'd already decided to get her master's. Soon, we'd completely forgotten about the Broken Cupid and were swept into our adult lives."

Was that a hint of longing laced in her voice or his imagination? She seemed completely focused and happy with her job, but he'd noticed her crazed schedule and workaholic ways. Was she wishing sometimes for something else? Something . . . bigger? "Do you regret going home and not giving it a shot?"

She seemed to think about the question seriously before answering. "No. Even though I was a different person then, I still believe I was always meant to do this. I get a joy and satisfaction from my job I couldn't imagine anywhere else. I just regret . . . Never mind."

He stopped walking and turned. Her gaze lifted and crashed into his. His breath tightened in his chest at the look in those hazel eyes. An intense hunger seemed to spark from a place deep inside him, a place he knew too well. His voice deepened, urging her to spill her truth. "What do you regret, Avery?" he asked.

She took her time, but the words seemed plucked from a memory she rarely visited any longer. "I regret not remembering that girl," she said softly.

The connection between them surged, peaked. He stumbled back a step, desperately needing the distance. *WTF?* Why did he suddenly have the desire to yank her into his arms and soothe her? To stroke her hair and tip her chin up and take her mouth to see how she tasted? To soak up her moan and know he was the reason for it? Confusion blasted through him, along with a rising arousal that threw him off-balance.

Oh no, he was so not going there. It was ridiculous and messy and . . . dangerous.

A couple strolled past them, bumping into him and apologizing, and he held up his hand in acknowledgment. When he looked back at Avery, the moment was gone.

And he was glad.

Avery opened the door to the bakery. The scents of sugar, chocolate, and happiness filled the air, and she perked up as she greeted the young girl behind the counter and asked for Maria. She wanted to forget about that strange encounter with Carter, and her sudden, awful urge to close the distance between them and . . .

Well, she didn't know. And she didn't want to find out.

Carter browsed past the display cases filled with butter cookies, cupcakes, and various pastries tempting onlookers with swirls of chocolate ganache, fresh whipped cream, and flaky pastry. She caught sight of the last chocolate croissant lying in the tray. It looked lonely. Madison's Bakery had been all sold out the past few mornings, so she hadn't had her fix in a while. She licked her lips and promised herself a reward for when the appointment was over.

Maria came out and shook Carter's hand. She was an older woman with permed brown hair that looked like a helmet, and strong, blunt features. With a stocky build, thick hips, and hands known to whip the best batter in the Cape, she was a master of her craft and well known for her custom wedding cakes.

Avery opened her bag and removed a stack of designs. She already had a basic idea of what her friend wanted, so today was about narrowing to specifics and taste. Carter sat across from her, lounging with ease in the small chair that barely held his length. Her glance touched on his muscled thighs, then quickly jumped away. His presence was becoming more than a nuisance. He was beginning to edge right into the distraction phase—a deadly place for a coordinator who had to juggle a thousand details.

She cleared her throat and focused. Time to implement her plan and show him tasting endless cakes and launching into an analysis of each one wasn't fun. He was definitely the no-nonsense type. The one to see a shirt on the rack and buy it without checking for something he might like better. Hopefully, this would be their last appointment together before he cried surrender.

Maria came back with a tray of samples and bottles of water. "It's always nice working with the bride's family when I can't be with the bride directly. I hope you've brought your appetite."

Carter winked. "I made sure not to eat breakfast or lunch due to your reputation."

A laugh tinkled from the older woman, and Avery tried not to gag at his obvious flattery. "There's eight samples here, which will give you both a spectrum of flavors and combinations. I've included some classic, my most popular, and a few designer types, as I like to call it."

"Sounds great. There are a few things Ally doesn't like, so that may help us limit the options," he said.

Maria nodded. "Yes, Avery already gave me a list, which is why we're staying away from red velvet, cherries, and any type of banana flavors."

Carter grunted, as if bestowing a point. He really didn't think highly of her if he believed she wouldn't know her best friend's likes and dislikes after years of hanging out together.

"Let's start with a twist on the basic. We have a vanilla butter cake, paired with caramel buttercream. Instead of the usual frosting, this one has a torched meringue to really intensify the flavors."

Avery and Carter reached for the same fork at the same time. Their fingers brushed, and Avery jerked back, not wanting to experience any skin-on-skin contact. Hell no. She refused to feel any type of attraction to her friend's overbearing older brother. It was too damn weird.

She grasped the other fork and popped the bite into her mouth. The gorgeous moist cake and subtle sweetness of caramel was soothing and pleasant on her tongue. She half closed her eyes, concentrating on the entire experience while she funneled Ally's particular tastes mentally.

Carter turned toward Maria. "I apologize."

The older woman frowned. "For what?"

"I questioned Avery's decision to deal with only one bakery. I thought we needed a broader amount of choices, but obviously I was wrong. This is truly amazing."

Maria smiled, pleasure sparkling in her brown eyes. "Thank you. That was the nicest apology I ever received."

Avery held back a groan. *Another female bites the dust.*

Maria narrowed her focus to Carter, enthusiastically explaining each sample and engaging in a lively discussion of baking compared to creative art.

"How did you come up with the idea of including lavender in the buttercream? It's subtle, but the lingering floral wakes up my mouth."

"Yes! That's exactly what I wanted. What do you think of it with the carrot cake?" Maria asked excitedly.

"Love it. But you know what's true brilliance? Pairing both with a Grand Marnier cream-cheese filling. If someone told me those flavors would work, I would've never believed them."

Maria leaned over the table, putting their heads close together. "We must break the barriers of the mind and concentrate on taste as essence. Even though the brain tries to anticipate what you will be eating, twisting the classics with surprising elements allows the taste buds to explode."

"Genius."

Barf.

Avery cleared her throat. "Um, Maria, I really think the coconut with the orange buttercream should be in the top three. It's a beautiful combination."

Maria nodded. "Excellent choice. Do you agree, Carter? After all, she's your sister. You know her best."

Avery firmed her jaw to keep it from falling open. *Son of a bitch.* He was doing it again. Pouring on hidden charm she'd never seen before—maybe because he'd never bothered to show her. The master baker was practically blooming under his attention and had cut Avery off from the consultation.

"Yes, we definitely should send her a sample, but personally, I think she's going to go with the carrot and lavender. It's unique."

"I agree, it's wonderful, but carrot isn't her favorite cake. She never orders it in a restaurant. I think she'll prefer a classic with a subtle twist," Avery said.

Carter arched a brow. "I disagree. I think she's going to want a cake that's a bit daring for her big day."

Irritation coursed through her at his dismissive tone. "But she hates carrots. Why would you think she'd want a carrot cake for her wedding?"

His voice chilled. "Because, as Maria explained, it's bigger than the actual carrot cake. It's the Grand Marnier and lavender that will make her forget it's carrot."

She snorted. "Sorry, dude, but carrots are carrots, no matter how you mask them. She won't pick that cake."

"Did you just call me *dude*?"

Maria glanced back and forth between them, her face fascinated. "Well, I love a lively debate, but why don't we just send her samples of both and let her choose? I'll include our third choice—the chocolate with chili-infused fudge buttercream—and we'll see what she picks."

"Fine with me," Avery said, trying not to sound defensive.

"Thank you, Maria, for your clear thinking. I'm glad my sister will have the very best cake for her wedding."

The baker beamed with pride. "It's a pleasure to meet someone who's not only charming and polite but understands exactly what I do here. Honestly, Avery, why can't you bring me more clients like Carter? It would make my job so much easier."

Avery forced a smile. "Oh, he's a joy, all right."

Her sarcasm was lost as Maria gathered up the tray and cleaned the table. Carter shot her a glare, and just like that, they were back to their feud.

Carrot, for God's sake. Like Ally would ever choose it, no matter how good it tasted. She reminded herself it would be a sweet victory when she picked the coconut and orange.

Maria sat down again. "Now, why don't you show me some of the designs you'd like. What are her colors?"

"Silver and lavender, but we're doing some black raspberry for contrast. These are some of the pictures I think would work," Avery said. "I'm looking to pair three squares that resemble gift boxes. We can add these types of elements," she said, pointing at ropes of pearls in shimmery silver and giant bows spilling down from each tier. "Once we pick her flowers, we can weave them here."

Carter nodded. "That's pretty."

She almost fell off her chair. Finally, he agreed with her. Maybe they'd be out of here soon. "Wonderful."

"But it's a bit boring, don't you think? Predictable?"

Her heart sank. "Most cakes revolve around basic shapes, but we can add any accents you'd like. Did you have something specific in mind?"

"No. Sorry, I'm not an expert. Maria? Any ideas?"

Avery snapped her teeth together and tried not to wince in pain. "I do have these other designs, which combine the square in a diagonal manner, giving it an almost-modern take. Ally mentioned she liked that setup."

Maria was nodding slowly, her fingers brushing across the glossy designs from the book. "All of these are classic for a reason. They work beautifully with every type of cake. With seventy-five guests, we don't want it to be lost with too many layers. There is a new technique I've been trying out for certain weddings, but I'm not sure about your budget. It's a bit pricey."

"There's no limit on budget," Carter said. "I'm paying for the cake."

Maria shot him a look full of affection. "How lovely. Well, there's a technique called bas-relief. Basically, I carve designs into the actual cake to give it a more architectural feel, but it ends up looking like a sculpture. Here, let me get you some pictures. Be right back."

The moment she disappeared, Avery leaned in. "What are you doing?" she whispered fiercely. "Are you trying to torture me on purpose?"

"No, I'm trying to get my sister the best cake possible," he hissed back. "Funny, I thought that was your job."

"I already spoke with Ally, and she loves the square-box design! You're mucking up everything just because you're a control freak."

"You're not pushing boundaries," he said. "You want to do the same stuff for every client. Doesn't my sister deserve something spectacular?"

Temper washed through her. "How dare you? I'm giving this my all, like I do every wedding. You're just a judgmental, arrogant prick!"

"Here we go," Maria sang as she returned to the table, laying a stack of photos down.

The two pulled back and glared at each other from a distance.

"We can keep the square shape and do two layers, but the wow factor would be in the design. When I carve designs into the cake, it gives it almost like a 3-D effect." She pointed to a gorgeous cake with intricate leaf carvings popping out from the surface. "I'd stay away from leaves or berries since that's more of a fall theme, but I can do roses, and then incorporate silver- and lavender-foil designs on the outer edge."

Avery took one look at the design and knew it was the cake her friend would want. Maria had never mentioned this new technique before. Guilt rippled. Was Carter right? Was she on autopilot, matching her clients with the same ideas instead of looking to be innovative? Was it her fault because she'd never asked Maria before if she had anything new to offer?

"That's it." Carter jabbed a finger at the design. "It's a work of art. You can actually do that?"

Maria laughed. "Yes. It takes a long time, so it's expensive, but if you have the budget, I can do it."

"Even with the time constraint?" Avery asked. "Usually, I'd give you months of advance prep. Is this something you can actually deliver on for an August event?"

Maria tilted her head and regarded Carter. "To be honest, this is pushing my schedule to the maximum. Normally, I wouldn't have even suggested it, but I'd like you to have something special, Carter, because I know you're appreciative. I'll be happy to do it."

Carter reached over and grabbed her hands. "There are no words, Maria. My sister is the only family I have left. This is a true gift."

Maria patted his hand, eyes filled with emotion, as Avery stared at him with a grudging respect and a growing worry that she'd underestimated her opponent. He'd won over the cake designer, gotten her to commit to an ambitious design on a tight deadline, and come out looking like a hero.

She added her thanks to Maria and gathered up her things. Carter strode to the bakery display. She opened her mouth to ask for the last chocolate croissant to go, but it was too late.

"Maria, can I get that to go?" He tapped the glass pane, targeting the lonely, beautiful pastry. "Those are my ultimate weakness."

"Of course! Take it, on the house."

Avery watched as it was wrapped in crisp paper, stuffed in a bag, and handed to Carter.

With a broad grin, he stuck his nose in the bag and sniffed. "Smells delicious. Gotta love a good chocolate croissant, right, Avery?"

That's when she realized he knew.

He knew she'd wanted that pastry—bad. He knew, and he'd deliberately snatched it, just like he'd overtaken her appointment and shown her they were playing by his rules.

On cue, his gaze crashed into hers. A tiny smile curled his lower lip.

He'd won this set because she'd underestimated him. Again.

But she wouldn't allow him to win the war. This was just one tiny battle . . .

They walked out of the bakery. "Well, that was fun." *Not.* "I need to go back to the office, so I'll be in touch," she said.

"Why do you look so cranky?" he asked.

She shot him a look. "Like you don't know."

"Seriously, what'd I do?"

She rolled her eyes. "Besides the whole cake thing? You took the last chocolate croissant. *On purpose.*"

He blinked. "I like them."

"Me, too. Sometimes the only thing I look forward to at my morning meetings is that damn pastry," she grumbled.

"You want it?"

He offered it to her, but she rolled her eyes. "No. I wouldn't enjoy it now."

"Why?"

A frustrated sigh escaped. "Because you really don't want to give it to me. It'd be a guilt-eat, and I'm no martyr."

Those full lips tilted in a half smile. "You really are a puzzle."

"Just don't try to solve me and we'll get along fine."

His laugh pleased her more than it should. She liked when he relaxed and stopped being so damn robotic. He was more fun and a tiny bit sexy.

As soon as the thought registered, horror slammed through her.

No. He was definitely not *sexy*. He had taken over the entire cake appointment, disrespected her job, and stolen the last chocolate croissant. He was the devil, a control freak whose goal was to ruin her summer, and she could never forget it.

The mantra played in her head as she marched down the sidewalk ahead of him.

Chapter Nine

"Want to go to dinner?"

She stared at him like he'd announced he wanted to take her to bed. Ever since they'd left the bakery, she'd gone back to the freeze treatment and just grunted at his occasional efforts at conversation. "No."

He couldn't help his gaze from lingering on the curve of her ass as she stalked in front of him, her heels clicking fast over the uneven sidewalk in her desperate need to be ahead. In the fashionable pencil skirt, her hips swayed, and her lush buttocks were framed by the tight black fabric.

When had he begun thinking of her as sexy? She'd always been this annoying female hellion he wanted to keep in check around his sister. But these last few encounters, he'd felt a physical connection between them he'd never noticed before. Was it just the anger? Or something more?

He didn't intend to back down easily. He had a need to explore this strange dynamic a bit more. "Why not?"

"Because I don't like you."

He grinned at her stark honesty. "You owe me dinner," he reminded her. "Unless you renege on all your bets."

That statement made her stop in her tracks. Her head jerked around, and she glared at him with an intense loathing he found kind of hot.

What did they say about anger and passion being closely linked? Was it possible she felt the same odd connection but refused to acknowledge it?

"You are a horrible person. Are you seriously going to force me to take you to dinner? How about I give you my credit card and I just pay for it? You're probably used to dining by yourself."

He cocked his head and allowed her remark to sink in. "That was kind of mean."

She muttered something under her breath. "You're right. I'm sorry."

"Apology accepted. Why don't I make reservations at Peter Shields for tonight?"

"I'm sure they're booked," she said between gritted teeth. "Besides, I have to work."

"Till what time?"

"All night."

"When are your usual days off, then?"

She rolled her eyes as if he was ignorant. "None. I rarely take a day or evening off—there's no time."

He frowned at that. He worked a heavy schedule, too, but enjoyed unwinding with a book or a long walk with Lucy in the evenings. "Fine, let's combine work with dinner. I'll pick you up at eight. We can go over booking the bachelorette party."

"You're not listening. I have a big wedding this weekend, and I need to make sure every detail is covered. Besides, I should speak with Ally's bridesmaids before solidifying any plans."

"I already did. They decided to let me be in charge of the whole thing. They want to be surprised, so they gave me carte blanche on the whole thing. Isn't that great?"

The look on her face almost made him laugh. She was so obviously not pleased with their decision. Those too-wide eyes filled with hot anger, and her mouth pressed into a tight line. Funny, he'd never noticed her lips made a plump bow, almost like a gift, painted in crimson red.

The sudden image of those lips opening under his crashed through his brain, and his body stirred.

"I can only imagine how you got them to agree," she said. "Are you really going to bust up your sister's last chance to cut loose? Why don't you gracefully bow out and let me handle it? The women really want to have fun."

He shot her a hurt look. "I'm fun. I have some great ideas I wanted to run by you. And if you want to guarantee Ally will have a good time, you need to help me plan it."

She blew out a breath. "Fine, but after this, the slate is wiped clean. Just so you know, you'll never get a reservation, and I'm not free until eight thirty."

"I'll handle it. Pick you up later. I better get back to Lucy." He strode away before she had time to change her mind.

The rest of the day flew by. A quick call secured dinner reservations. He took Lucy for a walk, read a few chapters of his book on the deck, and analyzed a proposal for his next project. By the time he'd showered and changed, he was ready for good food and some feisty conversation.

He whistled while he drove to Avery's house and parked. Glancing at his GPS, he confirmed the address. Of course she'd live in a cottage straight out of a Disney fairy tale. It was girlie and quirky, from the mismatched stone and bright-yellow door to the heavy ivy threading up and down the walls. The gate squeaked as he walked to the front porch, where a variety of endless, fascinating junk littered the space: watering cans, potted plants in various colors and sizes, statues of frogs and fairies, and mismatched wicker furniture with brightly colored pillows. The sound of multiple wind chimes caught the light breeze and lifted a wash of tinkling to his ears. It was as if spells could be cast in this small cottage close to the beach, and he wondered why a part of him sighed with pleasure at the happy, freestyle surroundings.

His whole life had been built on organization and planning. He'd needed to know exactly what to put on the table for meals. He'd needed to know how to budget for bills, get Ally to her various clubs or sleepovers, make sure she did well in school, and fit in work, all while keeping a low profile. He'd refused to have his sister be pegged as *the one with no parents*, so he had become both to save her from ever feeling she was different. A lofty goal—one he'd failed at multiple times. But after each mess-up, he'd tried harder. Looking at Avery's home reminded him of being playful again, with no thought to how a house of cards can crash with just one soft, misplaced tap.

He shook off his musings and pressed the doorbell.

Avery opened the door. Her chin was tilted, as if ready to meet an opponent rather than her dinner companion. His gaze swept over her casual jeans, flowy white top, and low-heeled sandals. She'd let her hair go free, and the natural curls sprang around her head with cheerful abandon. Other than a touch of color on her lips, her face held little makeup. A large canvas bag was thrown over her shoulder.

"Hi," she said.

He reached over, snagged the bag, and put it on his own shoulder. "Hi."

"I can carry my own bag, you know."

"My mother would scream from the grave if I allowed such a thing. I promised to open doors, pay for dinners, and help with oversized bags."

"It's a different time. Us womenfolk can take care of ourselves."

"I know, but I do it to honor her. She believed it was about respect."

Avery pursed her lips, seeming to consider his statement. "That's actually nice."

"Thanks. Your house is purple."

She rolled her eyes, and the quick truce ended. "I happen to like purple. I bet your house is still gray. And the interior is black and white—all neutrals. Little color. And very tidy."

Other than Ally's room, he'd put little thought into the house after their parents were gone. There was no need. It was just a space needed to accomplish his goal to raise Ally in a safe environment, and the less stuff the better.

"Yep, still the same. Do you still have the habit of leaving glasses half-full of water everywhere like the little girl from the movie *Signs*?"

Annoyance flickered over her face. "Of course not."

He grinned, pegging her in the lie. "At least you'll be prepared for an alien attack."

She ignored him, slamming the front door and marching past to his car. "Where are we going?"

"Peter Shields."

She slid into the passenger seat, and he climbed into the car, pulling smoothly away from the curb.

"Wait, how did you get a reservation? Even weekdays, it's impossible in the summer, especially last minute," she said.

He shrugged. "I had no problem." Especially after he'd used her name and basically told the hostess it was a business appointment so Avery could impress a client. That had secured him a table in record time.

"Hmm, must've gotten lucky. I just spoke with Ally a few hours ago. Told her the cake samples are on the way, and to let us know when she makes her choice."

He knew he should let the whole thing go, but the words popped out of his mouth. "Care to make another bet?"

She snorted. "Like what?"

"If she picks my cake, you come to the beach with me."

Her mouth dropped open. "That's the stupidest bet I ever heard. First of all, I have no time to go to the beach, and if I did, I wouldn't want to hang out with you."

"I'm going to begin thinking you don't like me by such harsh comments."

She shook her head, a laugh ripping from her chest. "And I think you just want to make these bets to get a rise out of me."

He did. Like right now, her cheeks were flushed, and the air conditioner was blowing over her gauzy top, lifting the skimpy material up to bare a nice flash of her midriff. Her scent had already permeated the car—teasing and seductive in its light floral with a hint of spice. He liked the idea of hanging out on the beach with her. Imagined kicking back on a blanket and trading barbs under the hot sun, a wash of icy ocean water over their toes. Not that he'd admit it. She'd either punch him in the face or run away.

"Actually, I've been concerned with something you've said a few times," he said. "When was the last time you took a day off?"

"Hmm. Maybe last year? Oh, wait, I got really sick last winter, and I missed a whole weekend."

"Sick days don't count. How can people get married every weekend all through the year? I figured you'd have plenty of downtime in the winter."

"We do in terms of actual events, but I use the time for planning the spring and summer weddings. There's really no downtime to discuss details, and planning is always a good year ahead. And of course, there's the occasional surprise wedding thrown in that I take on, like Ally's."

He'd figured she had all winter off to relax and recharge before taking on wedding season. It seemed he was wrong. His interest peaked. "What about holidays?"

She shot him a look. "Are you kidding? We always have multiple Christmas weddings to deal with, plus New Year's Eve. Then we get into Valentine's Day, and I have the month of March to scramble for spring, which starts in April."

"Have you thought about hiring more staff?"

"Of course, but it's harder than you think to get a qualified worker who wants to live in Cape May year-round. We get students and interns and part-timers, but my sisters and I are the only ones capable of truly handling the big clients. Gabe has been wonderful, though. He'll be promoted soon."

"Gabe?" Annoyance stirred. "Who's he?"

"My assistant, but he's ready to get his own clients. He's charming, patient, and women adore him."

Was that her idea of a perfect guy? Sounded boring and trite to him. Most men like that were hiding some nasty stuff underneath such a shiny exterior. "I see. Is he married?"

She laughed and waved her hand in the air. "Gabe? God, no. He's like Jake Gyllenhaal—gorgeous but a longtime bachelor. I doubt there's a woman out there who can tame him. He hates commitment."

Carter picked through this new knowledge and found himself a bit pissed off at this perfect assistant of hers. Maybe they were sleeping together. Which was fine. It wasn't as if he was looking for anything with Avery.

"How long have you been working together?"

"A few years. He's been an integral part of the team, so it's nice to see him succeed. We spend so much time together; it will be strange not being with him on a daily basis, though."

The thought of her with some hot playboy charmer *assisting* her did something strange to his insides. They got all twisted and burned like acid. Maybe he needed some damn TUMS. "Sounds like you're real close."

She shot him a look, and he realized he'd emphasized his last word. "Yes. We are. Like I am with all my employees."

Her voice told him he was walking on the edge, and though he'd like to know for sure if they were sleeping together, there was no way he was going to ask. That meant no more talking about Gabe and his Gyllenhaal-like charm. He shifted back to his original topic. "Seems a shame you live in a beach town but rarely use it. What about your niece? Do you take time off to be with her?"

Her face softened. He liked the transition and wondered what it'd be like to stare into those eyes when they were all misty and needy. Imagined her chin tilted up as she waited for a kiss, lips parted and welcoming. She'd make a man feel like a fucking superhero. "Zoe is my only distraction from work," she said. "Bella has a part-time nanny to help, but all of us put Zoe as a priority. So yes, if she wants to go to the beach, or the ice-cream store, or the library, I carve out the time."

"What about Zoe's father?"

A ragged sigh filled the air. "He died when Zoe was only six months old. Car crash. He was coming home from a business trip and got hit by a drunk driver."

He muttered a curse. "I'm so sorry, Avery. That must've been a bad time for your family."

"It was. I didn't know if Bella would get through it. Took her months to just get out of bed. Matt was her childhood sweetheart— they grew up together and got married right out of college." She shook her head as if the painful memories clung. "But she's strong, and eventually, she came back to all of us. We're lucky to have one another."

"Did that factor into your decision to stay here and not pursue the Broken Cupid?"

She nodded. "Once I got home, I realized how much I enjoyed being back. Then Zoe was born, and I couldn't imagine leaving her. By the time we lost Matt, I knew my life was here, with my sisters."

"Family is everything," he said simply.

She glanced over, and a charge of energy buzzed between them. This time, it was more than just physical—it was an understanding that they'd both experienced losses and used family bonds to battle through. He respected her choice. Many would have remained selfish and pursued their own interests, but he'd learned from his own tragedy that there was more to life than thinking of oneself. Ally had been worth the price of growing up fast, and he regretted nothing.

But he'd never pay such a price again. The cost of loving someone that much, and that intensely, was a choice he'd long ago decided not to pursue.

Love wasn't always kind. Sometimes it tore you apart and broke every fragment of the heart. Bella had experienced it firsthand. So had his father, who'd chosen to be weak instead of strong when his wife died.

Carter would never allow himself to experience that type of pain again.

Ever.

"You okay?"

Her question startled him. He gripped the steering wheel and refocused. "Yeah, sorry. Daydreaming."

She smiled. "About getting me to the beach? Dream on, because you're going to lose."

"Ah, so you are taking on the bet?"

She shrugged. "Why not? I know I'm going to win. What do I get when you lose?"

"What do you want?"

She tilted her head, considering. The heavy weight of her curls slid down over her shoulder, which was partially bared by the flimsy top. Her smooth, golden skin looked soft and touchable. "You get a full beach day."

He frowned. "Thought that was my prize."

Her smile was slow and triumphant. "With Zoe. You spend the whole day with her and take her to the beach."

"Doesn't seem so bad. I like kids."

She looked startled. "You do?"

"Yeah, why wouldn't I? Besides, I promised I'd hang with her at the beach. Works for me." He almost laughed at her dejected expression. "Sorry to disappoint you. I can pretend it's a horrible punishment."

"I'm not disappointed, I'm surprised. Most men consider spending hours with a five-year-old torturous. I figured you didn't mean it when you promised her."

He pulled into the restaurant lot, parked, and cut the engine. Turning to face her, he made sure her gaze locked on his. "I never break

113

a promise, Avery," he said, the words as resolute as the vow he'd made years ago. "To anyone."

Those hazel eyes widened, and he heard the small gulp of air as she sucked in her breath. For endless seconds, they stared at one another. Carter fought the impulse to lean over and kiss her. He imagined she'd taste like the spiced wedding cake he'd sampled—a bit of sweet, a bit of savory, and a whole lot of sass. The silence stretched. His muscles tightened. He moved an inch. One more.

Then pulled back. Shook his head. No way was he going to muck up his sister's wedding by getting involved with the planner, who happened to be her best friend.

It was best to remember that.

"Let's go eat," he said.

He turned and got out of the car.

Chapter Ten

What the hell had just happened?

Avery sipped her wine and tried to relax. The restaurant was packed, but they'd scored a table on the porch, overlooking the sprawl of sandy beach and ocean. Golden lights glowed in the darkness, battling against the bright shine of endless stars stretched out in the sky. The entire aura reeked of romance and first dates, and here she was with a bag full of wedding work and a funny feeling in the pit of her stomach from their conversation in the car.

For just a moment, she'd experienced intense attraction. When Carter spoke his vow about keeping a promise, the implacable truth and determination shone from his carved features, sizzled from those misty blue-gray eyes, left free from his usual glasses. Within his words laced a passion that seemed hidden under the surface, and for a few precious seconds, she'd connected with that part of him.

And she'd wanted him to kiss her.

Holy crap.

She took a big gulp of wine and fumbled with the bag. Better to focus on work. Her fingers closed on a thick folder, but his deep voice made her freeze. "Later. Why don't we order and enjoy our wine first?"

Reluctantly, she tucked the bag away and tried to avoid the low flicker of candlelight, soft violin music piping in from the speakers, and the sensual wash of breeze caressing her body. She cleared her throat. "I'm still shocked you got us a table tonight."

"Your name is important around here."

She rotated her wineglass in her hand. "Wait—what? You used my name for the reservation?"

His grin was filled with male satisfaction. "Of course. I told them we were dining tonight so I can try out their menu for a possible rehearsal dinner. They squeezed us right in."

Oh, he'd played her well with this one. Implied he had magically snagged a reservation on his charm when he'd just lied and used her name. "You're unbelievable."

"I try. After all, this was one of the restaurants I mentioned in my texts you never replied to." He flipped open the menu. "Any suggestions?"

She rolled her eyes at the unsubtle dig. "No. But I heard the fish-eye soup is good."

He wrinkled his nose. "Sounds awful."

"Ask the waiter. It's highly recommended here."

They took a few minutes to peruse their choices. The waiter glided over, smartly dressed in black, introduced himself as Nate, and began to dive into the specials. His voice was low and cultured, and the list went on for a while. When he finished, Carter spoke up. "I heard your fish-eye soup was excellent. Can you tell me about it?"

The waiter looked confused. "Fish-eye? I'm sorry, sir, we don't have that on the menu."

"Is it sold out?"

Avery stifled a giggle.

"No." The waiter shook his head. "To be honest, we've never served that type of soup. Personally, it sounds a bit controversial."

With a tiny frown, Carter considered the waiter's words, then shot her a look.

Uh-oh.

The realization hit him, and his gaze narrowed. "Never mind. It seems I was wrong about the soup. I'll begin with the lobster salad, please."

She pressed her lips together, trying not to laugh out loud. The intimate scene from the car drifted away, and things were back the way they should be between them.

"Did you say you had a crab appetizer?" she asked when the waiter turned his attention to her.

"Yes, ma'am. The chef made them special tonight. Crabby balls."

She coughed. "Crabby . . . balls?"

Nate nodded. "They're quite delicious. Crisp on the outside, creamy on the inside. Very popular. Our chef is known for his balls."

Carter glanced at her in disbelief. A giggle rose up. Was she trapped in a *Saturday Night Live* skit? "Good to know," she managed. "I think I'll skip the balls."

"But, darling, you adore balls! You really should order them," Carter announced. "Much better than fish eyes, you always say."

Shocked, she stared at him. His eyes danced with mischief.

The waiter had no clue what was going on, and had probably missed watching a lot of comedy in his years, because he babbled on. "You'll love them. The balls are fried, but not greasy at all. Firm to the touch. I guarantee they taste amazing."

The laughter ripped from her chest and exploded from her mouth before she could stop it. Eyes filled with tears, she waved her hand in the air and gasped out the words, "Fine, yes, bring the crabby balls. Thank you."

"Of course." He shot them a puzzled look, but his training held. He didn't comment on her hysterics or the way Carter had his hand over his mouth like he, too, was about to explode. He gathered their menus and pivoted on his shiny heel.

They collapsed into laughter. "He didn't get it," Carter said. "Poor bastard."

"It was better that way." She took a deep breath, finally calming down. "God, I forgot how fun it is to be silly. I didn't even know you had it in you, robot man."

He smiled back. "I've got a few surprises, including a sense of humor."

"I guess I always remember you being so serious all the time."

He tapped his finger absently against the white tablecloth. "I had to be. I was worried if I wasn't strict with Ally, she'd get lost."

"The first time we met, I recognized she knew exactly who she was. She had an inner strength I was drawn to immediately. Reminded me of my sisters," she said with a grin. "For someone who lost both parents young, it tells me your hard work paid off. Ally simply adores you. Hell, she promised me I'd be her MOH, and look who she replaced me with."

His mouth twitched in amusement. She had a sudden impulse to drag her fingers over those plump lips to see if they were as soft as they looked. She enjoyed making him laugh. Maybe because it was a rare gift she didn't see often, so she cherished it when it happened.

"Appreciate that. I still remember when I had to accompany her at a father-daughter dance. She didn't want to stay home because all her friends were going, so we put on our fancy clothes and showed up at the school gym. There were all these old guys hanging around the punch bowl. I swear, it looked like a scene from *The Godfather*, and they used a dance to make arrangements on hits." He took a sip of pinot noir and shook his head. "So I'm there with my poor sister, and these guys are staring at me like they're ready to throw the punk kid out of the gym. Ally grabs my hand and marches up to them."

"Oh my God. What did she say?"

"She told them I was her brother and her guardian, and to be nice to me. Said I didn't know anyone and asked if they'd have a glass of punch with me while she looked for her friends. I almost fucking died. But you know what? Those guys patted my shoulder, brought me into their group, and handed me some punch. They made me feel accepted, and by the end of the night, I'd made friends. And I needed friends in Ally's school. It was hard taking care of her when I wasn't an official parent, especially at my age. It was almost as if everyone else felt they knew what was best for her."

"How old were you when you were named her official guardian?"

"Nineteen. She was in fifth grade." A flicker of pain crossed his features, but was quickly hidden. "Too damn young."

Avery thought of being nineteen, fresh out of high school, and becoming a parent. Even worse, he'd had his own grief to deal with, and no parental support. "So were you," she said softly.

"I was old enough."

"I know your mom died of cancer. Ally told me your father died of a heart attack. She said the grief of losing your mom affected his health."

His muscles stiffened. A shadow passed over him, dark and ravaged and angry. She sucked in her breath at the glimpse of raw emotion and wondered what had caused it. Something bigger than his parents' death? A secret he refused to share? Curiosity stirred, and she almost pushed, but the waiter came back and set a plate down in the center of the table.

"Crabby balls," he practically sang in a falsetto. "Enjoy!"

Their gazes met and locked.

She burst into laughter again, and he shook his head, reaching over to stab a ball with his fork. They ate and fell into casual chitchat, catching up and sharing stories about Ally and their highlights of the good old days. By the time dinner was complete and she was sipping a cappuccino, she'd almost completely forgotten about planning Ally's bachelorette party.

"Time for work," she announced, pulling out her files. "This afternoon, I spoke with Ally and the bridesmaids to get a feel for what type of trip they wanted. They requested relaxation, beach, and pampering. No big-city trips, and no one wants to deal with additional airfare, so it needs to be drivable."

"Wait, I told you they'd given me carte blanche on planning this trip."

She refused to look guilty for doing her job. "Yes, I know, but I thought it would be a good idea to ask what type of getaway they were specifically looking for to make the job easier. And then Ally suggested I could help you since I know more about the area and options."

He shook his head. Irritation flickered over his features along with a strange type of amusement. "I should have known you'd try to hijack the bachelorette."

"Just listen, I did a bunch of research. I looked at dates, cross-referenced them with possible outings with the criteria they requested, and came up with this list right here."

She whipped out the spreadsheet that detailed her data. The final page showed the top three destinations that had evolved from her research. "As you can see here," she said, pointing to the picture, "Dewey Beach in Delaware is a popular bachelorette destination if she doesn't want to stay in Cape May. They have a fun place called Bottle & Cork that has eighties cover bands if they want to venture out."

"What else?" he asked, flipping through the various printouts and glossy brochures.

"The Hamptons. It's at the tip of Long Island, extremely popular in the summertime. Plenty of spas, shopping, and pampering. I have a contact there who can get them all a summerhouse for the long weekend. It's an impressive mansion with a pool, hot tub, and it's secluded. Close to the beach."

She waited for his reaction. He just nodded, a slight frown creasing his brow. Impatience fluttered through her. Did anything impress him? For once, couldn't he be enthusiastic and excited about her choices?

"The third option is right here. Cape May. I can book spa appointments and get some fabulous rooms at Congress Hall. Think gourmet dinners, vineyard tours, and complete pampering, plus no travel. I just need to confirm she doesn't want to go someplace new with the girls."

He continued perusing the paperwork, as if waiting to be dazzled. "That's it?"

She narrowed her gaze. "Yes, that's it. I'm not sure what you expected, but I think these spots cover what everyone is looking for."

"Yes, you've done a fine job."

And just like that, she was back to wanting to strangle him. "That sounded sarcastic to me."

He held up his hands in surrender. "Sorry, I'm just thinking of something different for Ally. She's extremely social, and I think she'd like to get dressed up, use one of her endless pairs of fancy shoes, and go dancing."

"Once again, I think your maleness is interfering with your ability to know what women want," she said sweetly. "I doubt her dream bachelorette party includes squeezing into Spanx."

"Do I want to know what that is? Sounds like a weapon."

"More like a needed torture device. So what would your pick be, then, if you seem to know it all?"

"Atlantic City."

She frowned and shook her head. "No, that's party central. Gambling, clubbing, concerts. Definitely not what Ally requested."

"When does she ever have the chance to let loose and have some fun? She should have a weekend with some excitement and edge. That's what I want for her."

"But she won't like it."

"Why?"

She blew out a breath and ticked off the points on her fingers. "Because they want a spa! Wine and food and girl talk. Not club music, high heels and short skirts, and socializing with strangers."

He grinned. "That's exactly what Ally needs."

"I'm sorry, Carter, but I'm vetoing your choice."

His expression morphed into mule stubbornness. "You can't veto me on this. I'm the man of honor, and I get to plan the bachelorette party. We're doing AC."

"And I'm telling you, if you insist on this course, you'll disappoint your sister."

"Care to make another bet?"

Her jaw dropped. "Are you kidding me? Is this a game to you? Because I've made a living organizing events like this to allow a bride and groom to experience the perfect wedding. You're a damn hacker who spends most of his time with his dog!"

He ignored her outburst and grinned. "You're just scared I'll win again."

She flung up her hands. "Oh my God, you are impossible. If you do this, I'm out. I refuse to help plan something she didn't specifically request."

"Fine, I'll do it myself. And I guarantee she'll love it."

She shook with frustration. "Oh, I'll take that bet. Because I guarantee she won't."

"I disagree."

"I mean it, Carter. You tell her I had nothing to do with this one. I refuse to get blamed when her friends find out instead of massages and hot tubs, they're getting sloppy drunks and blistered feet."

"I'll tell her. Will be easier when I take all the credit."

She huffed like the Big Bad Wolf and grabbed all the papers, shoving them back in her bag. "At least I can check this off my to-do list."

The waiter dropped the bill in front of Carter, and she quickly grabbed it. "I got this," she declared, whipping out her American Express. "It was a bet," she confessed to the waiter. "I had to buy him dinner."

Carter grinned. "I made an excellent choice."

"You certainly did, sir," the waiter said, shooting them an odd glance before quickly disappearing.

"I think this place will be perfect for the rehearsal dinner, don't you?" he asked, taking a last sip of his cappuccino. "Why don't you go ahead and book it?"

She couldn't help the evil smile that broke out. "This restaurant isn't available. They're fully booked, but I spoke with Ally and we decided on Aleathea's. I already emailed her the tasting menu we finalized, hired a piano player for ambience, and created a custom cupcake bar for dessert."

She almost laughed at his shocked expression.

"You did all of that already? Without letting me know? I chose this place tonight to try out the menu before we confirmed."

She shrugged. "We were lucky to have any openings at this late date, but once again, I was able to pull some strings and get Aleathea's. You'll love it. I'll send you the menu."

The waiter dropped off the receipt. "I hope you'll join us again soon. It was a pleasure."

Carter placed his napkin on his plate. "Thanks. And compliments to the chef on his balls. Not that I got to have many."

Nate cocked his head, not understanding.

"She busted them all before I even got a chance." Carter got up from the table. "Ready to go?"

Damn him. He'd made her laugh again, which made it harder to hold on to her annoyance. Shaking her head, she followed him to the car. The evening had definitely been surprising. He'd been a more engaging dinner companion than she expected. Who would've imagined there was a sense of humor hidden behind the robot mask? She was beginning to think Carter Ross held more layers than she'd originally given him credit for.

She waited for him to turn onto her road, but he kept driving straight and parked on Beach Avenue. "What are you doing?" she asked.

"Thought after such a big dinner we'd take a walk on the beach."

"Oh, we can't. The beach is closed."

He regarded her in amusement. "I'm sure that's never stopped you before."

"You think I'm a hardened criminal because I was in jail for a few hours over ten years ago? Seriously?"

He grinned and got out of the car. He came around, opened her door, and waited. "I think you're a woman who appreciates the occasional rule-breaking. It's a beautiful night full of stars. Let's have some fun."

She climbed out. "I'll walk with you, but not on the beach. There are signs posted everywhere."

He stuck his hands in his pockets and matched his pace to hers. "Don't disappoint me, Avery. We're not teens looking to vandalize. I'm sure no one would pay attention to a lone couple enjoying an evening stroll."

She snorted. "You don't live here. If I got busted, that's all I'd hear in this town."

"The beach is heavily patrolled at this hour?" he asked.

She hesitated. "Well, no. But why take a chance?"

"Because sometimes doing something you shouldn't feels good."

His husky words whispered across her ears, like an intimate kiss. A shiver shook through her. She never broke rules. Not anymore. Her sisters teased her about how much she'd changed over the years, becoming good old reliable Avery. It was easier to make everything about the business and not about herself. Longing rose up inside, and the voice she'd quieted years ago broke its silence. She used to live big, love hard, and break more rules than she should. That's the girl Carter remembered.

The woman who stood beside him had changed. The daily grind of routines and the passing of time had eroded that raw edge that always burned inside her. It never bothered her because she didn't think of it.

Until now.

"I'm different now," she said defensively. "You're thinking of a college girl who had nothing to lose. I grew up. I would've thought you'd be glad I'm not trying to drag your sister into any of our shenanigans or go skinny-dipping in the ocean after midnight."

"Hmm, never said anything about skinny-dipping, but that could be fun, too."

She shot him a look. "Now I know you're just messing with me. I think we should go back to the car." She turned but his hand shot out to grab her wrist.

"Wait."

Her skin tingled at the contact, and her heart did a crazy leap.

"I'm sorry. I didn't mean to make fun of you. It's just—" He stopped, and his fingers squeezed gently, his thumb pressing into her palm. "I know I disapproved of your friendship with my sister in college because I thought you were a bit wild. But you were good for her. I know that now." His misty eyes gleamed in the shadows, and she was transfixed by the intense heat and emotion glimmering in their depths. "She needed lighthearted fun. See, I thought I needed to be the parents, and to me, that meant discipline. Responsibility. Making sure she was on the right path. I didn't understand I could do both, because I was just too damn young and in over my head."

She nodded, touched by the naked vulnerability on his face. "I understand. You made the hard choices for her, and it all worked out in the end."

"But I lost a part of myself through it, too. That part that skipped over being a rebellious, selfish teenager to find my own dreams. I have no regrets, and I'm not whining about it, but sometimes, like tonight,

I want to do something silly and crazy for me. I guess I was just trying to drag you into it. Stupid, right?"

Her axis shifted as a piece of the puzzle snapped into place. Suddenly, his words made sense. He hadn't chosen his role. The death of his parents had forced it on him, and instead of rebelling or not accepting responsibility, he'd quietly stepped in to take care of Ally. He wasn't allowed to be the crazy older brother any longer, who allowed her to stay up late, or hid her drinking at a party, or hung out with her boyfriends. No, he'd chosen to be someone else—a man who was capable of raising a ten-year-old girl in the best way possible.

Maybe Carter Ross had a wilder soul than she originally believed. He'd just never had the opportunity to show it.

"Come on, let's go." He dropped her hand and began walking toward the car, but she stepped in front of him to block his path.

"The same thing happened to me," she blurted out. "I can't remember the last time I broke any rules, or did something crazy fun just for the hell of it. All I do is work and take care of my clients and build the business. I have no regrets, either. I'm exactly where I should be. But sometimes I want . . ."

"A spark," he finished. "To feel alive."

"Yes. So we're going to sneak onto the beach. Follow me."

She grabbed his hand back, and they ran down the path. She picked the entrance on the south side that was always less crowded and away from the main center of town. A flimsy wooden gate snaked its way around the edge of the beach, and the entrance was barred by a low chain with a sign that said No trespassing! Beach closed from 9:00 p.m. to 6:00 a.m. Subject to fine!

A thrill tingled through her. They looked back and forth, but the path was deserted, and there was nothing but the sound of the waves crashing over the shore. They ducked under the chain, took their shoes off, and ran toward the water.

A laugh burst from her lips. It was such a little thing, sneaking onto the beach, but she was suddenly pumped with adrenaline. She snuck a glance at Carter and caught the same satisfied expression on his face, shadowed in moonlight. They reached the shoreline and slowed their pace. She rolled up the legs of her jeans and hooked her sandals over her fingers. Her toes curled into the packed, firm sand, the bite of cold water tickling her flesh and flirting with her ankles. The air was sharp and clean. The stars spilled over a black velvet canvas, highlighted by a heavy, ripe half-moon hanging low.

"I used to do this with my sisters," she said, breaking the comfortable silence. "We'd sneak out at bedtime and come to the beach. Sometimes we'd meet boys, sometimes it'd be just us. Bella loved to swim, but then I'd hum the *Jaws* tune, and she'd get scared and run out."

"Mean," he said with a laugh. "Were the three of you always close?"

"Yes. We'd have the usual fights over clothes and who borrowed what, and who was Mom and Dad's favorite, but it never passed the barrier into cruelty. We loved each other, but like in all families, we got stuck with certain tags."

His fingers brushed hers and lingered. He'd pushed up the cuffs of his shirtsleeves to bare sinewy arms. He stood close, his hips pressed lightly against hers, their feet almost touching. "What kind of tags?" he asked.

"I was the oldest, so my mother was always pushing responsibility at me. I think that's another reason I wanted to go to college at Georgetown. I needed space to grow and play on my own. I was the practical one. The leader of the group, as my parents would say. Bella was the beauty—my dad calls her Goldilocks. She fell in love, got married early, and wanted a ton of kids to raise. Poor Taylor got stuck with the rebellious tag. The troublemaker. She was always asking questions and challenging them at every turn. Drove them crazy. She has a wanderer's heart and always wanted to travel the world on her own terms.

After Matt died, we all pulled together to manage the business, and then my parents retired. Taylor got stuck here longer than she wanted."

"Will she stay?"

She shook her head. "I hope not. She promised to give us another year here, and then she's off. I don't think the wedding business is for her. But she wanted to prove to my parents that she could do the right thing."

He let out a long sigh. "It's funny how we become the way others perceive us. It starts with families, goes into school, social media, everywhere. No wonder everyone's on antianxiety meds and desperate to be happy. We don't know who we are anymore."

His words stirred deep inside her, touching a part that had been long buried and forgotten. She turned sideways and tilted her chin up. "You're right. Maybe more people need to sneak onto a beach and figure it out."

He smiled. God, he was so different like this. Open and relaxed, bare feet in the sand, his face emanating a sexy warmth that heated her blood. The vast quiet and isolation around them lent itself to sharing secrets and being reckless. She moved closer on impulse, angling her body so she could study the sharp curve of his jaw, the stubble hugging his lips, the mysterious, misty depths of his eyes. His dark hair blew in the breeze, tumbling over his forehead. Her nipples tightened and pushed against her flimsy shirt, and suddenly her body ached for something more . . . something to fill the emptiness. It had been so long since she'd felt like this. Alive, and free, and hungry to experience something wonderful and new.

His smile faded. The easy camaraderie drifted away, and the energy shifted, kicking into high awareness. He stiffened, his sharp gaze raking across her face, probing for answers. "Avery?" he whispered.

"You're different like this," she said softly.

His jaw clenched. "I'm the same. I just don't get to show this part."

Her hand seemed to move on its own, reaching up to touch his biceps, her fingers trailing over the hard-muscled length in an exploratory caress. "I like it."

He sucked in his breath.

A thrill coursed through her at his obvious arousal. She leaned in a few more inches, raising up on her tiptoes. Their gazes locked.

"What are you doing?"

"I don't know." The night surrounded her, and the ocean roared, and his scent filled her head, musk and male and spice. Her insides clenched with a longing. He gripped her upper arms and stared down at her. Blistering heat seethed between them, and a drunken headiness made her body soft and pliable, leaning into his strength.

"I think you do." His breath raked over her trembling lips. "I'm way past the age of impulsive decisions and late regrets."

Avery licked her lips. "Maybe we both need to relax our standards."

His palm cupped under her chin, holding her still, and he muttered a soft curse. "Maybe you're right. God knows I'm no damn saint. And right now, I want this more than I've wanted anything in a long time."

His mouth covered hers.

The shocking heat and softness of his lips rocketed through her. From the first moment, he was in control of the kiss, sipping from her mouth like tasting a fine wine, savoring her texture and flavor with a leisurely pace that throbbed with an undercurrent of ferocity. His arm slinked around her waist to pull her up and close, his body flush with hers so every muscle pressed against her curves.

She opened her mouth in invitation, and his tongue slipped inside, each slow, silky thrust causing her toes to curl in the sand. A moan rose from her throat, and he captured and swallowed it while he explored and conquered every secret crevice.

Her head spun. She clung to him, helpless under the sensual mastery of his mouth and lips and tongue, her body craving more. Her fingers thrust into his hair, and her hips arched, the thick, hard length of his arousal against her inner thigh. He took the kiss deeper, devouring her with a raw hunger that made a matching need explode within and scatter through every cell of her body.

"You taste so good," he muttered against her mouth, nipping at her bottom lip. His hands moved to stroke her body, cupping her buttocks to lift and hold her tight.

"So do you."

"I want more."

"Take it," she breathed against him, the madness of lust edged into her voice.

He groaned, kissing her again, and hooked his fingers inside her jeans, caressing her through the thin silk of her panties. His touch burned, and she shuddered. Her core dampened and ached for his fingers, mouth, cock, and she dug her fingernails into his shoulders with a punishing fierceness. He ripped his mouth away, breathing hard, then ran his tongue down her neck, nibbling, sucking, driving her mad until his teeth sank in and she cried out.

The waves crashed and roared. The stars dripped like thick honey from the sky. And the night urged all her inhibitions to fall away under the wickedness of his hands and mouth on her body. He tugged on her shirt, edged the lace of her bra down with his teeth, and sucked on her nipple.

She ground out his name the same time she ground her hips against his, looking for relief. He murmured dark, sexy words as he pleasured her breast, and she wrapped her arms tight around him, urging him down to the sand.

She didn't register the flash of light until it was too late. The bright beam lasered over her face and into her eyes, startling her out of the sensual fog. Carter immediately placed her behind him, his large body blocking her from the intruder.

It was only when she heard the voice that she realized she was in big trouble.

"Sir, ma'am, the beach is closed after hours. The sign is clearly posted."

Oh. My. God. She was going to die.

Carter sounded calm, not as if he'd just gotten caught making out on the beach illegally like some horny teen. "I'm sorry, Officer. Our mistake. We just wanted to take a quiet walk. We'll leave now."

Avery ducked her head low as Carter took her hand and began leading her toward the police officer.

"We have rules for a reason," the policeman said in a thick Jersey accent, his tone registering disapproval. "There's been drownings at the beach at night, and we want to keep our people safe."

"I understand."

Crap, crap, crap . . .

She stumbled over the sand. The light wavered and came to focus on her full force, and it was all over.

"Avery?"

Slowly, she raised her head. She wondered how bad she looked—with her lips swollen, hair wind-tossed, and her eyes still glassy from the kiss that was so much more than a kiss. "Hi, Ron."

Ron Livery looked a bit like Ed Sheeran. He had a baby face, short red hair, and a jovial personality. They'd grown up together, and he was now a full-time police officer in Cape May. He was also a terrible gossip and loved spending aimless hours sharing stories with the tourists at the cafés. He was literally one of the worst people to catch her making out on the beach with a stranger.

"I can't believe it's you! Darlin', you know better than to be out here at this hour. Wait—are you here of your own free will?" he suddenly asked, his gaze sharpening on Carter with suspicion.

"Yes! Um, we finished dinner, and it was such a pretty night, I figured no one would notice if we took a quick walk. This is Carter, by the way."

Ron glanced back and forth between them. A slow grin transformed his face. "Yeah, sure, I get it. A walk, huh?" He laughed and shook his head. Her cheeks burned, but she knew there was worse to come. "Are you a weekend visitor, Carter?"

And let the torture begin . . .

"My sister is getting married, and Avery is the wedding planner," he answered. "I'm here for the summer."

"The whole summer, huh?" Was that a wink or a trick of the light? "Where are you staying?"

She cleared her throat. "Um, Ron, we should get going. It's getting late."

"Sure, sure. So where are you staying?"

"Jackson. It's a beach cottage by—"

"The Virginia Cottages. Yep, I know it. Which color? Pink?"

"No, white."

"Nice. Love the views. Where'd you go to dinner?"

Avery wanted to scream in frustration. "Peter Shields." She tried to walk a few steps and urge Carter ahead, but Ron just crossed his arms in front of his chest, his uniform neat and pressed and all official-looking.

"Wow, nice place. Fancy. You like the food?"

She caught the amused lift of his lip. Great, he thought this whole exchange was funny. Sometimes she hated small towns.

"It was excellent. We had crabby balls."

A sudden silence descended.

Then Ron burst out laughing. "Crabby balls, huh? Son of a bitch, that's funny. Well, come on, let me escort you back so you kids don't get into further trouble."

She barely bit back her comment that he'd been the one sneaking onto the beach with her when they were young, but she managed to behave. Ron chattered with Carter, asking a million more questions and shooting her grins that told her he approved of her choice in make-out partners.

By the time they reached the car, her head was pounding. Dear God, she'd kissed Carter Ross. And not just kissed. Felt up, stuck her tongue in his mouth, moaned his name. She'd been about to drag him down on the sand and let him do anything he wanted. Ron could have walked up to a scream-worthy scene she would've never been able to live down. Taylor had once been caught in a compromising situation in the back of Ugly Mug restaurant, and she hadn't heard the end of it for years. As far as she knew, her sister still refused to eat there to avoid the teasing.

"Catch you around, Carter," Ron said. "Avery, we'll talk later." He winked again, then strode off with a jaunt in his step.

She slid into the car seat and turned her head toward the window. She prayed Carter wouldn't try to talk about what had just happened. It was too much to process. She needed to get home and think about it all in blessed isolation.

She felt his heavy gaze on her, but after a few seconds, he started the car and drove her home. This time, the silence was agonizing, bursting with unspoken questions. She clasped her damp palms in her lap, counting down the miles until they pulled up to her house.

"Thanks for dinner. Oh, wait, I paid." She shook her head. "Okay, I'll see you for the florist appointment this week."

"Avery, we need to talk."

She gave a crazed half laugh. "Oh no, we really don't. In fact, I think we should forget this ever happened. Blame it on the call of the moon or the pull of the ocean or something like that. Bye."

He repeated her name again, but she jumped out and slammed the door behind her. The purple cottage had never looked so welcoming.

She hurried inside, slumped against the wall, held her breath, and waited him out. Eventually, the headlights dimmed and the car disappeared.

Her lungs collapsed. Tomorrow, they'd both wake up, laugh about the incident, and move on. They'd shared an impulsive kiss. It didn't have to mean anything. Not every kiss meant something. Maybe it was even a strange experiment they needed to have in order to move forward planning this wedding together. All that locked-up, backed-up, sizzling attraction could lead to nowhere.

The ridiculous explanations soothed her. She got ready for bed, watched a bit of television, and collapsed into sleep.

Too bad she dreamed of making love to Carter Ross on the beach.

Too bad it was so damn good, when she woke up, she tried to go back to sleep in order to do it again.

Chapter Eleven

She wanted to forget it.

Carter scratched his dog's rump and watched her little leg begin to kick in ecstasy. No wonder he adored Lucy. She was simple, loved him completely, and allowed him to make her happy. In reality, he'd just kissed a woman who'd made his head spin like moonshine, and she'd frantically told him to forget about it.

Irritation pulsed through him. He didn't just recklessly kiss women under the stars. His life had been stringently controlled for so long, he'd forgotten what it was like to let go. Maybe it was a lesson that doing impulsive things was a bad idea. Because the first time he tried, he got rejected.

Lucy whined when he took a break, pushing her damp nose into his palm, then licking him. Instantly, his heart was soothed. He resumed scratching, his mind sifting through the memory of last night. She'd literally burned up in his arms. There was no way Avery Sunshine was being polite, or having some harmless, reckless fun. No, that kiss had been sheer intensity, ripping through every one of his walls and rocketing toward his core.

Not just the physical core. The emotional one.

Much more dangerous.

He remembered the taste of her, sweet like raw honey dripped over his tongue. The breathy moans from her lips, the sting of her fingernails as she dug into his flesh, the way her body had madly pressed against his, seeking more. That kiss had consumed them both and been more than either of them expected. It had burst open feelings he'd never thought possible.

If Ron hadn't interrupted, who knew what would have happened.

But he had, and she'd run. Wanted to forget. Thought it was easier to ignore his texts today, pretending the kiss was nothing. Because if they acknowledged there was something more between them, there'd be a mess on both of their hands.

She was a woman who probably believed in weddings, love, and forever. He was a man who'd sworn to never allow such emotions in his life, because he'd experienced firsthand how poisonous the result could be. She was his sister's wedding planner and best friend. He was eight years her senior. They lived in completely different states. The only thing they could possibly have was a short summer affair, and he bet Avery would fight him every inch of the way.

Unless . . .

Unless he could convince her it was the perfect setup. Her work schedule had little downtime for dates or relationships. He could be the one to scratch an itch. Fit into her life as she wanted him. He still had a month in Cape May ahead of him, stretched out with nothing to do but help with the wedding and lie on the beach.

It was possible he'd be able to tempt her with him being at her beck and call, whenever she needed him. He wouldn't mind being used. Not by her.

Not after that kiss.

"What do you think, Luce?" he asked, stopping his servitude to take a swig of beer. The television murmured low in the background, and he was sprawled out on the sunporch, enjoying the view of the ocean in the distance. Not a bad vacation at all. But it would be better with Avery in his bed. "You think I can seduce her into seducing me?"

Lucy threw her head in doggy annoyance, her pink bow bouncing merrily. Her nose tipped up in arrogance. She took a long time to warm up to women, especially if they got close. It had taken his sister a while to get her to finally accept she was part of the family, too.

"Bitch," he said fondly, patting her head. "I'm going to try anyway. I know it's been a while, but I've never experienced a kiss like that."

Lucy growled.

He laughed, cuddling her, and drank his beer while he studied the ocean, thinking of Avery. Her fierceness and passion for her work. Her sharp mind and refusal to lose a bet. Her joyful laughter.

But most of all, that gut-stirring, explosive, perfect kiss.

And how much he wanted to experience it again.

When he walked into the room, her stomach tumbled.

Not a good sign.

For the past two days, she'd been desperately trying to forget the kiss. She'd ignored his texts, figuring she needed a bit of distance to reset before she saw him again. They had an appointment with the florist on the schedule, so there was no reason to see or talk to him beforehand.

Guess the distance hadn't helped.

He had that ridiculous man purse over his shoulder, and Lucy peeked over the edge to check out the surroundings. His hair was damp and gleamed coal-black in the explosive sunlight. He wore his glasses today, but somehow, ridiculously, they looked sexier than usual. Was it the newly sported stubble? The casual clothes consisting of shorts, a muscle-hugging T-shirt, and canvas boat shoes? Or did he exude a simmering intensity she'd never seen before? Dear God, she was doomed. From now on, she'd think of their relationship in terms of BK and AK.

Before Kiss and After Kiss.

She forced a sunny smile that matched her last name and chirped out a good morning, which came out way too fake. Still, he smiled back, allowing her to keep a healthy distance of space between them.

"Why doesn't she walk?" she asked.

He frowned, glancing down at his dog. "Why walk when you can ride?"

A laugh escaped. "Can you say *spoiled*? Hi, Lucy. How are you?" She reached out tentatively, holding her fingers up.

Lucy stuck her head out, sniffed, then disappeared back into her tote.

She'd been dissed. Again. "Guess she doesn't like me much."

"Eventually, she will. If you keep trying." His gaze narrowed on her, and suddenly there was little air in her space. It all got taken up by his big body, glinting blue-gray eyes, and seething male energy.

"R-Right. Well, let's get inside. Devon is one of the best florists in the Cape, and she squeezed us in. I'm assuming you don't know much about flowers?"

His grin made her pause. "Oh, I've been studying up," he said casually.

She had no time to panic at his words as a door opened. Devon greeted them in her usual zen manner. She wore denim overalls, a white T-shirt, and old pink sneakers. Her dark hair was braided and fell to her waist. Devon was proud of her hippie mother, who'd birthed her after a hookup at Woodstock, and was the ultimate flower child a generation later. "I have everything set up. Come to the back," she said in her singsong voice. "I'm thrilled to be working with purple—it's such a great chakra color to incorporate in a lifelong commitment."

Avery ignored the look Carter shot her.

Sketches, books, and photos spilled over the contemporary glass desk. The air smelled like lavender and sage. They sat down, and Devon faced them with a smile. "Carter, it's wonderful to see the man of honor take such an interest. It speaks well of how much you love your sister."

"Thank you. Do you have sample bouquets for us to look at?"

"No, I rarely have all the flowers I need right here at the store. I'm a visual florist, so I like to sketch out the entire design of the wedding; then I create a floral concept for the bouquets, tables, beach, and anything else she needs."

Avery turned toward him. "I already spoke with Devon regarding your sister's color scheme, but Ally is torn between going with tall centerpieces or shorter ones. I advised her to go with the taller ones, since they'll offer a bit more presence and elegance to the space."

"Can I see some examples?" he asked.

"Of course. I have a sketchbook, and here are some photographs to give you an idea of what I've come up with." Devon turned the photographs around and tapped a pencil against the first picture. "First off, I'm looking at doing narrow crystal vases and using a blocking effect with water and short-cut blooms. See, this one shows the lower half has water and blooms of purple peony; then glass beads will go on top and separate the top half of the vase. This is where I'll use various roses, lily of the valley, and hydrangeas for a lush effect, interspersing them with birchwood painted silver. It's for the wow factor."

Avery was always humbled by the creative artistry of the vendors she worked with. The idea before her was simply stunning, combining Ally's bold personality along with classic simplicity. "Will people have trouble looking through the vase to talk?"

Devon smiled. "No, that's why we do the blooms at the bottom, and water at the eye level. The flowers hit the perfect height, so it's not intrusive to the table."

"It's beautiful," Carter said slowly. "I think Ally would love it, but I'd like to see the shorter centerpieces for comparison."

"Of course." She shuffled the new papers and placed them down in order. "Here's the second concept. We use a square base with a silver-encrusted basket-type vase, with a black-raspberry satin ribbon. There'll be a slight shimmer of sparkle to give it a rich sheen. Then we keep the bouquet tight and neat, and use colors as our statement. Dark purple, lime green, and white looks lovely with the silver base. I'd go with lavender and jade-green roses, white Asiatic lilies, maybe some freesia. These are some combinations."

Avery watched his intense expression and was slammed back to the night on the beach. He'd been no robot—not even close. Sensuality had dripped from his voice and gleamed in his eyes. When was the last time she'd been kissed with such pent-up hunger and passion, as if she were the most important woman in the world?

Never?

"I think Ally would prefer this version," he said, tapping the glossy image. "The taller ones give off an air of ostentatiousness."

And just like that, all the warm feelings toward him leeched out. She snapped in annoyance. "'Ostentatiousness'? It's classic elegance with a vibrant twist. Sorry, but I disagree with you. I guarantee Ally will prefer the tall ones."

He lifted his gaze and stared back at her. The chilly, judgy look was back, and it only made her want to take him down a peg. When had he become the wedding expert? Brother or not, he was butting into every decision she'd carefully analyzed and helped select with her vendors. Hours of work, and he bestowed opinions like she was his lowly employee, ready to do his bidding.

Funny, she'd dealt with all sorts of PITAs in every family relation, and always kept her cool. But the longer she spent with Carter, the more she wanted to prove she was right.

His smile mocked her. "And of course, I value your opinion, but I'm quite sure if you send both options to Ally, she'll choose mine."

"I don't think so."

Devon cleared her throat, her eyes wide with fascination. "How about we move on to the bouquet? We'll put these two aside for now and secure the bride's approval a bit later."

Avery gathered her composure and nodded. "Of course," she said brightly.

"I'm excited about this arrangement. Our main showpiece will be the lisianthus, which is a beautiful Kyoto-purple color. It's a bell-shaped flower that looks like this." Devon showed them a picture of rich violet spilling down in a vinelike flow. "I'd surround them with a white lily of the valley, some roses, and frame the bouquet with some wild greens. The dresses are lavender, correct?"

"Yes," Avery answered.

"Perfect. We could do a smaller version with the bridesmaids. What do you think?"

Carter tapped his lip. "Do you have any of those in stock so I can see what it might look like?"

"I actually do. Give me a moment and I'll be right back. I can put together an extremely rough frame for you." She slid out of her seat and disappeared.

Avery turned with a snarl. Lucy sensed danger for her master and popped out of her carrier, a warning growl on her lips. "Why are you being such a jerk?" Avery hissed. "And keep your guard dog back."

"She's just protective, aren't you, baby?" he crooned, picking her up and cuddling her on his lap. The dog settled, licked his hand, and shot Avery a triumphant look.

Unbelievable.

"And why am I a jerk? Because I care what Ally's flowers look like for her wedding?"

She kept her voice to a harsh whisper. "You just want to disagree with me to bust my balls."

He grinned. "Kind of impossible to do that, isn't it? I'm just offering an alternate opinion. Do you call all of your clients jerks when they speak up?"

She squirmed in her seat. "No, just you."

"I'm honored."

She knew she was being unprofessional, but he was trying to sabotage her choices on purpose. He just wanted to win. "You don't care about flowers and cake and all this other stuff—I know you don't."

"I care about a lot of things you don't give me credit for," he growled, leaning in.

She sucked in a breath at the naked gleam of want in his eyes, and suddenly her body was on full alert. The room shimmered with raw energy.

"How come you never returned my texts?"

"There was no reason."

"Oh, there were plenty of reasons. You just took the coward's way out."

"I don't want to talk about the kiss!"

His expression practically seethed with hunger and heat. "Neither do I. I just want to do it again."

Her mouth fell open.

Devon sashayed back into the room with a small bouquet. "Here we go! Here's the lisianthus, and these are some other flowers we can pair them with. What do you think?"

Avery stayed silent as Carter studied the flowers with an intense scrutiny. His features slowly softened, and in that moment, she imagined him picturing his sister walking down the aisle for the first time.

"I love it," he said.

"Oh, good."

"But there was this other flower I thought might work better for Ally. It's called a vanda—have you ever heard of it? I have a pic on my phone." He whipped out his cell and handed it to her. "Scroll through. I found these on Pinterest."

Devon promptly shot him an excited look. "I adore the vanda, but it's extremely expensive and hard to get."

Avery wondered how this man had once again ended up hijacking the appointment. "What's a vanda?"

"It's an exotic orchid. Highly unusual but powerful. Gorgeous scent. Here." Devon angled the phone toward her. Of course, the flower was the same vivid purple, but it had a lush sensuality that the lisianthus didn't.

"It's quite beautiful, but I'm sure it would be impossible to get on such late notice," Avery said.

"Definitely difficult but not impossible." Devon's face lit up with excitement. "I'd love to arrange a bouquet with vanda. Maybe some Pittosporum greenery to encase the orchards?"

"Yes. Or even stephanotis?" Carter suggested.

Devon's green eyes sparkled. "And we wrap it around and let it trail to the ground! Definitely some parrot tulips." She grabbed a pencil and began sketching out the bouquet on her pad.

He nodded. "Maybe some striped roses?"

The pencil scratched madly over the paper. "I'll use a silver bow and construct the shape like a horn to accent the flow."

"I love it!" he declared, and Devon squealed.

Avery had never seen the florist get so excited over an appointment. And she'd never been ignored to this extent before.

"This is brilliant, Carter. It's so nice to talk with a client who knows his flowers."

Oh. My. God.

Caught in a nightmare, Avery watched as Carter smiled with pure charm and tipped his head. "Thank you. It's wonderful to work with a florist who listens and isn't afraid to change her vision."

Avery winced at the direct hit. Her hands clenched into fists, and she counted slowly to ten so she wouldn't reach across and try to strangle him. After a few minutes of them exchanging praise for each other, she jumped in. "I'm glad we came to a decision," she said with a tight smile. "Why don't we send Ally all of our choices and have her confirm?"

"And let her choose between the centerpieces," Carter reminded her.

Avery refused to look at him as she gathered up their final picks and texted pictures of them to Ally.

Devon and Carter launched into a deep discussion on the ceremony flowers for the beach, and she agreed with the decision for a floral archway and tall baskets for accent. By the time the appointment ended, Carter and Devon were chatting like old friends, and even made arrangements to meet for drinks later that week for fun. If Avery didn't know the florist was in love with her current partner, Lily, she would've thought the woman was trying to hook up with him.

They walked out into scorching heat. Immediately, her wraparound jersey dress stuck to her, and she felt strands of hair pop out and escape the tight clip.

"Well, that was fun," he said. "Want to grab lunch?"

She stared at him. "No."

"Dinner?"

"No."

"Avery, I think we need to—"

Her phone shrieked. She glanced down. "It's Ally." Without pause, she answered the call and put it on speaker. "Hey, sweets, how are you? How's Jason's mom?"

Her friend's voice sounded tired. "Doing much better. We'll get her to walk down the aisle just in time. I got all your goodies from the bakery and the texts with the flowers. Do you have time to go over everything?"

"Yes, of course. Your brother's here with me."

"Perfect! Hi, Carter. How's your beach vacay?"

He grinned. "Good, but we miss you, Ally-Cat. I hope you're not stressing about anything. Avery has it under complete control. She's been amazing."

Avery blinked, staring at him, but he'd sounded sincere. Probably just trying to be nice to his sister.

"I told you she was the best," Ally said.

"She is," he answered. "Listen, we're standing outside the florist, and it's a hundred degrees. Why don't you stay on the phone while we walk over to McGlades for lunch and some cold lemonade? Avery needs a break after that long appointment. Then we can go over all the details."

Avery sputtered. "No, I don't. I need—"

"That's a great idea! Get the shrimp salad on a croissant, Carter. It's my favorite."

"I will." He scooped Lucy out of her carrier, hooked on a pink leash, and set her on the ground. "Avery, you lead the way."

She was going to murder him.

She looked like she wanted to kill him.

He kept up a steady stream of nonsense chatter with his sister to keep Avery distracted, and settled in at the restaurant. Situated with a beautiful view of the beach, McGlades boasted fresh sandwiches and salads, fruit, and tart, sweet lemonade that he was beginning to crave on a daily basis. It was quiet, but busy enough to be able to hold a conversation on the phone while they had lunch. Too bad the woman by his side looked like she'd rather be anywhere than with him.

Maybe his plan had backfired.

He hadn't meant to act like an arrogant ass at the florist. He'd been looking to impress her with his knowledge, but the woman was competitive as hell. Her need to dismiss him only spurred his need to prove her wrong. Of course, she didn't know that before every vendor meeting, he called his sister and went over each detail. He gave suggestions, Ally tweaked them, and they sent pics back and forth.

Was that considered cheating?

Maybe.

Avery impressed him more every day. He'd had no idea how many choices went into a wedding day. Each pick was both thoughtful of the bride and groom, price, vendors' capabilities, and her obvious need to please everyone involved. She had a vast knowledge on all subjects, and each vendor's respect had seemed well earned. Tricking her into lunch seemed the only way to gain some private time with her. There was one thing he wanted with Avery Sunshine.

More.

More time. More conversation. More kissing.

He switched his focus back to the phone conversation. His sister was speaking. "I can't believe everything is coming together so fast! We're down to only a month now—it's crazy."

"Wedding planning usually goes faster than imagined," Avery said with a smile. "Did you make any final decisions on the items we sent?"

"Yes, I tasted the cake samples with Jason. It was such a hard decision because they were all amazing, but we decided on the carrot cake."

He caught Avery wince. "That's great. Um, I'm surprised, though. I didn't think you liked carrots."

Carter raised a brow at the obvious challenge, but also admired her for the subtle hit. The woman did not surrender easily. "I know! But I never had carrot cake before—I always avoided it because it sounded like a health thing. The moment I tasted it, with the hint of bourbon and the cream-cheese frosting, I thought I'd died and shot to cake heaven. You're brilliant, Avery. I never would've imagined sending me something so risky."

Carter pressed his lips together to keep from laughing.

Avery shot him a glare, huffing a bit, but kept her tone chirpy like the excellent planner she was. "To be honest, that was your brother's choice."

"Big brother always knows best, huh?" Ally teased.

"Something like that," he said, trying to keep the triumph from his voice so he wouldn't piss off Avery any further. Still, it felt good he'd been right. He liked pleasing his sister. "So the cake's done. We've also been back and forth on your bachelorette party. I know you told Avery you wanted something low key and relaxing, like the spa, but I think this is an important time for you to get out and party. Have some fun with the girls. I say let's nix the spa and head to Atlantic City."

Avery chimed in. "There's a bunch of restaurants and clubs we can hit if you want to dance and drink a bit. We certainly don't have to go to AC."

"But I think we should," he added.

A pause hummed over the line. "I never would've thought of AC as an option," Ally said slowly. "Figured we'd just stay in Cape May and keep it low key, but maybe you're right, Carter. Maybe we should take the opportunity to party. God knows it's been forever since I had a real girls' night out."

"Exactly," he said.

Avery tilted her chin up and gave him a steely stare. Why did he find her annoyance with him so damn sexy? Was it the challenge to see if he could take all the prickly fire and turn it into pleasure? Since their kiss, he'd thought of nothing else.

"It's up to you," Avery said through gritted teeth. "But I still think the ladies may prefer a relaxing evening before the wedding. Get pampered. I'm sure Carter doesn't want to pressure you."

"I can't believe I'm saying this, but let's do it. Let's party in AC and make it a night to remember."

"Good choice," he said. The waitress came by and set their plates on the table. "Ally-Cat, our lunch just got here. Anything else you decided on?"

"I flipped through the floral options and think the bouquets are to die for. And the centerpieces were so different—I loved having a choice."

"Which one do you prefer?" Avery asked.

Carter leaned in.

"Definitely the tall. It's unique, and I think it makes a stronger impression."

"I thought so, too," Avery said with triumph. "Good choice."

"Thanks, guys. I cannot believe you've been working so hard together for me. I owe you big-time."

Avery lifted her gaze and locked with his. Electricity rippled through the air, ramping up a sweet sort of tension he was beginning to get used to around her. Even look forward to. She shifted in her seat, and he could practically feel the imprint of her lips over his, the taste of clover and honey coating his tongue. Her cheeks reddened, and a satisfaction surged through him. *Good.* She was just as aware of him and their connection. He bet she couldn't get the kiss off her mind, either.

"No worries, that's what I'm here for," Avery said. "After all, it's my *job.*" Her emphasis on the last word flicked at him in warning. "I'll take care of all this. Let me know if anything else comes up. The final proof for the favors should be in this week, and I'll shoot them out to you ASAP."

They exchanged love and goodbyes, and Avery clicked off.

"I think that went well," he said.

She shot him a look and concentrated on her plate. For the next few minutes, she ate in silence. He decided not to push and gave her space to settle. He broke off pieces of bread to feed to Lucy, who ate with an aristocratic grace and calm that allowed him to take her everywhere.

"I'm sure you're quite satisfied with yourself," she finally said. She nibbled on a watermelon slice, the rest of her plate clean. "I guess you won."

He forked up a bite of potato salad. "I'm satisfied Ally's happy with our choices. Don't you think we both won?"

She narrowed her gaze. "You know what I mean. This little competition between us? You scored on the cake and the bachelorette party."

"And you successfully picked the centerpieces and the rehearsal dinner. I'd say we're even."

She shook her head. "No, I booked the rehearsal dinner without you knowing. Plus, you found her dress. Maybe you're right. Maybe I've stopped looking for a fresh perspective for my clients." She nibbled her bottom lip, seeming defeated.

Guilt hit. *Ah, hell.*

He cleared his throat. "Well, to be honest, I had a bit of help." She tilted her head, waiting. "I, uh, spoke to my sister at length before each appointment."

"Yeah, but I've spoken to her, too. You listened better."

He shifted in his seat. "Actually, we sent pictures back and forth. Did she tell you about her private Pinterest board?"

She squinted in suspicion. "No."

"That's where she saves all of her ideas so she won't forget. I pull a bunch of them, and we go back and forth until we narrow it down."

The slice of watermelon dropped from her fingers as the dawning knowledge hit. "Wait. Are you telling me this is how you knew about those special flowers and the cake design and the AC thing?"

He winced. "Kind of. I go through her pins and find a common theme, then research a bit. She kept saving these bouquets with vandas, so I lasered in. And she had a bunch of websites with designer dresses, shoes, and trendy clubs, so I figured she really wouldn't want a spa. I just know my sister. Sometimes what she says out loud isn't what she really wants."

"You cheated."

He shrugged. "Not really. I just used the information at my disposal to help you out. The bottom line is we made Ally happy."

She jabbed a finger at him. "You made me think I was beginning to lose my mojo! I should've known you couldn't be this good. For God's sake, you're a guy!"

"A smart guy. But I'm glad you know everything now. We can move on with a clean slate."

Her laugh made him nervous. It wasn't really filled with genuine humor. "Oh, we'll be moving on, all right. This little partnership is officially dissolved. We're done. Everything's been picked and confirmed, so there's no need to see each other until the bachelorette party."

His gut lurched. "I need to meet the photographer this week," he reminded her.

"No need. We booked Pierce Powers because he's the best and was willing to pull a twenty-four-hour shift just to squeeze Ally in. I don't need you grilling him or whipping out some crazy ideas for the wedding. I'll take care of it."

"I thought you were going to help me with AC?"

She smiled so sweetly, he wondered if she'd get a cavity. "No. You wanted that job all for yourself, remember, ManOH?"

"What about the DJ? That's too important to skip."

"Already sent Ally a few CDs so she can make her choice."

"My tuxedo?"

"I'll be happy to make an appointment and send over Gabe. He's my expert liaison for groomsmen."

He was running out of excuses. Time to throw her off-balance. "Fine, I won't bother you about any further wedding activities."

Surprise flickered in her hazel eyes. "Really?"

"Really." Her shoulders relaxed, and she took a sip of lemonade. "I want you to go on a date with me."

She choked and spluttered, grabbing a napkin and pressing it to her lips. "What?"

"A date. I think we should date. I think that kiss proved we have a connection, and we owe it to ourselves to explore it this summer."

"You are unbelievable. Do you just always state your feelings for the record?"

He blinked. "Sure, isn't that what women want? For a man to tell her what he wants or thinks or feels? That's what magazines and television are always groaning about—that men don't share or explain their needs and intentions."

This time, a genuine smile curved her lips. He wished he could kiss her again now and ingest all that warmth. "I guess. But, Carter, we don't even like each other."

"I like you. Well, I didn't like you before, but now I do."

She groaned and rubbed her eyes. "We're completely different. And I can't date my best friend's brother."

"Why not? We're all adults here. Ally won't care."

"It'll be too confusing, especially while planning her wedding. Besides, I'm too busy to date anyone."

"I understand your schedule, and I'm happy to work around it, whether it be a late-night cocktail or a simple lunch. All I know is that I enjoy being around you, and I felt something when we were on that beach together. Something I haven't felt before. Wouldn't it be nice to take advantage of the summer and my time here? Unless you didn't feel anything with our kiss . . ."

Her breath skittered, and a flare of vulnerability shone in her eyes. Relief crashed into him. Thank God. She wasn't going to lie, which made this a hell of a lot easier.

Her nails tapped against the table in a steady rhythm, as if considering how much to reveal. "The kiss was good," she finally said.

He grunted. "'Good'?"

Her eyes half closed. "Fine, great. The kiss was great. But you and me? I don't know."

His male ego stung, but he wasn't about to waste time stewing. "Give me a chance. Hell, maybe we'll spend more time together and I'll agree with you. But I'd like a shot. We can start with me collecting on my bet."

Uh-oh. The softness fled and was replaced by her hard, glittering gaze. "Excuse me?"

He barreled through. "Remember you lost the bet for the cake? You have to spend the day at the beach with me. Won't that be a great beginning for us?"

Her lips tightened into a thin line. Carter realized he'd made a big mistake when she stood up, grabbed her purse, and glared. "Sure. Blackmailing me by citing a bet to spend time together is a great start. I've got back-to-back weddings this entire weekend, so Monday looks like the only option. Why don't you text me when my punishment begins and how long I need to be there with you? I'm really looking forward to our first *date*."

"Wait, Avery—"

"And how about a special secret tip straight from a woman's lips?" She leaned in and practically snarled. "Sometimes not saying exactly what you feel is much smarter. Sometimes being a mystery can be a damn good thing."

Lucy gave her another warning growl, not liking her tone.

Avery shot a glare at the dog, spun on her heel, and marched out.

Ah, shit. He'd done it again.

He'd been an asshole.

Chapter Twelve

Avery flung open the door to her sisters' house and marched in. "I cannot believe what a jerk he is! I'm done. From now on, if he needs something, you have to handle it." Huffing in frustration, she opened the refrigerator, grabbed a bottle of chardonnay, and poured herself a glass.

"Did you just come into my house without knocking again?" Taylor asked, grabbing back the bottle and refilling her own glass. She wore jeans with rips at the knee and a minuscule black halter top. Her pink hair was messy and gave her a bit of a rocker look. Paint dotted her clothes and smeared her hands. In her spare time, Avery's sister practiced art and loved creating bold, intense paintings on canvas meant to challenge the onlooker. "What if I'd been getting laid?"

Avery froze. "Wait—are you in a relationship you haven't told me about?"

She rolled her eyes. "News flash, babe. You don't need to be in a relationship to sleep with someone. I don't have your hang-ups."

Avery shot her sister a look. "Fine, I'm sorry, I keep forgetting you demand privacy. Where's Bella?"

"Probably putting Zoe down for bed. What's got you all stressed out, oh mighty leader? Haven't seen you this riled up since the best man puked all over the groom right before the Hoffman ceremony."

The memory hit and still had the power to put her in a bad mood. "I'd put out a puke bucket because I knew he'd gotten drunk the night before, but he didn't even use it!"

Taylor grinned. "It all worked out. Switch out a new shirt, a bit of seltzer on the pants and jacket, some Febreze, and he was good to go. Who's the guy pissing you off now?"

"Carter Ross." Avery slid her butt onto the trendy barstool Taylor liked, then wondered if she needed to squeeze in more time at the gym. Her rear seemed to have an overabundance of flesh compared to a week ago. Was it all those chocolate croissants? "He's been torturing me this entire summer, making stupid bets about whose picks Ally would choose, and I'm done. Can you take care of him, please?"

Taylor considered her and took a sip of wine. "No."

"Why not?" she whined. "I'll take over one of your clients—we'll do a switch."

"Ally's your best friend, you took this on last minute, and now you have to deal with the consequences."

She shook her head. "Why are you such a bitch?"

Taylor grinned. "I work hard at it."

The inner door banged open, and Bella strode in. "Is there wine?" she hissed frantically. With her golden hair pulled back in a ponytail, yoga pants, and a white T-shirt that said JUST BREATHE, she seemed to glow from the inside, a natural beauty Avery had always envied.

"I didn't hear a knock," Taylor said between clenched teeth. "Honestly, Bella, do you want my poor niece scarred for life? I could've been rolling around on the couch out here."

"Oh my God, are you in a secret relationship? Who are you seeing?"

Taylor groaned. "You are both hopeless. Wine's over there."

Bella filled her glass and took the third stool by the granite island. Avery noticed that her butt fit perfectly on the tiny cushion. Figured. "Wedding season is killing me. Zoe is full of energy and running me ragged. And my vibrator finally broke, so now I need to find a new one."

"That's what I call a bleachable moment," Avery said.

Taylor looked serious. "There's a few new ones on the market since 2010."

"You're a real comedian. All I need is for it to be small, mighty, and quiet."

"Underachiever," Taylor muttered.

Avery couldn't help but laugh. "You guys are bonkers."

"Even worse? We're celibate," Bella said glumly, taking a sip of wine. "How do you meet someone when your entire day revolves around committed men?"

"Hey, what about Carter?" Taylor suggested. "Avery's looking to get rid of him because he's driving her crazy. Why don't you spend some time with him doing the rest of the wedding appointments? He's great with Zoe, he's cute, and he's single."

A stab of jealousy lanced through Avery. Gripping the glass with a too-fierce hold, she tried not to glare daggers at her sister for suggesting it.

Bella tilted her head in consideration. "What's his deal, Avery?"

Avery cleared her throat. "Trust me, you don't want to get involved with him. He's pushy and opinionated. I doubt you'd be a good match."

Bella crossed her long, graceful legs. "Hmm, he seemed really nice when we met him. At first, I thought you two would be cute together, but I could tell you weren't into him. He's here for the rest of the summer? What does he do? Is he definitely single? Zoe really liked him."

Heat seeped under her skin. Uneasiness stirred. Was Bella seriously interested in him? She hadn't dated in so long, closed off to the idea of moving on from Matt, but five years had passed now. She deserved to find some happiness. Was Avery being too quick to discourage her sister because of her own opinions? *Could* Carter be a match?

Hell no, the inner voice inside whispered with an edge of nasty. *Because he's yours.*

The image of their searing kiss burned hot and bright. She shook her head, trying to clear it. "He's a hacker. He's here for the rest of the summer, and then he'll head back to DC. He's definitely single."

They waited for more, but she had nothing further to give. The idea of Bella and Carter together danced in her brain. Of course he'd fall for her. Bella was one of the most beautiful people she knew, inside and out. They could get married, and he'd be a stepfather to Zoe, and Avery would have to deal with the secret of their kiss and these ridiculous feelings hidden deep inside. Maybe one day she'd explode, and she and Bella would have a huge fight and never speak again. All because she'd allowed Bella to date Carter.

"Dude, what's up with you?" Taylor asked, narrowing her gaze. "You look sick."

"I just don't think Bella dating Carter is a good idea," Avery said.

Her sisters studied her for a while in silence. She arranged her face into a pleasant mask, waiting for the subject to change, and then everything exploded.

"Holy shit, you're into him!" Taylor yelled. "You've got the hots for Carter!"

"Do not!" she shouted back instantly. "You're being stupid!"

Bella laughed. "Oh my God, T is right. You like him and that's why you're acting all weird."

"No wonder you're so mad at him," Taylor said. She turned to Bella. "Before you came in, she was droning on about what a jerk he was, and how she doesn't want to work with him anymore. It was the first time she's ever asked to switch a client."

Bella nodded. "Yep, proof. Now, tell us everything. Don't leave out any details."

She blew out a frustrated breath. "There's nothing to tell. I'm just . . . confused. I don't think I like him, but then after we had that dinner at Peter Shields, we—"

"Wait, he took you to dinner?" Taylor asked. "Why didn't we know that?"

"Because we're all running ragged with work, and I didn't mention it in our morning meetings. Plus, I paid because I lost a bet, so it wasn't a date."

"What bet?" Bella demanded.

"Remember when he picked Ally's dress? He told me if she chose his option, I had to treat him to dinner."

Her sisters shared a meaningful look. "Oh yeah, he's definitely interested," Bella said.

"So, after dinner, he suggested we walk on the beach and—"

"It's illegal to walk the beach after nine," Bella interrupted.

"I know." She tamped down a groan. "We snuck under the chains."

Taylor's jaw dropped. "You? The ultimate rule follower? I can't believe it. That's the craziest thing you've done since you moved back home."

She glared. "Can I finish my story, please?"

"Sorry," Taylor said.

"We snuck on the beach, and before I knew it, we were kissing."

"But you said you didn't like him," Taylor pointed out.

"I didn't think I did, but there's this intense chemistry between us. Freaks me out. And when he lets his guard down, he's different and sort of sweet and I want to get close and comfort him."

"So romantic," Bella said with a sigh. "How does he kiss?"

"Really, really good. Who knows what would've happened if Ron didn't break it up?"

"No way," Taylor breathed. "You got busted by Ron?"

"Yep." She told the rest of the story, all the way up to yesterday, when they'd made the beach date. "Now I'm supposed to go to the beach with him, but I have the Mitchell wedding and a million things to do, so I'll probably end up canceling."

"No."

Avery looked over at Taylor, whose face was set in the serious lines that showed she was not playing.

"You're going. This man actually interests you, and even better? He challenges you, Avery. I'll switch my day off and cover for you Monday."

Bella chewed on her lip. "Uh-oh. I need some help with Zoe on Monday. I was going to ask if you could watch her just for a few hours, T."

"Damn," Taylor said.

Bella waved her hand in the air. "I'll find someone else. Trust me, a man is much more important at this point. I agree with T. You need to spend some time with him and see if there's anything there other than intense dislike and sexual chemistry."

"Absolutely not. I refuse to lounge on a beach while you scramble to find a sitter for Zoe. Unless . . ." She trailed off, the plan forming perfectly in her mind. "I have an idea. A way to really test things out."

"What?" Bella asked.

"I'll take Zoe with me to the beach. He promised her a few weeks ago, anyway, and this will be a great way to see how he is in a relaxed environment. Stick a man with a preschooler for a few hours in the sun and you see the truth."

"That's kind of mean," Taylor said. "But it may work. Especially if he's trying to mask the bet as a way to get you alone. Teaches him a lesson and gives you the chance to see things more clearly."

Bella sighed. "I think you should just skip the beach date and sleep with him."

Avery laughed. "Sleeping with your best friend's brother is so . . ."

"Cliché?" Taylor asked.

"Tropey. It screams romance novel and chick-flick movie. Maybe it was just a hot kiss and together we'll be one hot mess," she said with a sigh.

"Better to find out now," Bella said. "I will allow you to borrow my daughter for your wicked plan. Just make sure you tell us everything afterward, and don't leave out the good stuff." She finished her wine and stood up. "I gotta get to bed. I'm exhausted."

"And I have to finish this painting," Taylor said. "Pierce said he'd hang one in his studio and try to sell it for me."

Avery paused, studying her sister. Her cheeks were a bit flushed, which was unusual. "Hey, you didn't tell me you wanted to try selling them. We can put some up in the conference room, too, if you want."

Her sister shook her head. "Nah, that's overkill. No one's going to buy them anyway. Pierce just thought it would look nice behind his desk when he meets clients."

"That's nice. And don't say that about your work. I always told you to try and go commercial or make a website."

"Agreed," Bella said. "I've always thought you had amazing talent."

Taylor glared, a normal reaction when she was beginning to feel vulnerable. "Give me a break. Family doesn't get to have an opinion, because they can't see clearly. I should've never mentioned it." She stormed out and shut the door behind her.

Bella sighed. "Mom always said she had a nasty temper. She really wants to be an artist, but she won't admit it."

"Probably afraid," Avery said thoughtfully. "At least she felt comfortable enough to give one to Pierce."

"Well, you know how close those two are. I always wanted a male friend like that. Preferably gay."

"Remember when you thought Gabe was gay?" Avery asked with a grin. "I've never seen him so upset."

"Well, I didn't know! I rarely see a male working full-time in the wedding industry, and then he wore those leather pants. I feel terrible about how I judged him. I don't think he's ever really forgiven me for that assumption."

"He never wore those pants again," she said.

They giggled. Bella shook her head. "Okay, I'm going. Hopefully, you'll sleep with Carter and give me every dirty detail. I'm tired of having celibate, boring sisters. Even Taylor is all talk and no action."

Avery stuck out her tongue. "Just make sure to have Zoe ready bright and early Monday morning for our beach trip."

Her sister gave a thumbs-up, and the door closed. Even though privacy was sometimes a problem in a town like Cape May, Avery loved having her sisters on the same block, and since they shared a house, it was the perfect way to see both in one visit.

She washed and recycled the wine bottle, cleaned her glass, and tidied the counter. Then she headed home to plan for her big date.

Chapter Thirteen

When Carter saw the two females tripping over the sand—pushing a large stroller filled with endless towels, buckets, shovels, toys, and an umbrella—he realized he'd been had.

His first date included a preschooler.

God, she was ruthless.

Still, as he walked over to meet them, he couldn't help his gaze from roving over Avery's flash of naked leg, or the luscious curves beneath her filmy red cover-up. Her curly hair was pinned up tight, but already the wind tugged a few honey-colored strands free and whipped them at her face. She seemed to be chattering away with her niece, but once Zoe saw him, she squealed and took off running over the sand, throwing a tide of grains at her aunt in a flurry.

He knelt down and swung her around, enjoying the high-pitched giggles. She wore a ruffled hot-pink bathing suit, a pink hat, and glittery pink sandals encrusted with jewels. Bangle bracelets filled up a wrist. Amusement skittered through him. "I didn't know we were supposed to wear our jewels to the beach," he said, feigning frustration. "I left my tiara at home."

"You don't have a tiara," she said with a toothy grin. "Boys don't wear those, silly."

"Oh, then it's a good thing I didn't. Wouldn't want anyone to laugh at me."

Her face pulled into a serious frown. "That's bullying, and it's very bad," she whispered. "I won't let anyone do that to you, Carter."

His heart melted into a pile of goo. "Thanks, princess. But you may have to watch your aunt. Sometimes she can say mean things."

"I'll make sure Aunt Avery is nice to you."

The woman in question rolled her eyes, huffing slightly from pushing the stroller over the sand. He reached around and gently nudged her out of the way to take over. "Already brainwashing her, robot man?" she asked.

"Just looking for a little protection." He leaned in, out of Zoe's earshot. "After all, you brought her to be your guardian, right? So you wouldn't have to be alone with me?"

She sputtered in outrage, and he grinned in delight, pushing the stroller ahead. "Bella needed some help, so I offered to bring Zoe. You promised her, remember?"

"That I did."

"See, we bang out the bet and the promise in one shot."

"Not the bang I'd hoped for," he muttered. He stopped at the wide-open spot he'd picked to settle in for the day and began tugging things from the stroller. Zoe immediately plopped in the sand and started burying her legs, ignoring them.

Avery's lips pursed into a tiny little O. "What did you say?"

His gaze raked over her slowly, deliberately, and he heard her catch of breath as the attraction between them caught fire and sizzled to life. "A different bang from what I'd hoped," he repeated slowly. He admired the rosy color in her cheeks as his meaning sank in. "I'm fine having Zoe here today. We'll have a lot of fun. It's just going to be more difficult for us."

She blinked. "Difficult how? Watching her? She's very good."

He gave her a lazy grin. "No, stealing another kiss. But don't worry. I'm a pretty smart guy. I'll work it out."

He ignored her gasp, peeled off his shirt, and knelt in front of Zoe. "Race you to the water?"

"Yeah!" She jumped up, grabbing his hand, and they ran past the lifeguard into the waves.

He didn't have to look back to see the simmering heat in Avery's hazel eyes, or the frustration emanating from her gorgeous body. The image was clearly outlined in his imagination, so he focused on playing with Zoe and ignoring the woman who was wrecking his peaceful vacation.

He hadn't experienced this much fun in a long, long time.

Why did the man have to look so hot in a bathing suit?

Avery tried not to gawk at the endless amounts of olive-toned skin, with the perfect sprinkling of hair dusting his chest, arms, legs, and tapering to that silky line that disappeared into his waistband. How were his abs so cut for a man who sat behind a desk? Those biceps and calves were taut and muscled. His ass was tight. But the biggest surprise was when he turned around and displayed the magnificent tattoo on the back of his right shoulder. An intricate compass inked his skin, seemingly with great detail she couldn't study from this distance.

The compass fascinated her. Not only because she'd never pegged him as a man who'd ever get a tat but also because of his choice of ink. It was a symbol that seemed to contradict the man she thought she knew. She couldn't stop staring at it, or the way his muscles bunched when he moved, or the sexy sheen of sweat glistening on his bare skin.

Her body was going haywire in the company of a five-year-old.

She was losing her damn mind.

Pulling out a few fresh peaches from her bag, she adjusted her chair in the sand and pushed her sunglasses up her nose. "Want some fruit, sweetie?" she called out.

"Yes!" Zoe barreled over, reaching out with sandy hands.

Avery laughed. "Go wash them in the ocean or your peach will be crunchy."

"Ew!" She took off, and Avery kept watch while she rinsed her hands, then got distracted by shells littering the shoreline.

"Can I have one?"

Avery looked up. In the glare of the sun, Carter's eyes crinkled at the corners, and those full lips held a sexy tilt, like he knew she'd been ogling him before but refused to admit it. "Sure." She handed it over, pretending his half-naked body wasn't interesting at all.

He bit into the ripe fruit, and a trickle of juice spilled over his chin. Her throat tightened as she imagined licking over the same trail and ending with her lips on his.

"Now that's a thought I want to know," he drawled. Amusement danced in his misty-blue eyes.

She ripped her gaze away and rummaged in the cooler for a juice box. "Trust me. You'll never know."

He laughed and took another bite. "Nothing like a good challenge to spur a man on."

"Is that what this is to you—a challenge?" Suddenly, all the twisted feelings inside her leaked into her voice with pure frustration. "Is the sudden flirtation and interest in me boredom? An itch to finish out your vacay with some fun in the sack? Why don't you tell me what this is really about, Carter?"

He finished his peach, and wiped his hands on a napkin. Then regarded her with an intensity that made her squirm. "None of the above." His voice came out like sand and gravel, raking across her ears. "But I don't have all the answers yet. I'm attracted to you. I want to spend more time with you. I want to kiss you again, and touch you in all your secret places and give you pleasure. This is all brand new to me, too. But if none of this interests you, I'll respect it and back off. Just say the word."

She opened her mouth, but nothing came out. God, it'd be easier to just send him away and get back to her busy, crazy life. But deep inside, she wanted all of it. The idea of exploring this attraction was too appealing to turn down. Maybe it was time to take a chance and see what they could be together.

He waited for her response. Patience and a fierce demand mingled in his gaze, daring her not to lie. Sexual awareness skittered through her.

But she wasn't ready to admit it. Not yet.

She took the safe route and avoided the question entirely. "You're very good with Zoe," she finally said.

She held her breath, wondering if he'd push, but his shoulders relaxed, and he allowed her the space. "I like kids. They're honest and pure with their intentions. I like the way they look at the world without blinders."

She tilted her head. "I guess I figured you'd find them messy, emotional, and a bit inconvenient."

His rich laugh made her belly drop. "Sometimes. But the good outweighs the bad. I love the way all three of you banded together to support Zoe after her dad died. I know his death will always affect her, but she's a happy, vibrant little girl."

Her heart softened. He seemed to always be surprising her. "I think we were all lucky to have one another. Just like Ally was lucky to have you."

Surprise flickered over his face, but before he had a chance to respond, Zoe came rushing back up to the blanket, her little hands full of shells. "Look what I got! Mommy says when I bring home a unique shell, it can go in the garden, but we can't have any of the sames," she babbled. "Can you help me find the good ones?"

"Definitely. Here, let me take them so you can eat your peach first. Looks like you got sandy all over again, princess." He transferred the shells to her pail of water, grabbed a clean towel, and dusted off her fingers. Zoe ignored her *Sofia the First* beach chair and plopped her tiny butt next to Carter.

Smiling, Avery handed her the peach and juice box, watching while they chatted away and Carter began sifting through the various shells. The warmth and genuine interest on his face told her there was no pretense. He wasn't trying to show off to get Avery into bed. This was a man who knew how to relate to kids and owned who he was. What a beautiful surprise.

A stirring in her gut rose up and crashed over her like a wave. Her dream of a future husband and father had always been a misty fragment of perfection—a list of black-and-white traits on paper that added up to a man worthy of her. But right now, a longing clawed to the surface, and the only sharp image in her vision was Carter Ross.

Shaken, she buried her thoughts and focused on the moment. It was a beautiful day at the beach, and she rarely got time off. For today, she'd have fun and soak in every ray of sunshine. Gabe was on call for emergencies if Taylor needed him, her phone was switched to silent, and the hours stretched before her like a gift.

Carter seemed to sense her shift of energy. They picked out their shells, Zoe finished her peach, and he stood up. "Ready to jump some waves, ladies?" he asked, extending both of his hands.

Zoe bounded up and grabbed at his fingers. "Yes! But not too far, because the water tastes yucky."

"I'll keep you safe. Avery? Ready to jump?"

She froze. The words stirred in the hot air with a much deeper meaning. His gaze dared her to join them. Her hesitation was brief, but enough to show her next actions weren't done on impulse.

She stood up and took his other hand.

Their gazes locked. His grip tightened with a searing warmth and security that made her soul sigh. His slow smile made her heart swell, and she smiled back, a lighthearted happiness flowing through her body.

"Let's go," she said.

They ran down, hand in hand, to the shore.

The next hours passed in a joyous blur. At first, the shock of the freezing water hitting her bare skin stole her breath and her nerve. Carter and Zoe called out encouraging words, and eventually her body adjusted to the frigid temperature, and she waded in to her waist. The classic game of jumping waves brought her back to her childhood days with her sisters, when every weekend was spent in the water until their skin pruned and they shivered with cold. Then they'd wrap themselves up in towels and sit together, watching the vast expanse of beach where ocean met sky.

Carter kept Zoe high in his arms, careful to watch every incoming wave for intensity so the little girl never got a mouthful of water or sand. Her hands wrapped around his neck, and she squealed in delight. Emotion hit Avery while she watched them together, wishing Bella could find a man for her and Zoe to love, and wondering if Carter had snuck up to snatch all the secret parts in her heart she didn't realize she had.

Too soon, the hour grew late, and they began to pack up. They rinsed the toys, shook out sandy towels, and piled up the stroller. The trudge back was slow, but they were all smiling as they reached the burning concrete and put on their sandals.

"Let's wash our feet, honey," she told Zoe, guiding her toward the showers.

They cleaned up and started heading toward the car. "Aunt Avery! Can I get the free fudge and say hi to Lenny?"

She turned, waving at the young teen working his summer job by handing out free fudge in front of the Fudge Kitchen. "Sure, we'll wait here. Don't take too much."

"I won't." She raced off, and Lenny leaned down to chat with her, his gloved hand picking out a few choice pieces.

Avery shook her head. "She's got most of the town charmed."

"I'm not surprised. The Sunshine girls are hard to resist."

He stood close. He'd propped his sunglasses on his head, revealing those gorgeous blue-gray eyes that called to her like a rising mystical storm. His nose was burned. Grains of sand clung to his cheeks. Stubble hugged his jaw. He'd shrugged on his T-shirt, which clung to his damp skin and outlined his broad shoulders and chest. He smelled of ocean salt, peaches, and man.

The words popped out of her mouth. "I had a good time."

"Me, too."

"Even with Zoe?"

"Especially with Zoe. I like seeing her with you. Your face lights up when you look at her. I keep wondering what it'd be like if you looked at me like that."

Her breath caught. His voice seared like a brand. "You're doing it again," she said.

His hand slowly reached out. He stroked her curls back, and she wondered briefly how bad she looked. Crazy ocean hair, sweaty face, and sand-encrusted skin. But his fingers were gentle when he stroked her cheek, and his eyes burned so bright, with a need that called to her primitive soul. "Doing what?"

"Making me confused. When you talk like that, it makes me . . ."

His thumb stroked over her lips. "Makes you what, Avery?"

She shuddered. "Want."

He muttered a low curse. His face tightened, and he leaned in so close, his breath grazed her in a caress. "Me, too."

And then he was kissing her, the lightest brush of his lips sliding over hers, as fragile as a butterfly's wings. His fingers cupped her cheeks, and his mouth sipped at hers with a delicacy that contradicted the bolt of raw hunger rushing through her in a demand for more. She rose up on tiptoes, but he was already stepping back, staring down at her with a male need that ripped a moan from her lips.

The pounding of Zoe's footsteps clamored in her ears. The ground shifted underneath her as she tried to refocus.

"I had three, Aunt Avery, but they were little, and look—I brought back some for you!" Zoe stuck out her hand, which held two tiny pieces of fudge. Smushed.

Carter grinned and tousled her golden locks. "Thanks, princess, but I think you should eat mine. I'm really full."

Those wide blue eyes turned to Avery, full of innocence. "Do you want yours?" she asked sweetly.

Avery shook her head, laughing. "Nope. Why don't you eat those last two pieces, wash your hands, and come right back?"

"'Kay!" She popped them both into her mouth at once and raced to the fountain.

"Will you let me take you to dinner?" he asked in a low voice. "Or do I need to win another bet?"

She sighed. "No more bets. I'd go to dinner, Carter, but my schedule is insane. I have back-to-back appointments all this week, and a wedding this weekend."

He nodded, a frown creasing his brow. "Is there a night I can cook for you? You can bring your laptop to my house and do some work, then break for dinner."

She nibbled on her lower lip in thought, then paused when she caught his hungry stare. Her belly tumbled. Right then, she knew she'd do anything to see him again. In private. "Wednesday. Eight o'clock. Will that work?"

"Yeah. It's a date."

"Don't forget Gabe is meeting you at the tux place tomorrow. And the favors will be done—I'll bring over a sample Wednesday."

"Sounds good."

Zoe appeared by their side, wet from head to toe. "Hi."

Avery gasped. "How did you get so wet? You were supposed to wash only your hands."

Zoe gave a little sigh. "There was a bug in my hair, so I wanted to get it out."

Carter laughed and grabbed a towel from the stroller. "You definitely drowned the bug, along with yourself." He rubbed her hair dry, chucking under her chin, and she gave him a quick hard hug.

"Can you come back home with me, Carter?"

"Not tonight, princess. But soon. We'll make another playdate, okay? Right now, Aunt Avery has to take you home."

"'Kay! Bye!" With another hug, the little girl smiled and skipped ahead of the stroller.

Avery said goodbye, heading back to Bella's, and wondered how the man had managed to capture both of their hearts in one short day.

She couldn't wait until Wednesday.

Chapter Fourteen

Carter knew the moment he met Gabe that he didn't like him.

Gabe was young. Well, younger than he was. He strolled into the tux place with a male grace that pissed Carter off. His dark hair was thick and shiny. He was stylishly dressed in a white summer suit that should look ridiculous on anyone but Robert Redford in one of his old-school films. But no, this guy pulled the whole thing off, shaking Carter's hand with a firm grip, his dark eyes quickly assessing his build and probably finding him lacking. God knew his one lousy hour lifting weights and running on the treadmill was nothing compared to this guy's bulging biceps. How could he be a wedding planner? He didn't seem the type.

"Nice to meet you, Carter," Gabe said, his voice deep and cultured. "I've got a few choices I'd like you to try first, if you don't mind? Avery told me Ally wanted you to have a different tux from the other grooms-men. Are you open to colors?"

"I've worn pink before," Carter said, slightly defensive. The moment he uttered the words, he wanted to groan. Why was he acting like an idiot? Because the thought of this guy working endlessly next to Avery drove him fucking nuts?

Gabe laughed. "Don't worry, I'd never stick you with pink. But I think lavender would work with the bridesmaid dresses without being overpowering. I have a few shades of gray picked out and various styles, too. Let's get you suited up."

He began to walk toward the dressing room with Carter. "Oh, I got this. I'll just come out and model."

Gabe's dark eyes sparked with humor. "Of course. I just wanted to show you which room you have."

Ah, shit.

Gabe opened the door to the one on the end. A line of tuxedos was neatly hung up, balanced with various shirts, ties, and two pairs of shoes. "Work from the right to the left. These three styles will accent the rest of the bridal party. I have two shoe sizes in case one runs tight. If you need help with the buttons or cummerbund, let me know."

"Got it."

"Want something to drink?"

He deepened his voice. "Sure. Whiskey. Straight."

Gabe pressed his lips together. "Um, I was going to offer water or coffee since it's ten a.m., but I can probably get you a cocktail if you give me a few minutes."

Fuck. "No, it was a joke. Sorry. I'm good."

"Great, I'll be out here waiting."

Carter rubbed his head and told himself to get it together. Why was he intimidated? The guy was just a worker bee. Good-looking, yes. But if he was interested in Avery, wouldn't he have made his move already?

He needed to find out.

He got himself into the first tux, hoping he'd hate it. Unfortunately, the style was nice—a bit conservative, with a narrowed jacket and tighter pants, but longer in the back, with some flair. The smoke gray accented the lavender shirt. He exited while Gabe assessed with a sharp gaze.

"Good cut. Fits your body shape perfectly. You like the colors?"

"It's okay," he said grudgingly.

"Alex, can you come here and take some measurements for me?" Gabe called out.

An older man with spectacles and gray hair walked over with a tape measure in hand. "Hello, Mr. Ross, I'm the owner, Alex. This style suits you."

"Thank you."

"Is it acceptable if I take measurements?"

He waved his permission, his gaze studying his competition. Carter cleared his throat. "How long have you been working at Sunshine Bridal?" he asked casually.

Gabe tapped his lips in deep thought, walking in a circle. "Oh, a good three years now."

"Do you like it?"

"Yes. Contrary to popular opinion, it's an exciting career."

"I'm finding that out lately. Been shadowing Avery a bit for my sister's wedding."

The man smiled, flashing the whitest, straightest teeth he'd ever seen. "Avery's the best. I learned the whole business under her direction."

Carter's muscles tightened. Alex frowned, snapping the tape and remeasuring as his body jerked. "Sorry," he coughed out. "Avery does seem supportive. Do you work with Bella and Taylor, too?"

Gabe seemed to have no idea he was being grilled. He clucked under his tongue at something with the pant line, and got into a dialogue with Alex regarding brands and each one's tendency to run a different size. "I help out everyone, but I work mainly with Avery. I'm her right-hand man. Her ride-or-die, you could say."

His smug grin ripped at Carter's temper. "Seems like you're close friends."

"Very close. Can you try on the next one for me? I want to get a comparison so you can make an informed choice."

"Sure." He got off the pedestal and changed into the second monkey suit while irritation scratched at his nerve endings. Was Gabe insinuating he was more than friends with Avery? Was he disrespecting her?

He had to get more information. Pump him, then kill the bastard if he said anything lurid.

He stepped back out and resumed his place in front of the mirrors. The two men poked and clucked like mother hens rather than men hanging out without a group of women directing them. Damn, they took their jobs seriously. Still, he had to admit the second suit was even nicer. A lighter gray, breathable fabric paired with a deep-purple shirt that seemed to complement his color and emphasized the muscles he did own. The shawl collar had a deeper silver tone for contrast.

"Hmm, I like this better. What do you think?" Gabe asked.

"Me, too. More comfortable."

"Can you turn to the right?" Gabe asked, fussing with the jacket. "Shoulders back, please."

He did as directed. "Close business partnerships can sometimes get personal. Has that happened with you?"

A deep laugh sounded out. "Let's just say my advances were ignored . . ."

Carter's muscles eased. "She wasn't interested?"

"Not yet. But you never know what will happen in the future. Okay, let's try the last one. Not many men can pull it off, but I'd like to see it on you."

He went back into the dressing room and tried not to lose it. What did that comment mean? That he was still hoping to date Avery? Maybe the asshole was trying to seduce her, using the closeness of work as an excuse. He tugged on the final tux and realized his chest was tight with the effort of not punching Gabe and telling him to leave his woman alone.

What the hell was happening to him?

He wasn't the jealous type. There'd never been anything or anyone he was terrified of losing, except Ally and Lucy. No one had ever gotten that close. He'd only spent a few casual weeks with Avery. How could a connection be formed so quickly? And why did he feel in his very soul that she was meant to be with him?

By the time he reached the pedestal, his head throbbed with confusion and an overabundance of testosterone.

Gabe stood beside him in the mirror, grinning proudly. "Wow, man, you pull this one off well. Looking sharp. I tell you, not too many can wear the gingham gray, but you have the confidence to do it. You'll make a hell of a statement, my friend. Thoughts?"

"Yeah, it's good." Carter barely glanced at his appearance. Immediately, Alex began tugging at the fabric with his magic tape measure. "You dating anyone now?"

"Me? Nope. I'm staying focused. Need to convince one special woman to give me a chance. She's worth the wait, and I better have the decks clear, so when she's finally ready, I can dazzle her and make her fall for me. Know what I mean?" He winked like Carter was involved in his conspiracy to seduce Avery.

A roaring rose in his ears.

Alex stepped back with a proud expression. "All done."

"Great! You're all set. How do you like your new tux?"

Carter blinked, the red mist clearing, and looked into the mirror. The suit was a pale gray with a bold gingham pattern that made him look like a tablecloth. A wide bright-purple cummerbund swallowed his waist. The pants rode up his ass and made him look like a twelve-year-old boy.

What the hell was Gabe thinking? Unless he wanted Carter to look awful at the wedding because he sensed his interest in Avery?

With a low growl, he stepped off the pedestal. "Fuck no, I'm not wearing this clown suit. I'll take the second one." He stormed into the dressing room.

Taking his time, he breathed deep and told himself to calm the hell down. He had no right to beat up Gabe's pretty face because he was interested in a beautiful, intelligent, funny woman. He'd be crazy not to be in love with her.

But he'd be too late. Because Carter was going to make sure he closed that door and locked it tight.

Avery Sunshine was his.

He came out, cutting a glare at Gabe. "What do you need? My credit card?"

The man stared at him for a long time. Then a delighted grin transformed his face. "Damn, you got it bad."

"What are you talking about?" he asked rudely, barely keeping his shit together.

Gabe threw his head back and laughed. "Come on, dude. It's close enough to noon now. I'm buying you a beer."

"Why would I get a beer with you?"

He slapped Carter's upper arm in a gesture of camaraderie. "Because I'm gonna tell you everything you want to know about Avery and how to dazzle her. We're just friends, man. She's not the one for me." His handsome features shadowed. "I was talking about someone else. A woman who doesn't even see me as a man, let alone as a future husband."

The realization dawned. Gabe wasn't after Avery at all. He frowned. "Why'd you try to hook me up with that butt-ugly tux?"

Gabe shrugged. "Wanted to see if you were worthy of her. Too many guys aren't strong enough to have their own opinion. They want to please people who don't even matter, like buying a crappy suit because some guy tells you it's cool. Avery wouldn't put up with that. Make sense?"

Slowly, Carter nodded. "Yeah. That's fucked-up, but it does make sense. I think you do owe me a beer."

Gabe laughed and they headed out.

Wednesday night, Avery arrived at the rental beach house and took a deep breath. It had been a long time since she'd had a date, let alone had a man cook dinner for her. She'd reminded herself all day it wasn't a big deal, but the flip-flop of her tummy told her the opposite. Tonight, she'd spend time with Carter by choice, stripped of her previous excuses and denials he was just an annoying ManOH.

Vulnerability hit. She hated being unsure, but she wasn't about to run away now. Like Taylor and Bella had told her, they needed some time together to see if there was anything between them other than surface attraction.

The porch held two rocking chairs and a wide blue-checkered awning for shade. He'd picked a rental ten blocks from the beach, so the road was a bit quieter and more residential. After a few more moments of psyching herself up, she knocked.

He opened the door, and his pleased smile made her relax. "I'm glad you made it," he said, ushering her in.

The small cottage was decorated in the usual beachy theme, with lots of bright-white paint, bleached gray floors, and various knickknacks that livened up the rooms. There were wooden signs that screamed "I'D RATHER BE AT THE BEACH," wicker baskets full of books and magazines, and comfortable furniture in yellow and blue that gave the place a true vacation feel.

"Cute place," she said.

Lucy trailed in Carter's wake, tail wagging frantically, and damned if the dog didn't jerk back in surprise when she saw who'd entered her master's home. Avery took in her displeased gaze, the tiny nose in the air sniffing with distaste.

The tail fell still.

Great. She had a possessive canine to deal with along with her own confused emotions. Better to make friends than enemies, right?

She placed her laptop bag down and knelt, putting out her hand in a gesture of goodwill. "Hi, Lucy. How are you, girl?"

The Yorkie took a step forward. Her nose twitched. Her pink bow flopped to the side of her head.

Hope surged.

Then the dog backed up, stuck her ass in the air, and walked away.

Carter frowned. "Lucy, that wasn't nice. Honestly, I don't know why she's so cold to you. Are you sure you like dogs? She's very sensitive to emotion."

Avery stood up, practically snapping in defense. "I told you—I love dogs! She thinks I'm competition for your attention."

He waved a hand in the air and laughed. "That's ridiculous. Lucy knows I'd never choose anyone over her."

She choked out a gasp. "Gee, thanks."

He must've realized what he'd said, and shook his head. "Sorry, that came out all wrong. I just meant I made a commitment to her, and I take that seriously. I'm not one to give up on someone I love for anything."

Heat surged through her at the simplicity of his statement. This was a man who had no problem with love. How had she missed such tenderness and ferocity behind his cool, distant surface? How had she been so very wrong about him?

Having no clue he'd just blown up her world, he faced her with a smile. "Do you want a glass of wine? I can delay dinner if you want to work first."

"Thanks, white, please. I actually got a lot accomplished today, but I need a good half an hour to clean up some tasks for this weekend."

"Of course. You can work at the table over there while I finish cooking. I'll bring your wine over."

Uneasiness flowed. Some hot date. Work seemed to cram up every moment of her life. She couldn't even enjoy a nice dinner during wedding season. Why would he want her here if she couldn't focus her attention? She bit her lip, suddenly questioning this whole ridiculous idea. "I'm really sorry. I'm sure this isn't your idea of a fun date—you cook while I work. Are you sure you want me here?"

He regarded her from across the high granite countertop, hands on hips. Those gorgeous dusky blue-gray eyes sparked. "Actually, this will be one of the nicest dates for me. I'm a homebody, and I enjoy cooking. I understand your workload, Avery. I respect the hell out of a business owner who does what she needs to do to be successful, and you never have to apologize for that. Not with me."

The tension eased and she smiled. "Thanks. Then I'll bang out the rest of this work so we can enjoy the meal."

He winked. "Bang away."

She set up her laptop, pulling up various spreadsheets and checklists for the Bankses' wedding. In minutes, she was swept away in a tide of endless details and the quest to make the event flawless. She murmured a thanks when Carter brought her wine, enjoying the cool fruity taste of sauvignon blanc on her tongue. She tapped out texts to her upcoming bride, combed through final schedules with vendors and made sure they had what they needed, and confirmed all reservations for the upcoming weekend festivities. The wine was gone when she finally surfaced, satisfied she'd gotten ahead on any issues ready to sidetrack her tomorrow. Slowly, she stretched and turned toward Carter.

He was humming under his breath as he moved around the small kitchen. The rich scents of lemon, basil, and garlic filled the air, along with the pleasant sounds of sizzling oil and bubbling water, but it was Carter Ross himself that held her transfixed attention.

God, he was gorgeous. How had she ever overlooked the earthy sexiness of the man? He wore faded jeans that cupped his taut ass and showcased the lean length of his legs. A white short-sleeve shirt was unbuttoned at the neck, giving her a tantalizing glimpse of his chiseled chest covered with dark hair. His bare feet moved soundlessly over the floors as he checked and stirred pots and pans, relaxed and at ease with his task.

Her heart fluttered like a schoolgirl's. She'd never had a man cook for her before. All her dates consisted of formal dinners or the occasional movie, and rarely led back to cocktails at home. She'd never craved that type of intimacy before—happy with the crumbs of romance and the occasional making-out session. He was beginning to stir up all sorts of longings in the short time he'd been here. If he wanted to take her to bed tonight, would she let him?

The thoughts whirled in her head as she packed up her laptop, grabbed her glass, and headed into the kitchen. "All set," she said lightly, sliding onto one of the cushioned chairs. "Can I help? It smells amazing."

His smile was warm and gave her all the tingles. Had she really called him *robot man*? She'd been so wrong. "No, it's under control. Will be ready in a few minutes. Did you get all your work done?"

She propped up her elbows on the counter. "Yes. Taylor and Bella have other events booked, so it's just me and Gabe handling this wedding. Besides a large wedding party, demanding MOB, and anal groom, I need to make sure nothing gets overlooked."

He stirred the asparagus, which looked nice and crisp, just the way she liked it. "MOB is Mother of the Bride, right? Do you use acronyms for all your clients?"

"Pretty much. It's our shorthand for all those long titles," she said as he refilled her wineglass. "MOBs can be a nightmare, even more so than the bride. For instance, this one undercut the bride's choices on everything, and made her doubt her instincts. As the planner, it's my job to protect the bride and encourage her to keep her vision alive while dealing with stubborn relatives who believe they can do it better."

"And the anal groom?"

She took a sip. "The groom insists his dog be the ring bearer."

His lip quirked. She had the urge to run her fingers over his mouth to see if his lips were as soft as she remembered. "Doesn't sound too weird. Plenty of people have their dogs involved in weddings."

"Yes, but the ceremony isn't outside or at the beach. It's in a church where we needed to get special permission to bring the dog in. I've also heard the dog misbehaves, which makes this a challenge. Of course, I'll try to gauge how bad it will be at the rehearsal dinner. The groom promised to practice with Gus so he's not nervous."

"Gus, huh?"

"Yep. Plus, the groom demanded a gluten- and nut-free cake."

"Well, people have allergies."

She sighed. "But no one he knows at the wedding has any allergies. He just wants to be prepared. He also insisted no roses be used anywhere in the ceremony or reception because it's bad luck. I guess his ex-wife used roses everywhere, and he believes it'd be a curse to his new marriage."

Carter lifted a brow. "I think *anal* is the wrong word."

"Eccentric?"

"Crazy."

She laughed. "Well, at least I'll have Gabe with me. I forgot to ask you about the tuxedo appointment. Did it go well?"

Something danced in his eyes, but he turned quickly so she couldn't study him further. "Yep. Found a good tux."

"And Gabe? Did you both get along?"

"Better than I imagined."

She sighed with relief. "I'm so glad. Gabe is simply amazing. I don't know what I'd do without him."

He turned and pinned her with his gaze. Heat flared between them. "He said the same thing about you." She sensed more to the story, but he smiled and said nothing more.

"Oh, I forgot to show you the favors we settled on. Want to see?" she asked.

"Absolutely."

She shot him a suspicious look. "You're not going to suggest an alternative and then challenge me to another bet, are you?"

He held his hands up. "Promise. No judgment or helpful comments."

She muttered an assent and grabbed the wrapped item from her bag. Carefully removing the fabric from the plastic-wrap protector, she withdrew the tea towel.

Carter frowned. "A shirt?"

She rolled her eyes. "Of course not. Unfold it."

He smoothed out the fabric and stared at it. Avery hoped he saw what she did. The tea towel was silver gray, soft to the touch, and had an Elizabeth Barrett Browning quote embroidered in calligraphy:

I love thee with the breath, smiles, tears, of all my life; and, if God choose, I shall but love thee better after death.

Underneath were Ally's and Jason's names with the wedding date.

He stared at it for a while.

"You don't like it?" She tried not to show disappointment. "Before you begin going off in a new direction, your sister approved them, and they're already paid for. Nonrefundable."

He looked up and smiled. "It's beautiful."

Relief cut through her. "Thank God. Ally really wanted to use the quote on something that wouldn't be thrown away, and everyone loves a tea towel. I had no idea your parents were such romantics," she teased. "Did they both love poetry? I never asked Ally about the true meaning behind the poem."

His jaw tightened. "My parents were like lovesick schoolkids. Crazy about each other. They'd met in college in an English class, so their love for words bonded them. Dad would read poetry to her late at night. That was Mom's favorite quote. When Dad got in trouble, he'd find ways to use it as a reminder that he loved her."

The thought of such devotion shook her to the core. "You were lucky to have them," she said quietly, sensing his tension. "They showed you and Ally what's possible."

He turned, jerking the pan from the stove and turning off the heat. His shoulders tensed into a straight line. "I learned many things from my parents' relationship," he said with a touch of bitterness. "But I'm glad the quote makes Ally happy. She should have something to remember them by during the wedding."

She frowned, feeling as if she'd stepped over a personal boundary he let no one cross. Was it the pain of losing them that caused the edge in his voice? Or something she didn't know? Something deeper?

When he faced her again, the smile was back, and his face had softened. "Dinner's ready."

She helped him serve, and they began to eat. She practically moaned with pleasure at each perfect bite. The roasted chicken was tender and juicy. The asparagus, slightly burned and garlicky. The baked potato was filled with butter and chives, with firm skin and a soft center. He'd even made dinner rolls with shiny, buttery tops that leaked steam when broken open.

"This is amazing," she finally managed to say between bites. "You're not a cook. You're a chef."

"Flattery will get you everywhere."

She laughed and watched him share his food with Lucy with a separate fork. Her little face tipped up, big brown eyes filled with pleading he seemed unable to resist. She ate like an aristocrat, sliding the food carefully from the fork and chewing slowly, sighing in happiness and waiting for the next morsel. "You spoil her."

"I pamper her," he corrected. He turned and tilted his head, studying Avery's face with his searing gaze. "I enjoy pampering my women."

His husky voice made goose bumps pepper her skin. Her belly tumbled, thinking of all the dark meanings in his words and how badly she wanted them. "Are there many?"

"Many what?"

"Women," she said lightly. "Women in your past who you've pampered."

His grin told her the question amused him. "Not many. Like you, I'm very involved with my work. My main focus has always been raising and providing stability for Ally. My relationships have been short and far between."

"Have you ever been in love?"

He paused, placing his fork down on the plate with intention. The clink vibrated in the air. Avery didn't know why his response was so important. His face grew shadowed. She sucked in her breath at the naked pain she spotted, before the barrier quickly slammed down and his gaze cleared. "No. I don't believe in love."

Shock filled her. She blinked, staring into his face. "How can you not believe in love? You adore your sister. Lucy. Certainly there are others you love."

His expression turned grim. "I should have clarified. I know love exists, and you're right, I love many people in my life. Friends, family. But I choose not to fall in love and get married. To give myself over to another with the expectation she alone will make me happy and fulfilled. I believe you can have a healthy, happy relationship without the trappings and expectations of romantic love or marriage. Personally, I think it's dangerous pushing couples to believe in that all-consuming emotion poets and artists and filmmakers write about."

The room spun as she tried desperately to piece together his words and get the full picture. *Impossible.* She'd seen the range of emotions within him. How could he choose not to believe? "But your sister is getting married. You're going to stand beside her as the man of honor and watch her commit to an institution you don't even believe in?"

He nodded. "I am, because that's her choice. I don't have the right to put my beliefs on her, but I've seen firsthand how love can ruin lives. It can tear people apart and break them so hard, they can't be put back together."

She shook her head and gripped the edge of the table. The evening had been so hopeful, and with his words, she found her hopes shredded in tatters. "What type of life do you expect to lead without the hope of love or marriage?" she whispered.

His voice was gentle, but firm. "An honest one. It doesn't mean I can't experience things such as passion and romance and beauty. I just choose not to follow a road that I don't believe in." He leaned in and took her hands, clasping them in his warm, strong grip. "Is this a make or break for you, Avery? Would you be able to open yourself up to a man without the promise of marriage and happily ever after? Can you grasp the moment and steep yourself in it without trying to define what we feel for each other? I can offer you so many other things."

A shudder racked her as a ravenous need to touch him clawed through her, to press her lips to his and let herself get carried away by her body and the sweet promise of passion. To be in his bed, naked underneath him, and allow herself to fall apart under his talented fingers. She wanted it all so badly, she almost pretended his words didn't matter. Almost convinced herself she'd be able to handle a decadent summer affair with no promises except for physical delight.

But that would be a lie.

A lie for both of them.

She brought his hands up to her lips and pressed her mouth against his rough skin. "Who hurt you so badly?" she asked. "What happened to you that tore you apart?"

He jerked. She tightened her grip, staring deep into those beautiful, stormy eyes, and urged him to share. But he either couldn't, or chose not to. She could practically feel the distance between them, as if the walls were closing in around his heart to barricade him into safety. He didn't answer, his pain trapped in a place she couldn't get to.

Her own heart breaking, she told him the truth. "I can't, Carter. Being a wedding planner isn't just a job to me. It's a belief in everything I do. I want to fall in love and get married and have a crazy, messy, joyous life. I believe in all of it, and that my happy ending is out there. And I'm afraid if I let myself open up with you, I'll fall hard, and you won't be there to catch me. Not because you don't want to, but because you don't believe enough to be there."

He muttered a curse. Sadness and loss twisted inside her for something she hadn't even tasted yet. She couldn't imagine what type of pain she'd go through if she allowed herself to give in and follow his path. It was as if the more time they spent together, the harder she fell, her soul seeming to recognize his.

No. He was too dangerous. Better to know now their relationship could go no further. Better to protect herself against the one thing he didn't believe in.

Forever.

An aching silence stretched between them. They held each other's hands, realizing they were at a crossroads, until Lucy got fed up with waiting for her next bite and let out a whine.

Avery's eyes burned, but she forced herself to speak. "I should go."

"I don't want you to."

His plea made her shiver, but there was no happy ending here. "Neither do I. But we can't change who we are, or what we want. It's better not to make it more complicated."

His hands slowly fell away, and she stood. Gathering up her stuff, she walked to the front door and turned. "Thanks for dinner."

He stood close. The delicious male scent of him rose to her nostrils. Her gaze fell to his lips, and she fought the treacherous need to kiss him one last time so she could hold it in her memory forever.

She tipped her chin up, meaning to keep her goodbye brief, and suddenly they were in each other's arms. Her hands gripped his shoulders and his forehead pressed to hers, his breathing ragged, while he waited for her to step back and shut the door behind her.

She didn't.

Their mouths fused together, and her arms tightened around him as she surrendered to the embrace, her breasts pressed against the hard wall of his chest. Her lips opened under the sweet thrust of his tongue, kissing him back deeply while her fingers stabbed into the silky blackness of his hair to keep him from pulling away. He groaned her name and dove his tongue deep, gathering her taste, and his erection notched between her thighs, making her grow wet and achy.

His hands slid down her back, cupped her butt, and brought her up high. He backed her up against the wall, and she clung to him as wildfire flowed hot in her veins, driving her to take everything from him in that perfect heartbreaking moment.

His teeth nipped, and his tongue soothed. His fingers bit into her flesh, and he rocked his hips against her, driving her mad with lust and the need for more. She moaned his name, and he swallowed it whole while her hands roamed over his body, enjoying each hard muscle and desperately trying to touch his naked skin. She yanked his shirt up and slid both palms over his chest, the crisp hair tickling her, his ab muscles jumping under her caress.

"I want to touch you," he growled, dropping stinging kisses over the vulnerable curve of her neck. He snaked one hand to her front and cupped her breast. Her nipple hardened under the scratchy lace of her bra, begging for contact. "I want to please you."

A shudder worked through her. She arched up for more, and his fingers slid under her top to stroke and play, scraping her nipple with his thumb. Her breasts swelled, and he muttered her name in question. She paused, on the verge of mind and body warring together, but then his fingers tightened on her nipple, and a bolt of pain and pleasure shot through her and weakened her knees.

"Yes."

His mouth reclaimed hers. He tugged her bra down, exposing her bare breasts, and teased the tight tips, the strength of his body holding her pinned against the wall for leverage. His fingers tweaked and played and tormented, until her breasts were swollen with need. Their tongues tangled together, and his hand moved downward, fingers hooking under the elastic of her panties and parting her swollen folds. She dampened, a demanding heat between her legs fogging her brain and making her crazy as she lifted her hips and allowed him full access.

His teeth nipped her bottom lip at the same time his fingers surged inside her tight channel. She cried out his name at the exquisite pleasure, and he growled blistered curse words in a symphony while his thumb rubbed her throbbing clit.

She dropped her head onto his shoulder and rolled it back and forth, helpless to fight or stop him. "I need—" She gasped, caught in the rising tide of pleasure that threatened to push her over.

"I know, sweetheart." His fingers worked faster, diving so deep that shimmers of heat gripped every muscle. Her core wept and squeezed around him. "Come for me." The demand was matched with one final thrust of his fingers while his thumb pressed hard on her clit.

She convulsed around him, her body writhing while he held her and milked out every last bit of her orgasm. He whispered her name, and when the shudders began to slow, he removed his hand and pulled her into a tight embrace, pressing kisses in her hair.

Her knees stopped trembling. Her breath evened out.

And Avery realized what she'd just done.

The full implication of surrendering to an orgasm with a man she'd planned to walk away from blasted into her. She'd wanted him badly enough to damn the consequences. But it hadn't changed anything between them. Even worse? She'd spend the rest of her life wondering what making love with Carter Ross would be like.

She lifted her head. His gaze locked with hers. Her lower lip trembled. "What did I do?"

He pulled back, face ravaged with arousal and regret. "I'm sorry. I shouldn't have pushed."

"No, I am," she tore out. "We can't do this. We'll only hurt each other in the end, and I don't want that for us."

Eyes stinging with tears, she kissed him one last time, then grabbed her bag and hurried out. The echo of her name drifted in the air, but she didn't look back, knowing she might not have the strength to leave again.

The door slammed behind her with a finality that reminded her that sometimes happily ever after didn't exist.

At least, not with Carter Ross.

Chapter Fifteen

"What do you mean you're sick?" Avery whispered frantically into the phone. She quickly ducked into a quiet corner amid the chaos of the bridesmaids fussing with the final touches to the bride in the back of the church. "I can't do this alone, Gabe."

His voice came out weak. "I know, dammit, and I tried. But every time I get up, I get dizzy and puke. There's no way I can get to the wedding."

She filled her lungs with air and cleared her mind. "I'm sorry, I don't mean to sound like I don't care. I just freaked out. Go back to bed and rest."

"You can't do it alone; there's too much room for error with only one person on duty. I'm sending over someone to be your bitch for the day."

"I thought Jessie was out of town this weekend," she said with a frown. Their receptionist was known to cover in tight circumstances, but she'd booked a trip away with her boyfriend. It'd been on the calendar for weeks.

"She is. I found someone else. Don't worry about it. Good luck."

The phone clicked.

Poor Gabe. Maybe he was sending over one of his friends to help. Even sick, he always looked out for her and the business.

Tamping down a sigh, she began lining up the bridal party, and positioned the two mothers who'd be escorted down the aisle first. The groom, bridesmaids, and groomsmen were ready and waiting at the altar. From the middle of the aisle, Pierce nodded—the signal he was ready to begin shooting the pictures.

"Hi."

She whirled around and her jaw dropped. Carter stood before her, dressed in a sharp, conservative black suit. His hair looked thick and slightly damp as it curled over his forehead. He wore his glasses, and his stormy gaze slammed into hers, reminding her of their intimate encounter.

Shock froze her for a moment. "What are you doing here?"

"Gabe sent me. Said you were short-staffed and to do what you tell me."

Yeah, she was going to strangle Gabe when she saw him. What the hell had he been thinking? "Why would he call you?" she asked.

He shrugged. "We're friends now. What do you need?"

The music cued. The bride's hissing voice rose in her ears, breaking her out of the trance. She snapped to attention. "Pretend you know what you're doing even if you don't. Keep your eyes and ears open to any potential disasters, and tell me immediately. I'll get you a wireless mic later so we can communicate." Damn, she was thrown off by Gabe's absence and Carter's disturbing presence and needed her head in the game. She couldn't afford shredded nerves at this point. This wedding needed her full attention.

"Avery?"

Her voice cracked on a high pitch. "What!"

"I got this. Just tell me exactly what you need me to do right now."

The quiet confidence in his tone and reassurance of his gaze loosened her tight muscles. "Okay. Go down the line and check in with the bridesmaids, making sure they're calm and have their flowers. We're on live time."

She pivoted on her heel and headed to her stressed-out bride, praying it wasn't a dress issue. They were the worst. She channeled her calm, hypnotic voice that helped in every situation. "Selena, what's the matter? We're ready to go. Do you need a few more minutes?"

The bride blinked furiously behind her veil, but, thank God, there were no tears to mess up her makeup. "That dog is going to ruin my wedding—I swear it."

Avery glanced over at the canine ring bearer. The pug looked clueless, his fat body scrunched into a tuxedo that matched his master's. His tongue lolled out as he sat on the floor, his black eyes peering out from a face full of thick rolls of flesh. The rings were secured to his collar in a velvet pouch.

"Gus is going to be fine," she said firmly. "You've practiced with Adam, and the dog knows exactly what to do."

"I wanted him to have someone walk him down with a leash, but Adam insists he's trained to do it on his own. What if he stops walking? What if he runs around?"

Knowing all of that could possibly happen, Avery smiled with reassurance. "Gus knows what to do," she repeated. "I'll be standing by to handle anything. Now, look at me, Selena. This is your wedding—your moment. Don't let Gus take that from you."

The bride nodded, her chin tilted up as if to be strong. "It's just that he hates me. Has hated me since Adam and I began dating. If he's in the bed first, he growls at me and pretends to be sweet when Adam comes in. When we're alone in a room, he turns his back and refuses to acknowledge I exist. I think he wants to kill me to have Adam to himself again."

Her mind flashed to Lucy and her possessive glares. Before, she would've laughed and figured the bride was ridiculous. Now she wasn't too sure. Dogs were smarter than anyone imagined, and their love knew no limits for their owners. But this was not the time to fuel her suspicions. "Gus loves you, too. You're his new mom, and you'll have a beautiful, happy family together." Knowing Selena did better with a firm hand, Avery looked her in the eye. "Now, are we ready to do this?"

The bride seemed to calm. "Yes. You're right, I'm overreacting. Let's do this."

Avery smiled, smoothed Selena's train, and dragged the FOB from outside, where he was trying to sneak in one last cigarette. "Mr. Banks, we're ready for you," she said, getting him set up next to his daughter. She double-checked the line, and saw that Carter was charming the bridesmaids, keeping them in position. She rushed to the front, shooting him a grateful look, and cued for the mothers to begin walking and take their seats.

Carter moved to stand beside her. The delicious scent of soap and spice rose in the air. With all the heavy perfume and cologne in the church, his smell was like finding home. She swallowed past the tightness of her throat.

The aunt and flower girl made the trip down the aisle perfectly. One by one, each of the bridesmaids followed. Selena and her father were tucked behind the heavy carved doors, out of sight for the big reveal.

Saying a quick prayer, she bent over and said the magic word to Gus. "Showtime."

The dog got up from his perch and shot her a look. Yawned. As panic teased her nerves, he began to slowly move, heading straight down the center of the aisle just like he'd practiced.

"That the crazy dog?" Carter whispered.

"Yeah. Come on, Gus. You're almost there."

The crowd tittered and laughed, kids pointing as the fat pug jiggled past, gaze on his master, who watched him with a prideful grin.

Halfway down the white runner, the dog paused. Looked to the right. Glanced to the left. More chatter and giggles. A childish voice yelled, "Look at the doggy, Mommy!"

The sense of impending disaster hit her before it happened. In slow motion, she watched in horror as the dog slowly began to lift his leg.

And peed.

The church erupted. The groom's face turned to horror and fear, telling her that he was deathly afraid his bride would walk out. The music stuttered, then kept going, and everyone seemed to look around to see what would happen next.

Gus finished emptying the last of his bladder and trudged the rest of the way without pause, settling beside the groom and plopping his ass on the floor.

Holy shit. The bride was about to walk into a puddle of pee.

"Holy shit," Carter said, echoing her sentiments.

She'd trained her mind and body to not only see any impending crisis but also take only precious seconds to solve it. Selena still hadn't seen the debacle, so she needed to move fast.

Mind clicking on the endless trinkets, tools, and emergency supplies in her giant bag, Avery turned and grabbed Carter's arm. "My bag is in the little room to the right," she instructed. "There's the tea towel from your sister's favors. Can you get it as fast as possible and cover that pee stain while I distract the bride?"

He didn't bother to take the time to answer. He headed to the room, and she lifted her hand with two fingers up, giving Pierce, the musicians, and the priest the signal she needed two minutes. The organist began to play a new song, and the singer launched into some generic tune.

Avery dove through the doors with a wide smile. "Almost ready?" she sang, pretending to fuss with Selena's gown.

The bride frowned. "That's not the entry song. Is everything okay? Did Gus get down the aisle? I heard laughing."

"Gus was a big hit," she said. "He's sitting nicely by Adam's feet. We had a tiny tear in the runner, so we're just patching it so you don't trip."

"A tear? How? Did someone trip? Oh my God, was it Gus's paw?"

Her father patted her arm. "Sweetheart, calm down. Avery said it's all fine. Now, are we ready to walk down the aisle?"

She gave a prayer of thanks for good FOBs and watched her bride settle in. "Ready."

She hoped it was enough of a stall, because they both began moving toward the front doors. Wrapping her grip around the heavy latch, she counted to three in her head, then slowly opened them. Everyone stood.

The aisle was clear.

The singer saw her, nodded to the organist, and the classic strains of the "Wedding March" began. From here, Avery could see the pale-silver outline of the tea towel covering the bad spot, but they'd done their best under the circumstances. She looked around and spotted Carter standing off to the side, hands clasped behind his back, his tall, lean length a quiet, supportive presence.

He winked.

Her heart melted.

Selena walked toward her groom and didn't seem to notice or care about the tea towel. Her father lifted her veil, kissed her cheek, and gave her hand to Adam. As the bride turned, Avery caught the look of pure joy and magic on her face as she stared at the man she loved and claimed as her own for life.

Emotion choked her throat.

Too bad it was something Carter didn't believe in.

She shored up her defenses, got her head back in the game, and concentrated on giving the bride and groom their perfect happily ever after.

She was magnificent.

Carter watched Avery weave her way through the crowds like a ninja—ready to battle at a moment's notice, but invisible to the general crowd. The reception was in full swing, and he'd never felt so damn tired in his life. He'd been running around nonstop, taking care of endless tasks that popped up. Everything ached, from his head to his feet, and through it all, the woman never lost her cool or her charm.

The idea she did this every weekend the entire spring and summer was more than impressive. And this was just "live time," as she'd termed it. All the months of prep work led up to this one day. All her efforts and sweat and time were for the purpose of making one couple happy as they embarked on a life together.

The entirety of her work humbled him. There were so many layers he itched to explore, so many secrets to uncover with this fascinating woman, and he would never get the chance.

He remembered how she'd burned up in his arms a few nights ago. The honeyed taste of her mouth and feel of her pussy squeezing his fingers. The look on her face when she came and arched for more. The hazy sheen of satisfaction in her hazel eyes when he held her afterward, making him feel like a god.

But she'd walked away, and he didn't blame her. He wasn't what she wanted. A woman who embarked on relationships with the goal of marriage and white picket fences didn't belong with a man like him. He'd made that vow long ago, when he saw how love destroyed and ripped apart his own family.

Yet . . .

She haunted him. When Gabe called, he'd been caught between the raw need to see her, and the fear he wouldn't be able to watch her leave again. Gabe had been trying to do him a favor by allowing him a peek into her world. Carter was damn grateful. Gaining a front seat to watch her in action was a gift, even though being close to her was slow torture.

He stood in the back of the room and chugged water. The cake was done, and the bulk of the party was behind them. The alcohol and music had done their job well. Dancers crowded the floor, throwing up hands and stomping feet to a classic disco song that made Carter wince. Still, watching the families and friends make sentimental toasts, share first dances, and cheer on the new couple affected him more than he'd imagined. For the first time seeing a wedding close-up, he began to understand why Avery would find it important.

"Hey, you the new assistant?"

Carter turned. The photographer—Pierce—checked him out with a frank assessment that made him instantly tense. Was he another of Avery's admirers? Or like Gabe, was he just part of her day-to-day world at Sunshine Bridal? "Hell no. I'd get fired within the week." He put out his hand. "Carter Ross. We haven't met, but Avery's planning a wedding for my sister, Ally. Been wanting to stop by and introduce myself."

Pierce shook his hand. "Yeah, I remember now. I'm doing Ally's wedding in two weeks. Sorry for assuming you were a new hire. I'm burnt, been a long day."

"No problem. It was actually nice to see you in action today. I know my sister will be in good hands."

"Thanks." Pierce rolled his neck and groaned. "Nice save with the dog debacle, by the way."

Carter grinned. "Credit for that goes to Avery's quick thinking."

"She always has something in her pocket. She's got a better save record than a major-league relief pitcher. What happened to Gabe?"

"Got sick. He called me to see if I could help out."

Curiosity sparked in the man's pale-green eyes, but he just nodded. He wore his dark hair long and tied back at the nape of his neck. He was built stocky and solid, but moved with grace and speed with a camera in his hand. "You must know Avery well, then. She doesn't trust many people to work a wedding, even as an assistant."

Pleasure speared through him. He liked the idea of her trusting him. "How long have you been working with her?" he asked.

"I grew up with her sister Taylor. Been part of the Sunshine family forever. Seemed natural to work for them as their primary photographer after college. Are you here till the wedding?"

He relaxed, sensing no interest in Avery from Pierce other than as a friend and business partner. "I rented a house until Labor Day. Gave myself some vacation time after the wedding before I get back to DC."

"Nice. Well, I better get back to work. Listen, why don't you stop by my office this week? I'm free late afternoons. I know your sister wasn't able to see my portfolio personally, so I'd be happy to go through them with you and answer any questions. We can grab a beer afterward."

"Thanks, I will."

After Pierce walked away, Carter decided to go look for Avery in case she needed him. The reception was being held at Congress Hall, a pale yellow-and-white building that sprawled out on endless acreage. The hotel boasted rich dark woods, expensive antiques, and an old-world elegance that made it perfect for celebrations.

He searched the reception hall and headed down the stairs, where the loud music faded. He was just about to turn the corner when a faint sob rose to his ears. Alert, he backtracked and found the flower girl curled up on one of the chairs. If he remembered correctly, her name was Brianna. Knees up, her pretty face streaked with tears, she gulped and wiped at her cheeks when she spotted him.

His heart stopped. "Sweetheart, are you okay? Do you need me to find someone for you? Your mom or dad?"

She shook her head hard. The floral crown had long ago been disheveled and now lay drunkenly to the side. Her hair was tangled and her shoes were kicked off, and her dress held a streak of chocolate from the cake. "No. Mommy and Daddy are dancing with Aunt Selena. And I don't wanna talk about it."

He knelt down in front of her. "Okay. Your name is Brianna, right?"

She nodded.

"My name is Carter. It's my job here to make sure everyone is safe and has a good time at the wedding. But you don't look happy, which means I failed at my job, and that makes me pretty sad. Are you sure I can't help?"

A small frown creased her brow. Big blue eyes stared back at him.

He assumed a sad face and patiently waited.

The little girl lifted her head, opened her mouth, and pointed. "I lost my toot."

He smothered a smile at her mispronunciation. She was so damn cute with the bloody hole in the front. "That's wonderful news! Now the tooth fairy can come and visit you tonight."

Her face screwed up, and she began crying again.

Shit. What had he done?

He kept calm, but if she kept crying, he really needed to get her parents. "Sweetheart, what's the matter? Does your mouth hurt?"

"I can't find my toot!" she sobbed. "I lost it when it fell out!"

The pieces of the puzzle came together. Trying not to laugh, he cleared his throat. "I see. And you're afraid the tooth fairy won't come visit because you have no tooth to put under your pillow?"

She nodded miserably. "And I don't want to tell Mommy and Daddy I lost it, because I lose things all the time, and sometimes they get mad. But I looked and I looked, and it's gone forever."

He nodded. "I understand. But I know for a fact your mom and dad won't get mad about the tooth. When I was little, the same thing happened to me. I was playing baseball, and when I got home, my tooth was gone but I couldn't find it anywhere. I cried, too, but then my mom told me all I had to do was write a note and explain it to the tooth fairy."

Her mouth fell open in fascination. She leaned forward, her watery blue eyes blinking. "A note?"

"Yes. If we explain you lost it, the tooth fairy will still come visit. How about I get some paper and a pen and we write it together?"

"Yes! I know how to write my alphabet and a lot of words, but I may need help with the big, big ones."

He smiled. "I'm good at big words. Now, let me get you some tissues, and I'll be right back with paper, okay?"

"'Kay."

He grabbed tissues from the bathroom, and asked for a pad and pen from the front-desk attendant. He figured it'd be easier to keep her occupied while her parents enjoyed themselves, and when they were done, he'd explain. He returned quickly, dragged over another chair so they were seated side by side, and gave her the pad. "Ready?"

"Ready."

"Okay, let's start with 'Dear Tooth Fairy . . .'"

Where was he?

She'd scoured the main reception area and the bar, but Carter was nowhere to be found. She wanted to let him know he could go home, but so far, he'd disappeared. Had he left already? That didn't seem like him, though, not without letting her know.

Her heels tapped on the polished floors as she wandered past the reception area, and the sound of his deep voice echoed down a side corridor. She walked around the corner and stopped short.

He was sitting on a chair next to Brianna. The little girl had her feet tucked under her dress, which was now wrinkly and stained. Their heads were bent together, talking softly, and she was staring up at him with complete hero worship. The sweet image seared Avery's vision and made all her girlie parts tingle. God, he was so good with children.

Avery walked toward them. "Hey, guys. How are you doing?" She'd spent some time over the weekend with Brianna, who was a complete doll.

The girl brightened when she spotted her. "Hi, Avery! Guess what? My toot fell out!" She pulled open her mouth and flashed the gaping hole right in the center.

Avery laughed. "Congratulations! That means the tooth fairy will visit."

Carter's lips twitched, his eyes full of affection. "That's what I told her, but she was a bit upset since she lost the tooth. So we're writing a letter to the tooth fairy to explain."

Brianna nodded. "Carter said he did it when he was little, too, and it worked. Want to hear it?"

"I'd love to," she said.

"Okay. It says, 'Dear Toot Fairy, my toot fell out at Aunt Selena's wedding and got lost, so it is not under my pillow. Please understand and leave my money. Thank you. Love, Brianna.'" Her head popped up. "Does that sound good? Carter helped me write it."

His gaze swiveled to hers. Their eyes locked, and warmth flooded her body, her heart, her mind. He had the power to charm kids, dogs, and anyone else he chose. The man had helped her all night without complaint and respected her work ethic and her business. He'd gotten underneath her skin, revealed her vulnerabilities, and made her body sing. He didn't believe in romantic love, yet at that moment, Avery knew she was falling in love with the man.

She was so screwed.

Swallowing hard, she tore her gaze away and forced a smile. "It sounds perfect," she told the little girl. "Now, why don't we go find your mom and show her the note?"

"Yes!" She jumped up, paper clutched in hand. "Thank you, Carter!"

"You're welcome, sweetheart. Are you going to share the money you get with me?"

She burst into giggles. "I can't! You have to lose a toot first!"

He ruffled her hair. "Ah, that's right."

Avery took the girl's hand. "You've done an amazing job, Carter," she said quietly. "I have to wrap a few things up, but you can go home."

"I'll wait."

Her nerves tingled at the husky words that sounded like a sexy warning, but she just nodded and got Brianna back to her mother.

The last half hour flew by as the reception hall emptied and she closed out with the vendors. Pierce took off, the band packed up, and the room was finally, blissfully quiet. As usual, the high of the night leaked away and left complete exhaustion.

She'd done it again. The wedding had been successful.

Selena had hugged her and thanked her for a perfect day. Pride rushed through her. Once again, she was reminded of how much she loved her job. Many thought wedding planners were silly—impractical and expensive. She knew different. She knew to the brides and grooms she served, it made all the difference.

She knew she was important.

Groaning, she kicked off her shoes and uncrimped her toes. She grabbed her Tieks from her bag and slipped them on, breathing a sigh of relief. Guzzled half a bottle of water. Then limped toward the exit.

Carter was waiting for her.

God, he was hot. Those blistering pewter eyes staring at her from behind the black-framed glasses, giving him the sexy-nerd look. The sharpness and tight cut of his suit, emphasizing all those lean and yummy muscles. The clean line of his angled jaw and those pillowy lips she dreamed about kissing again.

Silently, he walked toward her, taking her giant bag and transferring it to his shoulder. "You did a hell of a job tonight."

"So did you."

They stared at one another. The steamy night air filled with longing and unspoken need. "Will you take a walk with me?"

There were a million reasons to say no: Her defenses were down. She was tired. The high of a successful event brought the usual crash of loneliness and craving for something beautiful for herself. He'd already been honest about his limitations, and a midnight moonlit stroll was not a good idea.

But she said yes anyway.

He put the bag in her car, took her hand, and headed toward the beach. The crash of the ocean became louder and drowned out the last of the wedding revelry at Congress Hall. His fingers were warm in hers, and the full moon cast a shimmery glow, catching the edge of the waves and spinning them to diamond-bright explosions of light. They walked down the pathway adjacent to the beach, past the line of Victorian bed-and-breakfast inns painted in Crayola-type colors, past the late-night crowds having last call at Harry's Bar, and into the hushed quiet of private residences.

"I cannot believe the dog peed in the church."

His words broke the silence, and a laugh broke from her lips. "Believe it or not, I've seen worse. At least it wasn't poop."

"And when the bride couldn't get the train to button? I watched the whole bridal party try to use safety pins, but nothing would hold it up. What happened?"

"The bustle tore and popped a few buttons, so I had to sew it back together. My mother made sure all of us knew how to sew—and sew well—for any type of emergencies."

"Impressive. Was that Uncle Bill who fell on the dance floor? Or Uncle Al?"

"Bill. I pegged him for the sloppy drinker at the rehearsal dinner. Thank God he didn't throw out his back."

"You know, they say weddings aren't like the comedies pictured in the movies, but I disagree. They're worse."

"At least you'll be ready for Ally's wedding and primed to avoid all disasters. ManOH is a serious role."

"I'm not worried at all."

She snorted. "Confident much?"

"Yep. Because I have you by my side."

Her mouth almost fell open, but she kept it locked closed. The simple truth of his statement caused pure pleasure to flood her. "No more fights or bets?"

"I call a truce. You still on board with my plan for AC, or do you really think the women would be better off keeping it quiet?"

It stung, but she told him the truth. In their last phone conversation, Ally had expressed that she was excited about the upcoming bachelorette party and was glad they'd switched it from a spa. "You were right," she muttered. "Ally deserves a bit of wildness before settling in. I think AC will be great."

"What was the first part again?"

"I said you were—" She stopped, tamping down a grin as he cocked his head, pretending to listen intently. "I said you were right. Enjoy it now, robot man. It won't happen again." The nickname rolled off her tongue with affection now, and no trace of mocking. She'd been wrong about him. He was nothing close to robotic or cold. The memory of his fingers thrusting inside her, slamming her into orgasm, shuddered through her.

"Are you cold?" he asked.

She shook her head. "No."

He stopped. Tipped her chin up and studied her face.

Heart stuttering, she stood still, helpless to move.

His voice was a deep rumble of sound, caressing her like fingers trailing lightly over naked skin. "I don't know how to stay away from you."

A shiver raced down her spine. "We don't have a choice. The bachelorette party is next week, and Ally will be back. We'll be busy, and then after the wedding, you'll go home to DC."

The pain of not being able to see his face, touch him, talk with him, crashed through her. But nothing had changed between them. He couldn't give her what she needed, and she had to protect herself.

"What if I tried?"

She jerked, staring up at him. His face seemed tortured, as if uttering the words had cost him. She pressed her fingers against his lips. "Don't say it unless you mean it. I'm looking for a man who's not afraid to love me and take a chance on a future together."

He reached up and released the pins in her hair, letting the curls tumble free. A moan rose to her lips as he pulled through the strands, his hands strong and soothing on her scalp. "All I know is I've never felt like this before. Not with any other woman."

A terrible hope ignited within, but her fear smothered the flame quickly. What was he promising? A two-week affair? A long-distance relationship? Would she be waiting for him in desperation to call, or spend weekends with her, until he slowly realized he didn't have enough to give?

Her voice shook as she raised herself on tiptoes. "What do you want?" she demanded.

"You. Damn you, Avery, for making me want." He gripped her head, and his mouth crashed over hers.

She kissed him back with a touch of violence and need. The dam within her broke, and she pushed her tongue in his mouth and sank her nails into his shoulders, then bit his lower lip. He cursed, reslanted his mouth, and took the kiss deep, forcing her to arch back under the ferocity of leashed male hunger.

They kissed a long time under the ripe full moon, until she finally managed to rip herself out of his embrace. Panting, she gazed at him like an opponent in the ring, ready for another round. "I need to go home."

He stepped back, his breathing heavy. He nodded. "I'll walk you back to your car."

They didn't speak or hold hands. The aching sexual tension throbbed between them like a mocking taunt, and she knew all she had to do was touch him one time before they both surrendered, damn the consequences.

She opened her door and slid into the front seat.

"I'll see you this week about the final plans for AC?" he said.

She nodded. The empty ache inside stretched and yearned for more. "Carter?"

"Yeah?"

She nailed him with her stare. "Figure it out."

Then she closed the door and drove home.

Chapter Sixteen

Avery picked at the healthy parfait in front of her filled with plain Greek yogurt, fresh fruit, and homemade granola. It was definitely good, but nowhere near the ecstasy of a chocolate croissant. But Madison's had been out, and she knew she should be more like Bella and eat healthier.

"Do we want to discuss anything before Gabe gets here?" she asked, trying to muster some enthusiasm. Her usual energy had been lacking the last few days since her kiss with Carter. She kept checking her phone for a text, and swearing she saw him around every street corner. She fantasized about him showing up at her doorstep and declaring he wanted a full-on relationship with her, then dragging her to bed.

So pathetic.

Taylor's pink hair shimmered in the light streaming from the window. "Yeah, what's going on with Carter?"

Bella looked up from the laptop, suddenly interested. "You owe us an update. Zoe couldn't stop talking about her beach day with him, and then Gabe recruits him to help you at the Bankses' wedding?"

She shifted in her chair. Usually, she told her sisters everything because nothing interesting happened in her personal life. But lately, she'd been close-lipped, afraid to tell them about the real feelings she was developing. She wondered how much she should share, and then realized it was too late.

They'd scented vulnerability.

"Did you sleep with him?" Taylor demanded, the diamond in her nose winking outrageously. "I swear to God, Avery, if you slept with him and kept it from us, I'm gonna be pissed."

Avery gasped. "Are you kidding? You were the one who said to start knocking and give you privacy."

"That's different. I'll happily share all my sex stories with either of you. I just don't want you actually seeing it."

Bella laughed. "Good to know, T."

"I didn't sleep with him," Avery said stiffly. "We just . . . kissed."

"Did you have an orgasm?" Bella asked.

She dropped her face into her hands and groaned. "Oh my God, we're not teenagers anymore, guys! I refuse to talk about this with you."

"Aww, babe, you *did* have an orgasm!" Taylor said proudly. "Good for you."

"Are you going to see him again, or was it a onetime thing?" Bella asked.

All the ragged emotions hit her at once, and she was suddenly fighting tears.

Her sisters sensed her shift in mood, and in moments, they were crowded around her. "Did he hurt you?" Taylor asked. "I'll fuck him up good if he did."

She sniffed and tried to laugh. "No. I'm just stupid and fell for him."

"But that's a good thing," Bella said, stroking her hair in a motherly fashion. "You deserve to have a relationship and be happy. What's the problem?"

"He doesn't believe in love. Or marriage. He won't tell me why, but he's so damn stubborn about not wanting to commit to one person for the rest of his life. And I'm not asking him to put a ring on my finger after a few weeks—but I need to know I won't get hurt!"

Bella clucked her tongue. "That is surprising because he's so wonderful with Zoe. And he raised Ally. Was he divorced before or something?"

Avery shook her head. "No. Maybe he got hurt in the past? I don't know. I told him I can't get involved when there's no possibility of a future together."

"Why?"

She looked at Taylor. "'Why?'" she repeated. "Because it makes no sense. I'm already falling for him. We'll have some type of long-distance relationship, I'll want more, and he'll end up breaking my heart. There's no happy ending here."

Taylor frowned. "Well, that's a lousy way to look at life," she said. "Are you telling me you say no to anything that doesn't guarantee a happily ever after? 'Cause that's just lame."

Avery stared at her sister, temper snapping. "Thanks for the support, T. Of course you wouldn't understand why I shouldn't explore a relationship with someone who'll end up walking away."

She shrugged. Her sister didn't even seem bothered by the jab. "Maybe he won't. Maybe he needs time to see if you're the woman he can take the leap for. I'm disappointed in you, babe. You quit before you even got to play."

"Um, T? Maybe you should back off a little," Bella suggested, likely seeing the look of fury on Avery's face.

How dare she make her decision seem careless? Avery jumped to her feet and faced Taylor. "Oh yeah? When was the last time *you* took a chance on anything?" she challenged. "We may not say it, but we all know you just use guys for sex to keep from getting involved. You pretend you're this worldly woman with no cares, but you lock yourself up tighter than any of us. What are you scared of, T?"

Bella took a step back, her blue eyes wide with shock. "Guys? Can we slow it down here? Take a breath? I think—"

"At least I don't bury myself in work and pretend I'm satisfied," Taylor shot back. "You spend your life planning and living for others, but one day you'll wake up and realize you let every opportunity pass you by. I'm stuck in this stupid small town for another year because of my promise, but damned if I'm not getting out and going after my own happiness the moment I can."

Bella stiffened. The usual light in her blue eyes turned flat and cold. "Are you saying you got stuck here because Matt died? I never asked you to stay and give up your dreams for me. And I won't be your damn scapegoat. Maybe we don't need you here for another year, Taylor," she said.

Taylor shook her head. "No, I didn't mean it like that. I wanted to be here with you and Zoe. It's Mom and Dad who trapped me into this promise, not wanting the business to fail."

"Because I couldn't work for so long," Bella said flatly. "It was my fault. I wasn't strong enough. I've never been strong enough—not like you two."

Avery felt her sister's pain like a punch in her stomach. "That's not true, Bella," she said quietly. "You are stronger than any woman I know. You chose to raise Zoe with joy and gave yourself time to heal. How could we possibly blame you for any of that?"

The fight drained out of her sister. "I'm sorry," she said. Her voice came out faint. "Sometimes I just don't know if I'm doing anything right. I try to be my best self every day, but I constantly question myself. I never feel confident like you both."

"Are you kidding? We all question ourselves. That's part of being human. Don't ever apologize for that," Avery said. They surrounded Bella and hugged her tight, and then Avery started crying, and Taylor patted her back hard in her own form of comfort.

When Gabe came through the door, he stopped short at the cry-fest in front of him. "Are you guys okay?" he asked.

They broke apart, sniffling, and Avery grabbed a tissue. "Yeah, we're fine. We needed a cleanse."

He wrinkled his nose. "We really need another guy around here," he said, shaking his head. "I can't be expected to deal with this on my own."

Taylor laughed. "That's what you get when you're late."

"Are you feeling better?" Bella asked.

For a moment, his gaze flared, and Avery studied the expression on her assistant's face. He always acted a bit different around Bella. He didn't joke with her in the same way, or throw his arm around her with affection. In fact, he usually kept his distance and acted more professional. She'd figured it was because he thought Bella was more fragile and sensitive than the rest.

"Yes, thank you. The virus passed. Must've been a twenty-four-hour thing." He walked over to his usual chair, then stopped. "Almost forgot. This was on the porch for you, Avery."

She opened the small white bag and withdrew a perfect chocolate croissant. Freshly baked, with crisp crust and a chocolate drizzle. Her mouth watered, and suddenly her mood skyrocketed. "Who is this from?"

Gabe shrugged. "Not sure."

"Wait, there's a note." She pulled out a square piece of paper and read it. Then burst out laughing.

Guilt is optional. —C

Her sisters shared a knowing look. "Remember what I said, babe," Taylor said. "Someone has to take a chance. It might as well be you."

"Aww, come on, what's that cryptic message mean? I'm part of this group, too," Gabe complained.

"We were just having a discussion about our periods. Want in?" Taylor asked.

"You're such a bitch," Gabe muttered.

"Thanks," her sister said brightly.

Avery dropped back in her chair, pushed her parfait away, and took a bite of her pastry.

Then thought about her sister's words all day long.

Carter walked into Pierce's photography studio and admired the space. It looked like an old loft that had been converted and gave off an artistic, comfortable feel. Light poured in from various windows, and wood beams crisscrossed the ceilings. The walls were painted stark white and filled with pictures of all sizes. Right away, Carter saw the man had talent. They weren't the normal cookie-cutter photos one expected from a wedding, but instead had fresh angles and ways of capturing the couple and wedding party that made one want to study the shot closer. Ranging from vivid color to misty black and white, the collage showed the broad range of Pierce's vision.

Avery was right again. There was no need to question her decision to book him as Ally's photographer, especially after seeing the man in action at the Bankses' wedding.

"Hey, Carter, good to see you again," Pierce said, walking over to shake his hand. "You recover yet?"

He grinned. "Barely. Working a wedding is not for the faint of heart."

Taylor came walking out from the hall, her pink hair slicked back, wearing a sleeveless black dress that hugged her trim frame and hit above the knee. Her nose ring winked, and she smiled in welcome. "Hi, Carter. Heard you were having a boys' lunch."

"I invited Gabe to hang with us, too," Pierce explained. "He heard we were grabbing a beer and said he needs a shot of testosterone. He works with too many women."

Taylor rolled her eyes. "Gabe complains, but he loves the drama. He's the worst gossiper I know."

Pierce snorted and shot her a look. "Taylz, you couldn't keep a secret for a million bucks."

She gasped. "Screw you! I didn't tell your mom you skipped school for a whole damn week in eleventh grade, did I?"

"No, but you told Ron, which was worse. He snitched to everyone, and I got busted. Remember?"

"Whatever. Go ahead and rewrite history if it makes you feel better."

Pierce laughed, and they shared a look of such understanding and intimacy, Carter figured they'd been fooling around in the office before he came in. It seemed Avery's sister had found her match.

Taylor turned to face Carter. "Hey, I heard you kicked ass at the Bankses' wedding. You made Avery really happy." Her words held a deeper meaning, especially paired with the intense stare she gave him, as if trying to tell him something important.

His chest tightened. Had Avery confessed what was happening between them to her sister? And even more important, had she shared her real feelings? Taylor didn't look pissed at him, so maybe it was her way of saying she approved.

And why the hell did he care?

Because her sisters were family, and he wanted them to like him.

"Okay, I'm outta here," she announced, hitching her tiny leather purse over her shoulder. She shut the door behind her, and the room immediately lost some of its vitality.

Pierce clapped his hands together. "Okay, want to see the office and a few portfolios before we head out?"

"Sure. This is a great place you have."

"Thanks. It used to be a marketplace, then a bike shop, but nothing could make it. I figured even though it's a bit off the beaten path, the space would be worth it."

They walked down a hall and entered a room with a large desk and red leather chair, a mishmash of photography equipment, and shelves filled with more pictures on canvas. A corner bookcase held an array of books and magazines and various wooden signs with quotes. The chandelier was a cool concoction of metal and silver lanterns stacked in different sizes, adding an artistic twist. But it was the painting behind the desk that mesmerized him immediately.

The ocean was a moody, stormy gray with waves hurling high above the surf. A lone girl sat on the beach, arms curled around her knees, her profile shaded as she stared into the water and faced the violence of the storm. Wet blonde hair tumbled down her back. Her face reflected a calm and aching loneliness that was only emphasized by the roar of nature ready to devour her whole.

It wasn't a piece of work he'd hang in his office when consulting with clients. It was a bit jarring, and had nothing to do with showing off the expanse of the man's work, but Carter hadn't seen anything like it before. The combination of raw emotion and graceful, sweeping lines made him confused. Made him think.

He jerked his head toward it. "Did you paint that?"

The man glanced behind him and laughed. "Hell no. Taylor did. She paints as a hobby, and I've been bugging her to get some of her work out into the shops to sell. She kept refusing but finally let me display this one. Amazing, right?"

Carter loved art, especially the type that evoked a reaction. Books and art were the only safe places he allowed himself to feel things without worry of a fallout. "I'm impressed. You know, I have a few friends in DC who collect art and love to discover new artists. Maybe I can speak to Taylor and see if she's interested."

Pierce dug out a thick binder and flipped through the pages. "That's really nice, but she'd never go for it. She'd think it's charity. I've never known anyone else with so much stubborn pride. She's a real pain in the ass." He uttered the words with pure affection.

Carter sat down opposite the desk and gazed at it thoughtfully. "I get it. Artists are temperamental. Is the painting for sale?"

Pierce looked up, surprised. "You really want to buy it?"

"Yeah. I've been poking around the art shops here, and there's a lot of nice stuff but nothing extraordinary. I'd love to have this hanging in my home."

The man's green eyes filled with pride. "Then it's yours. A hundred bucks."

He blinked. "A hundred?"

"Oh, sorry, you want it for seventy-five?"

He groaned and shook his head. "That's worth at least $500. Maybe more. You need to speak to her about pricing properly or she'll be wasting her time. I'll take it for $250. If she's only expecting a hundred and gets five, she'll just think you're bullshitting her."

Pierce grinned. "Sold. And hey, if you want to pay me double for my services, I won't fight you. I don't have a pride problem like she does."

Carter laughed, and leaned over to study the sample pictures. "That's why I have a wedding planner—to get the most bang for my buck. But I will buy you a beer."

"Deal."

It didn't take them long to go through the portfolio and target various shots his sister would probably love to incorporate in her album. He texted a bunch to Ally and told her he'd call her later. He loved the sophistication of Pierce's work—his photographs weren't the usual kitschy, overdone wedding keepsakes but were pieces of art.

Pierce locked up the studio, and they walked toward the Beach Shack. Even though it was early, party stragglers ready to start their evenings were already scattered by the outdoor tiki bar. Music came from a small band playing reggae, and people danced in the sandpit to the island-type music. He loved the casual atmosphere. Oversize picnic tables held big groups, and thick burgers were served on Frisbees. Various activities had been laid out for patrons to amuse themselves with, such as mini-golf, boccie ball, and giant-size wooden puzzles. Brightly colored Adirondack chairs were set up around the band and firepit, where people relaxed and sipped frozen cocktails.

They found three open barstools at the end of the tiki bar and didn't have to wait long for Gabe. Still dressed in a sleek summer suit, this time a comfortable cream linen, he greeted them and immediately shrugged out of his jacket. "Dudes, I had a shit day. I need a strong IPA, preferably in IV form."

Pierce raised his hand and ordered three beers. "What disaster befell you today, my friend?" he asked.

"I got harassed by the MOH at a bridal luncheon. She had too much champagne punch and tried to drag me in the bathroom to get laid."

Carter let out a short laugh. "Does that happen often?"

Gabe gave him a sour look. "Yep. Sometimes it's unfortunate. I'm not interested in hookups with clients. Plus, my body is sacred. She kept pinching my ass."

Pierce cleared his throat, and Carter could tell the man was trying really hard to look sympathetic. "That sucks, man. What'd you do?"

"My usual bit. Made excuses, avoided her, and flirted with Tony to make her think I'm gay."

"Who's Tony?" Carter asked.

"The waiter at Mad Batter. He's gay and has a crush on Gabe, so he probably didn't mind," Pierce explained.

Gabe snatched his drink the moment it was set down in front of him and guzzled a quarter of the beer. He let out a sigh. "I'm tired of being treated like the community stripper by some of these clients. I'm up for this promotion, and I don't want anything to screw it up."

Carter frowned. "Why don't you just tell Avery? She'll understand and help you work it out."

He shook his head. "No, I want to deal with this on my own. I need to learn how to handle the handsy clients, so this was a good test. I'm just fucking tired of it."

The amusement faded as Carter looked at his new friend. Society still had a hard time deeming men who got hit on as a problem, figuring they'd be happy to bang anyone or anything. But for Gabe in a professional environment, it must be hard to consistently convince so many women that he followed a strict code of conduct and took his job seriously. "I'm sorry, man. Beer's on me tonight."

"Cool, thanks." He settled, seeming to shake off his bad mood, and grinned. "So tell me what's going on, my dudes. Carter, you have your sister's bachelorette party this weekend, right?"

"Yep. I'm in charge of five wild women let loose in AC. Should be fun."

"How are you and Avery doing?" Gabe asked curiously.

Pierce narrowed his gaze. "Wait. You guys are together?"

He hesitated, not sure how much to say, especially since both men were close to the sisters. "No. Well, kind of. I'm crazy about her, but I'm only here for the summer. I'd like to spend more time with her and figure it out."

Pierce nodded. "Sounds like a plan. Avery works so hard and could use some fun. God knows she hasn't even dated anyone in the past year."

"She's definitely into you," Gabe said. "And you helping out at the Bankses' wedding? That was huge. It's obvious how much you respect what she does, and that means a lot to her."

"I just don't want to hurt her." Frustration laced his voice. "She's looking for a happy ending, and I can't promise her that right now."

"No one can promise that," Pierce said.

"Just be honest with her, but don't give up. I think you'll be good for her."

Satisfaction flowed through him. Knowing these two men approved of him pursuing Avery made him even more determined to try harder. Maybe it was time he pushed himself to give more than he thought he could. Avery was worth it. And after their shared kiss on the boardwalk, the need for her was eating him up like a virus, keeping him from sleep. He thought of her constantly. Could he really manage to walk away? Maybe a long-distance relationship was a possibility.

The bartender refilled their beers, and they ordered nachos to pick on. "You and Taylor seem really happy," Carter mentioned in between bites. "How long have you been dating?"

Pierce began to choke, and Gabe pounded on his back until he caught his breath. "We're not a couple. We've been friends forever."

Puzzlement made him cock his head. "Really? You seem so in tune with each other."

Gabe threw his head back and laughed. "Told ya."

Pierce glared at him.

Gabe turned to Carter and explained. "Every time they're together, he gets these moony eyes but swears there's nothing going on." He shot Pierce a knowing look. "I don't know how you can stand being just friends with a woman you're hot for."

Pierce jabbed a finger in the air. "You do it every day, man. How's that working for you?"

Gabe snapped his mouth shut and looked pissed.

Carter glanced back and forth between the two, sensing a challenge sizzling in the air. "Okay, what am I missing?"

"Nothing," they both said.

"Talk about feeling like the third wheel," he muttered, taking another sip of beer.

Pierce groaned. "Sorry, man. Let's just say I'm not willing to mess up the best friendship I ever had with sex. It's not worth it. As for Gabe, he's got his own issues working with a woman who doesn't seem to notice him."

Carter remembered the words he'd uttered in the tuxedo place. Something about being hot for a woman who didn't know he was alive. And if it wasn't Avery or Taylor . . .

"Ah, crap, you're in love with Bella?" he asked.

Gabe shrugged it off. "Nah, just got a soft spot for her. But she's got zero attraction for me. Thought I was gay for the entire first year I worked there."

Carter flicked a glance at the group of women currently eyeing Gabe with obvious interest. "I'm sure you have a lot of women to distract you," he said. "Avery said you were named most eligible beach bachelor."

Gabe rubbed his head while Pierce burst into laughter. "So fucking embarrassing," he muttered.

"Seems like all three of us have some challenges in our love life," Carter said. He raised his glass in mock salute, and they followed. "Here's to having each other's back. To friendship. And the future."

They clinked glasses, ate nachos, and proceeded to get a little bit drunk.

He'd forgotten how nice it was to have a night out with the guys. He remembered that empty feeling back in DC—the stirring in his gut that told him he wanted more in his life. Funny, he'd had to travel all the way to Cape May to find all the things he'd been searching for: friends and a woman who made his heart light up. He was actually more than content.

For the first time in a very long while, he was happy.

"Are we ready to party?"

Carter tamped down a grin as he watched the group of women clink their champagne glasses together and let out a whoop. The past week had passed by in a rush. Ally had flown in for her big weekend, bringing her three bridesmaids, who were all pumped for Atlantic City. Jason would be in Cape May on Wednesday with his family to help with any last-minute details and settle in, and then the wedding festivities officially kicked off on Friday with the rehearsal dinner.

He'd only communicated with Avery by text, trying to give her what she asked for—distance. He didn't want to push or upset her the week before his sister's wedding. Still, the moment she'd gotten into the limo and slid next to him on the cushioned leather seat, his body knotted so tight, Houdini himself couldn't untie it.

The snug, short black skirt she was wearing almost dropped him to his knees. The royal-blue top dipped to a low V in the front, the clingy fabric emphasizing the lush thrust of her breasts and skimming around her curvy hips. She'd worn her hair down, so the wild curls fell over her shoulders with abandon, practically daring him to wrap his fist in the silky strands and tug her head back. She'd gone with red lips. Her eyes had some type of smoke effect, and when she turned to gaze at him, the hazel depths shattered the last of his fragile defenses. In minutes, he'd have done or promised anything just for permission to touch her.

Instead, he'd forced a smile and thought of nuns with puppies to keep his erection under control. Dear God, this was going to be a long weekend.

"Carter, what are you drinking? You better drink up—you're part of this bridal party, too," Ally said, her voice already a bit pitched from the shots done in the car. But her face glowed with an excited animation that confirmed he'd planned the right trip. She was wearing a black cocktail dress and high heels and had a tiara perched on her head. She'd refused to wear banners or signs saying "Bride to Be," and he'd agreed with her decision. There was a line between having fun and being tacky.

He threw up his hands. "I'm drinking. Just not champagne. I need my masculine whiskey."

The women laughed. Judith patted his arm with affection. She was his sister's colleague and a professor of medieval history. Her long blonde hair was caught up in an elaborate twist, and she wore a glittery silver top like a disco ball that blinded him every time he looked at her. "I may join you. I like those Moscow mules. You think they have them here?"

"I'm sure they do. Ready to hit the casino for a bit, ladies?"

Another whoop and he guided them into the heart of the Borgata. Multiple tables of craps, roulette, and blackjack were set up amid blaring and pinging slot machines in full diversity. From *The Walking Dead*, *Superman*, *Sex and the City*, and *Wheel of Fortune*, the choices were endless in ways to lose money. Most of them were more interested in the slots than the tables, so he figured he'd let everyone roam and herd them before their dinner reservations at Bobby Flay's.

Ally took off, arms hooked with Judith and Jason's sister, Maddie, giggling like a schoolgirl. Noelle was another close friend Ally had met in Texas, who was proudly single and began chatting up a guy sitting at the *Family Guy* slot machine. With her red hair and bright-red dress, she was the one who'd begged for strippers.

Yep. He'd need to keep a close eye on her.

"Do you need any help checking reservations?"

Heart battering his chest, he turned at the silky voice he heard every night in his dreams. Head tilted, Avery regarded him with wary fascination, as if she were trying to figure something out that remained a puzzle.

Figure it out.

Her words echoed in his head like a constant chant. But he'd sworn not to do anything this weekend to push or make her uncomfortable. He'd concentrate on giving his sister the best party weekend, and deal with the rest later.

"You're off the clock, remember?" he said, shaking his head. "No wedding planner. You're Ally's best friend and need to cut loose. I've got it under control."

Those teeth reached and nibbled on her defined lower lip. His dick wept. "Honestly, it's no trouble if something goes awry. I can help. Oh, and make sure the chef knows to present the seafood tower with the special light display—it really makes the presentation pop. Were you able to secure the private booth at Premier? VIP service is great, but I find confirming in case of miscommunication is helpful and—"

"Avery." He rested his hands on her shoulders, and she stopped. "I have it covered. I promise."

She let out a breath.

He released her shoulders, his palms itching to slide under the lace and touch bare skin.

"Sorry." She shifted her weight, as if not ready to leave yet. "I forgot to ask you: Who's watching Lucy?"

"Gabe."

She stared at him in shock. "My Gabe?"

His voice was a low growl of sound. "I hope he's not *your* Gabe. I hope he's *our* good buddy Gabe."

Her lips twitched at his obvious jealousy.

He wondered why this woman caused him to revert to a primitive caveman.

"I just didn't realize you two had gotten so close over one tux appointment," she said.

He shrugged. "We had a beer and nachos. He likes my dog. I think that's good enough for a decent friendship, don't you?"

She laughed, and the sound pumped the room with joy.

The words popped out of his mouth before he could stop them. "God, I love your laugh. It makes me feel so . . ." He trailed off. No need to embarrass himself further.

She stepped closer and tilted her head. Those hazel eyes urged him on. "So what?"

He locked his gaze with hers and told the truth. "Alive."

Her lips parted, and he almost reached for her, but the sudden shout and scream of the machines announcing a big winner ruined the moment.

She cleared her throat. "I guess I'll go gamble."

"Need a cocktail?"

"Still working on my champagne." She hesitated, then turned. "I'll see you later."

He watched her walk away and disappear into the throngs of excited, happy people looking for a big hit. Too bad the emptiness in his gut made him feel like the loneliest person there.

He clenched his fists and headed toward the bar.

He was with a girl.

Avery reminded herself it was his right. She was having a great time. Finally, she wasn't in charge of everyone else's happiness and was free to dance and have fun with her best friend. The girls in Ally's bridal party were easy to get along with, and after a few hours, it felt like they'd known each other forever. Noelle kept up a steady stream of dance partners, and when Judith and Maddie pulled her onto the dance floor, Avery remembered how much fun it was to cut loose and let her body lead. The DJ played a variety of high-energy hits mixed with hip-hop and just enough rap. The VIP service kept snacks and drinks flowing at their table.

So far, Carter had done an amazing job.

And he was talking to a girl right now. A pretty one, too. She had smooth, straight blonde hair and big Barbie-doll blue eyes. Leather pants and some type of fringe top that would look ridiculous on Avery, but the woman at the bar had a perfect sleek, skinny body that probably made all clothes seem model perfect. Probably the regular type of women Carter went for. Not extra-curvy, wild-haired workaholics who made every decision based on practicality.

Avery slumped in the booth and sipped her champagne. She was happy for him. The blonde wouldn't have rules about long-term relationships or expectations. Maybe they'd sleep together tonight. No strings and no hassles. Just the way he liked it.

He'd dressed casually tonight, but sharp. The navy button-down shirt was designer, with flipped-up paisley cuffs. The material clung and emphasized his molded chest. He'd put some type of gel in his hair so it was sculpted back away from his brow. The look made his eyes appear more intense—the blue-gray depths pinning an onlooker with a serious gaze, unbarred by his glasses. His dark-washed jeans were tight and made his ass drool-worthy. Every time she got near, the delicious scent of spice and whiskey teased her senses. Yeah, he was ready to get laid, and that woman was practically licking her chops.

On cue, the blonde threw back her head and laughed at something he said. Their faces were close together, probably trying to hear each other above the loud music. Carter grinned with pride at making her laugh, and the woman squeezed his biceps in a familiar gesture. He did nothing to shake it off or discourage her.

Asshole.

Avery brooded and drank and watched.

Noelle appeared with a big smile and leaned over the table. "Why aren't you dancing?"

She laughed, averting her gaze firmly from the man a few feet away. "Just hydrating. Having fun?"

"Always." Her blue eyes gleamed with pure mischief. Noelle practically exuded sex appeal and emanated confidence bigger women usually didn't own. It was obvious she loved her curves, and dressed to accentuate every single one. Men were consistently asking her to dance and seemed to want to soak up her presence. Avery had adored her at first sight and wished she lived closer so they could be friends.

"Noelle, I didn't get to ask what you do for work."

The woman raised her voice to be heard above the music. "I'm a producer. I worked in New York for a while, but got transferred to Austin to do an indie series on Netflix. I'm employed by LWW Enterprises—they're based in Port Hudson."

"Oh, I've heard of them! They got Kyle Kimpton's book made into a movie, *A Brand New Ending*. Did you see it? I couldn't stop crying, it was so damn good."

"Yes! That . as my girl Presley Cabot's doing. I was in the same sorority as her, and she's done amazing things at LWW. Hey, when you come to visit Ally, make sure you invite me out! Sometimes I have a hard time making friends, and I just clicked with you."

"Same."

They smiled at each other, and then the DJ mixed into another song. Noelle shouted and began swaying her hips. "Come dance with me!"

Avery focused on the slow bluesy-type sound. Couples began pairing up on the dance floor, arms and legs tangled together. "It's a slow song."

"Who cares?" Noelle grabbed her hands, dragging her out. Only then did she notice Ally and Judith dancing together, laughing hysterically.

"Girl power!" Ally declared with a slight slur.

Maddie joined in, and they began a giant group hug that slightly resembled dancing.

Suddenly, Carter cut into the circle, grabbing his sister and spinning her into his arms. "Come on, Ally-Cat. Show me your moves."

Ally's face lit up under her brother's attention. "I love you, bro," she said with a sigh, making him laugh while he guided her in tight loops around the crowded floor. "Best man of honor ever."

"Man HO," Avery popped in, shooting him a glare. The champagne had loosened her tongue. "In my world, it's *Man HO*."

Ally cracked up. "Imagine my brother as a Man HO. Maybe you'll get lucky tonight," she teased her brother.

The look he shot Avery held little humor. In fact, his gaze narrowed with such intensity, she shivered and hid a bit behind Judith, who was still bouncing back and forth in an imitation of dancing.

"Maybe I will," he said, his dark voice making lava bubble through Avery's veins. Suddenly, he traded off Ally to Judith and reached for Avery. "Switch," he said. "I'd like to dance with the wedding planner."

Ally giggled, and the ladies drifted off toward the right, getting closer to the DJ booth.

"What was that about?" he asked, lowering his mouth to speak close to her ear. "Did I miss something?"

Temper and embarrassment and alcohol mixed together in an explosive cocktail. "You missed dancing with your hot blonde," she said. Heat rushed to her cheeks. It was awful to know she was acting like a jealous girlfriend and unable to stop it. "Didn't she want to dance with you?"

Amusement glinted in his pewter eyes. Her body tensed, and her nails dug into his upper arms. Did he think that was funny? "Actually, she did. I told her I had a bachelorette party to take care of and wanted to dance with my sister."

"I'm not your sister."

He sucked in a breath and leaned in. Sexy stubble clung to his jaw and hugged his lips. "No, you're not." He paused. "You jealous?"

"No. I don't care if she turns you on. Go sleep with her. Isn't that exactly what you're looking for? A bit of fun with no strings?"

His lips firmed. "Sweetheart, holding your hand gives me a hard-on. That woman could strip naked in front of me and I wouldn't be interested."

His words pummeled her defenses like rocks against glass. She didn't speak, caught between the need to believe him and the awful ache tearing her apart that urged her to move in and claim him. Touch. Pleasure. Possess.

Love.

He lowered his head and spoke against her mouth. "I haven't stopped thinking about you or what you said. And I need to figure this shit out soon because I need you too damn bad. Now, let me hold you for a little while, sweetheart. Dance with me."

She shivered and moved closer, her body giving up the fight and melting against him.

He growled her name and pulled her in, his hips cradled against hers, his arms wrapped around her waist, palms on her ass. In the dark and the neon flashing lights, they were just blurry silhouettes, mashed into a crowd of strangers. His lips coasted over her cheek, his breath a warm rush of air, his lips inches away from hers. Surroundings drifted away until she was caught in a cocoon of warmth and want, his scent in her nostrils, her fingers in his hair, drowning in a wave of hunger she no longer wanted to fight.

When the song ended, it took a long time for them to break apart. The release of his hold pained her, until they stood staring at each other on the crazed dance floor.

Ally and Maddie danced in between them, grabbing her wrist, and she was pulled away to disappear back into the crowd.

But his words haunted her.

She didn't know if it was one hour that had passed or three when she realized the group had reached its limit. Ally was slurring, Judith was screaming from being music deaf, and Maddie had a wasted smile on her face. Noelle was a happy drunk and kept hugging everyone. Avery was just about to go find Carter and let him know they were done, when he appeared with one of the smartly dressed VIPs who held chilled bottles of water.

"Drink up, ladies," he said cheerfully. "We'll get you to your suites so you can relax and get some sleep."

Everyone nodded, hydrated, and headed up to the elevators. Carter tipped the guy and personally escorted each of them into their rooms, which were all right next to each other. Avery had stopped drinking champagne after the dance with Carter, so she was more tired than tipsy, but she helped him make sure the ladies were okay by themselves and weren't about to be puking all night.

Finally, the last door was shut. Avery stopped in front of her own room and slid out her key card.

"You okay?"

She swallowed and tried not to look at him. "Yep. I switched to water a while ago, so I'm fine."

"You think they had a good time?"

That made her swivel her head to meet his gaze. She smiled. "Yeah. They had a great time. It was the perfect evening. I can't remember the last time I had so much fun dancing."

"Me, either. Sometimes I get caught up in all the *dos* and *don'ts* and forget how to live."

She stiffened. His words pummeled her like sharp, tiny stones, tearing at her defenses. "I do that, too," she admitted. "I'm in my head a lot and like to plan things out so there are no surprises. It's good in my career. But lately . . ." She trailed off, afraid to finish her statement.

He moved closer. The leashed heat and strength of his body pulled her in. "What?" he asked softly. The masculine scent of spice and whiskey surrounded her.

She swallowed. Poised on the edge, she uttered the truth. "Lately, I wonder if I'm missing out from all my self-inflicted rules. I haven't allowed any space for mistakes. For stolen walks on the beach after hours, and magical adventures and passion." All she could think of were Taylor's words, urging her to take a chance, to grab the opportunity for pleasure even with an unknown future. Was she so scared of living she'd rather lock herself up into a safe relationship and miss out on being with a man who rocked her world? All this time, she'd hidden and been safe. Where had that gotten her? Content, but lonely. Satisfied with her career, but not her personal life. Was it finally time to stop doing the right thing and grab what she wanted?

Grab *who* she wanted?

As if sensing her inner struggle, his breath rushed out, and he laid his hands on the door beside her, trapping her in but not touching. "Avery." Her name was a whisper and a shout, a mixture of longing and need and hunger that called to her, promising her endless ecstasy. "If I step in that room with you, I'll be in your bed. I won't be able to stop myself. But you need to be sure. I can promise you till Labor Day. I can promise to open myself up to you and see what happens between us. It needs to be enough. And it needs to be your choice."

the key card, and the door clicked. He removed his hands and stepped back. Avery opened the door, turned, and reached out her hand.

Their gazes locked, and sexual energy crackled and seethed between them, a warning of what was to come.

Carter took her hand and walked inside, kicking the door closed behind him. For a few endless, aching seconds, he stared into her face as if needing assurance this was what she really wanted. And then, a tiny smile touched his lips. Without another word, he scooped her up into his arms and carried her to the bed.

Chapter Seventeen

Carter's hands shook as he laid her gently on the king-size bed. The moment she outstretched her hand, a deep sense of fated purpose rose up inside him, as if all his endless moments had led up to this.

Ridiculous. He didn't believe in poetry or cheesy admissions of finding *the one*, but right now, he was helpless to fight the voice. So he pushed it aside and concentrated on the woman lying on the bed, waiting for him.

Deliberately, not breaking eye contact, he reached in the pocket of his jeans, slid out a condom, and placed it on the bedside table. He noticed the tiny shiver that shook through her, the lust shining in those gorgeous hazel eyes. Oh yeah, that turned her on. He couldn't wait to find out how many ways he could make her come in one night, and what other things brought her pleasure.

His dick was already painfully hard. He deepened his voice and reached out to touch her hot cheek. "Do you know how long I've fantasized about you laid out for me?"

"As long as I've fantasized about you," she said simply, shivering.

Not wanting to scare her or lose control, he moved slowly, sitting on the edge of the bed to look down at her. He pressed kisses over her face, arranging her hair so it fanned out over the pillow. She lifted her head, searching for more, but he kept up the easy pace, his lips sipping at hers like a fine wine he wasn't ready to drink yet. "You taste so sweet."

She made a needy sound. "Give me more," she demanded, her fingers twining around his neck.

"Want to be sure I go slow," he said. His mouth slid over hers with deliberate motions. "Not rush you."

"You scared of me, robot man?" she teased, her teeth nipping at his lower lip. The quick bite of pain made arousal roar in his blood. "Am I too much to handle?"

Oh yeah. This woman wouldn't break easily. She could take his rough, almost-primitive hunger burning to get out and devour her whole. The thrill of the hunt shot through him.

He thrust his tongue deep in her mouth, holding her head still as he ravished her with all the raw hunger he'd been fighting to tame. When she lay boneless underneath him, clinging to him while her hips arched for more, he slowly pulled back and gave a slow grin. "Funny, I always fantasized about you begging me. Especially after all the insults and trouble you put me through."

Her snort was delectable. "You wish."

His dick hardened at the unspoken challenge. "Care to bet?"

Cheeks flushed, lips already slightly swollen, she wrinkled her pert nose. "Thought we'd left bets behind us."

His hands tugged off her skimpy top, baring her lace-covered breasts to his eyes. "This one could be a win-win for both of us. I make you beg, and you give me an entire free day of your time to do as I wish."

Her hazel eyes widened. "Like I'm your slave?"

"Exactly." His gaze raked over her half-naked body. "Always wondered what you'd look like in a French maid costume."

An outraged gasp escaped her lips. "Hell no. That's never gonna happen."

"So no bet?"

He loved the fire that lit up her eyes with the prospect of a good challenge. "Fine. But if I don't beg, you're on call for me. You either babysit Zoe or serve drinks shirtless at one of my bachelorette parties." An evil glint in her eyes flashed. "My choice."

Damn, she was ruthless. God, he loved it. He lowered his mouth to hers and growled. "Done."

Then he kissed her hard.

She gave it all back, opening her mouth to his and wrapping her legs tight around his hips.

He slowly broke the kiss and peeled her skirt up so it bunched around her hips, then stared at the tiny scrap covering her sweet pussy, sucking in a hard breath. "God, you're so damn beautiful." His finger traced the sensitive crease of her thighs, running a teasing path over her shivering skin. "The things I want to do may shock you, sweetheart."

She wriggled her hips and began unbuttoning his shirt. "You don't scare me." Her bravado contradicted her trembling fingers as she ripped the fabric open, then dug her nails into his chest. He hissed in reaction, and it made her feel bolder. "I didn't wait this long to be safe now," she challenged.

In one swift movement, he dragged her panties down her legs and threw them on the floor. Slowly, he parted her thighs wide, opening her up to his hungry gaze. He took a while to stare at her, arousal squeezing his dick at her gorgeous swollen, pink lips, already wet for him.

"Carter." Her voice tore at him, slightly ragged, slightly nervous.

He grinned, and lowered himself down to the bed, his shoulders braced between her legs. "I can't wait to hear you beg," he whispered.

"You bastard. I—oh God!"

He licked her, gathering her spicy essence and exploring every slick, satisfying inch. Ignoring the bundle of nerves throbbing for attention, he took his time, savoring every cry and wriggle as he pleasured her. Curving two fingers, he pushed inside her tight channel, experimenting until he hit the spot that made her heels arch into the bed and her body tighten.

Yes, right there.

With a low murmur of satisfaction, he kept up the steady rhythm while he teased her clit, pressing light kisses that never satisfied, until he felt her entire body poised on the edge, his name chanting from her lips. Then he closed his lips over the nub and sucked hard.

She came, twisting in his grasp, but he held her down and never let up the pressure, extending her orgasm. Drunk on her taste and open, heated response, he waited until she'd collapsed onto the mattress, panting for breath, her muscles limp and useless. Then he slid back up, cupped her cheeks, and took her mouth in a deep kiss.

When he finally released her lips, she stared at him with dazed hazel eyes. "I didn't beg," she managed drunkenly.

He laughed, unclasping her bra and pulling it off so she lay gloriously naked underneath. "That was just a warm-up, baby. Now I'm ready to get serious."

He'd wrecked her, and he was just getting started.

Avery lay helplessly beneath his hard-muscled body as she tried to recover from the intense, mind-blowing orgasm. Oh, that mouth was skilled. She should have known he'd bring the same ruthless attention to detail in seducing a woman as hacking a computer program.

Even now, he was revving her back up. Plumping both breasts with his hands, he scraped his teeth against her tight nipple, then laved it with his tongue, bringing the peaks to such sensitivity, a sob caught in her throat.

Dear God, she didn't stand a chance. She'd be begging in another three seconds, just to feel the exquisite sensation of him sucking hard on her nipple.

Fighting the drugging lethargy, she knew there was only one thing left to do.

Rally.

"Carter?"

He looked up, his lips damp, pure male satisfaction glinting from his eyes. "Yeah, baby?"

"My turn."

Without warning, she hooked her ankle over his leg, mustered her strength, and flipped him over. Crawling on top of his body, she braced both legs around his hips and arched her back, displaying her naked body for his pleasure. Pride coursed through her at the raw hunger and lust in his gaze while he studied her, surrendering to her dominant position. Avery was amazed by how natural and free she felt in her sexuality with him. She'd never been a prude, but struggled with displaying her most erotic side to men, always a bit shy with her naked body and its curviness, wondering if they thought she was fat. But not with Carter. Every look and touch reminded her he wanted her.

"I can't get enough of you," he murmured, reaching up to cup her breasts as she undulated and shook out her hair. "You're so fucking beautiful."

"And you're overdressed," she said with a wicked grin. "Let me take care of that."

She unsnapped his jeans and tugged them down his legs. She took in the black briefs and the impressive erection that pressed against the soft fabric. Oh, he was so ready. She finished parting the folds of his shirt, and he lifted up to help her shrug it off his body. Her mouth watered, and she ran her fingers down his chest, exploring every carved muscle, loving the feel of his crisp hair tickling her palms. "How are you so fit for a computer guy?" she asked, stroking along the waistband of his underwear.

His stomach muscles tightened. "I work out an hour a day. Weights and cardio. It's in my schedule to avoid back and muscle issues from a repetitive-motion career."

God, he was nerdy. Adorable. And sexy as hell.

"That's hot," she breathed out, running her tongue over the same intriguing line she'd traced with her fingers. She cupped his hard length, squeezing him with the fabric barrier, and only when he groaned and thrust into her hands did she begin to peel off his underwear.

It was time to make him beg.

She lowered her head and took him into her mouth. He hissed her name into the air, and his fingers tangled into her curls. She used her hands to stroke while she sucked him hard, her tongue running up and down the underside of his swollen shaft, relishing the power of his need and the musky taste of him. She hummed low to give him the slight vibration of her throat, and with a vicious curse, he suddenly loomed up, grasped her hips, and flipped her back over on the mattress. His face reflected the primitive aura of a man pushed to the edge, and she panted for breath as he grabbed the condom from the side table, tore the package open, and sheathed himself.

She parted her legs wide, half-crazed with the need to feel him inside her. Dropping a kiss to her inner thigh, he lined his shaft up, his gaze hot on hers. He lifted his hips and pushed inside her. Inch by slow inch, the sweet invasion stole her breath, filling every part of empty space in her body and her heart. When he was buried to the hilt, he lifted her legs onto his shoulders. Silver-blue eyes glinted with satisfaction.

"Hold on, sweetheart."

In one swift motion, he pulled out and slammed back into her. She gasped, and her fingers clawed for purchase, caught between pushing him away and pulling him close. Buried deep, he paused to allow her to adjust to his size and girth, her breath coming out in choppy pants.

And with a slow smile, he did it again. And again.

Avery arched her head into the pillow as her body tightened and pulsed, all her focus sharpened on the empty, hungry ache that rose up in torturous waves. Her toes curled, and he kept hitting some magic spot that shot sensation straight to her clit and heated the blood in her veins to lava. His fingers began to pluck and play, and his hips rolled with each thrust, harder and harder. Squirming helplessly beneath him, she called out his name, the blistering need for release twisting through her.

"So good," he murmured, watching her face as he rubbed the throbbing bundle of nerves in too-light strokes. "God, I can't get enough of you."

Another deep plunge, scraping her clit just right and pulling a scream from her lips. "Carter. Please!"

His face tightened, as if he were struggling to hold his control. "More, sweetheart? Tell me."

"Yes, I need you. Please—"

With a roar of satisfaction, he lifted her higher and thrust inside her one last time. Then rubbed her clit.

The climax rolled over her and bit deep, throwing her muscles into mini-convulsions as the sheer pleasure exploded and burned through her entire body. Practically sobbing his name, she heard his low shout as he followed her over, his hips jerking helplessly.

Dazed and feeling half-drunk, she collapsed underneath him, and he rolled off her body. "Be right back," he whispered.

She heard him in the bathroom, and then he returned, slipping under the covers and pulling her tight against him. She cuddled into his chest, enjoying the feel of his sleek, damp skin, the scent of spice and sex lingering in the air, the heated cord of muscles tangled with her softness.

"You okay?" he asked.

She gave a small sigh. "Not really."

He tensed. "Did I hurt you?"

"No, but I lost the bet. I begged."

His laugh made her smile, and he tugged playfully at her curls. "I'm gonna call this one a draw, sweetheart. I say we're both losers . . . and winners."

"No wonder I love you—" She broke off, horrified by the words that had slipped off her tongue. "Oh my God! I didn't mean that, I just wasn't thinking. Holy crap, I'm sorry. I meant to say, um, I didn't—"

He shushed her with his lips over hers, kissing her thoroughly until her mind was mush and any logical words disappeared. She blinked up at him, his pewter eyes full of amusement and an intense emotion she didn't want to name. "I know what you meant. Now stop worrying and go to sleep. It won't be long before round two."

"Oh. *Oh!* Wow, I didn't know men your age could go again so soon. I—" She stopped short. And groaned. "I didn't mean that, either."

"Go to sleep, Avery. I'll meet your second challenge in a bit."

She wanted to hear more or argue, but exhaustion overtook her. With a happy sigh, she snuggled closer and did what he'd ordered.

She slept.

Head mashed into the pillow, she woke slowly through layers of sleep. The soft slide of lips trailing over her spine made her shiver, and she moaned, stretching under the glorious sensations of fingers stroking the back of her thighs and a hot tongue licking at the top of her buttocks. Already wet and achy, she tried to roll over, but he kept her pinned, tormenting her with his hands and lips and teeth.

He squeezed her ass, nipped at the curves, and slipped his fingers inside her dripping heat.

She bucked upward, needing more.

He gave a low laugh and tugged her hips up, kicking open her legs. Bracing her palms on the mattress, she heard the rip of the wrapper, and then he surged inside her, his hands cupping her heavy breasts, his muscled chest pressed to her back. She swayed back and forth, pushing against each of his slow, deep thrusts, and let him lead her straight to the edge, hovering at the drop-off. Her body tightened, poised on the brink of explosion, and then his hands slipped down her belly to rub back and forth, quickening his thrusts. She came, milking him tight, caught in the storm of her third orgasm. His fingers dug into her hips, and she felt his release, the groan of her name sweet and raw against her ears.

He rolled her to the side, tangling her limbs within his, and smiled down at her. "Hey."

She smiled a bit dopily, still stunned from the powerful release. "Hey. I guess you'd term that a power nap."

He chuckled, pressing a kiss to her nose. "Sorry, I can't keep my hands off you for long. I'm thinking you can become an addiction."

"I have less calories than a chocolate croissant."

This time, he laughed deep and hard, and she caressed his hair, her fingers trailing down the back of his neck. "I wanted to ask you something," she said.

"The answer is yes. To anything you want or need."

"Good to know. When did you get your tattoo?"

He blinked, as if just remembering he had ink on his back. "When I was young. Seventeen. I was a senior in high school, and my buddies had some fake IDs. We got into a bar, had a few beers, and ended up at a tattoo place. Thank God we all got something meaningful. I doubt anyone had regrets."

"It's beautiful." She urged him forward, and he leaned over so she could see the faint outline in the dim light flooding into the room. "Why is this symbol important to you?"

"It represents my belief that you have to wander in order to find yourself. Getting lost isn't an obstacle, but a way to experience an adventure."

Her fingers traced the ink in wonder. Surprise struck her as she fought to make sense of his choice. "I don't understand," she finally said. "This seems like a complete contradiction of the life you chose. I always thought you didn't believe in travel, or impulsive decisions, or having a wanderlust soul. Remember when Ally and I wanted to go to the Bahamas on break? You lost your shit."

"I didn't trust either of you would be safe on your own. There were rumors about rich guys drugging girls' drinks. I kept thinking about Natalee Holloway."

"Exactly. Yet this is inked on your skin, by choice. What happened, Carter?"

It took a while for him to answer. She sensed the struggle inside him, and her gut clenched in fear. He'd promised to open up to her and give what he could. But would her first request be brushed off with an excuse? Was he really able to share parts of himself with her?

Then he spoke, his voice holding a lifetime of *maybes* and *what-ifs*, tearing at her heart. "I was different before my parents died. I'd planned to go away to college and be a big-shot journalist. I wanted to travel and write and explore the world on my terms. I never wanted to go to a local community college, study computer science, and get a stable job. Before my mother got sick, I was just a kid who believed I could have it all. The compass was the symbol of every direction I craved to travel, and having it permanently inked was my *Fuck you* to everyone who thought I was going through a phase and would end up becoming practical."

In the silence, she heard the quiet sound of his breath, the faint whir of the air conditioner, the steady click of the bedside clock. The picture became sharp and startlingly clear—the life he'd once believed he'd live versus the one he'd chosen in order to raise Ally.

Jagged emotion tore at her insides, along with a humbleness of the strength of the man wrapped in her arms. God, he was special. And though he swore it wasn't in him, Avery knew he was wrong.

Carter Ross was meant to love.

But she said none of that. Instead, she pressed her lips to the precious ink, her tongue tracing the graceful curves and angles of the compass. Her hands stroked his back, slipped around his stomach, and squeezed tight.

Slowly, his breathing changed, and his erection pushed into her hands in demand. She touched him everywhere, her teeth sinking into the hard muscle of his shoulder, and with a curse, he turned toward her and pulled her against him.

He kissed her long and deep and hard, laying her back on the mattress. His gaze was wild and hungry, but she spotted the flicker of grief there, ready to be soothed, so she caressed his rough cheeks and gave herself up to him to use and fuck and savor.

To forget.

But he didn't. Instead, his hands were achingly tender, his lips gentle and reverent as he worshipped her body and made love to her until the darkness was gone and the hopeful flicker of dawn soaked the Atlantic City skyline.

Chapter Eighteen

Carter dragged in a breath and stepped into the room.

The groomsmen were getting ready to head to the beach for the official ceremony. He greeted Jason's friends and brother, grinning at the flasks lying out on the table. Jason turned and waved them ahead. "Be right there, guys," he said, glancing over as if he sensed they needed a private moment.

The groomsmen disappeared and left them alone.

"You're not here to tell me she ran off in a horse and carriage, are you?" Jason asked, dark eyes glinting in humor.

Carter laughed, but his chest felt too tight, as if he couldn't breathe. Jason stood before him, his elegant black tuxedo emphasizing his lean strength. His hair was slicked back, and his handsome face held an excitement that every man should show on his wedding day.

But it was his eyes that made all the difference. They were full of love and a kindness that Carter's sister deserved.

Carter thought of his parents and knew how much they would have loved Jason and trusted him with Ally. He wanted to tell his future brother-in-law so many things. That he was getting a woman who was fierce, and beautiful, and true. That he was happy Jason had chosen her to spend the rest of his life with. That he loved the way his entire family had welcomed Ally into their lives with joy. But the importance of the moment overwhelmed him, and the words twisted up and remained stuck and silent.

"I just wanted to tell you congratulations," he said gruffly. "I'm proud to have you as part of the family." He clapped his shoulder, smiled, and turned.

"Carter?"

He turned back and cocked his head. "Yeah?"

"Ally wouldn't be the woman she is today without you." He reached out and grasped his arm, his fingers squeezing tight. Jason's gaze met his, head-on. "You gave up so much for her. You taught her everything a parent should have, and she never lost that joy and zest for life that made me fall in love with her the moment I saw her in that crappy sports bar." He gave a half laugh, raw with emotion. "So thank you for accepting me as her husband. I swear to God, I'll never let you down. Either of you."

Carter's eyes stung, and he stepped forward and gave him a quick, hard hug. "Thank you. Now, I'm going to get your bride, and we'll meet you at the altar."

Jason nodded, not able to talk, and Carter left the room knowing his sister was about to get her happily-ever-after ending.

He made his way down the short hallway. The bridesmaids were giggling and chattering, beginning to line up outside as Avery snapped them to attention. He entered the second room and stopped short when he saw the sight before him.

His sister's voice wobbled. "Carter?"

"Yes, Ally-Cat?"

She gulped a breath, her eyes huge in her face. "I'm getting married."

Emotion struck him hard. He gazed at her, dressed in full glory, and his throat tightened. She was stunningly beautiful. The cream lace of the gown skimmed her figure, and the endless yards of veil fell behind her in a splendorous trail. Her hair was twisted up into a spill of elegant curls, and her face glowed. Diamonds winked at her throat and ears, giving her an air of royalty. She was almost to his height with the sky-high, crystal-encrusted shoes, and damned if his fingers didn't shake when he took her hand in his for the last time before she became Jason's wife.

"Mom and Dad would be so proud," he said, shaking his head. "First, Mom would bawl and Dad would try to comfort her, and then he'd start crying and it'd be up to me to fix the whole mess."

His sister laughed, eyes shining with unshed tears. "Yeah, I can picture it, too. And Dad would make me dance to that ridiculous song that's so sweet, it gives me a cavity."

"'The Way You Look Tonight.' A classic. Can't go wrong with Sinatra."

"But it's so overdone! Remember how he used to play it loud and make me step on his feet to try and teach me to dance?"

"Hokey."

"And then he'd begin waltzing with Mom and tell us the story of how they met for the billionth time."

The memories flickered before him. All of them laughing together and teasing as his parents moved gracefully around the small kitchen. A bittersweet longing pricked. "I remember."

She sighed. "Yeah, Dad was more sensitive than Mom. I always wondered if that heart attack was just his sadness over not being able to picture a life without Mom in it. Like he'd decided to give up. I loved him so much, but he was never—"

"Strong," he finished, tilting his head and studying her. Something shifted and broke inside him, almost as if he sensed that within Ally's words lay the answer, but Avery peeked around the corner and smiled.

"It's time."

He met his sister's gaze and smiled at her. "Come on, gorgeous. Jason's waiting for you."

He escorted her outside and toward the beach. The day was hot and clear, with a light ocean breeze that kept it from being faint-worthy. A gazebo threaded with flowers was framed against the ocean, and the officiant stood behind a white pillar, his black book clutched in his hand. Avery had set up a runner pinned down by various giant stone shells. He watched the wedding party walk down the aisle, flanked by white chairs filled with friends and family, all beaming and murmuring at the sheer beauty of the event.

When everyone had reached their places, the music piping in through speakers changed to the traditional "Wedding March." Ally squeezed his arm, and he stared into her beloved face, memorizing the moment. Then he began walking her toward Jason.

His future brother-in-law beamed down at his bride. Lifting her veil, Carter pressed a kiss to her cheek, then took her hand and placed it in Jason's.

As Carter stepped back into line, Jason gave him a nod, the serious intensity of his face bestowing the recognition of what Carter had done for both of them. The kindness of the gesture gave him both comfort and pride.

The ceremony was brief. Applause broke out when they were declared husband and wife, and the crowd whooped when they kissed.

As they filed back off the beach, he looked for Avery, knowing she'd be in the background, ready to step in to solve any crisis. The woman amazed him on a constant basis. Ever since the night of the bachelorette party, their relationship had changed. Barriers had been ripped away, and an easy intimacy now flowed between them. Their days were packed with endless details for Ally's wedding, but at night, she snuck to his house and spent the hours wrapped in his arms till dawn, making love until they collapsed together in exhaustion.

Carter finally caught sight of her off to the side, blinking furiously through tears as she watched the happy couple greet well-wishers. The longing on her face caught him like a sucker punch, knocking him slightly off-balance. What scared him the most was the immediate urge to walk over and take her in his arms, claiming her for himself. He imagined uttering his vows. Sliding a ring over her finger. Kissing her as the words *I now pronounce you husband and wife* drifted in the air.

He jerked back, tearing his gaze from her. What was happening to him? He'd never had a flash like that. Weddings usually caused old anger and pain to stir up inside him, making him shut down in order to control his emotions. Now he was imagining Avery in a white wedding dress, her face aglow as she stared at him and promised to be his.

Panic struck. He shook his head and concentrated on casual chatter with the guests, trying to lock the vision away for good.

But like Pandora's box, he wondered how long it'd be before he snuck another peek.

The entire wedding was a dream for Avery, as both Ally's best friend and a wedding planner. She'd never enjoyed a ceremony or reception as much. Her friend was a calm, happy bride, full of joy. The bridesmaids were now like family, and Noelle, Maddie, and Judith consistently tried to drag her away from her duties and get her to dance. The vendors had no issues, and Gabe had cut out early for a rare night off, his presence not even needed.

Every detail they'd incorporated brought a sense of beauty to the event, from the flowers to the tea-towel favors to the stunning cake and special dessert bar. Pierce had outdone himself with the photos. He'd arranged the wedding party on a magnificent staircase under a glittering chandelier, and captured the more natural shots of Jason carrying Ally into the ocean. The endless buffet of specially created tapas rotating throughout the night was a huge hit with the guests, who enjoyed dancing more than a formal sit-down. Knowing Carter had worked on each detail with her made everything more special. It was as if they'd created Ally's wedding together, the two people who'd loved her forever.

Midnight grew close, and the DJ spun into the Donna Summer classic "Last Dance" while everyone crammed onto the floor for one final celebration. Smiling, Avery headed toward the bridal suite to begin packing up.

A warm hand wrapped around her wrist. She turned and found Carter staring down at her, his pewter eyes gleaming with intensity. "Dance with me, Avery."

A shudder shook through her. She meant to tell him it wasn't a good idea with the entire wedding party on the floor, but the words never left her lips. Instead, she allowed him to lead her out and take her in his arms.

The slow strains gave them time to press close together. His breath stirred her cheek. His hands brushed her hips, causing heat to trickle in her blood. The delicious scent of ocean cologne mixed with citrus and expensive whiskey. "Thank you, sweetheart," he said.

Startled, she widened her eyes. "For what?"

"For giving my sister the wedding of her dreams. For being patient with me. For being you."

She melted against him, and a sigh skittered from her lips. "You can be so smooth," she said teasingly. "Who would've thought there was such a charmer under all those asshole moves?"

His laugh rumbled from his chest, deep and sexy. "I needed to ensnare you with a challenge. Make you work to find the gold, right?"

She wrinkled her nose. "Oh, that's awful. Trust me, robot man. Women like a nice guy up front. Better to know that the next time."

"Don't need a next time." He lowered his voice. "Just want to dazzle the woman I'm with."

Her heart stuttered, and for one endless moment, she was caught up in the heat of his eyes, the promise of his arms holding her close, and the fragility of the promise he'd uttered. But she didn't have time to dwell or analyze. The slow rhythm built, morphing into the classic blaring dance song as the Queen of Disco belted out the words everyone knew by heart.

With a wink, Carter spun her out of his arms and fell into the steps of a fast dance. With grace and strength and the perfect blend of humor, they threw themselves into the music and enjoyed the final pounding beat. The wedding party surrounded the bride and groom, stomping their feet and pumping their hands in the air, and Avery got caught up in the revelry, enjoying being part of the enthusiastic celebration of love.

It was a good hour before everyone finally left the reception. Sliding off her shoes and throwing them in her oversize bag, Avery headed outside, saying a few goodbyes to the leftover guests, who spoke about moving the party over to the Boiler Room at Congress Hall.

"Avery!" The squeal of her name was accompanied by a big hug full of veil and lace and jewels.

Laughing, Avery embraced her friend. "It was perfect," Ally said, and sighed. "I can't tell you how many people have been coming up to me asking for your card. They all said they've never seen a wedding so beautiful."

"Thanks, babe. It was everything I always dreamed for you."

"We're heading over to the Boiler Room for a few more drinks. Are you coming?"

She shook her head. "I wish I could, but I'm ready to drop. I'll see you at the breakfast tomorrow, though."

"I totally understand. I'm just not ready to have the evening end."

Avery laughed. "You're the bride—you need to close down the house for me, okay? Show this beach town how to party."

Jason drifted up, giving Avery a warm hug and gushing about everything she'd done.

"Well, Carter was a huge help," she said.

The familiar deep voice cut through the air. "We make a good team."

Ally hauled him into a group hug. "Damn right you do. Carter, no wimping out on me. You're coming to party more, right?"

Avery shivered as he met and held her gaze. "Sure, Ally-Cat. We'll let Avery get her sleep and see her in the morning."

She nodded, knowing there'd be no visit tonight. She was too damn exhausted, and Carter needed to spend it with his family. Maybe it was for the best. She needed some distance and time to think. His words on the dance floor stirred a longing that scared her. She needed to be careful of giving her heart to a man who had no use for it. Though each night since the bachelorette party they'd grown closer, sharing both their minds and bodies through the late hours, nothing had truly changed.

He was still a man who didn't believe in love.

She was still a woman who did.

Avery said good night and headed home.

Brunch at the Mad Batter was held on the front porch. The striped awning shaded them from the sun, and a giant table was set up for fifteen guests. Mimosas flowed, and their famous seafood omelets were a big hit, loaded with fresh crabmeat, avocado, and Swiss cheese. The party had gone till 3:00 a.m., but Ally and Jason looked fresh faced and happy, feeding each other with moony eyes and taking the teasing with laughter.

Avery sat next to Carter. Sometimes he'd slide his finger under the table and touch hers. The innocent contact caused her tummy to swirl like a flight of butterflies. She ate and drank, but every inch of her body was aware of his. She ached to touch the rough stubble on his angular jaw, smooth the hair from his forehead, and trace the lush curve of his lips. He wore his glasses today, and the casual jeans and navy-blue T-shirt showed off his lean muscles.

"Carter, are you heading back to DC this week?" Ally asked.

His voice was smooth and heated, like the whiskey he'd drunk last night. "Actually, I extended my rental to Labor Day. It's been nice taking some time off, so I'm going to enjoy the beach until my next project kicks off."

Avery stiffened, but he grabbed her hand under the table and squeezed.

Ally looked delighted. "Good for you! I'm so glad you're giving yourself more downtime. Maybe you can convince Avery to take some time off, too—she's a proud workaholic like you."

Avery forced a smile. "Unfortunately, wedding season in Cape May doesn't allow for much free time."

"I know, babe. And I hate that I added to your burden with my last-minute wedding. I just want you to have some fun like we did in Atlantic City," Ally said.

"Your wedding was not a burden," she said firmly, pointing her fork in the air. "But I'll make sure to take care of your brother for the next two weeks." She refused to feel guilt from her declaration, but the grateful way her friend looked at her made her want to tell the truth.

"Thanks," Ally said. "Jason and I are heading out tomorrow for Turks and Caicos before fall semester starts. I don't want to have to worry about my brother while I'm lazing on the beach with my new husband."

Carter shook his head. "I'm perfectly capable of taking care of myself, Ally-Cat."

"I know, but you're a hermit and forget that Lucy isn't a real human. Avery will make sure you get out, even if it's just for a meal."

"A few hours as a married woman and you're already getting bossy," he teased.

She stuck out her tongue and everyone laughed.

"Avery, are you coming to the beach with us today?" Ally asked.

"I wish I could, but I need to cover a small evening reception." She pulled a sad face. "I think I've used up all my favors with my sisters."

"But I'm leaving at five a.m. tomorrow, and I won't be able to see you again before I go."

Guilt hit her. She opened her mouth to try and explain, but Carter cut in. "Ally-Cat, you won't be on your honeymoon forever. And Avery already mentioned when the wedding season calms down, she'll come visit you in Texas. Right?"

Avery nodded. "I'd love that."

Her friend sniffed. "Okay, only if you promise. I was bummed we couldn't spend the whole summer together like we planned. I just miss you so damn much!"

"Me, too."

Avery went down the length of the table, hugging and kissing everyone and accepting their thanks with gratitude. "Call me when you get back," she said, holding Ally tight. "And if you remember, text me some pics. I love you."

"Love you, too."

Avery walked out and headed back to Sunshine Bridal. Better to let Carter have the day and night again with his sister. Better to have a break from being with him. With only two precious weeks left for them to figure out what they both wanted, she suddenly wanted to hide in the only thing that made sense and soothed her shaky confidence.

Work.

Chapter Nineteen

Avery walked into her sisters' house and stopped short at the delicious scent of butter and garlic. "What's going on?" she demanded, dropping her purse on the sectional and heading into the kitchen.

Taylor never cooked—that was Bella's domain. But here she was, her pink hair curling from the heat of the stove, and a cranky look on her face as she glared. "You didn't knock," she accused. "I thought we discussed this."

"T, you invited me to dinner. Figured that meant you weren't rolling around naked on the couch with some random dude." She looked at the dining table, which had the additional section inserted, and seven table settings laid out. "Why are you cooking? Where's the pizza?"

"I get no support in this family," she grumbled.

Avery grabbed the bottle of chardonnay and poured herself a full glass. Maybe some alcohol would help. She'd been deliberately avoiding Carter, and her nerves were shot. "Who'd you invite over?"

"Pierce and Gabe. Here, help me with this stupid pot. I burnt myself twice."

"Why is Taylor cooking?" Bella called out, walking in with Zoe bouncing on her heels.

"Not sure yet," Avery said, grabbing pot holders and spilling the water through the strainer.

Bella headed for the fridge. She slid out a Capri Sun for Zoe and handed her the lemonade, then went to pour her own glass of wine. "Who's coming over?"

"Pierce and Gabe."

"Why do we have to suffer? You can give them your cooking and let us have pizza."

Taylor gritted her teeth and began madly stirring an oily lemon concoction Avery was afraid to ask about. "You'd think my own sisters wouldn't be my own betrayers. Go get the bread out of the oven, Bella. I don't want it to burn."

"Mommy, why is Aunt TT cooking?" Zoe asked. "I thought it was pizza night."

"I don't know, sweetheart, but you like spaghetti."

"Yay, pasghetti! Cool!"

"Let me help your aunt, and you can watch Mickey Mouse cartoons while we finish, okay?"

"'Kay!"

Avery finished straining the pasta and took over the bread duty, pulling out a tray of crispy Texas toast. "Looks good. Now, are you going to tell me what's happening? You hate cooking. How'd you let those two bozos push you into this?"

Taylor tossed her a haughty look and stirred faster. Splashes of burning oil leaped out, and she cursed under her breath, dropping the spoon. "I'm trying to do things out of my comfort zone to get ready for my travels next year. I mentioned taking a French pastry–baking class in Paris, and Gabe started in on how I'll get kicked out because I burn water, and Pierce agreed with him, so I figured I'd surprise them tonight by cooking and show I have mad skills. After all, I can read and follow a recipe. Any idiot can cook if they want to."

Avery pressed her lips together to keep from laughing.

Her sister snorted and rubbed her burned hand. "Real funny. Just help me dump this stuff into that pot, and I'll get more wine, okay?"

Avery peered into the oil mixture. "Um, what is it?"

"The sauce for lemon spaghetti. I'm using Giada's recipe, but I put my own spin on it."

The sharp citrus scent made her eyes water, but she covered up her reaction and figured she'd get drunk first. God knew she'd eat anything after two glasses. "Looks great." She combined the pasta and sauce, found the parmesan cheese, and dumped a healthy portion over it. Cheese can cover up anything, right? "Who else is coming? There's seven places."

"Carter."

Avery dropped the oversize spoon, and it clattered to the floor. "What?" she screeched, staring with her mouth open like a guppy. "You invited Carter?"

Her sister shot her a smug, mean look. "Yep. I thought he'd enjoy a home-cooked meal with Ally off on her honeymoon. And since you don't tell me jack shit about whether or not you slept together, I figured I'd find out myself."

Bella shouted, "Language, please!"

Avery breathed deep and reached out to strangle Taylor. "You're dead."

The bell rang.

Her youngest sister grinned. "Better answer it. Your *lover* is here."

Cheeks hot, she stomped to the door and flung it open. Gabe, Pierce, and Carter stood in the doorway with matching grins. "Rumor has it there's free food here," Gabe said, stepping around her and walking in. "Holy shit, back it up, Carter. Taylor's cooking. Let's go out and grab some pizzas and beer and stay alive."

Taylor mouthed *jackass* so Zoe wouldn't hear, and the men laughed.

"Come on in," Avery said, her gaze roving hungrily over Carter. He wore soft khakis, an aqua-green button-down shirt, and white canvas boat shoes. No glasses. Jaw clean-shaven. He held a bouquet of sunflowers. God, she wanted to crawl all over him like an ant at a picnic.

"This is for Taylor," he said in his deep whiskey-like voice. "She invited me to dinner."

Avery winced. She hadn't returned any of his texts since leaving him at breakfast. It had been easier to be a coward. "Sorry, I was really busy."

His sharp gaze dove deep, assessing. "We'll talk later."

A shiver bumped down her spine at the sensual warning. He walked past her, greeting everyone and diving right in to see if he could help.

"I have everything under control," Taylor said in a blatant lie. "What beautiful flowers. Thank you, Carter."

Gabe not so quietly coughed "suck-up" behind a hand with a smile, while Pierce went straight into the kitchen and began sniffing around the pots and pans. "Why does it smell funky?"

Taylor slapped his hands away. "Don't distract me. I'm still mad at you."

"Well, this is some kind of revenge you got planned, Taylz." He grinned and pressed a quick kiss to her cheek. "I brought a cheesecake for dessert."

Gabe gaped at Pierce. "Dude! You need to tell me if we're supposed to bring stuff." He looked at Carter. "You, too, Judas."

Taylor stared down Pierce, who was still grinning at her. "Is it the turtle one?"

"Yep, so there's incentive to keep me alive at least until dessert or you get nothing."

Zoe jumped up from the television and ran toward them, stopping short. "Gabe and Carter and Pierce! You know each other?"

Gabe laughed, scooping her up high in his arms with an easy familiarity. He was like a mixture of father figure and older brother to Zoe. "'Course we know each other! I got him a cool tux and bought him some chocolate milk. Then Pierce took our picture."

She giggled. "I love chocolate milk."

"I love it more," Carter said solemnly. Gabe tossed her over, and Carter carefully lifted her up, a grin curving his lips. "How was your day?"

Zoe crinkled her nose and thought hard. "Good. I did coloring, and cleaned my room so Mama wouldn't get mad, and ate a peanut-butter-and-jelly sandwich with milk, but not chocolate milk, because we ran out of Hershey's syrup. Oh, and I played outside on my bike."

"Sounds like a perfect day," Carter said.

Gabe turned to him. "Hmm, I went skydiving, had tea with the queen of England, and ate frog-leg sandwiches. What'd you do, Carter?"

"I rode a purple kangaroo and had chocolate cake for lunch."

Zoe's eyes widened. "You got to have cake for lunch?"

They all burst into laughter. Bella plucked her from Carter's arms and patted her on the head. "TV off and get in your chair. Dinner's ready."

Zoe ran off, and Bella turned to Carter. "You're amazing with children. What a fabulous father you're going to make someday."

Avery watched emotion flicker over Carter's face, but it was Gabe's that threw her off. Raw frustration and a touch of anger glinted in his dark eyes as he watched Bella finish serving in the kitchen. She glanced back and forth between them, wondering what was going on. Gabe was part of the family. Was he jealous that Bella was giving Carter kudos instead of him? But he knew Zoe adored him.

She had no time to puzzle out the question. Bowls were plunked down on the table, glasses filled, and they all took their places. The men immediately grabbed for the Texas toast, announcing it was their favorite. Taylor muttered something under her breath about clueless men and how bread should be the accent of a meal, and Avery tried hard not to laugh.

"How did the wedding go, Carter?" Taylor asked. "Avery must've been busy since she never let us know."

She shot her sister a glare.

"It was amazing. My family couldn't stop talking about it, and we gave out a ton of your business cards."

"Nice," Gabe said. "I'm almost ready to take on my own clients, so we'll be able to increase our list."

Avery sighed. "I'm excited for the business, but how will I ever find another assistant even close to your capabilities? It'll be impossible."

"Maybe Gabe should stay on as an assistant until we're comfortable with our growth," Bella suggested. "It may be smarter to delay his promotion until next season."

An uncomfortable silence fell. Gabe stiffened and Avery glanced at Bella. But her sister seemed clueless to the dig, acting as if it didn't matter what position he owned at Sunshine Bridal. Avery bit her lip. Gabe had worked hard the past few years to prove he'd be able to handle a full roster. Bella's casual dismissal of his skills was bound to sting.

Taylor shook her head. "I disagree. Gabe is ready, so we'll just have to find another amazing assistant for Avery. Hey, Carter, you in the market for a new job?"

He gave a mock shudder. "No, thanks. She's a slave driver. I slept for two days straight after I crawled out of the Bankses' wedding."

"I'm a perfectionist," Avery said defensively.

Gabe snorted. "The first month, I almost quit. Figured she'd be my very own Miranda Priestly and drive me to madness."

Her mouth dropped open. "Are you kidding?"

"Nope. Taylor told me that charts and checklists were my new best friend. She was right. I think you have to be detail-obsessed to succeed in the wedding-planning business."

"But you also need creativity," Pierce added. "Plus the ability to flow with sudden change."

Bella nodded. "All true. Balance is the key. Do you enjoy your job, Carter?"

He nodded. "I do. When I started working with the government, I received some special clearance projects that kept my interest. Lately, though, I've been feeling a bit stagnant. It may be time to move on to a new challenge."

Avery's interest piqued. "What type of new challenge?"

His gaze drilled into hers. "Something that excites me again," he said. "I'm tired of playing it safe. Aren't you?"

A shiver worked down her spine. "Yes," she whispered, caught up in the moment.

A brief silence settled at the table, but she was helpless to break the spell. He was right. She shouldn't have tried to run away after their nights spent together. They had little time left, and damned if she wasn't about to seize every precious second. He smiled at her, as if sensing her thoughts, and a giddy pleasure bubbled up in her veins.

"Maybe it's time we all do something that scares us," Gabe said seriously. "What do you think, Bella?" His direct question snagged Avery's attention, but it was her sister's response that had her holding her breath.

"I already did," Bella said calmly.

Everyone stared at her, waiting for more.

"I've eaten half a bowl of this horrific spaghetti even though it scared the heck out of me. Sorry, T, but next time, we're ordering a pizza."

Laughter broke out. Taylor shot her a disgusted look but pushed the bowl aside with a sigh. "Fine. Dial up Louie's. This sucks."

Zoe gasped. "Aunt TT, *sucks* is a very bad word. And I love the pasghetti! It's the best I ever tasted!"

Taylor bent over and gave her niece a noisy kiss on the cheek. "Thanks, honey. You're the only one who gets dessert at this table."

The pizza was delivered, and everyone indulged. Carter swore it was the best he'd ever had, including New York. He'd just taken an extra-large bite when Taylor called out his name.

"Pierce told me you bought my painting." Her tone was defensive.

Avery cocked her head, surprised. Her sister hadn't told her anything about that. He'd bought her work? "You did?" she asked him.

He swiped his napkin over his mouth, seemingly unconcerned. "That's right. I liked it."

A fierce frown creased her sister's brow. *Uh-oh.* Taylor hated any type of pity, and she'd be enraged if she thought Carter bought her stuff just to be nice. Her voice was fierce. "You paid too much for it. I don't need any charity."

"For God's sake, Taylz, I told you he had no idea you were the artist!" Pierce said with complete frustration. "Did it ever occur to you you're talented?"

"No. I want Carter to look at me and tell the truth. Why did you buy that painting?"

Carter put down his pizza and calmly stared back at her. Avery held her breath, waiting for his answer.

"Because it was good. Really good. You need some help with blending, and the colors on the edges were a bit too jagged to work with the whole, but overall it was the first painting I'd seen in a long time that made me feel something. I got a deal because you still don't know your worth, which is cool for me, but I'd advise you not to make that mistake again. I don't believe in charity when it comes to buying art, and I don't lie. Ever."

The table grew silent. Warmth flooded Avery's veins when she realized this was a man of honor—a man who didn't believe in pretty lies to make life easier. But, God, he was kind. Her throat tightened with emotion, and she wondered if she could keep on fighting what she really wanted.

Him.

Taylor slowly grinned. "Okay. That's the last clearance buy you'll get from me, though."

He nodded and picked up his slice of pizza again. "Good."

The rest of the evening passed quickly, with hearty slices of pizza, more wine, rich cheesecake, and lots of laughs. Gabe left first, and Carter lingered, allowing her enough time to wrap up, say goodbye to her sisters, and make an excuse to leave with him.

As soon as the door shut, he turned to her. "Are you running away again?" he asked boldly. "Or will you come home with me tonight?"

"I needed some space to think," she said. "Are you trying to deny me that?"

Intensity shot from him. His jaw clenched. "God, no. I understand completely. I'm just being a selfish bastard because I mourn every hour spent away from you."

She softened at the stark truth on his face, the tiny gleam of panic in his eye. It had cost him to be honest with his feelings, but she was past thinking or analyzing or wanting space. She wanted him, and it was time to step off the cliff and take the fall, trusting he'd eventually catch her.

Forgoing words, she stepped into his arms, yanked his head down, and kissed him. He groaned, and she opened her mouth to taste and savor, relishing his flavor and scent and feel of his hard body pressed against hers.

When they broke away, his pewter gaze glowed with purpose. "Let's go."

She took his hand and followed him to the car.

Carter made love to her for hours. He touched and tasted every sweet inch of her body, spread naked on his bed, reveling in her throaty cries and slick, hot need. When they collapsed together on the tangled sheets, the silence was broken by the faint scratching on the door.

"Poor Lucy," she groaned, pressing her face into his shoulder. "She hates my guts."

He laughed. "No, she doesn't. But when she hears you scream my name, she gets confused. She wants to see what's going on."

"I do not want Lucy to see me naked."

He laughed harder. "You need to make a truce. I want us to be one happy family together, okay?"

She rolled onto her back and stared at the ceiling. After a few moments, he noticed her silence was different. Troubled.

Leaning over, he turned her chin toward him and looked into her hazel eyes. "What's the matter, sweetheart?"

"Nothing."

He traced the frown lines marring her brow. "Tell me what brought this on. Do I need to give you another orgasm?"

She smiled, but it was weak. Shadows danced in her eyes. "It doesn't matter."

Normally, he'd accept her dismissal, not wanting to stir up worries or problems best left untouched. But with Avery, he wanted her to share her heart, her worries, her feelings. He wanted to steep himself in her body and mind and try to give her the same. "It does to me," he said quietly.

"How can you not want children? I see the way you are with Zoe, and how you interacted with Brianna at the Bankses' wedding. Your fierce affection for Lucy. You're full of love, Carter. What happened for you to stop believing in that?"

The words plowed into him like a sucker punch. All those ugly, messy feelings he'd locked up tight rumbled for freedom, bringing him back to his decision so many years ago, when he'd found his father. The grief and loss on Ally's face when she had realized both her parents were gone. The struggle to give his sister enough security and love so she'd never find out the truth, and the constant worry he'd never be enough. Children were casualties of love all the time. How could he ever trust himself not to hurt them like his own father had hurt him?

The memories stirred, unsettled. He tried to retreat behind his usual barrier. "Something happened that affected me when I was young. It changed the way I looked at things like love and marriage. I don't like to talk about it."

"Well, that's too bad," she said, sitting up in bed and tossing him a fierce glare. "Because I'm naked in your bed, and falling hard, and you promised to give me your best. I have a right to know what made you so sure no relationship is worth fighting for."

Shock held him immobile. Then he shook his head. "Why are you pushing me?"

"Because it's important!" she said, grabbing his arm. "You're important. I'm not about to just meekly accept your decision to hide and pretend it doesn't matter. Dammit, it does matter! You deserve more, and so do I!"

Dear God, she wouldn't stop. She'd just keep pushing, sensing something about to break inside him. Another woman would've retreated and left him to his secrets. But not Avery. She would never allow him to run and hide in her quest for answers. And in that staggering moment, the truth he'd never uttered to a single soul before rose up and begged for freedom. The secret broke free and shot from his lips: "My father killed himself."

Shock filled her eyes. Her hand dropped from his arm. "Ally said he had a heart attack."

A bitter smile curved his lips. "Because I never told her the truth. After our mother died, our father fell apart. He was so damn in love, he didn't want to live without her." The anger rose back up—a living, breathing thing that he'd shoved away a long time ago and refused to feel. Until now. "Ally and I didn't seem to matter. We weren't enough for him. So, one day, he locked himself in his office and overdosed on sleeping pills."

He spoke the words with a calm, controlled voice. The ice closed back up again, numbing the rawness of memory. It was better this way. No need to waste time on grief or fury for a man who didn't care enough to live for his children. A man who refused to look past his own selfish needs to join his beloved wife and forget about his responsibilities. God knew his mother had fought so damn hard to live for them. Ironic that her husband found it so easy to give up.

He watched Avery try to process his words, wondering if she'd want to talk it through or analyze it. Exhaustion leaked into his system. For so long, he'd kept his secret. Giving it space to breathe deflated him like a limp balloon devoid of its air and essence. He'd tell her everything now. It no longer mattered, and at least she'd finally understand his choices.

"I was in my first semester of college. Came home for the weekend to check on him. Mom had only been gone for four months, so it was still fresh. Ally was at her friend's for the weekend at a sleepover." The day flickered past his vision in slow motion. "I couldn't find him in the house. Called his name, but no one answered. I figured he was out. I took a shower, made some calls to my friends, got something to eat. Meanwhile, he was in his office, dying."

He noticed her beautiful hazel eyes were full of pain. How odd she felt it and he couldn't.

"Finally, I realized he rarely shut his office door, so I went in. He was collapsed on the desk. There were empty pill bottles and my mother's picture clutched in his hands. I called 911, but I knew it was too late." He dragged in a breath and finished up. "I knew it could break Ally. She was barely coping with Mom's death, and knowing her own father took his life would've put her over the edge. I decided to hide it. Told her it was a heart attack—which technically it was, due to the overdose. After that, I made the decision to drop out of school. The life insurance set us up for a while, and I applied for guardianship of Ally. I'd gotten into trouble for hacking before, but eventually, a start-up company came looking to hire me. It was easy after that. I was good at hacking, so I made a name for myself. I was able to be home most of the time to raise Ally. The rest is history."

She remained silent, her gaze delving so deep, a shiver shook through him. It was as if she saw things he'd allowed no one else to view. A secret part he'd kept from everyone.

He forced a smile, looking to reassure her. "I know it's a terrible story, but honestly, I'm fine. Ally's fine. But that's the main reason I made those hard choices. I never want to love someone so much I'd sacrifice everything for them. Sounds like a worthy, romantic cause, but in real life, it's just wrong."

"You carried this by yourself for all these years?"

He shrugged. "I was old enough to handle it."

It was then he saw the tears in her eyes. His heart stopped as he studied her in almost-wonderment. Why was she crying?

"Sweetheart, don't cry."

A sob caught in her throat, and suddenly, she was in his arms, wrapped tight around him. Head tucked by his shoulder, she squeezed him as if trying to protect him from harm. Her wet cheeks pressed against his chest, and he returned the embrace, dropping kisses on the top of her head and whispering her name. She cried for a long time, cried for him and his past, releasing all the grief and anger on his behalf. And as Carter comforted her, his chest began to ease. A lightness he'd never experienced before settled over him. It was almost as if the tears he'd never been able to cry had finally released. Through Avery.

They held each other tight even after her sobs had eased. The soft, solid weight of her broke the icy numbness, and slowly, heat seeped back into his body. Hours or minutes or seconds later, she tipped her head up.

Carter froze.

The naked longing and need in her luminous eyes rocketed through him. His hands cupped her damp cheeks, his thumb tracing the trembling curve of her lower lip.

Her words wrecked him to his very soul: "I love you, Carter Ross. I know there are a million reasons you don't believe in it, and you'll never be able to say it back to me, but it's the truth, and you deserve to hear it. I love the boy who protected his sister and had the bravery to sacrifice his youth and dreams. I love the man who makes Zoe laugh and writes a letter to the tooth fairy for a stranger. I love the man who spoils his dog, and brings me chocolate croissants, and looks into my eyes when he makes love to me." Her smile wobbled, but her face was lit with a giving joy that stole his very breath. "So there it is. And you're just going to have to deal with it. Okay?"

His world shredded and a new path opened before him. A path with thorns and brush leading to an unknown track he'd always avoided. But looking into her face, everything inside him sighed and opened and wanted for the first time. Fear and need warred inside him, battling for dominance.

Carter closed his eyes. This woman had given him everything without expectation. He struggled to say the words in his heart and mind and soul, the same words that had destroyed his father. The words he'd spent his life rejecting to protect himself. The words he hoped and feared were his new truth.

But they died on his lips, unspoken.

He opened his eyes. Gazed down at the woman in his arms. And took her mouth with his. This, he could give. His body could give her everything, and maybe, it would be enough.

He pressed her back into the mattress and spent the next few hours showing her his heart.

Chapter Twenty

"He'll be right back."

Lucy stared back at her in dismissal. She whined again and circled by the door, obviously upset that the love of her life had left her with his new squeeze.

Avery sighed, tugging down the shirt she'd borrowed from him, and refilled her coffee mug.

For the past week, Lucy had been making it crystal clear she was unwelcome. When Carter was in the shower, she'd jump up on the bed, curl onto his pillow, and show her teeth in warning when Avery tried to join her. If Avery tried to explain the behavior to Carter, he stared at her in disbelief and asked Lucy if she was being nice.

Yeah. Like the dog could answer him. Even if she could, Avery knew she'd lie.

Yesterday morning, she'd discovered a surprise in her shoe. Lucy's punishment consisted of a light scolding and an extra walk, peppered with excuses that she hadn't been walked enough last night. But when Lucy turned back and nailed Avery with a stare, triumph glimmered in her big brown eyes.

She was beginning to understand exactly what Selena had been talking about with Gus. Lucy was out to get her, but she couldn't let the dog win.

Avery rummaged through the cookie jar, knelt down, and offered her a treat. She planned to kill the dog with kindness until she was finally accepted. After all, since Carter had confessed the truth to her, their relationship had grown stronger. Understanding how he'd gotten twisted in his mind over his ideas of love helped her be patient. In her heart, she knew the man was capable of being a great partner, if only he faced his fears and left the past behind.

But first he needed to heal. Believe. And let himself love.

Was she the woman meant to be part of his journey toward healing, or would she be unable to truly break through?

She pushed the disturbing thoughts away and tried to concentrate on bonding with her nemesis. "Lucy, want a treat?"

She'd watched the dog gobble them up from Carter's fingers, but now, Lucy just gave an annoyed sigh and plopped her butt down by the door to wait.

Avery dropped the biscuit on the floor and stretched out her legs in front of her. "If someone tried to take away the man I loved, I'd be upset, too," she said. "But there's something you need to know. I will never try to get between you. You loved him first, Lucy, and he loved you."

The dog cocked her head, giving her a sidelong look as if she were listening. Even though Avery felt ridiculous, she continued her speech.

"I just want to make him happy, too. I know you'll be rid of me in a week when you go back to DC, but is it wrong to hope for more? Can you give me a chance if I promise to never hurt you or try to control your relationship? Because you're everything to him, and that will never change. I think we can both make him happy. Don't you?"

Lucy blinked. Considered. Then dropped her head to rest between her delicate paws, as if telling her she needed some time to think about it.

"Fair enough," Avery said, getting up from the floor. "I guess trust is earned, not given. I'll work harder."

The door opened. Lucy jumped with joy, and damned if the man didn't get straight to his knees to give her love and affection. Avery's heart mushed and her head spun, and she watched his tenderness with a longing that roared up from her very soul.

When he straightened up, he tossed her a sexy grin and walked over, pressing a hard kiss to her lips. "You look so fucking hot," he growled, eating her up with his gaze.

"It's just a shirt," she teased, cupping his rough cheeks.

"It's my shirt. I'm all over you. Turns me on."

She laughed and stepped away, grabbing the bag from his hands. "Everything turns you on, but right now, all I can think of is food." She pulled the chocolate croissant from the bag and moaned, crossing her legs in ecstasy. "Oh God, it looks so good. How do you keep finding them? Each time I go, they're all out."

He grabbed a paper plate and napkins, and slid his own pastry out of the bag. "When I found out how much you love them, I asked Madison's to keep one to the side every time they baked a batch and text me." He took a bite. "You're right. It's so good."

The pastry dropped from her fingers. She blinked, staring at him. "What did you say?"

"It's good."

"No, about Madison's."

He shrugged. "Told them to put one aside. No big deal."

The knowledge he wanted to please her and had gone out of his way to make her happy struck hard. If only he realized how much he had to give. If only she could help teach him.

She leaned forward, making sure the shirt gaped open and flashed her bare breasts. "After you finish your breakfast, I want you naked. I'm about to show you how grateful I am for being so sweet."

He stared back, slightly dazed. "I'm done now."

She laughed and shook her head. "After. Can I give some to Lucy?"

"No, chocolate isn't good for dogs."

"I can give her this crunchy end. It's plain."

He smiled, glancing back and forth between them. Lucy gave a tiny whine, sensing she was close to the treat. "Sure."

She offered the bite, but Lucy sat stubbornly, waiting for Carter to give it to her. "Dammit, she's stubborn."

He deepened his voice. "Lucy, you can take it from Avery or you get nothing at all. Your choice."

Lucy whined and looked away in refusal.

"Okay, your loss."

Avery kept it aside. Carter dumped the plate, rinsed his hands, and turned. "Now, you were saying?"

She laughed. "Meet you in there, robot man."

He disappeared in a flash. Arousal tightened low in her belly, mixed with a joy she'd never experienced before. She dried her hands and turned, ready to join him.

Lucy sat before her. Paws in front, head cocked up, she looked like an adorable posed doll.

Avery sucked in a breath. Her heart beat. Was this just a ploy to mock her? Slowly, she took the edge of the croissant and bent down, offering it to her.

The dog gently accepted the bite, chewing politely. When she was done, they gazed at one another with a new understanding.

"Girl power," she whispered with a big smile. "It's something I'm going to teach you, Lucy."

And damned if she didn't catch a twinkle in those big brown eyes.

"Please don't make me watch this."

Avery gave an impatient sigh and turned to face Carter on the couch. "But you've never seen it! I swear, it's not mushy. It's really funny, and it's my favorite movie. Can't you give it a try?"

He glanced down at the cover of the DVD for *Notting Hill* and looked miserable. "Does it have any of those stupid one-liners that women like to swoon over and repeat endlessly?"

She averted her gaze because it was very difficult to lie to him. "Not really."

"What about *Baby Driver*? It's a new classic. The soundtrack kills."

They stared at one another in a battle of wills. Lucy cranked her head around to stare at them from her position at Carter's feet, as if sensing a war. Finally, Avery sighed. "What if we watch my movie first, then your movie?"

He narrowed his gaze in suspicion. "You're not going to fall asleep during my movie and claim tiredness, are you?"

She giggled at his adorable frown and pressed a kiss to his lips. "No. I'll make popcorn while you put it on."

He grumbled, but set up the movie on the ancient DVD player while the merry sounds of popping corn echoed in the air.

She returned to the couch with the bag, and snuggled under the comfy crocheted afghan. "I promise you're going to love it," she squealed. "Lucy, wanna come up and sit with me? I'll share."

Lucy gave her a long look. Ever since the croissant episode, they'd been slowly bonding, and Avery wasn't afraid to admit she used bribery to help her along. Still, she was surprised when the dog got up from her spot and jumped up to settle on the extra patch of blanket beside her.

"Good girl," she crooned, stroking her silky back. "Here, have one."

The dog took the kernel with a gentle bite, then slowly chewed, as if savoring the salty taste with class.

"That's my girls," Carter said happily, putting his arm around her shoulders. Then he hit the "Play" button.

Two hours later, the credits rolled past, and she risked a glance at his face. Lucy was snoring happily, the popcorn was gone, and darkness had fallen.

His eyes were closed.

She punched him in the arm. "You were sleeping!"

He jerked and blinked madly. "Nope, I was awake the whole time."

"Liar!"

"Oh, sweetheart, there's only one liar here, and it's you."

A shiver worked down her spine at his sexy growl. She huffed out a breath. "What are you talking about?"

"You said it had no stupid lines, but that one gets the award for worst line ever spoken."

She wriggled her butt on the couch and glared. "It wasn't stupid."

He snorted. "'I'm a girl, standing by a boy, asking him to love me'? Really? That's the most ridiculous thing I've ever heard. Holy crap, how do they create this stuff that would never be spoken in a million years? This is why men never want to watch these movies. It's completely unrealistic."

She sniffed. "You said it wrong. And it's not unrealistic. You can't be sure you'd never say anything like that if you were desperate to prove your love to someone you were afraid of losing."

"Yes, I can. Nothing could make me say that shit."

"That's horrible! What if it was the one line that would make everything better? You wouldn't say it because of your male pride?"

"Nope."

She nibbled at her lip, desperate to make her point. "What if you had to say it to gain a million dollars?"

"Not worth it. It's too stupid. Can we watch *Baby Driver* now?"

She got up and stalked into the kitchen. "Fine. Do you want some water?"

"Can you grab me a beer, please?"

She cracked open an IPA, filled a glass of water with ice, and came back to resettle. Lucy was snoring softly, and she cuddled into the crook of Avery's arm as soon as she sat back down. "This better be good," she warned.

"Oh, it is. You'll love it. It got extremely high reviews from all the critics."

"So did *Notting Hill.*"

He grumbled something, but she got quiet and swore she'd have an open mind.

Two hours later, she was ready to scream. "You call *that* realistic?" she hissed furiously. "Nothing in that movie could have ever happened."

He looked at her with complete astonishment. "What do you mean? He's a getaway driver! That's how they drive. And there was even a hot romance in there."

Her disbelief grew. "That was a romance? I think it was a train wreck. I'm sorry, I didn't like it."

"Impossible. Wasn't it exciting and pumped you with adrenaline? Didn't you love the music?"

She wrinkled her nose. "No."

They stared at one another in shocked silence. The movie clicked off, and the television went to a blank screen. The room was quiet and hushed. "I don't like your taste in movies," he finally stated.

"I don't like yours."

He nodded slowly. "Duly noted. How do we get past this serious test in our brand-new relationship?"

Her lips quirked. *Damn him.* He was sexy and funny and nerdy, and she was crazy about him. She stretched, making sure her loose T-shirt fell off her shoulder and flashed a half-naked breast. His gaze became attached to her bare skin, and he licked his lips. "We can make up in bed. That was a horrible fight," she said.

"I agree. Awful. It's time for make-up sex."

Very slowly, she smiled; carefully extricated herself from Lucy, who gave a slight jerk, then settled back into sleep; and stripped her shirt off. "Let's go, robot man."

He plucked her off the couch and carried her into the bedroom.

Avery hoped all their fights would end just like that.

Three more days.

Carter dropped his phone on the table and rubbed his head. It was official. He'd just been sent a new project, and they wanted him at a meeting Tuesday morning.

His time in Cape May was officially up.

Chest tight, he scooped up Lucy and headed outside. The sun was high and bright, and the street was quiet other than the occasional passerby or bicycle. He slid into the oversize rocker on the porch, put his feet up on the rail, and settled Lucy in his lap.

He'd never thought he was a beach-town type of person, but Cape May had subtly weaved itself into his heart. He loved the small-town charm, reminding him he worked too much indoors and had forgotten what it was like to be closer to nature. The ocean soothed him, and he enjoyed taking morning runs on the boardwalk with Pierce. He'd made friends with some business owners and was greeted by name at Madison's Bakery and Louie's Pizza. He had a regular lunch and beer date with Gabe and Pierce at Ugly Mug, and had been able to take Zoe to the beach one more time.

He didn't want to leave Cape May.

He didn't want to leave Avery.

He stroked Lucy's belly, and tried to take comfort in her warmth. He'd known this day would come. He couldn't stay here forever—he'd made a life for himself back in DC. But he didn't want to end the relationship with Avery. These past two weeks together proved she was special.

She loved him.

God, she was sweet. And passionate. And giving. Everything he'd always dreamed of in a woman, and he still wasn't able to say the words back. Each time he tried, panic rose up and wiped out his voice. Maybe he'd never be able to say them.

Maybe his father had ruined him.

He squeezed his eyes shut and groaned. He needed more time. Tonight, he'd tell her he wanted a long-distance relationship. He'd commit to regular visits, texts, phone—hell, he'd happily do FaceTime. September and October were still busy for weddings, but they'd be able to spend more time together in November. He'd take his laptop with him and work from here on long weekends. He had no interest in other women. Avery was the only one he wanted. She had to know that, and be happy with the next step moving forward.

His breath eased as he reminded himself the arrangement could work for both of them. It made sense.

He'd explain tonight, and everything would work out fine.

She was losing him.

Avery stared at the man she loved across the table and knew her time was officially up.

His new job began on Tuesday. He'd laid out his plans for a long-distance relationship, even sliding over a color-coded calendar where they could both keep track of their available times. She didn't know whether to laugh or cry. The relief on his face was almost tangible. He'd be able to ink her into the spaces and open slots of his life, yet keep a safe-enough distance to avoid the day-to-day messiness of a true relationship.

She looked at the charts and listened to his well-rehearsed speech and felt her heart slowly break into pieces. What had she expected? That he'd declare his love and announce he'd move to Cape May? Things like that only happened in the movies and novels. Real life was hard and meant compromise, like organized spreadsheets and phone sex. Why did she have a sinking sense she'd lose him for good once he left?

"Sweetheart? You look upset. What do you think of my ideas?"

She forced a smile. "It seems you worked it all out. I'll download my wedding schedule into the spreadsheet and we'll sync it. I've always wanted to go back and visit the capital."

He nodded with enthusiasm. "Exactly. We'll make this work for both of us. We don't have to lose anything."

Heart bruised, feeling extremely vulnerable, she asked the only question she needed answered: "Do you want this to work, Carter? Because I understand if it's too much. We'd agreed only to the summer. Are you sure you're willing to try and take on a long-distance relationship and its challenges?"

He leaned over and laid his hands on her knees. Those misty blue-gray eyes flared with hot emotion and a fierce command. "I'm not letting either of us walk away from this. You're too damn important to me and can never be termed a summer affair." His voice broke, and she sensed his need to tell her more, but his gaze dropped. "You changed my life."

The naked truth in his words gave her hope. It was more than he'd given her before, and she needed to be patient. They'd bonded after he confessed the secret about his father. She understood how the experience had changed him. Maybe having control would have the opposite effect. Maybe he'd realize what they could be together, and distance would make them closer. Praying she was right, she reached for him. "Then we'll make it work."

Her fingers skimmed his soft lips, loving his smile. And then he carried her to the bedroom and made all the doubts go away, for a little while.

Chapter Twenty-One

The day Carter left, the sky didn't weep, she didn't get a sick gut instinct she'd never see him again, and it was a regular workday.

His car was packed. The rental house was locked up. Lucy was loaded up in her carrier case. And Avery stood on the porch, wondering how to express so much feeling into a few words of goodbye.

"We're on for September twenty-first," he said firmly. "It'll give me plenty of time to get a handle on the new project, and then spend a long weekend with you."

"Sounds like a plan. Text me when you arrive safe."

"I'll call."

She smiled and caressed his rough cheek. "Yes, call. If I don't answer, I'll call back when I get a break. The wedding will run late."

His phone blared and he glanced down. "Can you give me a sec? It's work."

"Of course."

He handed her Lucy's carrier and walked a few feet away, engaging in deep conversation.

She sighed and took a seat. Propping the carrier on her lap, she gazed down at Lucy. "You probably don't believe it, but I'm going to miss you, girl. Take care of him for me, okay?"

Tears stung her eyes, so she lifted her gaze and stared out at the ocean, reminding herself they'd work it out. People engaged in long-distance relationships all the time. It was common in today's age with technology to help out, and there was no reason to act dramatic or weepy. She needed to show him she believed in them.

The warm lick of a tongue on her palm startled her. Looking down, she watched Lucy bestow tiny doggy kisses, as if sensing her distress.

Avery gulped and smiled, patting her tiny head. "Thank you, girl. I needed that."

"Sorry, I'm all set. Ready, Luce?" He picked up the carrier and placed her in the passenger seat. Then turned.

"I love you," she said.

He ran a knuckle over her cheek, his eyes whispering what he couldn't yet say. Then he kissed her long and deep, bending her backward and devouring her mouth, giving his body entirely in a final, blistering embrace.

He pulled back. Raked his gaze one last time over her face. Then got in the car and drove away.

Avery wondered why she was already grieving the end.

Three weeks later, her sisters stormed into her house in a forceful invasion. Avery had been on the couch, watching TV, and devouring an entire chocolate-explosion Peace Pie. "What's the matter?" she demanded. "Did you even knock?"

Taylor snorted and dropped into the oversize chair. "No need. Carter isn't here this weekend, and you've been like a hermit these past few weeks. Something's up, you're not talking, and we're here to get the dirt. Spill."

She blinked. "Are you nuts? I'm fine. There's nothing to tell."

Bella shook her head and gracefully took a seat next to her. "We've never seen you like this before. You're like a wedding demon come to life, buzzing from event to event and working all hours. If you're not

Jennifer Probst

working, you're sitting at home, watching TV and eating. It's not like you."

"You said I should take more downtime," she pointed out. She popped the last piece of ice-cream sandwich into her mouth. "I'm doing what you said."

"We meant to go to the beach and play with Zoe and travel. To have fun. Not to be miserable. You're going against your normally cheerful nature. It's painful," Taylor accused. "For all of us."

She stiffened. "Sorry to inconvenience you by not being Mary Poppins every damn day. Maybe if you'd pick up more of the slack and get me a new assistant, I'd do better."

Bella sighed. "Oh, it's worse than I thought. She's getting mean like you, T."

"Dammit, we're your sisters! Ever since Carter left, you've been spiraling, and it's our right to know why!"

"I'm sad, okay?" Avery battled the raw emotions and tried to keep herself calm. "This isn't working out like I wanted it to."

Immediately, her sisters moved to flank her. "What happened?" Bella asked.

Avery squeezed her eyes tight, willing the tears back. "I fell in love with him. I know it was a short time, but I know the difference between lust and love—between an affair and a man I want forever with. He's it."

"Babe, that's wonderful. I'm so proud you went for it even though you were scared. How does he feel about you?" Taylor asked.

"I think he loves me, too, but he's too afraid to say it. He's got these ideas that are still lodged in his mind. He's scared, and I'm not sure if time is going to make a difference. Things have been . . . different since he left."

Bella frowned. "Like what? You looked happy to see each other last weekend."

Avery thought back over their time together. She'd gorged on his presence, intent on hibernating in bed and spending endless hours in

276

his company. But there was something between them she hadn't felt this past summer. He'd begun to pull back, as if rebuilding the wall that had crashed down a month ago. Oh, they talked, and made love, and planned for their next visit, but Avery knew he wasn't fully present and open. He'd blocked off an important piece of himself. The breakthrough after he'd confessed the truth about his father seemed to have faded. She'd prayed the distance would benefit their relationship, but last weekend had proved her fears.

They were already growing apart.

"He's not able to give me what I need," she said softly. "Is it wrong to want to share your intimate self with someone you love? To hope for a future? To want a partner?"

"No," Bella said. "You deserve that, Avery."

"How long do I need to fight for him? How can I give up so soon? I have this awful fear that we don't have a chance unless we're together."

"You need to talk to him," Taylor said. "He deserves to know exactly how you feel and the doubts you have. And if he's not ready to fight for you, too, then you have your answer."

"Love hurts," she whispered, bowing her head.

Her sisters hugged her tight, and Avery leaned into their support, taking comfort in the strength and bonds of family.

Taylor was right. She needed to be honest with Carter. She needed more, and pretending things were fine the way they were wasn't fair to either of them. She only hoped she could explain it in the right way and show him what he meant to her. God knew she didn't want him to feel trapped or bullied into a relationship. But she deserved his whole heart and not pieces of it.

She just hoped she was strong enough not only to fight for him—but to walk away if it was the only choice left.

♥ ♥ ♥

Carter was working on important code when his phone rang. He glanced down, saw Avery's name, and experienced an odd mixture of eagerness and reluctance, joy and fear. It was a cocktail he despised because it only clouded his mind and gave him no clear-cut answers.

He didn't know what was wrong between them.

Last weekend, the moment he saw her, his heart did a crazy jump in his chest. So many emotions bubbled up to the surface, but instead of allowing himself to let go, he'd begun to clam up. Sure, he talked and made love to her and held her close, but it was as if the familiar wall inside him he'd lived with since he'd found his dad had reappeared. He watched her from an odd distance, analyzing her words and her affection with judgment.

He'd truly believed the distance would work to their advantage. But if he was honest, he realized it'd become easier to slip into his old ways. He dove deep into work, getting lost in endless code and the puzzles of unlocking each layer of his new project. Work was a shelter, a distraction, and a reminder that there was no emotional upheaval when he was focused.

Avery was a bright light in his drudging existence, and that fact scared the shit out of him. Because if he got used to her, what would happen to him if she left? Would he become exactly like his father—unable to cope, weak under the idea of love?

He wasn't stupid. He knew she realized things weren't the same, but he tried to cover it up, and when he finally retreated back to DC, he may have been empty, but God knew he was safe.

Jerking himself out of his computer mode, he picked up his phone. "Hey, sweetheart. How are you?"

Her voice vibrated with an undercurrent of tension. "Okay. I had to deal with a ring-bearer tantrum, and a fight between a best man and groomsman over a girl at a bar the night before. Nightmare."

He pictured the roll of her eyes and smiled. "It's always about a girl, right?"

Silence hummed over the line. "I don't know, Carter. Is it?"

Her soft question seethed with the threat of a serious discussion. He tried to tamp it down, not sure he could handle in-depth questions tonight. "If it's a woman as beautiful as you, then yes. Every time. How's Zoe? Is she liking school?"

"The girl has a bigger social life than I do. Bella is driving her back and forth to playdates, and now she's in dance lessons. Lady Gaga's got nothing on our Zoe."

He missed the little girl's infectious giggles, and the way she ran to him with open trust. Who would've thought he could've gotten attached to them all so quickly? The fact only solidified his decision to take it slow. Yes, he had deep feelings for Avery and her family, but taking their time was key in controlling the overabundance of emotion. She'd told him she loved him so soon. Too soon?

"What about everyone else? Gabe texted me his promotion went through."

"We announced it this week. He said he'd call you later. He wants to get you out here for a celebratory beer with Pierce."

"Sounds good. I know our next scheduled meeting is October eleventh, but if I sink hard into this coding, I may be able to finish quicker and take a few extra days to spend with you."

"I'm grateful I can be properly scheduled in," she said tightly. "Have I now been relegated to a meeting status?"

"You know what I meant." Annoyance flickered. "Are you tired? You seem . . . off."

A humorless laugh came over the phone. "Funny you should ask. I've been thinking that this relationship has been a bit 'off' lately. You promised total honesty and openness, Carter. It was the only way to move forward with us, so I need to know. What's really going on?"

Panic grabbed at his throat. She wanted to back out already. After only three weeks of being apart, she was ready to give up.

He should have known. Relationships were too hard. The path was filled with challenges and thorns that made you bleed. It was so much easier to be alone.

His voice chilled, and he felt the blessed numbness begin to come back, the same he'd experienced after seeing his father's dead body. "I don't know what you're talking about," he said. "Are you trying to pick a fight? I thought things were fine. We had a good time this past weekend. We're on the schedule for another visit in two weeks. Isn't everything going according to our plan?"

"I'm not a damn *plan*, Carter! I'm not looking to fit nicely into the calendar of your life." Her voice shook with intensity. "This summer, I fell in love with you. We were connected. But since you've gone back to DC, I feel this barrier between us, as if you're afraid to let go. What are you scared of? That I'm too important? That I'll wreck your orderly existence? Or that I'll break your heart?"

He sucked in a breath. It was too much. Her words pushed and prodded and probed until he only wanted to protect the rawness inside. He reacted like a wounded animal being threatened. "Does saying you love someone make all the issues magically go away? You plan weddings and happily ever afters for people on a daily basis. Did you ever stop to think that it could all be an illusion—and that behind the curtain is disappointment? I'm trying to take it slow here, Avery. Let us catch our breath after an intense summer. Get to know one another on a regular basis to see if we fit. I'm not sure what else you want from me."

"You're not your father! He made his choices, and now it's time for you to make yours—to live your own life. Can't you see you're punishing yourself for something that's not your fault? That you're strong enough to love someone and not lose yourself?"

The mention of his father made him shudder with rage. "The only thing I see is you trying to push me to say something I don't feel," he shot back. "Will those three words finally make you happy?"

The tiny gasp sliced through him.

His gut churned. He gripped the phone, wanting to take it all back, but he remained silent.

"I'm sorry," she finally said. "You're right."

"Good. Now, are we still on for the eleventh?" He knew before she spoke he'd made a terrible mistake.

"No, Carter. I can't do this anymore."

"Avery, please—"

"You want to know what I want from you?" She spoke with a strength that humbled him, even as his heart shattered in his chest. "I want everything. Not pieces of you doled out in perfect proportions to keep things neat and tidy. I don't just want to fit properly into your life. I want you to love me. I want you to take the leap with me and believe you're strong enough to handle the flight, or the fall. But you won't even try. And I can't stay with someone who has given up before we've even begun."

He shut down, sensing the end of something beautiful and good and hopeful, and he wondered if he'd ever know what it was like to be whole again.

"You're breaking up with me," he stated.

"I'm letting you go," she corrected. "If I thought time and fighting for you would make a difference, God knows I'd do it. But you have to want all of me, and I don't think you're ready." She paused and he held his breath. "I don't think you'll ever be ready."

"I won't chase after you." His words dropped like hard stone between them, and he flinched, knowing he'd hurt her.

"I know," she whispered. "I want you to be happy. You deserve . . . everything. Goodbye, Carter."

The phone clicked.

He dropped it on the desk. Stared at the computer. And tried to tell himself it was the only way their relationship could have ended. It never would've worked. They'd had a magical summer, but real life proved it was all an illusion.

His hands trembled. Nausea punched his gut. His head swam. He wondered if he was getting sick, so he stumbled to the couch and lay down. Lucy sensed his distress and hopped up next to him, worriedly licking at his cheek. He cuddled her close, shutting his eyes, and telling himself not to think about it.

She'd done the right thing. For both of them.

A week later, he called his sister to check in. Ally didn't answer, but then a few seconds later, a FaceTime call came through. Shaking his head, he accepted it. "You know I hate video calls," he grumbled.

Her face was wreathed in a big grin, and she stuck out her tongue, making him chuckle. "I missed your face," she said cheerily. "Plus, I need you to give me an honest answer. You're the only one I trust."

"What is it?"

She held the phone all the way back and showed off her jean-clad body. "Am I getting fat?"

Instead of groaning and pretending she was crazy, he knew exactly what she needed. "Turn around," he directed, and she did a slow spiral. "Nope, not fat at all. In fact, you look great. I think marriage agrees with you."

She let out a relieved breath. "Thank God. And yes, marriage does agree with me, but that's why I've been eating more. I don't mind a few pounds, but I don't want to overdo my happy diet."

He grinned. "I hear you. Now, catch me up on things."

She chatted about Jason and her students, and he listened to her musical voice, loving the way her face lit up. She looked . . . settled. There was a calmness about her that shone right through the tiny screen, and he was glad he'd picked up the FaceTime call. Talking to his sister always made him feel better.

"Have you seen Avery?" she finally asked, switching topics.

Every muscle locked and tightened. He spoke carefully. "Why would I see Avery?"

Her eyes danced with mischief. "Do you think I'm an idiot? It was so obvious when you danced at my bachelorette party. I didn't want to push too soon, so when I got back from my honeymoon, I called Avery and demanded the truth. She fessed up and told me you guys were seeing each other. I'm so happy! You two are perfect together!"

Pain crashed through him. He'd figured a few days of mourning and he'd be back to normal, but the last few weeks had been brutal. He dreamed of her. He stared at his computer like a lovesick teen, sick to his stomach. It was like having the flu with no medicine and no assurances of getting better. Ever since she'd said goodbye, the life he'd fought hard to protect and maintain had shattered around him.

He debated lying, but he didn't want to do that. "We spent the summer together," he finally admitted. "Why didn't you say anything sooner if you knew?"

"It was obvious you were both crazy about each other, and honestly? I didn't want to interfere. I figured if I played dumb, you guys would just do your thing. I also know how weird you are talking about your love life, so I wanted to give you time before I pounced. Now, tell me everything."

"Unfortunately, we broke up," he said.

Her face dropped. "What? Carter, I'm so sorry. What happened? I've never seen you like that around a woman—it was obvious you were crazy about her. Oh my God, Avery never even told me you broke up!"

She hadn't even told her best friend? Hurt and annoyance warred inside, but he just shrugged and forced a smile. "We couldn't do the long-distance thing."

A frown creased her brow. "That's it? Dude, why don't you just move?"

"People don't just move and change their entire life after one summer. It doesn't make sense."

She snorted. "Love isn't supposed to make sense. Mom and Dad met and were married within six months. The moment Jason and I began dating, I knew he was *the one* in a few weeks. Sure, we took time getting engaged, but we both committed to the relationship immediately. It's a heart thing, Carter, not a brain thing. Love sometimes just doesn't make sense."

His heart pounded at the simple explanation. "You think I should sell my house, quit my job, and move to a small beach town after only *really* knowing this woman for a few months? You don't think that's impulsive, reckless, and foolhardy?"

She laughed. "Yes."

"I can't. I'm not like you, Ally-Cat. I don't believe in the things you do."

"Like what? Relationships? Love? Marriage? I call bullshit. And I think it's time you begin to realize this little martyr act you put on will only get you one thing—loneliness."

Temper pricked. She had no idea what he'd gone through because he'd chosen to protect her. But he wasn't about to let her think he hadn't tried. "I'm not a martyr, and I don't pretend to be. I made hard choices, and I don't regret any of them. And I did try with Avery. She was very clear that the distance between us wasn't what she wanted."

"The mileage? Or you?" She groaned and threw up her hands. "Carter, please listen to me. I've minded my own business because I trusted you knew what you were doing. But all those sacrifices you made for me? Quitting college, giving up travel, and making sure I was always your priority? They haunt me. You don't think I lie awake at night sometimes and cry, knowing everything you gave up?"

Shock barreled through him. He'd never imagined Ally had these feelings—he'd worked so hard at making sure she never thought of herself as a burden or sacrifice. Because she wasn't. "Ally—"

"No, wait. That compass tattoo you got before Dad died? It meant something to you. It was a symbol of freedom, right? But this past decade, when you finally were free, you chose to do nothing. You have the same solitary life as when I was young. I'm married and happy. I'm going to raise my own family. Why do you still cut yourself off from living? What makes you so afraid?"

It was the same question that Avery had asked. He'd told her the story about his father, but now he began to wonder if it had gone deeper. Had all those years of sacrifice for Ally become habit? Had he used her to hide, playing a martyr role so he'd never be tested or challenged to take risks? Why was he still in the same place, at the same job, when there was nothing holding him back any longer?

The thoughts spun in his head. "I don't know," he finally said. "Each time I saw Avery, I freaked out a bit. In some ways, I thought she was too good to be true, and then I worried if I fell hard for her, that I'd get hurt. Like Dad."

"How so?" she asked.

Knowing he was in tricky territory, he tried to navigate his answer in a way she could understand. "Do you remember what you said about Dad at your wedding? That you worried his heart had given out because he didn't want to live without Mom? What if you were right? What if he just gave up on his body and left his children because he was too weak to be alone?"

His sister shuddered out a breath, then took a while to answer. She looked deep in thought. "I always suspected that was the case," she finally said. "It was too soon after Mom's death to be a coincidence. I actually read plenty of articles on soul mates who let their body stop working because they couldn't bear a world without their spouse. But, Carter, you can't compare yourself to Dad. You're the strongest person I know. We were orphans too young, and you had to grow up so fast. You could have chosen not to do it. You could have walked away and put me in foster care. Do you understand that you chose love over selfishness?"

He shook his head, trying to figure it out. "It wasn't a choice. I'd never leave you behind, Ally-Cat. I love you too much."

"Exactly. Love makes you strong, Carter, not weak. Maybe Dad gave up, maybe it was coincidence—we'll never know. But if he did choose to give up, I know in my heart and soul you'd never do that." She touched her finger to the screen. "Love is the ultimate freedom. It pushes you to be the best, challenges your worst, and tests your strength. It gives the most reward because you risk the most. It's not exotic adventures and distant lands that you've been missing. It's love."

A shiver shot down his spine. He nodded, his throat tight.

"Do you love Avery?"

The question slammed through him. His sister stared at him with a piercing gaze, still touching the screen. He grabbed for excuses and his normal rationalizations, but a faint whisper rose up inside him that made him still.

Yes.

He'd known it all along. He just hadn't wanted to deal with the consequences. But his sister's words had given him a freedom he'd never had before—the realization that his constant comparisons to his father had been a way to protect himself. All this time, he'd been a coward.

His tat seemed to throb and burn on his skin as a reminder of the boy he'd once been, and the man he'd chosen to grow into. Ally was no longer his responsibility. It was time for him to make a life for himself free from the past.

He just hoped he could do it.

"Yes," he said. "I love her."

Ally nodded. "Good. I can only imagine the horrific things you said to her, so you probably have a long way to dig yourself out of the doghouse."

He winced. "Yeah, it was bad."

"She'll give you another chance, but it may take a while. You know what you need to do to get her back, right?"

"Quit my job and move to Cape May?"

She grinned. "It's a start. But if you want your own happily ever after, you have to go all in, Carter. Do you understand?"

He nodded, throat choked with emotion. "Yeah."

"Good. Now get to work. Love you."

"Love you, too, Ally-Cat. Thanks."

The screen went dark.

His sister was right. He couldn't fix this overnight, but he could damn well begin the process. Avery deserved more than the man he'd shown her. It was time to show her he had the balls to leap.

He opened up his internet search and began typing.

Chapter Twenty-Two

Avery walked into Sunshine Bridal in a bad mood.

Gabe had called in, citing an emergency, sticking her with a vendor appointment amid all her regular meetings. Bella had disappeared and wasn't answering her phone for backup, and Taylor had texted that she was in AC for her sacred day off and wished her luck. And to top everything off, Jessie, their receptionist, had called in sick, so she now had to spend the next hour going through messages to make sure they didn't miss anything important.

She hated today.

Muttering a string of curses, she handled the voice mails first, then printed out Gabe's worksheet for the Ackerman wedding. Her life was pathetic. This was all she had left to look forward to—planning everyone else's weddings while she grew into an old maid. She'd met the love of her life, and he hadn't wanted her.

Morphing into a pool of self-pity, she almost wished Taylor was here to kick her in the ass. Her sisters gave her a full month to grieve the loss, and then she wasn't allowed to eat a Peace Pie every night. She even had to begin eating kale salads again.

Her life sucked.

She heard the door open and close. Great, if she had to deal with a walk-in, she was going to seriously lose it. Gritting her teeth, she popped her head out of the conference room, praying she wouldn't have to pretend to be nice.

Her jaw dropped.

Lucy stood in the foyer, glancing back and forth as if trying to figure out what was going on. When her gaze snagged on Avery, her little doggy face lit up, and she began trotting toward her.

Avery dropped to her knees and held her arms out. "Lucy! Sweetheart, what are you doing here?" She hugged and kissed the wriggling bundle of fur, savoring her sweet licks and the sheer comfort of knowing such love. God, she'd missed her so much.

Then her brain gave her a jolt, reminding her if Lucy was here, it also meant Carter was here.

Her body shook. It'd been more than a month since their phone conversation. He'd never called her back. The pain was brutal and swift, and she'd spent endless nights crying with a hopeless longing to beg him to come back. But she refused to be with a man who'd never give his whole heart, no matter how much she loved him. As time passed, she got stronger, but there was still an empty ache in the pit of her stomach that hadn't gone away.

After some more snuggles, she noticed a paper tied to Lucy's collar. She pulled out the rolled-up note and opened it.

Avery,

Please meet me at the Merion Inn in 15 minutes. I'll be waiting for you at the bar.

PS: Please bring Lucy with you.

She hissed out a breath and grabbed for patience. How dare he? By giving her Lucy, he forced her to his terms. It would serve him right if she just took Lucy home with her and ignored his note. Her schedule was already packed, and she didn't have time to play games.

What was he doing in Cape May?

Anger warred with despair. Did he want to apologize? Try again? Or just clear the slate for his sister's sake? The questions haunted her, but she had little time to think. Exactly what he'd counted on—no time to call her sisters for advice or make a quick disappearance.

Fine. If he wanted to make nice, she'd do the same. She'd be cold, distant, and polite. She'd pretend she'd moved on. Anything to make him go away.

She checked her hair and makeup for vanity only, then scooped up Lucy. The Merion Inn was within walking distance, and the dog's pink leash had been attached to her collar. Though it was a gorgeous fall day, she refused to be charmed by the cooler air, the flight of crisp leaves, or the calming sound of the ocean waves.

When she reached the Merion Inn, she walked inside. It was an odd time between lunch and dinner, and the place was empty. With the gorgeous floral Victorian wallpaper, mahogany wood, and rich tapestry carpet, the restaurant gave off an old-world, elegant charm that was a favorite for guests. A beautiful piano gleamed with high polish, empty for now.

Carter was sitting at the bar, nursing a whiskey, his elegant fingers skimming the edge of the crystal-cut glass. Hank, the bartender, nodded to her and left his station, probably sensing something big was going down.

Carter's gaze delved into hers.

Trembling, she took a step back under the intensity of those stormy blue-gray eyes. The last time she'd stared at him, his gaze had been passionate but remote. Today, a raw flare of emotion glimmered in its depths, carved out his features.

He looked tired. Lines bracketed his eyes and mouth. He'd grown a bit of a beard, giving him an edgy, sexy look that stole her breath. No glasses. His outfit consisted of jeans, a gray pullover, and leather loafers. Her body wept to touch him just once, but she kept her distance.

Lucy wriggled in a mad dash to be reunited with her owner, so Avery was forced to cross the room and stand near him. He picked the dog up, kissing her and calming her down, then slipped her into his carry bag.

"Thank you for coming." His voice was smooth whiskey and rough gravel.

She curled her hands into fists to keep from reaching out. "You didn't give me much of a choice unless I wanted to be a dog-napper."

A smile touched his lips. He was staring at her so hungrily, it reminded her of how it'd been over the summer. Pain blew the thought away, like poking a sore tooth. "I was afraid to give you too much of a choice after how we left things."

A weary sigh shook from her. "Is that why you're here? To make things nice? You don't have to, Carter. I'm not mad, I'm truly not. We tried."

"I didn't."

Her eyes widened. "What?"

He turned on the stool and placed his hands on his knees. His face held the resolute lines of a man on a mission. And, God, the sexual tension burned and simmered between them, trying to knock her off-balance. Damn him and his guilt. She needed to get out of here.

"It's simple, really," he said. "I'm so damn sorry. You gave everything and I gave nothing. You were brave and I was a coward. When you tried to tell me, to reach out and ask why, I treated you like shit. Because I was messed up. Mixed up. Scared crapless. Pick one."

Her throat tightened, and her voice came out choked. "I get it. You told me why, and I thought I could just fix it by pushing you. Apology accepted. I swear, you can go home now and know I'm okay and I understand." She turned on her heel, desperate to leave, but his next words stopped her.

"I am home."

"What do you mean?"

He waited until she turned and faced him again. "I talked to my sister. Told her everything, and she gave me a come-to-Jesus moment. I've been protecting a life I don't even want anymore. So I made some changes. I sold my place and quit my job. I'm in therapy, so I can learn some tools to make sure I don't slip into my old ways."

She moved close, blinking back tears. "I'm so happy for you, Carter. You deserve to follow your dreams now. Where are you going next?"

"Nowhere. I bought a house in Cape May."

The shock barreled through her, and the ground shifted underneath her feet. She must've heard wrong. "You're kidding me."

He shook his head. "Nope. Also got a new job in Atlantic City. Never thought about working for the casinos before, but it's good money and a new challenge I desperately needed."

"Wait—you moved here permanently?"

"Yep. I knew words wouldn't be enough. Neither would intentions. Action was the only way I'd have even a chance of convincing you to take me back." He stood from the stool and walked over to her. Gently taking her hands in his, he stared into her face. "See, I happen to be in love with you, Avery Sunshine. And I'm tired of denying it and running away. I want the chance to gain back your trust. Be part of your family. And even if you say no, I understand, but I won't give up. I'll be here every damn day, to convince you I'm not only ready to love you, but I'll give you everything you ask for."

As she stared back into his beloved face, she saw the truth.

He loved her. It was in his eyes, in his smile, in the tender way he touched her. But more than that, there was no barrier any longer.

And then he sealed the deal: "I'm just a guy, standing by a girl, asking her to marry me."

Holy crap, he'd quoted *Notting Hill*. Well, kind of. He was ready to give her the gift of a rom-com in epic form, proving he was all in, offering her love and—

Wait, what had he just said?

She blinked through blurred vision as he dropped to one knee, took out a small box, and slowly opened it. The square-cut diamond ring sparkled and shone with spectacular glory. Shock barreled through her, tangled with a hungry need that made her entire body begin to shake.

Oh. My. God.

"Avery Alyssa Sunshine, will you marry me?"

She stared back at him helplessly. "You swore you'd never repeat a line from a rom-com. Not even for a million dollars."

His smile was gentle. "I'd do anything for you, Avery. I know that now."

She choked back a sob and put out a trembling hand to touch the ring.

"You still didn't answer my question."

She didn't need another second to think. Avery flew into his embrace and kissed him. She had to give him credit—he didn't even fall back under her joyous enthusiasm. When he finally lifted his head, she smiled. "Yes."

He laughed, and then he kissed her again.

Epilogue

Avery took a sip of her coffee and laid out her chocolate croissant in front of her. Flipping open her laptop, she glanced around the conference table and launched into her morning-meeting ritual. "Good morning, ladies and gentleman! Are we ready to have a great day?"

Taylor shot her a look and deliberately yawned. "No."

Nothing could dim her happiness today, though—not even her youngest sister's attitude. She could tell Bella would love to utter a snarky comment, but refused to destroy her yogic aspirations. "We'll certainly try," she said calmly. "I'll be able to take on a few more hours to fill in the gaps for the upcoming holiday weddings."

Gabe attacked his keyboard with his usual efficiency. "We're in good shape, Bella. No holes in the schedule for now, unless Avery wants to throw us another of her famous curveballs."

Taylor grunted. "I think she's learned her lesson. Now that she found her Prince Charming, maybe she'll actually start saying no to last-minute weddings."

Hmm, Gabe's and Taylor's comments seemed like a perfect segue to her announcement.

Savoring each moment, she took her time with the first bite of her croissant. The flaky, buttery crust melted in her mouth, replaced with the rich chocolate that sang in her blood. Sheer heaven. She blotted her mouth with a napkin and smiled. "Funny, it's like you're both mind readers. Something did pop up, and it was impossible to say no."

The three of them stared back at her. "What are you talking about?" Taylor asked in a threatening voice.

She refused to be bullied. Not today. "We need to add a wedding for September twentieth to next year's schedule. The groom was desperate and refused to wait any longer, so the bride agreed. Nine months should be doable."

Bella sighed, already flipping through her planner. "Avery, I wish you'd speak with us first before agreeing to cram in another wedding during high season. That was the only weekend we were keeping open for Mom and Dad to visit to celebrate their anniversary. Don't you remember?"

Taylor threw up her hands, gearing up for bitch mode. "No. I don't care how bad the groom wants to wed her. They can wait another damn six months when we have a decent opening."

"Too late," Avery practically sang. "I said yes and it's booked. I don't think Mom and Dad will mind at all."

Gabe used to remain quiet and let the sisters battle it out, but as a full partner now, he seemed ready to jump into the fray. "I agree with the majority. We say no. Call the bride and groom back and get us out of it."

"I can't. He's too damn stubborn."

"You live with a stubborn man!" Taylor growled. "Use your experience with your new fiancé and stand up for your family. We don't want another client."

"Even if it's me?" she asked softly.

Silence fell. Avery studied the people she loved and pegged the exact moment understanding dawned.

"That's your wedding date?" Bella breathed out in wonder.

Damned if silly tears didn't fill her eyes, but she was too happy to be embarrassed. "Yes. We finally picked the day, and Mom and Dad were thrilled we'll be sharing their wedding date."

Taylor grinned. "You got us good, babe. I was ready to blow."

Gabe slammed a fist on the table in celebration. "Carter didn't even tell me, and I got him pretty drunk last weekend. I'm so happy for you guys. That's a wedding I'll be happy to squeeze into our schedules."

They got up from their seats and gave her big hugs, and for the next twenty minutes, they spoke nonstop about the wedding in all its detail. When she glanced at the time, she realized they only had a little while left to talk business. "Okay, guys, I do have a few things to go over before we break. Unfortunately, we did get a cancellation for the Neeleys' New Year festivities. Seems like they decided to call the whole thing off."

"That's so sad," Bella murmured. "But I never liked him, so is it wrong to be glad?"

Gabe turned to her. "I never knew you didn't like him. How come?"

Bella's cheeks turned a slight shade of pink. "Well, he kind of liked to flirt with me. It made me uncomfortable."

Gabe scowled, and his voice iced. "You should have told me. I would have taken care of that immediately."

Avery glanced at him in surprise. Gabe was always laid-back and charming, and rarely lost his temper. Kind of like Bella. But she caught a swirling anger beneath the surface that told her if someone messed with one of his people, he'd get mean.

"I handled it myself," Bella said dismissively. "There was no need to tell you."

His entire body stiffened, as if he were trying to hold back his temper. "I respect you can handle it. I'm just pointing out that I'm here to support you."

"Thank you," she responded. But Avery could tell she had no intention of leaning on anyone, especially Gabe. The glimmers of frustration shooting from his aura told Avery he wasn't too happy about it, either.

Interesting.

Avery cleared her throat. "Well, no one get too excited over the cancellation, because I had Eloise Royal on the waiting list for a postholiday wedding, so she took their place. The bride and groom love Christmas so much they want to do it all over again."

"Yay," Taylor grunted.

"It's definitely a 'yay' for you, T, because I have you down as away that weekend to attend the wedding expo in Atlantic City. We get a ton of business from that, and Mom and Dad have had a booth there forever, so you need to cover it."

"I won't argue with that assignment."

Gabe laughed. "Gambling, alcohol, and hot men figuring out they just want to be single after all? We'll never get you back."

Taylor stuck out her tongue.

"Bella, Gabe, I need you both to work that wedding. Carter and I are flying out to Texas to visit Ally that weekend, so I won't be around."

Her sisters gasped. Gabe's jaw dropped.

"What?" Avery asked.

"You're taking an entire weekend off during holiday-wedding season?" Bella asked.

It struck her full force how much her life had changed since the summer. As much as she loved work, she didn't want to live for it any longer. She wanted to enjoy Carter and Ally and Lucy. And she realized the world wouldn't fall apart if she took a few days off.

"That's right," she said. "If you're okay to cover me."

"Good for you, babe," Taylor said.

Bella nodded. "Of course. I'll handle everything."

Gabe gave her a pointed look. "*We'll* handle everything."

Uh-oh. Something told her change was on the way—a slight simmer of tension, a swirl of emotion, and the way Gabe looked at her sister, like he was finally tired of being ignored.

She wondered what was going to happen next.

Avery finished the last of her chocolate croissant as her phone flashed. She smiled as she adjourned the meeting and took the call from the man she loved, pushing Bella and Gabe out of her mind.

For now.

AUTHOR'S NOTE

I've mentioned some real businesses in Cape May and created some fictional ones for convenience.

I began traveling to Exit 0 in my late teens with my best friend. From the moment I visited, it became a magical place for me. Every year we'd go down for a week and made a solemn vow on our friendship that no matter what happened—whether we were married, had children, or moved away—once a year we'd meet again in Cape May. We never broke the vow, even when our children were a few weeks old and we were terrified to leave them with our husbands!

One day I will own a house there and sit out on my rocker, listening to the horses' hooves clap past, the ocean roaring in the distance, and be at peace.

I've wanted to write a story in this setting for years, but like everything, patience is key, along with the right story.

This one was it.

ACKNOWLEDGMENTS

A huge thank-you to Catherine Walton from Weddings by the Sea for helping me learn the lingo and advising me on all the complicated details that make up being an amazing wedding planner. I'd definitely hire you if hubby and I decide to renew our vows! Any mistakes I've made are truly mine.

I want to thank the entire team at Montlake, especially Maria Gomez, and my AMAZING editor, Kristi Yanta, for whipping this book into the best it can be. A special shout-out to the team at Social Butterfly and Nina Grinstead, my go-to person for all things PR. Also to Kiki Chatfield at Next Step PR for her support and much-appreciated help. Thanks as always to my agent, Kevan Lyon, for all her advice and career guidance. A big thanks to my new assistant, Mandy Lawlor, for keeping me organized and supported on all fronts.

I adore my Probst Posse reader group and the Ladies Who Write. They inspired me by sharing all their wedding disasters for use in this series! Look for two of their stories in the next installment of the Sunshine Sisters series.

Finally, to my loyal, supportive readers who allow me to tell stories for a living.

Thank you. None of this happens without you.

ABOUT THE AUTHOR

Photo © 2012 Matt Simpkins

Jennifer Probst is the *New York Times* bestselling author of the Billionaire Builders series, the Searching For series, the Marriage to a Billionaire series, the Steele Brothers series, the Stay series, and the Sunshine Sisters series. Like some of her characters, Probst, along with her husband and two sons, calls New York's Hudson Valley home. When she isn't traveling to meet readers, she enjoys reading, watching "shameful reality television," and visiting a local animal shelter. For more information, visit her at www.jenniferprobst.com.